Cactus Flower

Cactus Flower

Alice Duncan

Five Star • Waterville, Maine

First Edition
First Printing: September 2006

Published in 2006 in conjunction with Tekno Books.

Set in 11 pt. Plantin by Christina S. Huff.

Printed in the United States on permanent paper.

Library of Congress Cataloging-in-Publication Data

Duncan, Alice, 1945–
  Cactus flower / Alice Duncan.—1st ed.
      p. cm.
    ISBN 1-59414-456-7 (hc : alk. paper)
    I. Title.
  PS3554.U463394C33 2006
   813'.6—dc22   2006016513

For my Rebel sisters.
I don't know what I'd do without you.

Chapter One

As soon as he heard the first whoop, Nicholas Taggart knew his uncle Junius was on a spree again.

"Aw, shit."

"What is it, darlin'?" a sleepy voice whispered as Nick swung his legs over the side of the bed.

Nick growled, "Uncle Junius," as he fumbled for his boots.

"Oh. I expect you gotta go get him?" Violet Watson, the sweet-natured, obliging, sporting girl with whom Nick had spent the last agreeable hour, sounded disappointed.

"I better. If the sheriff gets ahold of him, he might lock him up. He was pretty sore the last time Junius went wild."

Before his uncle cut loose, Nick had been peacefully recovering from his tumble with Violet, relaxing against the pillows and listening to the warm spring wind howl outside her window. Springtime on the high plains bore little resemblance to the pretty word pictures novelists painted of springtimes in other, gentler parts of the world. Out in the territory, spring was marked by forty-mile-an-hour winds, dust storms, and dry-as-an-old-bone weather for months on end. Nick liked it pretty well, although he preferred summer, when the thunderstorms came and things turned green. His uncle Junius, on the other hand, always went a little crazy with spring fever. Nick guessed he should have watched him more closely today.

"Yee-haw!" came, muffled, through the window. "Whooee! Ain't you a purty little thang!"

"Damn!" Nick grabbed his shirt, flung it on, and stuffed the tail into his trousers.

"Jeez, Nick, do you suppose he's captured himself another gal?"

"Sounds like it." Nick deposited a quick kiss on Violet's naked bosom and ran for the door, still fighting with his trouser buttons.

"Y'all come back again soon, honey," Violet called after him.

"Yeah," said Nick. "Right." If he didn't get Uncle Junius off the street, Nick feared the sheriff wouldn't let him come back at all, much less soon. In fact, the sheriff had threatened to run both Taggarts out of town the last time this happened. Nick ripped down the stairs, tore through the smoky room, and thrust open the batwing doors. He barreled out of the saloon and came to a screeching halt on the scarred boardwalk, blinking into the sunshine. "What the hell . . . ?"

Ah, damn. Junius was dancing with the poor girl, who was a stranger, and who looked like she was about to faint or scream or both. She was small and kind of thin—certainly no match for Junius—and at present was pressing a flowered hat to her head with one hand and had a wicker valise clutched in the other. Junius held her around the waist and was doing a polka without any help from her. A crowd had gathered to watch the fun, some cheering Junius, some on the girl's side.

"Put that girl down, Junius!" Nick made his voice stern. Sometimes Junius responded to sternness.

Not this time. "Hell, Nicky, let an old man have his fun!"

"Stop him!" the girl screeched. "Somebody stop him!"

Nick didn't blame her for screeching. Junius wasn't the sort of fellow to melt a fair maiden's heart at the best of times, with his long white whiskers and elaborate paunch. When he'd imbibed a gut full of rye, he could be downright frightening if you didn't know him. Hell, he could be frightening even if you did know him. Bearing that in mind, Nick moved carefully when he approached his happy uncle, not fancying a bullet in the head or any other portion of his anatomy.

"I swear, Nick Taggart, if you can't keep that man under control, I'm going to lock him up."

Nick's heart fell. He'd been hoping to disengage Junius from the girl before the sheriff came out of his office. Too late now. Sheriff Wallace glared at the scene being enacted on the main street of his town and didn't look happy. Nick wasn't happy, either.

"Stop that!" the girl shouted. "Stop it, you brute!"

"I'm trying to stop him, honey," Nick said in a soothing voice.

She clearly didn't want to be soothed. "Don't you honey me!"

"Whooee!" cried Junius, happy as a lark. "Yee-haw!"

"Come on now, Junius, let the girl go. You've had your fun, and she don't look like she's enjoying the dance." Nick smiled at his uncle, who didn't look at him. The girl did, and he could tell she was mad enough to spit horseshoe nails. At least she wasn't crying. Nick hated it when females cried during one of his uncle's toots. "Junius!" he shouted.

"Hell, boy, I'm just dancin' with the lady," Junius shouted back. He dipped her, Nick presumed to demonstrate his skill on the dance floor, even though they weren't on one, but rather on a dusty road running through Rio Peñasco, New Mexico Territory.

What happened next took Junius by surprise. It surprised Nick, too, as well as everyone else who was watching. It made the sheriff smile, so that was a good thing. Maybe he wouldn't lock Junius up for too long.

The girl lifted her wicker valise and bashed Junius over the head with it. From the fragile looks of her, Nick hadn't expected her to do anything so aggressive. Shocked, Junius let her go and staggered backward. Nick rushed up and grabbed him around the middle before Junius could draw his gun and shoot the girl's valise. Sheriff Wallace ran up, too, and managed to wrestle Junius's sidearm out of his holster while Nick pinned his arms at his sides.

Thank God, Nick thought. *Thank God.* Eccentricity was far from an unusual characteristic out here in the western territories, but every now and then Nick's uncle Junius carried it to extremes.

"Haul him over to the jail, Nick," Sheriff Wallace said as Junius continued to struggle. He didn't sound angry, which was damned near a miracle to Nick's mind. "I'm gonna lock him up until he sleeps it off."

"Hell, I only wanted to kick up a little lark," Junius said, sounding disheartened. He was strong as an ox, an attribute that came in handy at the blacksmithing and farrier shop he and Nick ran, but it was a distinct hindrance to Nick at the moment. Fortunately, Nick was strong as an ox himself, as well as several inches taller and a few decades younger than Junius, and he didn't lose his grip.

"He isn't going to sleep for a while yet, Sheriff," Nick told him, mostly because he didn't want the sheriff to get mad when Junius sang for the next two or three hours.

"I know it. But I'm not going to have him running loose on the streets and bothering no more ladies, either." For a young man, Wallace had always been kind of a stuffed shirt, more's the pity.

"I want to press charges," the woman announced.

Even though he was having a time subduing his uncle, Nick stared at her in surprise. She stuck her little chin in the air and repeated herself. "I want to press charges. That man assaulted me on a public thoroughfare."

Well, Nick guessed she had a right to do what she pleased, but he did think pressing charges was kind of mean, considering all Junius had been doing with her was the polka. He didn't argue, because he needed his strength to handle his uncle.

"Come on to the office with us, ma'am, and we can discuss the matter."

Nick recognized Sheriff Wallace's voice as the one he used when he was trying to impress a woman. Nick would have grinned if he weren't otherwise occupied. It took some doing, but he finally managed to muscle Junius over to the sheriff's office. Once they were all inside, Sheriff Wallace unlocked the single cell in the back room, and Nick shoved Junius into it. He was exhausted by that time, and sank into a chair in the front room as soon as he was sure Sheriff Wallace could get the cell door locked. He popped up again when he saw Junius's dancing partner frowning down at him.

"Sorry, ma'am." Nick removed his hat and gestured at the chair. "Won't you please have a seat?" He was hoping she'd soften in her attitude toward Junius if he was polite to her. When she sniffed and sat, his hopes died.

Junius had been hollering. Now he began to sing. Since he only sang bawdy songs when he was drunk, Nick shook his head and took to wishing they'd stayed home today. The girl stiffened in her chair like a pointer eyeing a duck. Sheriff Wallace shut the door, although the flimsy wood didn't appreciably muffle Junius's voice.

"Try to ignore him, ma'am," Sheriff Wallace advised, taking the chair behind his desk, which he generally did when trying to look official. He hauled out a red bandanna and wiped the sweat from his brow. "He isn't dangerous most of the time."

The girl huffed indignantly and followed it up with a furious, "I never!"

Nick thought that summarized the situation pretty well.

"Now, ma'am," Sheriff Wallace continued. "You say you want to press charges? Want a drink of water, first? You've had a shock."

"I should say I have. I've never been mauled like that in my life. And no, I wouldn't care for water. Thank you."

Nick watched her through slitted eyes. He wouldn't mind mauling her some himself. She was a ripe little thing, with a curvy figure, a fair complexion, and lots of dark reddish-brown hair. Her eyes were deep blue, not unlike a territorial sky when you could see it through the dust. Nick liked blue-eyed females. He couldn't fault his uncle's taste, even if Junius's approach lacked subtlety.

"I know, ma'am. It's a shame, but Mr. Taggart's uncle Junius can be a handful." The sheriff gestured at Nick to let her know who Mr. Taggart was.

"He's more than a handful. I believe the man is mad." She shot Nick a hateful glance, which Nick didn't appreciate. Hell, it wasn't his fault Junius couldn't handle his liquor. Nick had tried to rescue her, and it also wasn't his fault she'd rescued herself before he'd had the chance.

Sheriff Wallace eyed her doubtfully. "He didn't look mad to me, ma'am. He looked like he was enjoin' himself."

"Mad, in this instance, Sheriff, means insane," the girl informed Wallace.

"He's not insane," Nick muttered. "He just gets a shade lively sometimes."

"Lively!" The woman snorted. Hatefully.

"Yes, well, it's over now, ma'am. Is there anything I can do for you? You're new in Rio Peñasco, aren't you?"

After his speech, Sheriff Wallace smoothed his mustache in a gesture Nick recognized. The sheriff made a play for any pretty female who happened through Rio Peñasco. This one was pretty, but she wasn't real friendly. Nick preferred his females friendly, quiet, and compliant. No matter what a female looked like, every single one of them had the same equipment, and that's the only thing Nick cared about. If he wanted to look at something pretty, all he had to do was watch the sunset. If he wanted to talk, he could talk to Junius. Nick never wanted to argue, which was one of the main reasons he didn't cotton to proper females. Nick had never yet met a respectable woman who couldn't argue the leg off a lawyer.

"Yes, I just arrived a moment or two before that bear of a man grabbed me." She spoke in a cold voice. "My name is Miss Eulalie Gibb, and I have been hired to sing at the Peñasco Opera House."

The sheriff shot a look at Nick, who shot one back. This woman had been hired to sing at the Opera House? The very same disorderly house from which Nick had exited in order to save her from his uncle? Nick eyed her more closely. Maybe she was more his type than he'd first thought.

"Uh," said Sheriff Wallace, "did you say the Opera House, ma'am?"

"Yes." She sounded indignant, as if she thought Sheriff Wallace should pay closer attention to her than he seemed to be doing.

"Er, ma'am, did you know the Opera House isn't a real opera house? It's more of a saloon, if you know what I mean."

There went her chin again. "Yes. I know exactly what you mean. But a girl has to work somewhere."

"Where are you from, ma'am?" Nick asked, suddenly curious about this newcomer.

The look she gave him was one of the iciest Nick had ever received from a woman. "I," she said grandly, "am from Chicago, Illinois."

"Ah." Nick nodded. Maybe that accounted for it. He didn't expect a lady from Chicago, Illinois, would know much about the kinds of saloons in territorial villages like Rio Peñasco.

She might have read his mind, because her gaze thinned and she scowled at him some more. "I know the territory is rough, and I know I shall probably meet many rugged men who don't have any manners and who don't know how to behave. Your uncle is a prime example of that breed, I expect, Mr. Taggart."

"Aw, Junius isn't so bad. There are worse." Nick wondered what her point was.

"But, as you saw for yourself, I was able to defend myself against him. And I wasn't even prepared for his assault. I imagine I'll have to entertain lewd comments and perhaps even unwelcome advances when I'm singing, and I am fully prepared to fend off any number of men, even drunken inebriates like the man singing in that room. I," she concluded with a firm nod, "am a very determined person."

"Yeah, I can tell." She was beginning to annoy Nick, who didn't like boastful people. Nick was pretty determined himself, but he didn't go around telling everyone he met about it.

"I don't know, Miss Gibb," Sheriff Wallace said, scratching his chin. "The Opera House is kind of a hard joint."

"I'm sure it couldn't be otherwise in this awful place."

Nick didn't like people who walked into a new town, especially one in which he lived, and disparaged it, either. "So why'd you come out here if you don't like it?" he asked sharply.

She paused just long enough to make Nick wonder if she was going to lie. Then she turned on her chair and skewered him with the shiveriest blue gaze he'd ever seen. "Some people," she said slowly and deliberately, "may not understand this, but I have to make my own way in the world, and I *won't—*" she placed special emphasize on the won't—"be at the mercy of men."

It didn't sound like a lie.

Nick continued to watch her, still vaguely wondering if she had a point. She didn't continue, so he reckoned maybe she thought she'd made it. "So you're going to take up working as a saloon singer? That doesn't sound like a very good way to stay away from men, if you ask me."

"I didn't ask you. However, I am a singer, Mr. Taggart. The opportunities for singers in Chicago aren't bright because it, unlike the territory, is a civilized place where many, many talented people are vying for the positions available. I applied for the job in Rio Peñasco because I figured the competition wouldn't be as stiff for someone starting out in a career, as I am."

"Oh," said Nick.

"Oh," said Sheriff Wallace.

She stood abruptly. "I've decided against filing charges, however. I presume that man isn't vicious and was merely overcome by injudicious consumption of spirituous liquors. Therefore, I shall leave him in your capable hands, Sheriff." She smiled at Sheriff Wallace, whose Adam's apple bobbed up and down when he swallowed. "I shall repair to the Opera House and talk to Mr. Chivers." Doolittle Chivers owned and ran the saloon. "I told him to expect me around this time."

Again, Nick and Sheriff Wallace exchanged a glance. Dooley Chivers wasn't going to be pleased when this innocent young thing showed up to take the job he had open for a singer. Nick knew good and well Dooley had been expecting another sporting girl, one young and pretty enough and with a good enough voice to enable him to charge a high price for her other services. Nick hadn't met Eulalie Gibb before today, but he already knew she didn't fill that bill.

"Uh, maybe I should escort you over there, ma'am." Sheriff Wallace rose from his chair and tugged at his vest. "I don't think it's a good idea for a lady to walk into the Opera House all by herself."

She looked down her nose at him, even though she was shorter than he by at least a foot. "I intend to work there, Sheriff. I shall have to learn to walk alone among the patrons. I may as well begin as I intend to go on."

The sheriff appeared nonplussed, which seemed a sensible reaction to Nick, who really didn't like this testy little thing at all. "Let her go, Mike, if that's the way she wants it. She doesn't want your help."

Eulalie Gibb glanced at Nick. "That's right. And I don't want yours, either."

Nick held up both hands. "I wasn't offering it to you, ma'am."

She sniffed again, gave him one last mean look, turned, and walked out the door, her back as straight as a board. Nick shook his head.

"Hell, she isn't what Dooley's expecting, or I'll eat my hat," Sheriff Wallace said.

Nick suspected the sheriff's hat was safe. He also experienced a strong desire to see the woman put in her place—which wasn't singing in a saloon. Damned snippy thing. Through the sheriff's dirty window, he watched her walk

16

across the street, her bottom switching, thinking of all sorts of scenarios that might transpire in that saloon in which she'd get her comeuppance. He'd like to see it happen. He stood and stretched.

"Reckon I'll go over there and watch the fun."

She'd almost made it to the saloon. Nick experienced a funny sensation in his chest that felt a lot like worry, although he was sure it wasn't. He'd gotten over worrying about women years ago.

"Good idea," said Wallace. "Reckon I'll join you."

That made Nick feel a little better. It was, after all, the sheriff's duty to see to the safety of women in Rio Peñasco. Not that Nick's intention was to see to Miss Gibb's safety. Hell, he didn't care what happened to her. Still and all, he felt better knowing the sheriff would be there.

"And she said Toodle-oo as she pulled off her shoe . . ." rendered in Uncle Junius's rich if slightly off-key bass voice, followed them out of the sheriff's office.

Eulalie Gibb wasn't nearly as fearless as she pretended to be. In fact, she approached the battered batwing doors of the Peñasco Opera House with a good deal of trepidation and inner apprehension. Since, however, she also approached it with a Colt Lightning revolver in her handbag, a small Colt Ladysmith in her pocket, several long, sturdy, and extremely sharp pins in her hat, and a ten-inch Bowie knife in a scabbard strapped to her thigh, she figured she was up to it. She'd better be, since she was all the hope she and Patsy had left in this life. The thought of her sister waiting in Chicago for Eulalie to send for her stiffened her resolve. She thrust the doors open and stepped inside with resolution.

Her resolution suffered a setback when she walked straight into a thick, almost palpable cloud of smelly cigar

17

smoke only a second before she bumped into the thick, definitely palpable, back of someone Eulalie assumed was no gentleman. He turned around and grinned down at her while Eulalie was still sneezing.

"Well, look here, Petey. What do we have here?"

"Ain't you never seen no female before, Lloyd? That there's a gal."

Eulalie wiped her nose on a handkerchief hastily yanked from a pocket and frowned at the two men discussing her. They were excessively rude, but Eulalie had prepared herself for rudeness as well as lascivious suggestions and even physical assaults. She opted not to reach for her Ladysmith yet, but asked coldly, "Is Mr. Doolittle Chivers here?" Lord, she was going to have a time of it trying to sing in all this smoke. She hoped she could persuade Mr. Chivers at least to open a window or two when she performed.

"Dooley? I reckon he's around here somewhere," the man she'd bumped into said. "What you want with him, honey? I'm nicer'n Dooley any old day."

She wrinkled her nose. "What a dreadful thought. Where might Mr. Chivers be, my good man?"

Lloyd thumped Petey's shoulder. "Did ya hear that, Petey? She already knows I'm good. How about that?"

Eulalie huffed and gave up trying to get assistance from these two louts. She turned away from them and had begun to stalk across the smoky saloon in search of more helpful folks when she felt a beefy hand on her arm. She tried to snatch her arm away, but sausage-like fingers closed around it, squeezing into her flesh and hurting. With a sigh, Eulalie turned around to discover it was Lloyd who'd grabbed her. No surprise there. She ought to have expected as much.

"Release me, sir, if you please."

He leered down at her. "What if I don't please, yer majesty?"

He obviously thought his assessment of her demeanor was hilarious, because he roared with laughter.

Eulalie was not amused. She reached into her pocket and withdrew her Ladysmith. "If you don't please, then I suppose I shall have to shoot you."

Lloyd looked stunned, an expression Eulalie neither understood nor appreciated. As far as she was concerned, a man as uncouth and obnoxious as Lloyd should expect any number of distasteful things to happen to him before someone killed him.

"Hey," he said. "You don't have to shoot me."

She glanced pointedly at his fingers, which were still wrapped around her arm.

"Let her go, Lloyd," said a voice from the saloon's door.

It was a voice Eulalie recognized. She was, therefore, not alarmed when she and Lloyd turned to see who had spoken, and Nicholas Taggart stood there, looking like a large gray ghost wavering through the cigar smoke. She was somewhat surprised he'd come, however, since she'd received the impression from their first meeting that he didn't like her much. On the other hand, he'd probably merely come to the saloon for a drink. He looked the type; it must run in the family.

"Hell, Nick, I'm just havin' me a little fun," Lloyd said.

He still didn't release her arm, and Eulalie was growing peeved about it. His fingers were not only large and painful, gripping her that way, but they were undoubtedly dirty as well. Eulalie didn't care to have the sleeve of her traveling coat smudged.

"I don't think the lady's having any fun, Lloyd," Nick said calmly. "She's the new singer Dooley just hired. You don't want to damage the hired help now, do you?"

19

"I ain't damaging her," Lloyd protested.

"Really!" Eulalie said, incensed. "This is too much to bear."

And with that, she whacked Lloyd's fingers with the butt of her Ladysmith as hard as she could, which was pretty hard since she was a strong woman.

Lloyd bellowed and leaped away from her. Eulalie did not repocket her gun because she didn't trust him. In fact, she didn't trust any of these rough men. Because of this mistrust, she positioned herself so that her back was against the bar. She didn't aim to have anyone attack her from behind again.

"Why'd you hit me?"

"You'd rather I shot you?"

"Naw, but why'd you hit me?" Lloyd sounded as if he might cry.

"Because I do not care to be manhandled," Eulalie said tartly. "I won't stand for it."

She noticed Nick Taggart looked surprised, too. He'd drawn his gun, but held it at his side. The sheriff stood behind him. He hadn't drawn his gun at all, a circumstance she considered odd. She had assumed, before her arrival in this hellhole of a town, that if guns were drawn, they'd be drawn by the law and/or by outlaws, although she didn't really know much about how life went on out here in the territory.

A glance around the room showed her that everyone else in the saloon, except those men who seemed to be sleeping at various tables, had slid to the floor and flattened themselves out. That must have been the shuffling noise she'd heard right after she'd thumped Lloyd. Interesting. She'd keep this reaction to drawn guns in mind if she ever needed to clear a room in a hurry.

"What's going on in here?" a new voice said. When Eulalie turned to look, she beheld a large, solid man with a handlebar mustache, fluffy salt-and-pepper side-whiskers, and a florid face, standing at the door to a back room.

"This is your new singer, Dooley."

It was Nick Taggart who'd spoken. When Eulalie looked from Mr. Chivers to him, she saw him slipping his firearm back into its leather holster. She wasn't sure she should turn her back on Lloyd, but decided he probably wouldn't do anything as long as Nick Taggart and the sheriff were there. Besides, Mr. Chivers owned the place. People would probably behave themselves around him if they wanted to continue imbibing in his establishment. She stepped away from the long, polished bar, and put her Ladysmith back into her pocket.

"Eulalie Gibb, Mr. Chivers. We corresponded."

Dooley's eyes went round. "Er, yes, ma'am."

Eulalie waited, but he didn't seem inclined to continue speaking. Perhaps he was uncertain because of the unorthodox way she'd been introduced. Not that it was her fault. Yet she felt obliged to clear the air—in a manner of speaking. It would take a month of windstorms to clear the cigar smoke out of this place.

"I just arrived by stagecoach, Mr. Chivers, and I wanted to meet you first, before I searched for lodgings."

"You ain't got no place to stay?"

Eulalie considered telling him that no, she didn't have no place to stay; rather, she did have no place to stay, but she figured that would merely confuse him. Grammar seemed to be as uncommon as manners in Rio Peñasco. That was all right. Eulalie was ready for whatever the territory offered her.

"Yes. I need to secure lodgings, but I wanted to meet my new employer first and introduce myself."

Dooley Chivers had begun to frown at her, a circumstance Eulalie feared boded ill for her future employment. She braced herself, prepared to battle tooth and nail to hold on to

21

this job, such as it was. She and Patsy needed it. She'd be hanged if she'd let Mr. Chivers un-hire her after he'd hired her. Besides, she had no choice.

"Uh, I'm not sure about this," he said.

Drawing herself up as tall as she could, Eulalie said, "You were sure in your letter. We agreed to a salary."

"Well, yeah, I know it, but I didn't think you'd be—you."

"Who did you think I'd be?" she asked, irritated by his lack of logic.

He shrugged. "Well, I reckon I didn't mean that, exactly. It's only—" He broke off abruptly.

"It's only what?"

Muffled footsteps sounded on the saloon's plank boards. The room had been silent except for Eulalie and Dooley's voices. Slowly men began picking themselves up from the floor, dusting off their trousers, and resuming their seats at various tables. Eulalie supposed some sort of Western communication with which she was unfamiliar had taken place, and that the men sensed danger was over for the nonce. The danger wasn't over for her, however. Nor was it over for Patsy. It might never be.

That thought buoyed her flagging courage. She wasn't going to let Mr. Doolittle Chivers cheat her out of her job.

"You hired me, Mr. Chivers."

"I know it, but—"

"Yeah, Dooley, you hired her."

To Eulalie's surprise, Nick Taggart appeared next to her. She wasn't sure she wanted him there, even if he did seem to be on her side. Because she felt the need to fight her own fights, she said, "I sing very well, Mr. Chivers. You won't be disappointed."

"Well, but . . ." Dooley looked her up and down in a fashion Eulalie imagined she'd better get used to. "Well, but what about costumes. You can't go on stage dressed like that."

Ah, so that was it. The man dealt in flesh as well as liquor. Eulalie, who prided herself on her unflappability, was prepared for this, as she was prepared for everything. "I have a plethora of costumes, Mr. Chivers," she said in a voice as dry as the wind blowing the earth away outside. "Why don't you allow me to sing tonight so you can see for yourself? Your customers won't be disappointed, I can assure you."

This time it was Nick Taggart who looked her up and down, as if he were undressing her in his mind's eye. Eulalie did not react outwardly. Inwardly, she blushed up a storm.

"Well . . ." Chivers still sounded uncertain.

Nick, however, had evidently made up his mind. He said, "Yeah, Dooley. We won't be disappointed." To Eulalie, it sounded as though he'd enjoyed his visual inspection of her body.

"I just don't know, Nick. If you say so, mebbe it'll be all right."

Although Eulalie wasn't sure she liked Nick Taggart, she did appreciate his support. She even smiled at him.

With a huge sigh, Dooley Chivers acquiesced to forces stronger than himself. After a few more doubtful minutes, which included a discussion of where Eulalie would spend the night, he even took Eulalie's wicker bag. He then proceeded to lead her to the small dressing room behind the stage.

Chapter Two

Nick watched them go, his curiosity about Miss Eulalie Gibb acute. She didn't look like a saloon singer, most of whom wore lots of paint and dolled themselves up like tarts. Since he didn't want to go home, while Uncle Junius remained locked up in jail, he decided to wait until Junius had sung himself out, slept for a while, and woke up again.

While Nick lingered to escort Junius home, he talked to Dooley Chivers, who had reappeared not long after he'd led Miss Gibb backstage. Dooley sported a hangdog, harassed expression beneath the whiskers on his face.

"Hell, Nick, she's no more a saloon singer than I am."

Since Nick had heard Dooley sing once or twice, this was hard for him to imagine. He laughed. "Aw, give the girl a chance, Dooley. Maybe she'll be really good."

Dooley didn't appear much cheered by Nick's suggestion as he took a gulp of beer. "Really good. Yeah. For her sake, I hope so. And for mine, too. The boys ain't gonna like it if she stinks."

It was difficult to imagine Miss Eulalie Gibb stinking, in any sense of the word. Nick didn't say so. "She's a smart cookie, Dooley. She'll be all right. Hell, even if her voice isn't prime, she's prime to look at, and that's what matters."

"Prime?" Dooley looked like he wanted to run away and hide. "Prime, my ass. She's stiff as a board."

Nick shrugged. "She'll probably unbend when she starts singing. She sure looks good."

He didn't know why he was sticking up for the pungent Miss Gibb. He didn't like her. Yet when he'd pushed open the saloon doors and seen her there, holding big Lloyd Grady off with no more than her acid tongue, he'd felt a spasm in his heart that had hurt like a fit. He'd have shot Lloyd there and then except he feared the bullet might hit her. It galled him that he still felt a need to protect stray females. After putting up with what he'd put up with when he was a kid, he should know better.

"Hell, Nick, I don't even know how she looks. She says she's got costumes, but I ain't seen 'em yet. She looks like a schoolmarm to me. The boys hanker after skin."

"Yeah, I know they do." So did Nick. He was kind of looking forward to seeing some of Miss Gibb's, even if she was sharp as a cactus spike.

It had been decided that Miss Gibb would sleep in the saloon that night, upstairs in an empty room. Tomorrow, Nick had told her, he'd introduce her to Mrs. Johnson. Mrs. Johnson, widowed mother of five sprightly children, would be happy to rent her a room, even if she had to have her children build it.

Eulalie had argued at first. "Is Mrs. Johnson a respectable female?"

"Sure, she's respectable," Nick had retorted, nettled. Hell, he'd expected her to thank him and her lucky stars he'd come to her rescue again. "Anyway, she's likely to think it's you who's not very respectable, if you don't mind my saying so, Miss Gibb, singing in a saloon and all."

"I do mind your saying so, Mr. Taggart. And I am imminently respectable, thank you very much."

Nick had been able to come up with no rebuttal to that one, so he'd shut his yapper.

"I ain't easy in my mind about her sleeping here tonight,

either," Dooley said glumly. "What if some of the boys get frisky?"

Recalling Miss Gibb's belly gun, Nick said, "I expect she can take care of herself."

"Hell, yes, she can take care of herself. But I don't want her shootin' up the clientele, dammit."

That was a reasonable point to Nick's way of thinking. "If you want, I can stand guard, Dooley. I don't have to go home until Junius sobers up anyway." Nick and Junius lived behind their smithy at the north end of Rio Peñasco.

Dooley watched him slanty-eyed for a moment. "You got any plans for the female yourself, Nick? She ain't bad looking, but she's mean tempered. I don't want to have to mop up any man's blood if she gets mad and shoots him, especially not yours." He frowned and rubbed his chin. "Mebbe I should ask the sheriff to keep her in a cell overnight."

"Not necessary, Dooley."

"I dunno. Might be safer than here." Giving Nick a good hard look, he said, "But you ain't staying in her room."

Nick shook his head, nettled. "I don't have any designs on her, for God's sake. I'm offering to do you a favor, Dooley. Let her stay here tonight, and I'll stand guard."

"Not if you aim to sleep with Violet, you won't," Dooley said flatly. "I ain't havin' one o' my whores occupied for a whole night and not get no money for it."

"I wasn't aiming to sleep with Violet," said Nick, who had been. "Hell, I already slept with her once today, and I'm not a greedy man."

"Huh." Dooley sipped his beer and thought about Nick's offer. "I reckon you can stay here, then. It'll save you a walk in the morning."

So Nick whiled the rest of his day away playing cards in the

Opera House and wondering just what kind of costume Miss Eulalie Gibb would wear that night in her premier performance. He also wondered if she could let the starch out long enough to put on a good show.

There was much speculation about the new singer among the men in the saloon. Nick listened and grinned and didn't participate, although he couldn't account for his reluctance to do so. Nor could he account for the compulsion he experienced to shoot several men who were ruminating rather salaciously about Miss Gibb's anticipated charms. His reaction was nonsensical; he knew it. Therefore, he left his gun on the table—as a subtle warning that he wouldn't tolerate cheating—and maintained his composure.

Eulalie looked at herself in the mirror and frowned at the image she saw reflected therein.

"I've never seen anything so coarse and vulgar in my entire life," she muttered at her reflection. "Perfect. Exactly the image I was striving for."

Eulalie knew very well that coarseness and vulgarity were qualities much prized in the western territories. She'd studied up on the matter specially, when she and Patsy had decided they needed to get out of Chicago. She only hoped she could make plenty of money quickly, so that she could send for Patsy before Gilbert Blankenship found her. Patsy was still pretty well laid up for the time being, but once she healed, Eulalie wanted her here so that she could watch out for her.

Poor Patsy was too sweet for her own good, and look what it had gotten her. Eulalie was way past sweet; she'd learned the hard way that sweetness only earned a girl grief.

Although she hadn't told Patsy so, she'd decided during her trip to Rio Peñasco that she'd even sell her body if she had to, in order to protect her sister. Patsy would have been appalled and refused to let her go if she'd told her, so she hadn't. Patsy had enough to worry about already.

Rather short-sighted, Eulalie had donned her spectacles in order to make sure her costume fitted right and was indecent enough, and that she'd rouged her cheeks to a high-enough bloom. Putting her hands on her hips, she turned slowly in front of the mirror, looking at herself from all sides. Perfect. She plucked her glasses off and laid them on the dressing table.

"God bless Marjorie Dobson," she murmured, picking up her comb.

Marjorie Harrison had been a showgirl in Chicago before she'd married a Mr. Hilton Dobson, who'd spotted her in the chorus. Now Marjorie was a respectable and respected matron, and she'd gladly donated her costumes to Eulalie and Patsy when Eulalie had explained their desperate situation to her.

Fortunately, Eulalie and Marjorie were about the same size, except that Eulalie's bosom was somewhat larger than Marjorie's. In Eulalie's estimation this was a good thing, since it was sure to titillate the males who would pay to watch her parade her wares. Eulalie felt nothing but contempt for most men. She'd loved the one good man she'd ever met, and now he was gone. She was almost looking forward to teasing these beastly Westerners with her forbidden fruits for Patsy's sake. She worked her hair up in the way her mother had taught her, weaving faux pearls in it and then stabbing a perfectly garish ostrich feather through the knot on top.

She put down her comb and surveyed the result of her work. "There. I've never seen you look worse, Eulalie Gibb." She was so pleased with herself that she grinned.

In spite of the saloon's rough clientele and locale, Mr. Chivers had a well-appointed, if smoky, establishment. There was even a stage rigged with a purple velvet curtain and gold scalloped edging. If it weren't for the dust coating everything, that curtain might even be pretty. Eulalie didn't suppose there was much one could do about the dust out here, since the wind seemed to blow constantly, and there was nothing by way of trees or shrubs to stop it. Nobody'd warned her about the wind.

There was also an orchestra of sorts, consisting of a piano, a violin—fiddle, she supposed she should call it—and a horn. The piano player was a consumptive drunk, the fiddle player was a fifteen-year-old boy, and the horn player was a Mexican man who seemed to have trouble with anything that didn't have a Latin beat to it, but Eulalie didn't care. She could sing with them or without them. She aimed to make the whole town love her voice and her shape, if not her personality, so that she'd make a lot of money fast.

Her costume was low-cut in front, and Eulalie's bosom was more than ample. She had plenty of cleavage, in other words, and she stuffed her Ladysmith between her breasts. She wasn't going to take any more chances than she had to.

A knock came at the door, and she turned quickly, reaching for the Ladysmith as she did so. "Who is it?"

"It's me, Miss Gibb. Nick Taggart."

"What do you want?" She didn't bother to try to sound polite.

"Dooley wanted me to tell you it's almost time." He sounded offended. Eulalie didn't care.

"I can tell time, Mr. Taggart. And I know when I'm supposed to perform."

There was a several-second silence from behind the door. Then Nick said, "You're very welcome," and Eulalie heard him stomp away. Since she hadn't heard him stomp up in the first place, she presumed she'd annoyed him with her acerbity. She didn't care about that, either.

He was right, though. It was almost time. Eulalie replaced the Ladysmith, sucked in a huge breath for courage, and bowed her head for a moment of silent prayer. Then she squared her shoulders, opened her door, and marched to the wings.

Nick Taggart had met unpleasant people in his day, but he'd never met one as aggravating, mouthy, and crusty as Miss Eulalie Gibb. He'd like to turn her over his knee and paddle her bottom. And then strip her naked and tussle with her until she begged for mercy.

When, after a suitable and almost tuneful introduction by the Opera House musicians, she slithered out onto the stage, looking for all the world like a professional harlot, his mouth dropped open and his fantasies dried up and blew away like so much chaff. He ceased thinking entirely. In fact, for a moment or two, he didn't believe it was really her. The Miss Eulalie Gibb he'd met couldn't look like that in a million years.

Could she?

The moment of stunned silence that filled the saloon was followed by a din the likes of which Nick had never heard before. The noise, consisting of whoops, catcalls, whistles, stomping feet, and bellows of approval, jarred him out of his slack-jawed contemplation of Miss Eulalie Gibb's abundant charms.

She was . . . she was . . . Nick couldn't think of a word for what she was. Several came close. Magnificent. Shapely. Breathtaking. Gorgeous. Splendid. Stimulating. Arousing.

Arousing. That was it. In fact, she was so arousing in her present state of undress that Nick's prior wish that he could strip her naked thundered back into his head like a randy bull. When he could pry his gaze away from her, he looked at the other men in the room and decided they all felt the same way. Which made him angry. All at once, he experienced an almost overwhelming urge to rush up to the stage, wrap a blanket around Eulalie Gibb, and haul her off so that none of these other men could ogle her the way Nick was doing.

"Holy shit," Nick heard at his side. He shot a glance at Dooley Chivers and discovered him staring, bug-eyed, at Miss Gibb. Dooley's mouth hung open, too, and his cigar barely clung to his lower lip. Nick repressed the urge to shove the lit cheroot down the older man's throat.

His reaction was stupid. Nick knew it, and he forced himself to get a grip on his emotions. What the hell did he care if Miss Eulalie Gibb made a spectacle of herself in front of a mob of lustful men? It was no skin off his teeth. She was nothing to him but a pain in the neck. Or in another part of his anatomy.

Nick suppressed a frustrated moan when Eulalie, smiling provocatively and, posing with one pink-slippered, well-shaped foot poised in front of the other, lifted her arms for silence. He gulped hard. When she lifted her arms like that, her bosom damned near popped out of that teensy piece of bright pink material she had draped over it.

"Lord above, I ain't never seen nothing like it," Dooley murmured, awed.

Nick hadn't either. He didn't say so.

Dooley finally managed to drag his lascivious gaze away from his new singer and peered at Nick. "I swear, Nick Taggart. If I waren't lookin' at her with my own eyeballs, I'd never believe it was the same female. Did you think she'd turn out like that?"

31

Since he didn't trust his voice, Nick only shook his head and continued staring at Eulalie.

Looking as if she were the conqueror of the world, which she pretty well was in the very small world of the Peñasco Opera House, Eulalie smiled her seductress's smile at her ravening audience once more, and then signaled to the orchestra.

Nothing happened. When Nick glanced at the musicians, he discovered them gaping at Eulalie, too stricken with lust to play their instruments. He decided things had gone on long enough.

"Hey!" he shouted. "Get to playing, you fools!"

His voice was virile, deep, and loud, and it made everyone in the room jerk to attention. The whistles and stomps and catcalls stopped. Nick threw a cracker from the bowl on the bar at Griswold Puckett, the piano player, who immediately slammed his hands down on the piano keys, producing a chord that sounded like fifty cats screeching.

He recovered at once, however, and launched into the tinkly strains of *What Was Your Name in the States*, a song that had originated among the California gold-mining camps, but which held a good deal of appeal to the men populating New Mexico Territory nowadays. In fact, a new round of cheers went up from the men, many of whom, Nick knew, had been less-than-stellar citizens in the States and had left their original names behind when they moved to the territory.

When Eulalie began to sing, the room went quiet again.

"Sweet Lord, have mercy," Dooley whispered, which expressed Nick's sentiments to a T.

He'd never heard anything like it. Sweet and pure and as loud as the alarm bell on top of the sheriff's office, Eulalie's voice filled the air like sunshine after a storm. She had the most beautiful voice he'd ever heard in his entire thirty years of life. He felt like a pure fool when tears filled his eyes. Yet when he glanced around the room, he saw that most of the other men, those who weren't too drunk to be pervious, were sneaking hands to their eyes, too, and wiping tears away. A couple of bandannas appeared, even.

At least five minutes of thunderous applause followed Eulalie's rendition of *What Was Your Name in the States*. This time when she lifted her arms for silence, the men obeyed her. Nick had never seen a person, male or female, control an audience with such ease. He wondered if she'd been trained as an actress.

He decided she must have had some kind of training when she launched into *The Man on the Flying Trapeze*. She strutted and pranced on the stage like she'd been born on it. By the time she'd finished that one, every man in the house was drooling.

Nick himself had never seen a female kick so high. And her legs . . . Well, if he'd ever seen more delicious legs on a woman, he couldn't remember when. The fishnet stockings she wore didn't hurt any, either. Nor did the black-and-pink garter she'd pulled up to about mid-thigh. Lord on high. He discovered within himself a fierce desire to shoot all the other men who were lusting after her, and told himself to stop being an idiot.

From *The Man on the Flying Trapeze*, she went on to *Lorena* and *Streets of Laredo* and a couple of other tear-jerkers. Several men in the audience sobbed aloud. Nick was astounded.

Then she took a bow, and his eyes nearly bugged out of his head. She had knockers the size of watermelons. He heard Dooley suck in a deep breath. He'd noticed, too, Nick presumed. Who wouldn't? She was flaunting them for everyone to see and appreciate. Which, Nick gathered from the renewed chorus of whoops and hollers, everyone did.

"Jehosephat, Nick, it's a good thing you'll be stayin' here tonight. Otherwise, I ain't sure she'd survive the night."

Nick wasn't, either. Although she took several curtain calls, the noise didn't abate. Finally she stopped returning to the stage, and for a few tense minutes it looked as if the men might riot and tear the Opera House apart. Nick bounded onto the stage and drew his hogleg, however, restoring calm without more than several fights breaking out.

"She'll sing again tomorrow night, boys," he shouted above the din. Cheers erupted. He noticed Dooley was surrounded by men, all of whom, Nick presumed, were asking how much a tumble with Miss Gibb would cost. Nick saw red for a minute, and fired his gun into the planking of the stage.

Dooley Chivers said, "Aw, hell, Nick!" but Nick didn't feel very guilty about it. It wasn't the first time a gun had been fired in the Opera House, and it assuredly wouldn't be the last. At least this one had only made a hole in the floor. Usually, when a gun went off in the saloon, the bullet made a hole in a man. This was much less messy.

Again, men dropped like rain, flattening themselves on the dirty floor like lumpy carpeting. When Dooley had hollered at Nick, his cigar fell from his mouth and landed on the back of Jem Flick's neck. Jem hollered and swore, but he didn't get up. Any time gunplay broke out in the Opera House, most fellows considered themselves fortunate to escape with a cigar burn.

"Miss Gibb isn't for sale, boys," Nick called out. Groans and curses met his announcement. He was prepared for disappointment and didn't holster his gun immediately. "But Miss Violet and Dooley's other fine ladies will be happy to take care of you." He winked at the men on the floor, some of whom had lifted their heads to listen better.

Dooley, who had grabbed his cigar and apologized to Jem, nodded. "Nick's tellin' ya the truth, boys. Miss Gibb, she said she ain't in any but the singing-and-dancing business."

"That's right, boys. Miss Gibb's an honest-to-God actress, trained in Chicago." Nick didn't know if it was true or not, but it might as well be. She was surely good enough to have been trained somewhere.

Unhappy mutterings rumbled up from the floor. Men began to get to their feet and dust themselves off now that it appeared there would be no more guns going off.

Eulalie listened from behind the door of her small dressing room, wishing the door had a stronger lock. She had her own gun—the Colt Lightning this time—drawn, just in case. Her heart thundered like a herd of buffaloes stampeding through her chest. She'd never been so scared in her life as she was there for a second, when she'd wondered what she'd do if any of those men decided not to take no for an answer. One or two, she could probably handle with her Colt. More than that, and she'd be lucky to escape in one piece.

She and Patsy had formulated a contingency plan for conditions such as these that might arise, but Eulalie wasn't eager to implement it. For one thing, she'd hoped to get through this ordeal without having to depend on a man. She especially didn't want to acknowledge that she needed a man to protect her.

Aside from all that, she and Patsy had both learned the hard way that men were unreliable at best, even when they were working for money. More often than not, men were pure beasts. Eulalie wouldn't hire a bodyguard except as a last resort because she was done with beasts in this life if she could help it.

It began to seem like she might not be able to help it, however. She wasn't going to give up yet, but she decided she'd better keep her options open and her guns handy. If she had to fall back on her contingency plan, it looked to her as though Nick Taggart might be her best bet to hire as a bodyguard, but she couldn't be sure until she'd studied him a little longer. Which meant, of course, that she had to survive tonight in one piece. The wrong choice might be fatal to her plans.

A knock came at her door a moment after the noise in the saloon quieted to its more normal low roar. Eulalie kept her gun drawn. "Who is it?"

"It's Nick Taggart, Miss Gibb. May I come in for a minute?"

At least he was being polite. At this point in her career in Rio Peñasco, Eulalie didn't trust Nick Taggart a speck more than she trusted any other man in the damnable place, but she did consider his politeness in this instance encouraging.

She unlocked the door and pushed it open, holding her gun at what would be chest height on him. She also stepped back, in case he lunged at her. She'd had practice with this sort of thing, unfortunately.

Chapter Three

Nick frowned at Eulalie's revolver. "How the hell many guns do you own, anyway?"

"That's for me to know, Mr. Taggart."

"Well, you aren't going to need to use that one on me, Miss Gibb. I only came back here to tell you that I'll be watching out for you tonight."

Immediately suspicious, Eulalie said, "What do you mean, you'll be 'watching out for me'? What does that mean, Mr. Taggart? And where do you presume to be doing this watching?"

Nick's frown deepened into a scowl, which he directed at her Colt Lightning.

"I know how to aim and shoot it, Mr. Taggart, so don't get any ideas."

"Dammit, I'm not the one with ideas here. You're the one with ideas, if you think I'm going to do anything to you. I'm the one who saved you from those men out there, lady, or have you forgotten that?"

Eulalie searched his face. He was obviously offended, but she couldn't say that she cared much about that. What she cared about was whether he could do her the kind of service she might need of him. It did seem that the other men in town respected him. That was an auspicious sign. He was also good-looking, in a rugged sort of way. If she discovered she had to use him the way she thought she might, his looks might be a bonus, especially if she had to persuade him to help her by using more than mere money. She didn't want to mess up the sheets with any man at all, but a repulsive one would be beyond endurance. Life was hard enough without that.

She decided to give him a try and lowered her gun. "Thank you for that, Mr. Taggart. I beg your pardon if I seemed to misunderstand your intentions, but you must know that a woman's life as an actress isn't one of unalloyed peace and joy. A woman has to be able to protect herself."

He didn't look convinced. Nor did his scowl abate. "Maybe, but a fellow don't much like having a gun pointed at his belly by a woman he's just saved from being assaulted, either, in case you give a hang about that."

She gave him one more good, overall, penetrating look. "Actually, I'm not sure that I do. However, if your aim is to protect me from the rest of the men in Rio Peñasco, perhaps you can begin by guarding the door while I change my clothes."

His eyes went as big around as mush melons, and she noticed their color for the first time. They were a rather startling green, and quite lovely, shaded as they were with long, thick, dark lashes. Eulalie wasn't surprised. In her experience men were more apt to have beautiful eyes than women, which was about as unfair as everything else in life. Her own eyes were nice, which was a benefit in her profession, but they were a plain old everyday blue and not nearly as exotic as Nick Taggart's eyes.

"Don't worry, Mr. Taggart. There's a modesty screen in the corner." She gestured with her gun toward the Chinese screen blocking off a corner of the room. "You won't even have to avert your eyes."

Nick seemed to deflate. "Oh, yeah. I see it."

Eulalie couldn't tell if his tone reflected relief or disappointment, although she had her suspicions. Men were, after all, men. "Will you please lock the door, Mr. Taggart? Just in case." She made her eyes go squinty. "I presume you meant it when you said you were here to guard my person from marauding males."

"Of course I meant it. I told Dooley I would."

He didn't appreciate having his word questioned, either, Eulalie noted. Well, that was too bad. Eulalie wasn't about to take anything, least of all a man, and especially not one as large and intimidating as Nick Taggart, on faith.

"Thank you." She went behind the Chinese screen, where she'd already laid out the clothes she intended to change into. She was ravishingly hungry. After all, she hadn't eaten anything since the stage stopped a little before noon that day.

Since she was in a testing mode with Nick Taggart, she called out a question as she wriggled free of her costume. "Is there some place in town where a lady might get a bite to eat this time of the evening, Mr. Taggart?"

"Eat?" He still sounded annoyed.

"Yes. Eat. You do know what the word means, don't you?"

"Yes, I know what the word means. I'm thinking."

"Don't strain yourself." She pulled the ostrich feather out of her hair, gently disengaged the pearls, and began brushing. When she'd brushed out all the tangles, she wound her hair into a soft knot and pinned it up.

"You're a real peach, you know that, Miss Gibb? Do you have to practice being rude, or does it come naturally?"

"It comes naturally." Eulalie picked up her corset, and an awful thought struck her. Blast it, she was going to have to ask him to help her lace up the wretched thing.

"At least you admit it."

Nick Taggart sounded grumpy. Eulalie couldn't really

fault him much. She had, after all, been especially impolite to him.

"There's no reason not to admit it. I'm not ashamed to treat men the way they deserve to be treated." She eyed the offending garment, wondering where her brain had gone begging when she'd laid out her clothes. She should have chosen the one that laced in the front. But she hadn't, and there was no getting away from it. She certainly couldn't appear in front of the men she'd just entertained *sans* corset, or they'd never believe she was interested only in singing for them.

Of course, she could put her costume back on and go fetch the other corset from her trunk. She peered at the bright pink, and intolerably tight, garment she'd just removed and decided she couldn't bear it. She sighed deeply.

"You don't even know me. How the hell do you know how I deserve to be treated?"

"Simple," she said, thrusting her arms through the corset straps. "You're a man." She might have to get his help, but she wasn't going to give him more of a show than she had to. She paused to contemplate her conclusion.

On the other hand, this might be a good test. If he seemed intrigued by the sight of her bare flesh, and if she decided she needed him further, this would give her a chance to gauge his reaction to her charms. If he was like most men, he'd react like a rutting pig. That was the result she determined she wanted to achieve.

She stepped into her petticoats and tied the tapes at her waist. Then she walked out from behind the modesty screen, holding the corset to her bosom.

Nick Taggart looked as if he were enormously peeved. He stood at her dressing table, frowning down at her makeup pots and fingering a powder puff. "What does being a man have to do with—"

40

He made the mistake of turning before he'd finished his question. Eulalie was encouraged to see his mouth drop open and his eyes open wide. It looked to her as though whatever words he'd planned to say had been snatched from his head as if by a thieving magpie. She smiled at him, making sure it was one of her honey-was-no-sweeter-than-she-was smiles.

"I beg your pardon, Mr. Taggart. I don't believe you finished your thought." She waited, pressing the whale-boned instrument of torture to her bosom in order to enhance her cleavage. This was the second—maybe the third—time today she'd found cause to be grateful to her rather large bosom. Men were so predictable.

"What—" Nick had to stop and lick his lips. "What are you doing?"

"I was trying to get dressed, but I find I need help. May I get it from you? My corset laces in back."

Nick stood there for several more seconds, watching her as if he suspected her of ulterior motives. Which, Eulalie knew, she possessed in abundance, although he couldn't possibly know what they were. He probably thought she was trying to seduce him. Seduction, if it had to come at all, would come later. Eulalie planned to try every way she could think of to avoid it first.

"Well?" she said, to encourage him.

He straightened and took a step toward her. "Turn around." It was a command.

Eulalie obliged, although she still eyed him over her shoulder. She was glad to see he had to lick his lips again. "I'm sure you've had experience lacing up ladies' undergarments, Mr. Taggart." She made her voice go sultry. "And in unlacing them."

"I've had experience." He didn't elaborate.

And then he touched her. Eulalie had prepared herself for

at least a thousand contingencies before she'd set out for New Mexico Territory. She and Patsy had entered into this phase of their lives with their eyes wide open and with full knowledge of what they might have to do in order to escape from Chicago with their skins intact.

The one thing they hadn't prepared for was Eulalie's reaction to the physical sensation of Nick Taggart's hands on her bare flesh. She very nearly swooned on the spot.

Good Lord, this was terrible. She'd never had this reaction to a man's touch before. Perhaps it was merely because she was exhausted after enduring a long, tiring trip, awful worry, terrifying stress, a full day fraught with lumbering polka dancers and drunken louts, and her first performance in a strange and alien and half-civilized place. Not to mention near starvation.

Whatever the reason for it, she felt a tingling, goose-fleshy sensation spread over her skin as soon as Nick Taggart's large, rough hands brushed her shoulders. She gasped slightly, and barely thought fast enough to turn her gasp into a cough.

He smoothed his hands down her arms. He shouldn't be doing that. Even in its present scrambled condition, her brain knew that much. Eulalie opened her mouth to tell him so, but couldn't get the words out.

Good heavens, this was awful. She was the one who was supposed to be in control of this situation, not Nick Taggart. Nick Taggart was a rough-hewn man of the territories and, therefore, beneath Eulalie Gibb's contempt. She was a sophisticated actress; he was a lout. She, not he, was supposed to maintain the upper hand in any potential sexual dalliance.

So why, when his arms went around her, did she not resist? Why, when his fingers closed over hers and he pulled the corset away from her breasts, did she not utter a sharp protest, using the acid tongue for which she was justifiably famous in some circles? Why, when his hands covered her breasts and he gently squeezed them, brushing his thumbs over her puckered nipples, did she go weak in the knees?

"You want me to do what?" His voice was like roughened velvet. He drew her to him until her bare back rested against his chest and her bottom pressed against his thighs. He was fully aroused, hard as an oak log, and almost as big.

Eulalie, who had been fighting awful battles all by herself for a very long time, experienced a fierce desire to turn in his arms and have him hold her. She wanted to rub the juncture of her thighs against the bulge in his trousers.

No, no, no. This was not the way things were supposed to proceed. She had Patsy to think of.

"If you will please unhand me, sir, I believe you've made my corset fall to the floor." Eulalie was more proud of the tone she achieved—ironic and slightly humorous—than she was of anything else she'd done all day.

She felt his hot breath on her neck a second before his lips touched the skin of her shoulder. *Oh, Lord. Oh, Lord.* Eulalie's sexual experience was not vast, but just then she felt an intense desire to allow Nick Taggart to broaden her horizons.

No! She couldn't let a mere moment's pleasure ruin her plans. Patsy. She had to remember Patsy above all else.

"Mr. Taggart?" Again, she strove for lightness and achieved it. Eulalie was, first and foremost, an actress of the highest caliber. "I believe you've lost track of our purpose here."

"I don't think so."

If he didn't remove his hands from her breasts, she was going to scream. Not, unfortunately, in distress, but in pure, lust-crazed pleasure. When she'd made love with Edward, she'd been deeply in love, but she hadn't felt this pure animal desire. She hadn't really even believed women could feel this kind of overwhelming passion.

No. No, no, no. Patsy. She had to remember Patsy. And Gilbert Blankenship. And poor Edward.

"Mr. Taggart, I'm going to faint here and now if you don't stop that and feed me."

"I'll feed you. I'll stuff you full."

Trust a man. On the verge of panic, Eulalie spoke sharply. "That's not what I meant, and you know it. My body is not for sale, Mr. Taggart. Unhand me." His warm breath on her bare skin was about to send her over the edge. For the briefest second, Eulalie wished she could just give in to the sensation; to give herself, however briefly, to the keeping of this strong, warm, protective male.

By this time in her life, however, Eulalie knew such delicious feelings were only transitory—and in her case, they might well be deadly. No one would ever rescue her. She was on her own. She and Patsy.

It took an almost superhuman effort, but she slipped out of Nick's embrace, knelt, and scooped up her fallen corset. Then, her fingers trembling, she pulled it on again and dared turn and peer at Nick.

Mercy, he was something to look at. Tall and broad-shouldered, his torso tapered to a slim waist and narrow hips. The bulge in his trousers was huge, as were the massive, muscular legs supporting the rest of him. Eulalie would like to see him naked. And aroused. As beautiful and warmhearted as Edward had been, he'd also been kind of scrawny. As purely as Eulalie had loved Edward all those years ago, she still wouldn't mind seeing Nick Taggart naked.

Which was nothing to the purpose. "May I depend on you not to overstep the bounds of propriety again, Mr. Taggart?"

She smiled at him; a cool, aloof smile that cost her virtually all of her remaining composure.

"I can pay you." Nick looked as though the words had been pulled from him against his will and better judgment.

Eulalie shut her eyes for a split second. If only life were as simple as that. "My body is not for sale," she repeated softly, wishing things could be different, wishing she'd never had to leave New York, much less Chicago.

He watched her for a while longer, his eyes narrow, an expression on his face that Eulalie couldn't quite define. She lifted her chin defiantly. "And what's the matter with you, Mr. Taggart?" In truth, Eulalie knew exactly how he felt—both voluptuous and resentful—because she felt the same way about him.

"I don't like being teased, Miss Gibb," he said at last.

Oddly enough, Eulalie was a little ashamed of herself. She, who had planned her campaign ruthlessly, refusing to consider the feelings of anyone in the universe save herself and Patsy—and for good reason—felt guilty about having tempted Nick Taggart. She wouldn't let on.

"I'm sorry you feel that I teased you, Mr. Taggart. I was at fault for setting out the wrong corset, although it was an oversight."

"You were just trying to get me stirred up."

She didn't want to fight about it. He was right, and she was right, and they were both utterly wrong. "If you'd care to leave the room for a moment, I can fetch my other corset, fasten it myself, and we can avoid this discussion. I need to get some food in me, or I'm going to get a headache or faint, or both."

Nick huffed once. He still looked both angry and frustrated, but Eulalie sensed any danger was over for the time being. She had a more desperate feeling, however, that danger to herself and to her self-control would never be any farther away than Nick Taggart.

"Turn around," he said again. "I'll lace you up."

She eyed him for another moment or two, trying to judge if he meant it. She decided he did, turned around, and he laced up her corset. Her reaction to his touch still shocked her, but she didn't show it.

"There. Go get dressed. I'll wait here. Then I'll walk you to the chophouse down the street. Vern stays open late."

She could tell he was still unhappy, even angry, and didn't know whether to be glad of it or not. "Thank you, Mr. Taggart."

Nick wasn't accustomed to being outmaneuvered by a woman. Not as an adult, he wasn't. When he was a kid, he'd had no choice but to put up with their constant demands, fainting fits, and feigned helplessness. They'd nearly driven him crazy.

But he wasn't a kid any longer, and he didn't like this feeling of having been manipulated one little bit. The women in his adult life had been simple, often foolish, creatures, whom he could twist around his little finger with ease. He'd always been able to make females do what he wanted with them, which was why he only consorted with a certain type. No sense ruining virgins. Not only was it a dastardly thing to be doing, but it invariably got a fellow in trouble.

Not that he was ever mean to a woman. Hell, he had half the ladies in Rio Peñasco, married and unmarried, in love with him because he was always fixing things for them and so forth. But Nick never, ever, let himself get tangled up with one of them. He'd learned about women the hard way.

Since he'd grown up he'd never, not once, been manipulated by a female—until tonight, when he'd had the misfortune to become involved with Miss Eulalie Gibb, damn her soul to perdition. But that body. And that sassy way she had. He couldn't have resisted if all the angels in heaven had held him back when she turned around and he saw all that bare skin. She was as smooth as silk. And her breasts . . . Well, Nick wished he could stop thinking about them, was all.

His mood was as black as the night sky as he walked next to her down the dusty boardwalk to Vernon's Place. His thin gaze held everyone they met at a distance. Not that they met many people. Thanks to Dooley's worries about riots breaking out in the Opera House, there was a back door to the establishment. That's the one Nick had led Eulalie through when they'd exited. Nick didn't want to even try to imagine what might have happened if they'd walked out through the saloon itself. All the men Miss Gibb had stirred up with her performance wouldn't think twice about attacking her—or of shooting him to get at her.

Hell, and here he'd thought he was merely doing Dooley a favor by offering to protect her tonight. Dammit all, now Nick was the one needing protection—and from Miss Eulalie Gibb.

It wasn't fair, and Nick hated it. Not only was he as titillated as a bull pastured next to a meadow full of nubile young cows, but he had no way to escape. Eulalie Gibb wouldn't allow him into her bed, and he was committed to guarding her tonight. That meant he couldn't even relieve his lust with Violet.

"You're frowning, Mr. Taggart. Is something the matter?"

Nick looked down at Eulalie. She'd taken that silly feather out of her hair, and now her hair was piled up in a soft plop, as if she were a demure, maidenly schoolmarm. If he hadn't seen and felt her for himself, he'd never guess what alluring treasures lay hidden under that high-necked, prissy dress she wore. Lordy, he'd never realized how tempting clothes could be until now. At this moment he had a violent urge to pick her up off the boardwalk, take her home, and rip that dress right off of her.

"Oh, no. Nothing's the matter. I'm used to females flaunting their naked selves in front of me and then refusing to let me pay for what they're flaunting. Happens all the time. I'm fine. Just fine."

"I don't believe that for a minute."

"Why not?"

"I have a difficult time imagining that you don't usually get what you go after."

He squinted at her, wondering if she was making a play for him. If she was, why the hell hadn't she accepted his money? "Yeah? Well, I didn't get what I went after tonight, did I? Even after it was displayed in front of me, all ripe and ready for the picking."

She gazed up at him, a wry expression on her face. "That's not really fair, Mr. Taggart. I wasn't flaunting myself. I'd set out the wrong corset, is all."

"Sure it is."

"It's the truth."

"Like hell."

They walked in silence for another few moments. Nick gazed up at the sky. The wind had died down when the sun set, which it generally did this time of year. The stars looked like tiny points of light pricking the darkness of the heavens, and they twinkled up a storm. Sometimes Nick liked to ride out onto the plains and just sit on his horse and watch the stars twinkle. Tonight he wished he could crawl into bed, pull a blanket over his head, and hide away from those damned stars and everything else. They looked too blasted happy to him in his present state.

"I'm truly sorry, Mr. Taggart," Eulalie said after Nick had almost forgotten what they'd been talking about. "It wasn't fair of me to tempt you, I suppose."

"You suppose?" All of Nick's grievances against this woman stomped back into his head. "It seems to me I've been pretty nice to you today, Miss Gibb. I hauled my uncle away from you, kept Lloyd from attacking you right there in the saloon, prevented a riot from breaking out when Dooley told the boys you weren't for sale, offered to protect you all night long, and I'm now taking you to supper. What do you mean, you *suppose* it wasn't fair of you to tempt me? You're blasted right, it wasn't fair, and you know it."

She didn't speak again for a moment. When she did, she sounded almost contrite. "Perhaps, after we've eaten and we get back to the Opera House, you can—ah—visit one of the other girls who work there. That one named Violet seems to be quite pleasant, and she's very pretty."

"Violet's all right. At least she's nice, unlike some females I've met recently. But I told Dooley I'd watch out for you, and that's what I aim to do."

"I can take care of—"

"Yeah, I know. You can take care of yourself. Well, maybe you can and maybe you can't, but I promised, and I don't go back on my word."

"That's very good of you."

He couldn't tell for sure, but he suspected she was being sarcastic. "You're really something, you know that, Miss Gibb?"

She sighed. "I'm sure you have every reason to think so, Mr. Taggart."

"You're right. I do."

They'd reached Vernon's by this time. Nick opened the door and stood aside so she could enter the chophouse in front of him. She might not like him, and he might not like her, but Nick wasn't going to lower his standards because of their mutual dislike. He was a polite man, dammit, and that was that.

She swept past him like a queen, then stopped and looked around. Vernon's Place wasn't much; just a one-room eating joint in the territory that served steaks and beans and biscuits, but it was open, and she'd said she was hungry.

A few other men sat at the counter. Nick took a table in a far corner where he had a view of the whole room. He wasn't going to take any chances where Miss Eulalie Gibb was concerned. He pulled out a chair. "Sit here, Miss Gibb. I'll take the chair over there, with my back against the wall, so I can watch the front door and the room."

She sat. "Do you really think that's necessary?"

He glowered at her. "Yes. I do."

"Very well." Meek as a kitten, she settled her bottom onto a chair.

Nick had seen that lush bottom of hers in its skimpy costume, and he wished he could stop thinking about what he'd like to do with it. He sat, too, feeling abused and out of sorts, and set his hat on the chair next to him. Then he pulled out his revolver and laid it beside his knife and fork.

Eulalie eyed it curiously. "Do you always do that, Mr. Taggart? Is Rio Peñasco really so rough a place?"

He eyed her back, hard. "Not usually. Not in the daytime. And not when the boys haven't been teased to busting their britches by a new saloon singer."

She blinked, evidently startled by his plain speaking. "Oh. I see. I shall keep that in mind."

"Do that."

Vernon came over to them in his dirty apron. Vern was a nice enough fellow, but he didn't bother to fix himself up much. He had a stubble on his chin that looked itchy to Nick, and he had a dirty dishtowel draped over his arm.

"Howdy, Nick." Vernon glanced at Eulalie Gibb with patent appreciation. That's only because he didn't know her yet, Nick thought bitterly.

"Howdy, Vern. This here's Miss Eulalie Gibb. Dooley's hired her to sing at his place."

Vernon's eyebrows lifted. "You? You're the one everybody's been talkin' about?"

Eulalie smiled up at the restaurateur as if she were a great lady and he one of her lackeys. "I didn't know anyone had been talking." Her voice was cultured and sweet and soft, and if Nick didn't know better, he'd think she was nice. He did know better, though, and he thought she was being sneaky, cozying up to Vernon in this way.

"Yes, ma'am," Vernon told her. "They're all talkin' about how good you are. At singin', I mean."

Eulalie graced him with another smile. Nick decided enough was enough and said, "We want some chow, Vern. What you got tonight? The usual?"

His attention jerked away from Eulalie, Vernon turned to Nick, a blank expression on his face. "What?"

Nick uttered a warning growl.

Vernon snapped to attention. "Oh, yeah. Food. Sure, we got steak and beans and biscuits. I think there's still some of the apple pie I bought off Miz Johnson this morning."

"We'll take it," Nick said, hoping to get rid of the man.

Eulalie, it seemed, had other ideas. "Mrs. Johnson? Isn't that the lady to whom you're going to introduce me tomorrow, Mr. Taggart?"

"That's the one."

"You going to be staying at Miz Johnson's place, Miss Gibb?" Vernon asked, sounding more than a bit interested.

Nick eyed him narrowly. "Maybe she will, and maybe she won't. That's up to her and Mrs. Johnson, Vern, and we won't know until tomorrow."

"That'll mean you're stayin' right close to town, then, won't it?" Vernon reached up and tugged at his collarless shirtfront.

Nick wanted to holler at him. Then Eulalie fluttered her long eyelashes at Vern, and he itched to pick up his revolver and shoot the man dead. This was really bad. He had to get ahold of himself.

"I'm not sure what lodging arrangements I'll be making, Mr. Vernon."

"Call me Vern, ma'am. Everybody does. The back name's Howell."

"Mr. Howell."

Eulalie was smiling up at him as if he were the most wonderful man on earth. Nick, who knew better—hell, Vern didn't even bathe from one week to the next—interrupted the moment that seemed to be stretching between them. "Miss Gibb hasn't eaten since early in the day, Vern. She says she'll faint if she don't get fed soon. You want to get a move on?"

Vern started as if he'd been rudely awakened from a pleasant reverie. "What? Oh, yeah. Sure. I'll get them steaks going."

Nick frowned after Vernon as he walked off toward the kitchen to cook the food. "What the hell are you trying to do here, anyway, Miss Gibb? Get every man in the town lusting after you?"

She laughed. Her laugh was damned near as musical as her singing voice. "Heavens, Mr. Taggart, you're giving me much too much credit. I'm sure most of the men in Rio Peñasco don't know I exist and wouldn't care if they did."

Squinting over this blatant piece of disingenuousness, Nick muttered, "Don't press your luck, lady. Not all the men in town are as stupid as Vern or as understanding as me. You're apt to tease the wrong man one of these days and find yourself in a lot of trouble."

Eulalie shut her eyes for a minute and looked pained. Her attitude puzzled Nick, who figured she knew very well what she was doing and did it on purpose. "Mr. Taggart, I don't expect you to understand this, but my aim is not to frustrate a town full of rugged frontiersmen. My one aim in life is to earn enough money to send for my sister in Chicago."

Well, now, this was interesting. Nick wasn't sure he believed it. "You have a sister?"

She nodded. "Patsy."

"Why does she want to leave Chicago?"

"That's our business."

"Hmm. Wouldn't life be easier in Chicago for females on their own?" Nick remembered the explanation Eulalie had given earlier in the day about starting out in a singing career. "Oh, yeah. You said something about jobs being easier to get out here."

"Exactly."

As he pondered that one, Nick decided it didn't make any sense. He also sensed a withdrawal in his dining companion, however, as if she were determined not to reveal other than surface details of her circumstances to him. A trifle mysterious, Miss Eulalie Gibb. Nick wished she weren't, since mystery only added intellectual allure to her already potent physical charms. Of course, her prickly personality counteracted a good deal of that, thank God.

A booming voice startled both of them. "Aha, I've found you, my lovely prairie rose."

Nick glanced up, peeved. He recognized that voice. "Aw, hell."

Eulalie looked up, too, and glanced over her shoulder to see who had entered the small restaurant and addressed her thus. A fat, florid fellow stood at the door, beaming at her. He wore a brown checked suit, a string tie, and a tall beaver hat. He carried a cane with a carved horse's head handle.

Without much enthusiasm, Nick said, "Miss Gibb, that there's Bernie Benson."

Bernie strode over to Nick's table, giving Nick a conspiratorial wink as he did so. "Indeed, I am Mr. Bernard Benson, Miss Gibb. At your service." He gave her a flourishing bow, removing his beaver hat and damned near sweeping the floor with it. Nick shook his head and wondered sourly if Eulalie Gibb would have every man in Rio Peñasco acting like fools before she was through with them.

"Bernie owns the newspaper, Miss Gibb."

"Indeed, I do, and I aim to write a most complimentary review of your splendid opening night performance, Miss Gibb. May I sit with you?"

"There are only two chairs available," Nick pointed out. He wasn't about to remove his hat from the extra one for this tub of lard to sit in.

He should have known better than to think he could thwart Bernie with such an obvious ruse. At once, the fat man pulled up a chair from another table. "That's easily remedied." He gave Nick another jovial wink.

Nick, far from jovial himself, fingered his gun until he noticed Eulalie eyeing him in some alarm. He sighed and left his gun alone.

"My dear Miss Gibb," Bernie went on, ignoring Nick's overt hostility, "I can't tell you what a pleasure it is to see your delightful face and form and to hear your magnificent voice in Rio Peñasco. I'm astonished that such a lovely thing as you should have lowered herself to grace our shabby home with your glorious presence."

"That means he's happy to meet you," Nick said. He usually took pleasure in whacking the garbage out of Bernie's elaborate phrases, although tonight he wasn't enjoying it much.

Bernie laughed heartily. "Isn't our Nick here a card? Don't worry, though, Miss Gibb. He may look like a bumpkin, but he's not as doltish as most of the uneducated rascals populating the territory."

A bumpkin? Not as doltish? Nick glared at Bernie and shifted in his chair. He guessed it wouldn't be very nice to punch Bernie's nose in, but he might just do it if the man didn't quit trying to make him look like a yokel.

"Mr. Taggart? My goodness, no, Mr. Benson. Mr. Taggart has been my good angel today." Eulalie shot Nick one of her I'm-really-a-shy-and-oh-so-sweet-country-girl smiles. Nick frowned back at her, not believing it for a minute.

"A good angel, is he?" Bernie slapped Nick on the back, quite a bit harder than was necessary.

"That's me, Bernie." Nick slapped Bernie's back, too, and almost sent him tumbling over, chair and all. He followed up his slap with a warning look.

Bernie understood. He gave up trying to dislodge Nick by force or guile. They both knew he couldn't do it. "Well, well, well, I suppose wonders will never cease. Does Miss Violet know you're dining with Miss Gibb, Nick?" Bernie's piggy eyes squinted in Nick's direction.

Hell, the old fart was trying to make Eulalie jealous. As if such a thing were possible. She'd have to care about him first, and Nick knew good and well she didn't. "I expect Violet's got her hands full tonight, Bernie." Nick smiled another warning at Bernie, who again caught on.

He cleared his throat. "Ah, I see. Well, isn't that fine." He leaned toward Eulalie, who drew back slightly. Nick considered that a good omen. "Miss Gibb, it would be my great pleasure to conduct an interview with you for the *Rio Peñasco Piper*, our weekly newspaper. I can see the headlines now." Bernie spread his fat hands out over the table and half closed his eyes, as if he were picturing a pile of gold in his mind's eye. "Prairie Rose Comes to Town."

"Prairie Rose?" Nick guffawed rudely. "She's more like a prickly pear, if you ask me."

Eulalie kicked him under the table. Nick frowned at her. She frowned back.

Bernie's fleshy face, however, took on a thoughtful cast. "That's good, Nick."

"It is?" Nick stared at Bernie.

"It is?" So did Eulalie.

"New headline," Bernie announced, once again beaming. "A Rare and Precious Cactus Flower Blooms in Rio Peñasco."

Eulalie said nothing, but continued staring at Bernie.

Nick rolled his eyes.

Vernon came up to the table at that moment and plopped plates down in front of Eulalie and Nick. "You eatin' tonight, Bernie, or you just takin' up space?"

Unable to avoid the hint, Bernie rose reluctantly. "Alas, I've already eaten."

Nick stared deliberately at Bernie's broad belly. "That don't usually stop you."

Bernie didn't dignify Nick's pointed remark with an answer. Instead, he bowed low before Eulalie once more. "It's been a great pleasure, Miss Gibb."

"Likewise," Eulalie said. Nick got the feeling she didn't mean it. When she held out her hand for Bernie to shake, the bastard lifted it to his thick lips and kissed it. Then, with one last wink, he was off.

Eulalie, Nick, and Vernon stared after him.

"What an unusual man," Eulalie murmured before attacking her steak.

"He's unusual, all right," muttered Vernon.

"He's an ass," said Nick. Then he, too, dove into his meal.

Chapter Four

Eulalie did not spend a peaceful night. For one thing, a lot of noise filtered up from the floor below, not to mention cigar smoke. For another, men in big, heavy boots walked back and forth past her room all night long, she presumed on their way to and from Miss Violet or one of the other girls for sale at the Opera House. In the back of her mind, too, was the ever-present reality of her situation in life—and that of Patsy. Eulalie never allowed herself to forget why she'd traveled all this way and was now trying to sleep above a noisy—and noisome—frontier saloon.

Far, far away, in the deep recesses of her mind, Eulalie recalled older, more peaceful days; days when she and Edward had been young and in love and Patsy had been safe, and their family had been together and happy. Life certainly had a way of kicking the foundations out from under one's feet and leaving one floundering. Eulalie did not appreciate this habit on life's part, and not merely because those faraway, wistful memories made it difficult for her to sleep, as if the noise and smoke weren't enough.

Then there was Nick Taggart, who was stationed right outside her door. The mere thought of him sent strange hot flashes through Eulalie. She couldn't chalk up these sensations to hunger, since she'd eaten heavily, if not well, at Vernon's chophouse.

She was not pleased, either with herself or her circumstances, although she could tolerate the circumstances. She and Patsy had both decided to put up with the discomforts of the Wild West, and the relative lack of civilization prevailing there. But, at the ripe old age of twenty-five, with a good deal of experience, both pleasant and unpleasant, upon which to draw, Eulalie had believed herself long past the season when a woman mooned about a man.

Not, of course, that she was *mooning* about Nick Taggart, precisely. It was only that every now and then she experienced a compelling urge to open her door, reach out, grab Nick by the belt, and drag him into her room. Unfortunately, the mental images didn't stop there, but Eulalie did her best to drive them out.

She was helped in this effort by the occasional scuffle in the hallway. She assumed these episodes occurred when a man more drunk than his fellows attempted to get into her room past Nick, who wouldn't let him. Although Eulalie was as sure as anything that Nick Taggart wasn't a man with whom it would be wise to become involved, she appreciated his bulldog attitude regarding her safety. Not to mention his redoubtable physical attributes, which she wished she'd never noticed. Drat the man.

After what seemed like hours of wakefulness, which Eulalie spent alternately praying for her safety, praying for Patsy's safety, trying to remember Edward's sweet face—which had an unfortunate tendency to waver and dissolve into the face of Nick Taggart—and wishing she had Nick Taggart with her in bed, Eulalie finally fell asleep. The blissful condition lasted until a particularly loud noise from the hallway jerked her awake.

Sitting up and hugging the sheet to her modestly covered bosom, her heart slamming against her ribcage like waves at the Jersey shore, Eulalie tried to shake leftover strands of sleep out of her brain. Another loud noise made her start. This one sounded like a dozen bowling balls falling down several flights of stairs. Understanding that this was unlikely, but also quite curious, Eulalie glanced at the clock on her bedside table, saw that it was after three in the morning, and deduced that it might be safe to investigate the source of those unsettling sounds. Probably all the men who'd been drinking in the saloon downstairs had either drunk themselves into a stupor or gone home by that time.

She waited what seemed a prudent interval after the last loud noise before she crawled out of bed, grabbed the robe she'd thrown down at its foot, put it on, went to the door, unlatched it, opened it six inches, and peeked outside. She'd taken the precaution of putting on her spectacles since she didn't care to be surprised if anything untoward lurked in the hallway.

It was dark out there. She couldn't see a thing. Eulalie cleared her throat softly. "Mr. Taggart?"

Nick Taggart's voice came to her out of the gloom. "Yeah?"

He sounded grumpy. Oh, dear. "Um . . . I heard a big noise. It . . . ah . . . woke me up."

"Yeah? You're lucky you were able to get to sleep at all."

She hoped he wasn't going to be fussy about having to stay up all night in the hallway to protect her. It had been his suggestion, after all. Eulalie determined it would be better not to remind him. "Yes. I suppose so. Um . . . is everything all right?"

"Sure. Everything's fine and dandy. I just threw Gus Nichols down the stairs."

Aha. So that was it. She gulped. "Oh."

"Gus is an all right sort of fellow, but he don't take hints."

"Oh."

After a pause, Nick said, "You probably better go back to bed now."

"Yes. Thank you." Although she wasn't certain why she was being so cautious, Eulalie moved as softly and quietly as she could when she closed her door and latched it. She hadn't bothered to light a candle before she left her bed, so she had to feel her way back to it.

Sporadic scuffles continued to filter through the door to her ears, and it occurred to Eulalie that, while she and Patsy had read everything they could about the West and the people dwelling therein, they might possibly have underestimated the perils the West contained for youngish, single females. This might be especially true for females who were perceived as belonging to a profession not generally considered respectable. She took a few moments to decry the unfairness of life, but knew they were wasted. Whether it was fair or not, life was life, and it had to be dealt with.

Therefore, she pondered the man stationed outside her door and allowed as to how she might possibly have made a mistake with him. Not that she knew at the time that Nick Taggart would prove to be a big, lusty male with protective instincts. For all she'd known when they'd first encountered one another, he might have been as mad as his uncle.

She knew better now, or thought she did. One could never be absolutely certain about these things, and he still might prove himself to be a brute. Until she knew for sure, it might be worthwhile to mend a couple of fences as regarded Mr. Taggart. If it became necessary for Eulalie and Patsy to seek more protection than their weapons and wits could give them, it looked to her as though Nick Taggart was at the top of the list of candidates.

Eulalie huffed once, peeved that such a drastic possibility

might eventuate—and all because of a fiend like Gilbert Blankenship—then reminded herself that life was merely life and didn't have it in for her or Patsy in particular. She said a silent prayer that Edward, if his spirit lingered anywhere, would forgive her and understand.

Then she fingered her Colt Lightning on the night stand, and made sure her Ladysmith was nearby and her knife in its sheath under her pillow—just in case—and tried to get to sleep again.

Eventually she did.

Long before dawn, Nick was cursing himself as a damned fool. It wasn't his lookout if some prissy city girl was too stupid to prepare herself for rigors of the West before she ventured into it. Miss Eulalie Gibb was nothing to him but a pain in the neck, and here he was, giving up an entire night for her—and without even the benefit of enjoying her favors, if she had any. So far, it didn't appear likely, although he recalled the softness of her skin and the fullness of her breasts with something damned near akin to longing, idiot that he was.

And why? Why was he stuck here in the damned hall when he might be home sleeping peacefully—or having a nice romp with Violet? Because he'd succumbed to the irresistible urge to protect a female. *Damn* it! He'd believed he'd overcome his tendency to harbor chivalrous impulses years earlier. The good Lord knew he'd tried hard enough.

But no. Here he was, sitting in a hard chair and playing knight in shining armor to protect a female whom he didn't like and who didn't like him.

"Nick," a thick voice said. "How's about you take this gold eagle and lemme into that li'l lady's room for a few minutes."

Nick chuffed out an irritated breath. "No can do, Sam. Miss Gibb's not for sale. I already told you that downstairs."

"Aw, Nicky, be a sport."

"Get the hell out of here, Sam." No use being polite. Sam didn't care, and Miss Gibb wouldn't appreciate it.

"But, Nicky."

Nick allowed the front legs of his chair to hit the floor—he'd been leaning back against the wall, as if that would offer him a measure of physical comfort, which it didn't—grabbed Sam Bollard by his collar, turned him around, and shoved him back towards the stairs. He didn't expect he'd have to heave Sam down the stairs as he'd had to do with Gus, because Sam wasn't as stupid as Gus. After all, Nick had been working as a blacksmith and farrier ever since his father died fifteen years earlier. He had muscles in places Gus hadn't even heard of, and he was stronger than just about any other man in town except for his uncle Junius.

Speaking of Junius, Nick hoped Sheriff Wallace would keep him in jail overnight, because Nick couldn't be in two places at once, and he'd committed himself to playing guard dog for Miss Gibb, fool that he was. If Junius got out of the jug and did something else stupid, he'd be on his own, and Nick owed him too much to be comfortable with that, even though Junius's inability to handle liquor vexed Nick sometimes.

When he was sure Sam was gone for good, Nick sat back down in his chair, leaned the back against the wall, and tried to catch a nap. It was a difficult thing to do, and not merely because the chair didn't make a very good bed. Nick was annoyed with himself because he couldn't get Eulalie Gibb out of his mind. Actually, it wasn't his mind that was affected, damn it. And there wasn't a blasted thing he could do about his state of sustained arousal, either, because he'd been a fool and told Dooley he'd protect the new merchandise.

Nick couldn't recall the last time he'd gone and done something so damned stupid.

"Hey, Nick," came a whisper from out of the dark. "How's about you let me see that little gal for a minute or two."

Sighing, Nick let the front legs of his chair down, stood, and dealt with another fellow too stupid—or too titillated—to take no for an answer.

Since Eulalie couldn't think of a good reason not to, and she also had ulterior motives, she adopted a cheerful expression when she prepared to leave her room the next morning, praying she'd be able to find another place to stay, and the sooner the better.

Therefore, she dressed with care, selecting a sober gray gown, and pinned a lovely confection of a hat onto her hair. Because she'd read that parasols were a necessity to a lady's complexion here in the territory, she picked hers up and hung it over her arm. Pausing at the door, she sucked in a deep breath and prepared to greet the day—and whatever else lay in wait to pounce on her out there in the world.

As she had anticipated, what lay in wait for her was Nick Taggart, leaning back in a hard-backed chair, heavy-eyed, cranky, with his arms folded over his chest, dark stubble decorating his chin, and a frown on his face that made him look as if he'd welcome the opportunity to pounce on someone, most likely her. Eulalie gazed upon him in dismay. If he was as crabby as he looked, her ulterior motive might be difficult to achieve. Nick gazed back at her with antipathy.

"Oh, my, Mr. Taggart, you look as if you didn't sleep a wink last night."

"I wonder why," he growled.

Eulalie felt her lips tighten and endeavored to retain her smile. "I'm very sorry you had such a disagreeable night. Perhaps if you will be kind enough to introduce me to the lady whom you mentioned yesterday, I might make more suitable arrangements for my lodging."

"Huh." The front legs of the chair Nick had been sitting in thumped on the floor, and he rose, frowning magnificently. Slamming his hat on his dark hair, which was mussed this morning, probably because of his disturbed night, he said, "Yeah, I'll take you there right now," and held his arm out to indicate the direction in which he expected her to walk.

If Eulalie had not exactly forgotten overnight what a splendid specimen of masculinity Nick Taggart was, the reality of him made the breath catch in her throat. She didn't approve of this reaction, and she frantically tried to recall Edward's classical features to her mind's eye. She failed, although she did manage to suppress her urge to rise up on her toes, remove Nick's hat from his head, and run her fingers through his tumbled locks.

She was only suffering from fatigue, she told herself, although she suspected she might be a victim of self-deception. She suppressed a sigh. "Did you say this woman's name is Johnson?"

"Yeah."

Eulalie took another deep breath and tried again. "Thank you for guarding my door last night, Mr. Taggart."

"Yeah," he said. "Sure."

He was making it very difficult for her to engage him in polite conversation. She thought perhaps he'd appreciate a bit of humor. "Did you have to throw anyone else down the stairs?"

"No."

Very well. So humor was out. "It was very kind of you to watch out for me."

"Huh."

Annoying man! Well, Eulalie wasn't going to let him spoil her day. She hadn't met a man yet who wasn't a fool for flattery—except, of course, Edward, who had been perfect in every way. Eulalie thrust aside the niggling voice in her head reminding her that Edward had been a trifle on the spindly side. A man's physique had nothing to do with his character, she told herself. Nevertheless, judicious appreciation of his musculature might be used to win a man over, if he believed a woman to be enamored of his physical traits. Not that Eulalie would ever be swayed by so unimportant an aspect of a fellow's makeup as his muscles.

It was certainly warm in this revolting backwater. Eulalie wished she'd thought to bring along her fan.

However, that was nothing to the purpose, and she had work to do. Therefore, she said, "I imagine none of the men in town would dare challenge you, Mr. Taggart. You're so big and strong." She contemplated batting her eyelashes at him, but decided against it. No matter how much of a rugged Westerner Mr. Nick Taggart might be, Eulalie sensed that he was neither stupid nor a man to be easily manipulated by such an overt display of her charms. This was especially true since they hadn't exactly got off to a good start with each other.

From the way he looked at her, anyone would think she'd just told him to jump out a third-story window—not that there were any buildings that tall in this godforsaken place. "Yeah," he said. "Right."

Eulalie had been through a good deal of late. It had cost her a measure of self-respect to be coy with Mr. Taggart, since coyness was not as much a part of her character as was her sharp tongue. Her temper snapped. "For heaven's sake,

Mr. Taggart, anybody would think I'd spent last night torturing you! Can't you at least be civil?"

He eyed her coldly. "Well, now, ma'am, I don't know. Seems to me you haven't been awfully civil to me. Until now. I wonder why that is."

"It's because I didn't realize you were a gentleman until you proved yourself to be one," she said, lifting her chin and thinking she sounded like an elderly matron from the Upper West Side in New York City.

"Huh. You don't believe in giving people the benefit of the doubt, in other words."

Lord, no. Giving people the benefit of the doubt had been her and Patsy's downfall. What she said was, "I've discovered it to be prudent to withhold judgment."

"That's crap."

They'd been going down the uncarpeted staircase. Eulalie had just hit the bottom step when that comment smote her ear. She whirled around and scowled at him. "Well, *really!*"

Nick got to the bottom right after her. "You know I'm right."

"I do not!"

He towered over her, and he was an exceptionally large man. Eulalie wasn't accustomed to feeling little and fragile, and she didn't like it. Well, she *did* like it, but she didn't like it that she liked it.

"That's crap. You didn't like me from the moment you saw me—and I was trying to help you at the time, too."

Eulalie couldn't bear being loomed over like this. She feared for her self-control. Turning so that she wouldn't succumb to the temptation to leap upon Nick Taggart and beg him to take care of her, which she knew to be a foolhardy urge if she'd ever had one, she sniffed, whirled around, marched toward the door and said, "If you will recall the circumstances, I don't believe you can fault me for my leap to judgment."

"Huh. I guess I can understand why you might not take to Uncle Junius, although he's a good fellow once you get to know him, but that was no reason to be mean to me."

She felt him there, huge, beside her as she stamped across the scarred wooden floorboards of the Peñasco Opera House, and she spared a moment to be grateful that he was a good influence rather than an evil one. It was difficult enough having an enemy as physically unimpressive as Gilbert Blankenship after one. If Nick wasn't precisely a friend, at least he wasn't an enemy.

The outer door to the Opera House had been shut and bolted sometime during the night, although Eulalie couldn't imagine when. She knew for a fact, having looked at her bedside clock, that people were still roaming freely after three o'clock in the morning. She paused at the door, glaring at it, wondering how to open it, when Nick pushed past her. He lifted the bolt and shoved, and daylight streamed into the dim interior of the Opera House. Blinking into the sunshine, Eulalie took a deep breath and said, "Thank you, Mr. Taggart."

"You're welcome."

He pushed one side of the batwings and Eulalie sailed past him out into a new day that she knew from experience would be fraught with fear and frustration. Every now and then she succumbed to the temptation to bemoan her fate. That she did so on this occasion she chalked up to exhaustion.

Squinting, she hesitated on the wooden boardwalk that had been built along the street on either side, and gazed around her at her new domain. Some domain. The whole place was a study in beige and brown, with the occasional splash of red or blue being worn by a pedestrian. There wasn't a tree in sight, and the only bushes she saw were grayish green weeds of one sort or another. Eulalie presumed they were examples of some species of the hardy specimens that grew in inhospitable climes. Offhand, she couldn't recall seeing anyplace quite as inhospitable as Rio Peñasco, although she'd spent most of her days back East, so she had little first-hand experience upon which to draw. She heaved a sigh before she could stop herself.

"Not what you're used to," Nick observed.

"Um . . ." Eulalie contemplated lying and decided against it. As she'd observed earlier, Nick wasn't stupid. He'd surely catch her in the lie, and being the person he was, he'd probably call her on it. These Westerners. So brash. "No, it isn't. It does have a certain . . . um . . . appeal, however."

"Yeah?"

Catching a hint of amusement in the one word, Eulalie tilted her head and peered up at him. She wished she hadn't when she caught the full glory of his green eyes glinting at her from under the brim of his broad hat.

Before he could ask her to point out the charms of Rio Peñasco, which she wouldn't be able to do because it had none, she hurried to forestall him. "Well, I mean, this landscape has such a vastness about it." That much was true. The fact that she'd prefer her vastness broken here and there by stands of pretty green trees, a little grass, and the occasional bubbling brook, she didn't let on. "I've never seen so much . . . sky."

She felt, rather than heard, his chuckle. It was like a low vibration in the sweltering morning air. "Yeah. We've got lots of sky, all right."

"Yes." A fit of candor grabbed her by the tonsils and made her say, "And . . . honestly, Mr. Taggart, I've never been anywhere quite like this. It might take some getting used to."

"Yeah, I'm sure it will."

He took her arm, making her jump. She hadn't meant to do that. When she peeked up at Nick again, she was distressed to see that he was frowning.

"I won't bite, dang it, Miss Gibb," he growled.

"I know that," she said meekly. "I'm only . . . adjusting to my new circumstances."

"Yeah. Well, if you don't mind my saying so—"

Eulalie suppressed the urge to inform him that she undoubtedly would mind him saying so.

"—it don't seem to me as to how you planned this jaunt of yours very well."

"You have no idea how much preparation went into my decision to come here."

"True, but you obviously didn't expect what you found when you got here."

"That's not so. I had anticipated Rio Peñasco to be rough, Mr. Taggart. I hadn't expected to be attacked almost the moment I got off the stagecoach, and I hadn't realized exactly how . . ." Eulalie searched her brain for words other than *bleak, barren* and *godforsaken.* ". . . how . . . devoid of plant life the landscape would be." Or how the wind blew constantly, carrying with it fine grains of grit that sanded the paint off buildings and the skin from delicate Eastern cheeks.

"Yeah, well, people are beginning to plant stuff. Trees and the like. We even have us a few fruit groves close to town." He sounded a trifle defensive.

Eulalie seized an idea that had suddenly popped into her head, rather like a gun blast. "Yes! I'm sure that's so. And when more women move here, I'm sure Rio Peñasco will begin to bloom. Why, I've heard that women civilized San Francisco after the Gold Rush a few years ago. I'm sure the same thing will happen here."

Silence ensued. Glancing at Nick, she was surprised to see that his nose had wrinkled and he was frowning again. Oh, dear. And here she'd thought her notion so brilliant, too. It was becoming increasingly clear to her that Nick Taggart was unlike any other man she'd ever met, and the realization irked her.

"Well, Mr. Taggart? I'm sure you can appreciate the civilizing nature of the female of the species. Or are you one of those men who dislike women?" Discouraging thought, especially if she had to enlist his aid.

"I don't dislike all women. But I can live without a female's notion of civilization."

Hmm. Interesting. There was probably a story there, although Eulalie knew this wasn't the time to pursue it. Feeling a slight tug of desperation, she asked, "What about Mrs. Johnson? You like her, don't you?"

"Sure, I like Mrs. Johnson. But she's a widow lady with lots of kids to take care of."

"How does that make her different from the rest of womankind?"

He shrugged. "She don't want anything from me, is all."

She stared at him, nonplussed, but didn't get the opportunity to question him further because at that moment she caught sight of his uncle Junius, and she stiffened, lifted her furled parasol, and prepared to fend him off with it if it became necessary.

"It's all right," said Nick, evidently aware of her preparations. "He won't hurt you. He's sober this morning. Hell, he wouldn't have hurt you yesterday. He only wanted to dance a little."

Eulalie was not amused—if his comment had been intended to amuse. She didn't let down her guard.

"Nicky!" Junius's voice boomed through the momentarily still air.

"Hey, Junius. You feelin' all right?" Nick didn't leave Eulalie's side, but he smiled broadly at his uncle, who appeared a little worse for wear this morning.

Junius rolled to a stop in front of Nick and Eulalie and whipped off his hat. "Headache is all. Don't handle my liquor like I used to." Junius, who was a huge man like his nephew, only a little heavier and with a belly on him, peered at Eulalie, whose every sense was alert. "Is this the young gal I danced with yesterday?"

"It is." Nick still grinned.

She jumped a yard in the air when Junius suddenly stuck out his hand at her. She stared at it for a few seconds, unnerved.

"I'm mighty sorry, ma'am. I get a snootful and then I feel like dancin'. I didn't mean to scare you none."

It was an apology, however inelegantly presented, and Eulalie was touched. Her nerves still twanging, she took the hand Junius offered. It was a huge hand, and gnarled and tough, with gigantic calluses. Eulalie felt rather as if she were gripping old leather.

"This here is Miss Gibb, Uncle Junius. Miss Gibb, my uncle. Junius Taggart."

"How do you do, Mr. Taggart?"

"I'm right lively, ma'am, and I hope you don't mind my saying that you're the purtiest thang to visit these parts in a month of Sundays."

For once, Eulalie truly *didn't* mind one of the Taggarts saying nice things to her. This was probably because Junius, now that he wasn't reeling from having consumed a wholly indelicate amount of intoxicating liquors, possessed an innocent and childlike air about him. It was an air his nephew didn't share, but Eulalie found it charming, in a rough and rugged sort of way.

"Thank you, Mr. Taggart." She gave him one of the gracious smiles her mother had trained her to deliver to her audience. "You're very kind."

"Only bein' honest, ma'am." Junius clapped his hat back onto his head. "Reckon I'll get to the smithy, Nicky. No sense wastin' the day."

"I'm going to take Miss Gibb to Mrs. Johnson's place, Junius. See if she can rent a room there."

"Good idea. Mrs. Johnson, she's a fine lady." Junius executed an astonishing bow, considering his mien and the location, said, "See ya later, ma'am," and lunged off.

"Your uncle seems to be an . . . er . . . enthusiastic individual, Mr. Taggart."

"You got that right. Uncle Junius, he enjoys life."

Eulalie recalled that she'd once enjoyed life, too. The ability to do so seemed to have slipped away during the past couple of years. That wasn't surprising, she supposed, but she hadn't noticed it slipping away, it had happened so subtly. She sighed.

"You all right, ma'am?" asked Nick. They'd resumed walking on the dusty boardwalk.

"Yes. Just . . . remembering things."

"Don't appear to be happy thoughts."

"Some of them are." Especially memories of her family. And Edward. Dear Edward. Curious, she asked, "Do you have any family other than your uncle, Mr. Taggart?"

"None close by."

She sensed, although he didn't say so, that he'd have liked to add a *thank God* to that sentence. "Oh? Where does the rest of your family live?"

"Got a stepmother and a bunch of stepsisters in Texas. Reckon there's more family around there. I haven't been back to see 'em, and I don't aim to."

"Oh? Don't you care for your family, Mr. Taggart?"

"Well, now, I don't know that I don't *care* for them. I just seem to get along better with my uncle than with a bunch of females."

"There you go again, disparaging us ladies." Eulalie laughed a little and peered at Nick to see how he reacted. From the glower on his face, she gathered he hadn't taken it well. Difficult man.

"I had my fill of females when I was a boy. My daddy and I were the only males in the whole family and, believe me, those women drove us like a pair of mules. When my daddy died, I got out of there, and I'm not going back."

"I'm sorry you had such a bad experience."

"Yeah, well, it's over." He hesitated for a moment. "What about you, Miss Gibb? You got family somewhere? Besides your sister in Chicago, I mean."

"I have an aunt and uncle and several cousins in New York City," she said, thinking wistfully of the company she'd had to leave when Patsy was injured. "We were all part of an acting troupe." She hadn't intended to divulge that bit of information, although she didn't think it would do any harm.

"That so? That's interesting. I don't recall ever meeting a real actress before."

Eulalie considered asking if he'd met any imaginary ones, but opted not to. No sense in baiting a touchy man.

As they clumped along the boardwalk, Eulalie had been taking in the sights and sounds of Rio Peñasco. They were very unlike anything she was used to. In New York and Chicago there had been oodles of traffic, most of it in the nature of carriages and carts, and throngs of people, male, female, young and old. Here most of the vehicles were rustic wagons pulled by big, rangy horses. The foot traffic consisted primarily of males in dusty trousers and jackets, with the occasional person whom Eulalie assumed was what was known as a "cowboy" thrown in here and there for color. So to speak. Two women walking together on the other side of the street wore drab morning dresses. She assumed they were doing their marketing, or what passed for it in this remote village.

The softening influence of womankind on the place was depressingly absent. No flower boxes graced windows. No school bells clanged. No music swelled from church doors. For that matter, Eulalie didn't see any churches. A couple of the buildings had been adorned with false fronts, but they only made Eulalie's overall impression of Rio Peñasco that much more melancholy. She couldn't imagine Patsy being happy here. She couldn't imagine *herself* being happy here, if it came to that. She could kill Gilbert Blankenship for forcing them to take this drastic step.

Suddenly the dullness of the day was broken by the thunder of hoofbeats. Turning, Eulalie saw two men in bright blue coats riding down what seemed to be the main thoroughfare, if such a meager road could be so called, of Rio Peñasco. She stopped to squint at them—she was looking into the sun.

"Oh, my, Mr. Taggart, those men look like military fellows."

"Yeah," said Nick gruffly. "Fort Sumner's real close by."

A frontier fort! Imagine that. Eulalie's heart leapt slightly. Or, if it wasn't precisely a leap, it was at least a lift. "My goodness!"

The two men brought their horses to a spectacular stop in front of Nick and Eulalie, bringing to Eulalie's mind romantic notions of cavalry charges and sabers and so forth until the cloud of dust thereby produced made her sneeze.

"For crying out loud, Fuller," barked Nick. "Don't you know better than to show off in the middle of springtime?"

Eulalie didn't know which man Nick had spoken to. They both dismounted, smiling. The taller of the two fellows bowed low before her, almost sweeping the ground with his hat. "I'm mighty sorry, ma'am. Didn't mean to kick up so much dust."

Beside her, Nick grunted.

Sneezing again into the handkerchief she'd hastily withdrawn from a pocket, Eulalie couldn't speak, but she tried to convey her acceptance of his apology with a sweet smile. My, my, but he was a handsome fellow. He looked magnificent in his uniform, too. So did the other man, but the taller one outshone him in every particular. Both were ever so much more elegant and civilized looking than Nick Taggart.

"Lieutenant Gabriel Fuller, ma'am. At your service."

"She don't need your service, Fuller," said Nick in a menacing voice. "She's got mine."

Eulalie ignored Nick. Holding out her daintily gloved hand to Lieutenant Fuller, she assessed what she saw. He was a handsome man, if not quite so rugged as Nick Taggart, with blond hair that looked as if it had been bleached by the sun, a flowing cavalry mustache, and a tanned face. "Eulalie Gibb, Lieutenant Fuller. So happy to meet you." Turning to the other uniformed man, she said, "And this is?"

"Lieutenant Willoughby Nash, ma'am," the other man said, stammering a little, and blushing up a storm. Eulalie thought he was adorable, in a cuddly sort of way. While she appreciated cuddliness and had an uncle who was likewise endowed with the charming trait, she didn't need it at the moment. She needed spirit, grit, strength, and ruthlessness. While she didn't want to leap to conclusions, she sensed she'd still be better off with Nick Taggart than with either of these uniformed gents. Besides, they were soldiers and owed their first allegiance to the United States Army. If she decided to enlist the aid of a male, she wanted someone who'd be around when she needed him.

"I'm taking Miss Gibb to Mrs. Johnson's place," Nick said, his voice hard. "We don't have time to stand here in the heat and gab."

"Of course, of course. We'll just tag along, then," said Fuller, fairly oozing charm.

Eulalie didn't need charm any more than she did cuddliness, although she thought it was rather sweet of the fellow to be so blatant in his pursuit of her. Perhaps "sweet" wasn't the word she was looking for, come to think of it, especially if the lieutenant was laboring under the same conclusion most of the other men in town had made about her.

That being the case, and because she wanted to nip that sort of thing in the bud, she said, "Thank you, Lieutenant, but there's no need to interrupt your busy day. Mr. Taggart is doing a fine job of taking care of me."

Fuller stepped back a pace and eyed Nick with disfavor. "He is, is he?"

"Yeah," said Nick. "I am. Go on about your business, Fuller. Don't you have duties or something?"

The lieutenant didn't answer, but swept Eulalie another bow. "I'm sure we'll be seeing each other again, Miss Gibb. And I, for one, am looking forward to catching your show tonight. The men from the fort who saw it last night said you were a truly gifted artist."

"Thank you." Eulalie demurely dropped her gaze. Good Lord, she had a reputation already. She'd heard that word spread fast in a small town, but she'd never performed in one before, so this was the first opportunity she'd had to test the adage. It was, clearly, true.

She watched as Lieutenant Fuller and Lieutenant Nash led their horses away from her and Nick.

Nick said, "Fools."

Lifting her chin, Eulalie said, "They were both very polite."

"Yeah, they're polite, all right. But what's that Fuller said about you being an artist? You draw, too? I thought you only sang and danced."

"Singing and dancing are considered arts, Mr. Taggart. A fine dancer is an artist, as is a fine singer."

"Oh. Well, it sounded funny, the way he said it. But that's no more than I'd expect from that Fuller fellow. Always showing off."

Eulalie had the impression he felt foolish, and she wished she hadn't had to give him the lesson. She didn't want to antagonize him any more than was inevitable. "They seem like nice young men."

He eyed her, frowning. "You sound like you're a hundred years old, Miss Gibb. I'm sure they're both older than you are."

With dismay, Eulalie realized he was right. She had sounded like a little old lady. She felt a hundred, too. She sighed. "Please take me to Mrs. Johnson's house, Mr. Taggart."

"Yes, ma'am." And with her arm still attached to his, Nick stomped down the boardwalk. Eulalie had to hustle to keep up with him.

Chapter Five

Damn Gabriel Fuller and every other damned officer stationed at Fort Sumner. Show-offs. They were all a bunch of show-offs. Nick knew good and well that Fuller had put on that spectacular rearing stop in order to impress Eulalie Gibb. And he'd succeeded, too, damn his eyes.

Nick wasn't sure why that annoyed him so much, but it did. Yeah, it was true that Fuller was a good horseman, and yeah, Nick was too big for most horses, but that didn't matter, did it? Hell, Nick had other talents that Fuller completely lacked. He couldn't think of any of them offhand, but he knew he had them.

Anyhow, it was nothing to him if Miss Eulalie Gibb fell under the handsome officer's spell. Hell, the two of them could run off and get married and it would be nothing to him. He experienced a sharp pain in his chest and slammed his hand over it, wondering if he had indigestion. He doubted it. Not only had he not eaten anything since last night, but he never had indigestion.

His notion to have Eulalie Gibb stay with the Johnsons was a good one, and he was proud of himself for thinking of it. Mrs. Johnson was one of the few respectable women in Rio Peñasco, and she'd spiffed up her place with sunflowers and a vegetable garden and lots of civilized things like that.

And that was another thing. Until Eulalie Gibb came to town, Nick hadn't considered his little town lacking in any particular. Sure, it was kind of far away from any big cities, if you had a hankering for that sort of thing, but Nick didn't. He'd had his fill of big-city ways when he was a boy. His stepmother had cured him of any hankering he might once have had for high society. Not that the society available in Galveston, Texas, was all that high, but his stepmother had sure scratched and clawed to get to the top of the heap of what there was of it. And she'd yanked his poor father along behind her in her quest to conquer the societal mountain. Even thinking about those bad old days made Nick shudder.

He rapped more sharply on Mrs. Johnson's door than he'd intended, startling a squeak out of the poor woman, who must have been standing right in front of the door, because it opened a second later.

"Nick Taggart, you like to scare me to death!" A small woman with a face like a slightly worse-for-wear cherub, clad in a faded calico dress and men's heavy shoes, beamed at him from the open door. Her graying hair had been secured into a haphazard knot at the top of her head, and she looked as if she'd been scrubbing something, because she wore an apron and carried a scrub brush.

"Sorry, Mrs. Johnson," Nick said sheepishly, regretting that he'd allowed himself to show any sign of upset in front of Eulalie Gibb.

Before he could state the purpose of his unexpected arrival at Mrs. Johnson's door, several shrieks emanated from inside the house.

"Uncle Nicky! Uncle Nicky!"

And before he could warn Eulalie, an entire herd of excited children raced past their mother and leaped upon Nick. Damn. He liked the Johnson kids all right, but he'd sort of hoped he'd be able to preserve his air of dominant masculinity around Eulalie Gibb, at least for a little while. That was difficult to do with a bunch of kids crawling all over him.

"Charles! Clarence, William, Sarah, and Penelope! Stop bothering Mr. Taggart right this minute," their mother commanded.

As was usually the case with the Johnson children, they subsided almost at once, with William, the youngest boy, slowest to obey. Little Sarah, who had turned five years old the week before, clung to Nick's big hand. "Did we hurt you, Uncle Nicky?" she asked in her sweet, piping voice.

"It would take more than a little mite like you to hurt me, Miss Penny," Nick assured her.

Mrs. Johnson had been taking stock of Eulalie while she was disciplining her children. Now she turned to her and held out her hand. "I'm mighty sorry for the ruckus, ma'am. I'm Louise Johnson—Mrs. Ezekiel Johnson, who's gone on to his maker, God rest his soul—and these here are my children. They act like a pack of wolves, but they're not so bad once you get to know them."

Wide-eyed and staring, Eulalie gave a small start, as if she'd been transfixed by the swarm of children and suddenly jerked out of her trance. "Oh! Oh, yes. I mean no, I'm sure they're not. Bad, I mean." Eulalie flushed and took the other woman's hand. Then she flashed one of her patented, knock-'em-dead smiles. "I'm sorry, Mrs. Johnson. I just didn't anticipate them. I'm really quite fond of children. My name is Miss Eulalie Gibb."

Mrs. Johnson nodded. "I heard all about you, Miss Gibb. But here, there's no need to stand out in the sun. Come on indoors, and have a sit-down. It's not elegant, but it serves us all right."

She ushered Nick and Eulalie into her house, which

boasted a total of five rooms and a sun porch. The children slept on the sun porch in the spring and summer. Nick didn't know where they slept in the wintertime, but he began to question his wits in bringing Eulalie here. It was true that Mrs. Johnson had the kindest heart in the territory, and it was also true she needed money, but her comment about lack of elegance struck Nick where it hurt.

As he gazed around the shabby little house, he understood for the first time since he'd proposed the idea that Miss Eulalie Gibb, actress, from Chicago, Illinois, was probably accustomed to grander surroundings than this. She might not be thrilled to rent one of the only five rooms in this house, especially since the house came equipped not only with bedrooms and a kitchen, but a pack of unruly kids. Damn. Where had his wits gone begging?

"Have a seat, you two," said Mrs. Johnson happily, waving them toward a faded sofa that sagged in the middle. An obvious effort had been made to perk it up with homemade throw pillows and an afghan no doubt crocheted or knitted by Mrs. Johnson or one of the girls. "I'd offer you a cold drink, Miss Gibb, but I'm afraid there's no such thing to be had in this little town of ours. But I will take my apron off and put up my scrub brush." Taking the apron off and sinking into a chair that was as faded and saggy as the sofa, she called, "Charles! Come here and take this to the kitchen."

Charles Johnson, fifteen years old and excessively sober for so young a lad, probably because after his father's death he'd been designated as "man of the family"—a position that Nick had held, too, once upon a time—appeared in the parlor. All the Johnson children had reddish hair and freckles, and Charles looked particularly small and vulnerable to Nick, who'd always been big for his age.

Because, in spite of himself, he had a lot of sympathy for Charles, Nick smiled at the boy, who smiled back, shyly. "How're you doing, Charles?"

"Fine, Uncle Nick. Thank you." His gaze shifted from his mother, who had taken a chair, to Eulalie, who sat on the edge of a sofa cushion, as if to assess their willingness to put up with a kid. Nick's heart twanged.

"What projects you got going, Charles? Need any help?"

Another glance at his mother, who smiled indulgently, prompted Charles, clutching the apron and scrub brush to his breast, to blurt out, "Oh, Uncle Nick, if you could help Bill and me, we're building a tree house, only there's no trees, so we're going to have to stick it somewhere else. And Clarence," he added belatedly. Nick understood. Being the youngest boy, Clarence was kind of a pest. Nick figured that was only because he didn't get enough attention from his siblings because he couldn't do as much as they. Again his heart twanged. He wished like thunder it would stop doing that.

"I reckon I can do that," said Nick.

"Thank you, Uncle Nick!" And Charles fled the room, still clutching the apron and scrub brush, a huge smile on his face.

Nick flashed Eulalie a quick peek to see if she was sneering at his softhearted attitude toward the boy. To his surprise, he saw that her face had lost its set expression, and she appeared almost pleased with him.

He was probably imagining it.

After clearing his throat, Nick got to the point. "Say, Mrs. Johnson, Miss Gibb is going to need a place to stay while she's singing at the Opera House. As you can imagine, the Opera House isn't . . . um . . ."

"You don't have to explain it to me, Nicky." Mrs. Johnson

smiled at Eulalie. "We'd be right proud to have you stay with us, Miss Gibb."

"Naturally, I'll pay you for room and board, Mrs. Johnson," Eulalie said.

"I reckon you will, sweetie. I'm a charitable woman, when I've got it to give, but I expect you'll be earning enough to pay something."

"Of course. I'll be happy to give you a deposit."

Nick didn't want to offend either lady, but he felt compelled to intervene. "Are you sure you'll be all right here, Miss Gibb?"

"Good question, Nicky," Mrs. Johnson said with a grin. "I'll warrant this isn't what you're used to, Miss Gibb. We're a little rugged out here in the territory."

With perfect graciousness, which Nick ought to have anticipated but hadn't, Eulalie said, "Don't be silly, Mrs. Johnson. I assure you that I knew what I was getting into when I chose to move to the West." She shot Nick a glance. "Well, for the most part. I must say I hadn't anticipated some aspects of the New Mexico Territory."

Nick gave her a cold eye. "She's talking about Uncle Junius. I expect you heard that story."

With a hearty laugh, Mrs. Johnson said, "I do declare, Nicky, your uncle is a caution!"

"I don't think Miss Gibb thought so," grumbled Nick.

"As I said, while I was prepared for many . . . ah . . . circumstances that are not what I'm used to, I was unprepared for Mr. Junius Taggart." Eulalie lifted her chin in a gesture Nick was beginning to recognize as one she used when she was irritated.

"Why don't you go collect Miss Gibb's traps, Nicky, and I'll set the boys to cleanin' out the back room. Reckon Sarah and Penelope can share a room with me."

Eulalie's eyes opened wide. "Oh! I had no idea you'd have to oust your children, Mrs. Johnson. Please. I'm sure I can find another place to stay. I don't want to be a pest."

Both Mrs. Johnson and Nick looked at her in a way that made Eulalie's cheeks get pink. Mrs. Johnson said, "You're not a pest, believe me. It'll be a plumb pleasure to have another woman to talk to. There aren't a whole lot of us here yet. And as for finding another place to stay . . . well, I reckon I've heard folks talk about building a hotel here in Rio Peñasco, but it's not built yet. I expect we'll have to get a speck more popular with drummers and the like before a hotel could be considered profitable. I think I'm your best bet unless Nicky decides to build you a house." She winked at Nick, who didn't appreciate it.

"Build me a house?" Eulalie said blankly.

Again Mrs. Johnson laughed. "He's a mighty handy fellow, our Nick. And he's got the biggest heart in the world. I reckon if you asked politely, he'd build you a house, houses out here being on the small side and easy to build out of adobe bricks."

Peeved, Nick stood and said, "She's joshing you, Miss Gibb. I'll go get your bag."

Eulalie said, "Thank you," and steeled herself for the coming ordeal—being left alone to fend for herself with Mrs. Johnson.

Not that Mrs. Johnson didn't seem like a perfectly nice woman. But the notion that Eulalie was driving two little girls out of their bedroom made her feel just terrible. She didn't want the children to hate her. Life was already hard enough.

Eulalie wasn't a snob. She'd come from a theatrical family and was accustomed to making do. But these territorial residences were . . . different from what she was used to. Most of

85

the places she'd stayed in back East had been hotels or rooming houses of one sort or another.

With a sigh, Mrs. Johnson rose from the chair on which she'd been sitting, picked up a squashed throw pillow and endeavored to fluff it into life. "While Nicky's getting your things, why don't I show you where you'll be staying, Miss Gibb? It's not elegant, as I said, but it's safe. I reckon, what with your job and all, you might have to endure a few misunderstandings before Nick sets all the men in town straight."

The older woman's candor made Eulalie's cheeks get hot. She got up from the sofa and prepared to take the tour. She didn't anticipate that it would take long. "Thank you, Mrs. Johnson. Um . . . I assure you that I really am a singer. I don't do . . . anything else."

"Oh, my goodness, you don't have to tell me that, sweetie. Nicky wouldn't have brought you here if you were anything but a lady."

Eulalie decided perhaps she hadn't given Nick the credit he deserved, although her opinion had been colored by that embarrassing episode with her corset. Or without her corset.

Mrs. Johnson bustled ahead of Eulalie toward the kitchen. Following, Eulalie assessed her hostess. They were about the same height, although Mrs. Johnson was perhaps an inch taller than Eulalie's own five feet, two inches. Eulalie couldn't even guess at her age. She looked about a hundred and six, but Eulalie imagined she wasn't more than forty or thereabouts. The territory, clearly, was very hard on its women. That might have given Eulalie pause had she not already discovered that there were many ways in which life could be hard on women, and at least Patsy could probably be safe here.

Every now and then she experienced a compelling urge to shoot Gilbert Blankenship dead. Unfortunately she was prevented by distance from fulfilling her desire. Thanks to the lessons she'd taken in Chicago, however, she'd be ready for him if he ever showed up.

The kitchen was a large room, with a big wood-burning stove in one corner, a table and six chairs in the middle, and lots of cupboards. The sink and counters sat under a window decorated with pretty, frilly yellow curtains and that gave a perfect view of . . . nothing. Offhand, Eulalie couldn't recall ever being anywhere with less scenery, unless you counted scrub grass, rocks and cacti. If she hadn't been prepared, she might well have succumbed to melancholia.

"I'm going to plant me a garden out there," Mrs. Johnson said, indicating the ground outside the kitchen window. "I get durned tired of looking at dirt. I'm from Massachusetts originally, and I miss seeing green."

"I understand completely." Eulalie's agreement was heartfelt.

The other woman laughed. "I reckon you do. But don't worry. You'll get used to it. When I first moved here with my Zeke, I used to think I'd go crazy in all this open space. When I went back to visit my kin in Auburn ten years ago, I thought I'd die from being closed in. Everywhere I looked there was a durned tree in the way."

With a small smile of her own, Eulalie said, "I'm looking forward to acquiring your perspective."

"Reckon you are. Where are you from, Miss Gibb?"

"Chicago. By way of New York."

"Yup. You'll miss green, too." Mrs. Johnson shook her head. "You're a brave woman, to come all this way by yourself. Not many women would have the grit for such an adventure. But I have an idea you're going to do all right."

Eulalie didn't know how she'd come to that conclusion, but she appreciated it. "Thank you."

"It's a fact that women don't have much of a chance to

87

shine in the States," Mrs. Johnson went on musingly. "Out West is about the only place where a woman of spirit can find her own place in the world. Of course, having a good man on your side don't hurt any." She shot a grin at Eulalie over her shoulder.

With the conviction of experience, Eulalie said, "Good men are hard to find."

"You already found one of 'em. If you ever decided you need a man in your life, you couldn't do better than Nick Taggart."

Hmm. While Eulalie wasn't sure she liked Nick Taggart much, she was pleased to have Mrs. Johnson confirm her tentative opinion of his potential usefulness. Since the older woman seemed inclined to talk, she asked, "Your children called him Uncle Nicky. Is he a relative of yours or your late husband?"

Another laugh from her hostess. "Mercy, no! But try as he might, Nicky just can't help but be nice to my children. And helpful? That man would give you the shirt off his back if he thought you needed it."

The notion of seeing Nick Taggart without his shirt gave Eulalie pause. She shook the disgraceful idea out of her head. "Is that right?"

"You bet. He can't help himself, although I know he's tried."

Puzzled, Eulalie said, "Tried? You mean tried not to be helpful?"

"Yup."

How odd. She decided to say so. "How . . . odd."

"Not if you know his story, it isn't." Another chuckle carried Mrs. Johnson through the kitchen and out the other door. "Here's the room that'll be yours, Miss Gibb. I'll have my gals out of here in a couple of shakes."

Eulalie really wanted to know Nick's story, but didn't want Mrs. Johnson to think she was interested in him. Therefore, she remained silent as she peeked into a medium-sized room with two beds and a large wardrobe and a table pushed against the far wall, under a window. This window also looked out on a good deal of nothing, but was prettied up with pink-flowered curtains. Two little girls whom Eulalie judged to be perhaps five and eight, sat on one of the beds, their hands folded in their laps, their big blue eyes wide and staring. It was clear to her that they wanted to tackle her and ask her about a million questions. She'd never been around children much, but she smiled at them.

"Girls," said Mrs. Johnson, "this here is Miss Eulalie Gibb, and she's going to be renting this room from us for a while."

The little girls stood up and curtseyed. Eulalie thought they were adorable. "How-do, ma'am," said the older one.

"I'm quite well, thank you. What's your name?"

"Penelope. Folks call me Penny. This here's Sarah. She's only five."

"It's good to meet you, Penelope and Sarah." She turned to Mrs. Johnson, "I hate to have to disturb your daughters, Mrs. Johnson."

"Nonsense. They'll be thrilled to have a real back-East lady livin' in the place."

"We don't mind," Penelope assured her eagerly. "We don't mind at all."

Mrs. Johnson eyed her daughters, and creases appeared in her forehead. "I hope you don't mind if they bother you a bit. I'll do my best to keep 'em away from you, but they'll be curious."

"We won't bother you!" Penelope cried. "Honest, we won't."

"I'm sure of it," Eulalie murmured.

Mrs. Johnson said, "We don't get too many female visitors to Rio Peñasco. Respectable female visitors, that is."

"I'm sure that's so." And how respectable was she? Eulalie wondered. She'd run into prejudice against actors and actresses in the East, but generally it came from people who were excessively self-righteous. As of this very moment, she guessed she was a respectable widow lady. If she had to, however, she was willing to exchange her respectability for protection. Her mind and heart were both steeled to accept that possibility if it became necessary.

"Say, Miss Gibb," said Mrs. Johnson. "You got a special fellow in your life right now?"

Eulalie hadn't expected the question, although she didn't mind it since it would enhance her air of respectability even more. "I'm a widow, as you are, Mrs. Johnson. My Edward died four years ago, of consumption."

Mrs. Johnson shook her head sadly. "I'm mighty sorry to hear that, ma'am." She eyed Eulalie curiously. "Er . . . you still call yourself Miss Gibb?"

Smiling, Eulalie explained, "I come from a theatrical family, Mrs. Johnson. My great-grandfather, Mortimer Gibb, established the Gibb Theatrical Company in the early eighteen hundreds. The company has thrived since that time. My married name was Mrs. Edward Thorogood."

"I see. Well, now, that's right interesting. I'll warrant you have some pretty good stories to tell about all the plays you've been in and everything like that."

"Indeed." She had lots of stories, all right, and not all of them were fit for respectable company. She'd be happy to talk about her family, however, any time anybody wanted to hear about it. Talking might make them seem closer to her. At this moment, Eulalie felt very much alone in the world—but that was only because she was. She'd be so happy when Patsy could travel again. A pang of loneliness spurred her to say, "My sister will be coming to join me as soon as she's able."

"That so? Well now, isn't that fine! Wish I had some family here. Besides my children, of course. I do miss 'em. And I miss other things about back East, too. Clams and lobsters come to mind." She laughed softly, but Eulalie sensed there was real longing in the woman's words.

"Oh, my, yes," she said. "I can imagine that's so. The food here is . . . different."

"You don't know the half of it." Mrs. Johnson sighed. "I'd give my eyeteeth for a dish of real Boston baked beans. We used to eat baked beans and brown bread every Saturday night when I was a girl. Out here, all we can get is pinto beans, and they just aren't the same, although I do my best. Thank God for bacon and molasses. My sister sent me some white beans a year or so ago, but they were gone in a month." She laughed again. "We may get civilized one of these days."

"I'm sure of it," said Eulalie, who knew no such thing. In truth, she wasn't eager to have Rio Peñasco become civilized any time soon. The longer she could remain out of the limelight or any hint thereof, the better she'd like it and the safer Patsy would be.

A commotion at the door preceded a stampede of children. Mrs. Johnson sighed. "Reckon that'll be Nick with your belongings, Miss Gibb."

"Please," said Eulalie. "Call me Eulalie."

Mrs. Johnson gave her a big smile. "Thank you kindly, Eulalie. Please call me Louise."

Eulalie decided she was off to a good start in her new career as a runaway.

Chapter Six

My dearest Patsy,

Well, dear, I have arrived, and Rio Peñasco isn't half as horrid as we expected it to be. In fact, many of the citizens seem determined to bring civilization to the place (but don't worry. It won't happen soon). I understand the civic leaders even put on a town barbecue supper once a year, to celebrate the town's founding, although God alone knows why anyone would wish to celebrate the establishment of such a barren, desolate community.

Some of the natives are rather nice, however, and I am now renting a room from a very kind widow lady named Mrs. Louise Johnson, who has five children. It's a rather noisy house, but it will do for now. When you are well enough to come out, I will be sure we have a place of our own to stay. The people who live here build houses and so forth out of mud bricks, rather like the ancient Egyptians used to do, only these local bricks are called adobe, which is, I believe, a Spanish word meaning mud brick.

There is a fort nearby, and several soldiers come to town quite often. I have considered one of them, Lieutenant Gabriel Fuller, as a possible protector, if it comes to that, although there's another man in town who might fill the bill slightly better, except that he's rather a brute. On the other hand, that may be exactly what we need. His name is Nicholas Taggart, and he has an uncle named Junius. They both work as blacksmiths and farriers, and both are as big as houses.

My dear, please take good care of yourself. We are safe for a little while longer and, with luck and good timing, you will be long gone from Chicago by the time Gilbert Blankenship gets out of prison.

All my Love,
Eulalie

Eulalie had believed herself fully prepared for her new life in an upstart Western village. She'd not only studied all the newspaper and periodical articles she could find, but she read all the dime novels about cowboys and sheriffs and cattle rustlers she could get her hands on. And, for the most part, she discovered her education was valid.

She was pleased to find that Rio Peñasco, for all its lack of refinement, was not too difficult a place in which to live. This was true primarily because it had been settled, more or less, for better than thirty years, and people had instituted a few conveniences. For instance, Nick Taggart had installed a water closet and a toilet in Mrs. Johnson's house. Eulalie appreciated not having to go outdoors to use the facilities, since her presence in town was known, and quite a few men seemed to hang around Mrs. Johnson's yard. Ever since Nick had made it known that Eulalie was under his protection, none of the men had yet dared enter the yard, but Eulalie didn't want to tempt fate.

The local mercantile emporium couldn't hold a candle to the new department stores in New York and Chicago, of course, but Mr. Lovelady, who owned and ran the store with the help of his wife and various other relatives, compensated his customers for any lacks by providing them with both a Sears and Roebuck and a Bloomingdale's catalog from which to order anything he didn't stock. These "wish books," as the local ladies called them, were in a constant state of use and almost too well thumbed. When Eulalie glanced through the Sears catalog, she could scarcely read the print on some of the pages.

"We get new ones every year," Mrs. Lovelady assured her, treating her with a deference Eulalie hadn't expected. She'd understood that saloon singers weren't widely respected by the few ladies who survived in these backwater villages.

She was pleased to know she'd been mistaken and asked Mrs. Johnson about the phenomenon one evening just as she was waiting for Nick and Junius to accompany her to the Peñasco Opera House to begin her evening's job. "I'm glad no one thinks I'm a hussy," she said, after mulling over and discarding several other descriptive terms.

Mrs. Johnson, her hands dripping soapsuds, cried, "Good Lord, child, why would anyone think you're a hussy?"

Eulalie made a gesture meant to imply indecision. "Well . . . I mean, Mr. Taggart said you might not view me as a respectable woman, since I sing at the Opera House."

"Bosh. Nicky was only funnin' you, sweetie. Anybody can tell you're a fine lady."

"Really?" How astonishing. It's a good thing the few respectable ladies of Rio Peñasco couldn't see her perform. A glance at her scandalous costumes would make them change their good opinion in a heartbeat. Which reminded her of something. "Mrs. Johnson, I should like to attend church on Sundays. Are there churches in Rio Peñasco?"

"Why, bless you, child, of course there are!" Mrs. Johnson sounded surprised that Eulalie would even ask. Apparently she hadn't read the same books Eulalie had. "My children and I attend the Baptist church down the road a piece, because there's no Presbyterian church in town yet. But if you're a Roman Catholic, there's a Catholic church down the road in the other direction." She spoke the words *Roman Catholic* as if she didn't approve of them.

"I would be happy to attend church with you, if I may," Eulalie said demurely. If there was a piano or a choir or something, maybe she could even sing for the natives. She meant the congregation. She really wanted to be accepted by the good people of Rio Peñasco, primarily because she didn't want Patsy to endure any more unhappiness if it could be prevented.

The schoolhouse was a one-room affair, and Eulalie didn't envy the schoolmaster, Mr. Chalmers, mainly because he was small and spindly and most of the boys he had to teach weren't. His voice was kind of squeaky, too. Eulalie was of the opinion that a fellow built along the lines of Nick Taggart might be able to enforce discipline with more success than little Mr. Chalmers. She got the impression from the Johnson children that Mr. Chalmers needed help. However, from talking to Mrs. Johnson's children, Eulalie gathered that they learned their lessons in spite of their teacher. This might, in part, have been due to the fact that the only entertainment for children in town was garnered from books, and Mr. Chalmers was the only person in town who could provide the children with books.

Baths were something else again, and required heating water on the wood-burning stove and filling a huge tub. Mrs. Johnson made her children bathe once a week, on Saturday, and they all used the same water. Eulalie made do with bathing herself in her room, using a pitcher, basin, and washcloth. She stood on an oilcloth. It wasn't perfect, but it worked.

The one feature of life in Rio Peñasco that threatened to undermine her confidence was something about which no one could do anything: the weather. More specifically, it was the wind and the dust that were anathema to Eulalie. She'd grown up in New York, where one could see a tree every now and then if one wished to do so. Evidently, God had seen fit to withhold trees from the Rio Peñasco area, except along the river that had given the town its name. On the banks of the Rio Peñasco, one could actually sit under a cottonwood if one were so inclined. Of course, one had to fight off the huge red ants, mosquitoes, and gnats that also enjoyed the moisture. While Eulalie knew God was supreme, she did question His wisdom in creating the southeastern area of New Mexico Territory.

"It's because it's springtime," Mrs. Johnson explained to her one day when, in spite of her vow to make the best of her circumstances, Eulalie had mentioned the dust problem. They were in the backyard, hanging up laundry. Mrs. Johnson had told Eulalie not to help her, but Eulalie had insisted. It wasn't any fun, due to the aforementioned wind and dust. "We get real bad winds in the springtime."

"Ah. I see." Rather wistfully, Eulalie recalled the spring flowers of her youth. And the color green. She missed green. She flapped out a shirt and pinned it to the clothesline. One of its sleeves retaliated and smacked her in the nose. Stupid wind.

"Wait until the summertime. The winds will die down and we'll get rain durned near every night."

"In the summertime?" How odd. "We used to get our rain in the fall and winter back East. Not that I'm complaining, mind you."

Mrs. Johnson laughed heartily. "Aw, go on and complain, sweetie. You won't hurt my feelings any. Sometimes I get so homesick for Massachusetts, I just sit and cry."

Oddly enough, while she didn't wish Mrs. Johnson heartache, her landlady's confession made Eulalie feel slightly better. "I miss the grass," Eulalie admitted. "And the trees."

"You're sure not alone there. But Rio Peñasco's coming along. One of these days we'll have lots of trees." She sounded confident as she pinned a pillowcase to the clothesline.

"You really think so?" Eulalie dodged another sleeve and grabbed one of little Sarah's dresses.

"Oh, my, yes. Why, Nicky's already sent away to back East to get me a couple of rosebushes and a magnolia tree."

"How nice of him." She'd noticed before this that Nick Taggart seemed to be Rio Peñasco's good angel. He certainly didn't look much like one, but she supposed angels had to fit into their surroundings. "I'm curious about one thing, though."

"Only one?" Mrs. Johnson laughed again.

Eulalie joined her, but pursued her original thought. "Water. Does all the water used in this town come from the river? It's not . . . that is, it doesn't seem . . . Oh, dear."

Mrs. Johnson patted her arm. "Don't think a thing about it, Eulalie. Like I said, you won't hurt my feelings. But I know what you mean. When you're used to big rivers they have back East, this puny thing they call a river here is a real disappointment."

Eulalie wouldn't have put it in those exact words, although she'd thought them a time or two.

"But, you see, that river, along with everything else around here, is watered by underground streams. You have to dig down to get at it, but then you'll have water for as long as the supply lasts, and God knows how long that'll be. Artesian wells, is what they call 'em."

"I've heard of Artesian wells, but I didn't know what they were until now. Imagine that."

97

"Yup. That's why we have all these windmills. With all that water underground, I still don't know why we aren't greener on top, but there you go."

"Ah, I see." There were, indeed, a plethora of windmills in Rio Peñasco. They were among the first oddities Eulalie had noticed when she stepped off the stagecoach. She might have asked about them before now, but she'd been distracted by other things.

"The good Lord knows, we have enough wind to keep the windmills pumping."

That was certainly true. "When do you think the rosebushes will arrive?"

"Don't rightly know, but I'm sure looking forward to planting them."

Although Eulalie hated to admit it, Nick Taggart, Rio Peñasco's resident handyman and good angel, was also a huge help to her. And—this hurt her even more than admitting to Nick's usefulness—his uncle Junius was a help, too. Both men appeared at the Peñasco Opera House every evening for two solid weeks in order to ensure rioting didn't break out before, during, or after her act. They appeared periodically after that, too, and one of them generally walked her to work in the evening. Eulalie always felt safer on the nights they showed up to watch her act.

Less helpful, but rather endearing, were Lieutenants Gabriel Fuller and Willoughby Nash, who also caught as many of her evening shows as they could. Eulalie wondered exactly what their duties entailed, that they were able to spend so much time away from the fort where they were stationed.

Then there was Bernie Benson, owner and sole journalist for the *Rio Peñasco Piper*. Bernie came to all her shows, too, and wrote fulsomely complimentary articles about her. Eulalie wished he wouldn't, since the publicity drew more people every day, and she was going to have to put on two shows a night pretty soon in order to accommodate all the lust-crazed cowboys, soldiers, drifters, and townsmen who flocked to see her. Perhaps if the Gibb Theatrical Company had someone like Bernie Benson in New York, their audiences would have been bigger. At this point in her life, however, Eulalie would just as soon dispense with Bernie's effusions. They were not only embarrassing, but they gave people the wrong idea.

Two nights in a row, the entire Johnson family, not to mention Eulalie herself, had been awakened in the middle of the night by a drunken man demanding entry. Charles, Mrs. Johnson's eldest son, had had the devil of a time convincing the man that Eulalie wasn't available. The entire experience had been humiliating, although none of the Johnsons seemed to be holding it against her, which she appreciated more than she could say.

However, other than the occasional rude suggestion, Eulalie was not finding her experience in Rio Peñasco as arduous as she'd feared it might be. Oddly enough, it seemed that many people actually came here on purpose from back East. According to Nick, the warm, dry air of the region was considered to be healthful for people suffering from consumption—a piece of information that made Eulalie's heart ache painfully for a moment when she considered her dear Edward, who might have benefited from the atmosphere here.

Another moment's thought disabused her of this opinion. Poor Edward had been too fragile to exist in this rough place. His sensibilities had been exquisite. He would have suffered terribly.

Unlike Nick Taggart, who thrived in the inhospitable clime of Rio Peñasco.

Eulalie frowned and for a brief moment entertained the rebellious reflection that Edward had been quite the delicate flower and rather a whiner upon occasion. She mentally chastised herself severely for the thought.

However wholesome the air of Rio Peñasco might be for consumptives, Eulalie had a hunch more people came here to escape their problems in the States than for their health. She also had a hunch those problems ranged from pesky wives and families to pending felonious charges. She knew for a fact that she'd never experienced some of the problems back East that she encountered in Rio Peñasco, although that might have had something to do with the fact that back East she was surrounded by a loving family. Here, she had to depend on the kindness of the Taggarts.

After one show, as Junius waited at the foot of the stairs to ward off any fellows who were inclined to disregard Dooley Chivers' warning that Miss Gibb was *only* a singer, and Nick waited outside her dressing-room door, in case Junius proved unsuccessful as guardian of the staircase, Eulalie called out to him from behind her dressing screen. "Do you believe that man named Dwight Singleton is really wanted by the law in Massachusetts and New York?" She'd heard a rumor to that effect earlier in the day.

"Wouldn't surprise me any. He's pretty shifty."

Shifty. Eulalie liked that word. And she had to admit that it seemed to apply to Mr. Singleton. "Do you suppose that's his real name?"

"Doubt it," Nick called back. "Sometimes I think Junius and I are the only folks in town who kept their birth names. Well, except for the Johnsons. And probably Chalmers."

"My goodness." She unhooked the devices holding her costume together in front and sighed deeply when the garment fell away, allowing her to take a deep and unobstructed breath. These costumes, however much Eulalie appreciated them for other reasons, were torture devices. "I'm surprised that the two lieutenants are in town so often, Mr. Taggart. I should think their duties would keep them more closely attached to Fort Sumner."

"It's a frontier fort, you know. Now that the Indians have all been sent to the Bosque, there's not as much for the soldiers to do, I reckon."

Indians. Mercy. Eulalie hadn't even considered the possibility of Indians when she and Patsy decided the West was their last, best option for escape. Of course, the twentieth century was almost upon them, and the eastern states hadn't had an Indian problem—if it could be termed that. Eulalie suspected that white men had been far worse a problem for Indians than vice versa—for decades now. Why, New York, Boston and Chicago were as up-to-date and modern as London or Paris. The only reminders of the Indians were a few names of rivers and towns.

Which still left Rio Peñasco sitting all by itself out here in the southeastern edge of the New Mexico Territory. Eulalie could hardly imagine a more desolate place, unless she and Patsy took it into their heads to hide out in the Gobi Desert, which sounded as if it might be moderately worse than Rio Peñasco.

"I see. Er . . . what exactly do they do then?"

"Who?"

"The soldiers at the fort."

"Beats the hell out of me. Drill and target practice, I reckon. Every now and then I guess they have to quell a squabble in the town or between ranching factions."

"A range war," Eulalie said, her head filling with brutal images of gunfights being carried out on horseback while wild cows, frightened by all the noise, stampeded in the back-ground. Imagine that. A real range war.

"I guess you could call it that. And there are rustlers, I reckon. Incursions from outlaw gangs from Mexico from time to time. There's a fellow called Jesus Malverde who's been causing some trouble along the border."

"I do believe I've read about him."

"Yeah. I hear he's a real piece of work."

"I believe one of our newspapers back home called him a Mexican Robin Hood."

"He steals stuff, if that counts," Nick said in something of a grunt. "I haven't heard that he's given any of his spoils to poor folks."

"Another one called him a lone eagle." She'd thought at the time that the appellation was rather romantic, but she sensed that Nick wouldn't agree.

"More like a lone buzzard if you ask me," he said, con-firming her suspicion.

She smiled behind her screen. As much as she'd tried to detest Nick Taggart, she couldn't do it. They sparred verbally all the time. He still considered her a stuffy city girl and prob-ably no better than she should be, and she knew full well that he was a rough-edged oaf, but she couldn't help but like him.

The same went for his uncle. Junius, who was probably around fifty years old, actually reminded her of her uncle Harry, who was one of the finest actors she'd ever known. Harry could wring tears out of an audience with the same ease with which he made them laugh. And entertaining? Goodness sakes, Eulalie would never forget some of the evenings the company had spent being regaled with stories by Harry. Aunt Florence, Harry's sister, had often told Eulalie she despaired of Harry, but she always laughed at his stories along with ev-eryone else.

She missed her family like fire. But it wouldn't be too much longer before she could send for Patsy. It didn't take mail as long to get back and forth to Chicago as she'd feared it would, thanks to the stage lines and the railroad. Patsy claimed to be almost ready to make the arduous journey by train and stagecoach to Rio Peñasco. Eulalie needed to begin searching for lodgings for the both of them. Unlike most of the places she'd lived, there weren't boardinghouses or hotels on every corner. There were few corners, for that matter, in the town of Rio Peñasco proper—if such a term could be applied to so improper a place—consisting of one long main street. She sighed as she slipped into a modest blue dress, which was quite a pleasant change from the tight green monstrosity she'd worn for the show this evening.

Nick, Junius, and she made it a habit to stop at Vernon's chophouse for a meal before Nick and Junius deposited her at the Johnson place. Eulalie didn't think it would be fair to Mrs. Johnson to make her prepare a meal in the middle of the night, which was when she left work. The fare was monotonous but nutritious, and the good Lord knew, there was plenty of it, and Eulalie didn't mind too much. Once she and Patsy got settled in a house of their own somehow or other, they could fix their own meals.

They had just left the chophouse and were making their way down the road to Mrs. Johnson's house when Nick put a hand on her arm. "Just a minute. I hear something."

Eulalie wasn't sure why hearing something required becoming alarmed—she heard things all the time—but she honored Nick's request, having come to the conclusion that he knew more about life in the Wild West than she. Therefore, she stood still while Nick and his uncle hurried forward. When she listened harder, her brow furrowed and she understood Nick's concern. It sounded like a scuffle to her. Oh, dear. She hoped it wasn't about her.

"Here!" Junius shouted. "Stop that!"

"Dammit!" yelled Nick.

Eulalie started to distinguish the noises coming to her out of the dark, Rio Peñasco being too unsophisticated to have acquired streetlamps thus far in its existence. The only illumination available after dark was the faint light spilling from various doors and windows, and since it was after midnight, there wasn't much of it available this night. Thumps, grunts and thuds smote her ears. When she heard a boy's voice cry, "She ain't there, I tell you!" her blood ran cold and her heart sank.

That was Charles Johnson; she'd bet on it. She rushed toward the sounds, praying that some crazed cowboy wasn't beating Charles to a pulp. "Charles!"

"Izzat her?" a voice asked in the blackness.

"You can't have her!" Charles's voice cried. His declaration ended in a grunt.

A hand like a ham grabbed her arm, and Eulalie found herself jerked to a stop before she'd reached the scene of the fight. "Just a minute, girlie," slurred a voice. "What you think you're doin'?"

"Unhand me!" she shrieked, kicking out at her attacker with the pointy toe of her shoe, connecting with a hard part of his anatomy. She assumed it was a shin or something.

"Ow! Dammit, lady, that's not nice." And the fiend gave her a wallop to the face that would have sent her staggering if he hadn't had a grip on her.

Well, this was ridiculous. Not only was Eulalie now injured herself—she could taste blood in her mouth—but she feared for Charles's safety, as well. That being the case, she reached into the pocket of her demure blue dress, withdrew her Colt Ladysmith, and shot the man who held her; she wasn't sure where. He screamed and let her go, and all other sounds ceased, as if by magic.

Because she'd been struggling before the ham-like hand released her, Eulalie reeled away and would have fallen to the ground had she not bumped into something as hard, if not as dirty, as the packed earth beneath her feet. She heard someone say, "Umph!" and decided it must have been Nick's body that had broken her fall. She knew it for a fact when his hand, not unlike a ham itself, steadied her.

"Did you just shoot somebody?" Nick roared. "Shit!"

"He hit me!" Eulalie cried. "And don't use bad language! There's a child present."

"I'm not really a child anymore, Miss Gibb." Charles's voice was faint and a little mushy, but he sounded firm in conviction of his manhood.

"He hit you?"

Eulalie had never heard Nick sound so menacing.

"She shot me!" a whiny voice came from Eulalie's feet. "Damn it, she *shot* me!"

Eulalie had endured quite a bit of unpleasantness this evening, and the realization that her attacker believed *she* had abused *him* was too much for her to endure. Her temper snapped. "And I'll shoot you again if you don't be quiet this second!"

Gunshots weren't unheard of in Rio Peñasco, but they weren't as common as Eulalie had previously supposed, having read a good many yellow-backed novels in recent months. Therefore, at the sound of the shot the little village sprang to life. Doors opened, window sashes were thrown up, lamps were lit, and people cried out. Eulalie saw lanterns bouncing toward them, carried by folks whose faces she could not yet distinguish. The door to the Johnson home flew open, and Mrs. Johnson, followed by a swarm of children, hurried out to the scene of the action. William held a kerosene lantern to guide the way.

Eulalie sighed heavily, wishing she could live a less public life. This was especially true since she was trying to hide.

"Give me that lantern, Will," growled Nick when the Johnson contingent arrived.

The boy flinched but obeyed. "Sure, Uncle Nicky."

Nick held the lantern up so that he could see Eulalie, who shied away because the bright light hurt her eyes. "By damn, he *did* hit you!" He turned back to William. "Here, take this." He shoved the lantern at the boy.

William did, and Nick reached down and grabbed the man Eulalie had shot by the scruff of his collarless shirt. Heaving him to his feet, Nick drew back a lethal-looking fist and would have broken the man's jaw had not Sheriff Wallace shouted, *"Nick! No!"*

Three people, including his uncle Junius and Mrs. Johnson leaped upon Nick's arm. Eulalie didn't know why they were doing that; she believed the fiend who'd attacked and hit her deserved to be leveled by somebody, and Nick seemed like the best-qualified fellow to do it. By the flickering lamplight, Eulalie had seen another man on the ground, faceup, and guessed he was the one who'd been struggling with Charles. She presumed Nick had dispatched him, thereby rendering him unfit to continue the fight. She believed the villain who'd hurt her deserved the same treatment.

The attack on his arm forced Nick to let go of his prisoner, who dropped to the ground with a hard *whump* and mewed piteously.

Nick bellowed, "Damn it, he *hit* her!"

"Can't kill a man for that, Nicky," said Junius judiciously. "Leastways, not without a trial first."

Eulalie fingered her cheek and felt the inside of her mouth with her tongue. "I think he knocked a tooth loose. I'm going to be bruised for days." And that, curse it, would probably interfere with her job.

"She shot me," whimpered the man she'd shot.

"Oh, be quiet!" Eulalie had no sympathy for the lout.

"Oh, my, will you just look at that cheek!" Mrs. Johnson cried suddenly. She let go of Nick, rushed to Eulalie and put an arm around her.

The scene was vividly illuminated now, what with all the lanterns being held aloft as people gathered around the combatants. Nick took a better look at Eulalie's cheek, his eyes grew wide, and he tried and failed to shake off his uncle and the sheriff and lunge at the wounded man, who still sat on the ground with a hand pressed to his thigh. Eulalie frowned. How in the name of mercy had she managed to hit him there? Of course, she hadn't had time to aim. If she had, she'd have shot him a few inches to the left, and made a eunuch of him.

Goodness, she never used to harbor vicious thoughts. The West did that to a person, she guessed. "It hurts," she said to Mrs. Johnson, hugging her back and appreciating the warmth and comfort offered by another woman at that moment more than she could say.

"I should say so. You're going to have a terrible bruise and probably a black eye."

A black eye. Wonderful. Eulalie didn't have time to appreciate the full horror of her facial disfiguration because another roar rent the air. She and Mrs. Johnson both levitated a foot or so in the air before they realized the roar had come from Nick, who evidently didn't appreciate the news about Eulalie's impending black eye any more than she herself did. He tore himself away from his uncle and the sheriff and leaped on the man on the ground, who tried to escape, crab-fashion, but failed. Nick lifted him in the air until his feet were dangling. Eulalie was impressed, as the fellow wasn't small by any stretch of the imagination.

The wounded man screamed, "Help me!" a second before Nick punched him in the jaw, sending him over backwards. He dropped like a felled oak, and the ground beneath Eulalie's feet trembled. It occurred to her that she'd never had a man defend her—not, of course, that dear Edward wouldn't have tried to if the occasion had ever arisen, which it hadn't. She couldn't imagine Edward being quite so effective in the execution, however. God help her, she liked it.

She also hated the notion that a fifteen-year-old boy, to wit, Charles Johnson, had actually engaged in fisticuffs in order to protect her. Who knew how often something like this would occur? Certainly not Eulalie, but she didn't expect the rough men who populated this rough-edged place would change any time soon.

"That's enough, Nick." Sheriff Wallace grabbed Nick around the waist to prevent him from lifting the man off the ground and socking him again. "This is a job for the law to handle."

"He hit her," Nick said. "Let me at him."

Junius joined the sheriff. It was a struggle, but between them and a couple of other hardy souls who braved Nick's wrath, they subdued him enough to assure that Eulalie's attacker would probably live to attend his trial, should one occur. Eulalie hadn't noticed much in the way of trials since she'd moved to Rio Peñasco, but she'd heard of a circuit judge who came around once in a while. She was more worried about her job than the law.

"Calm down, son," Junius said soothingly. "Everything will be all right. The sheriff will lock the fellow up and the doc will tend him, and Miss Eulalie will be fine." Glancing at

Eulalie and wincing, Junius added a qualifying sentence, "She'll be fine pretty soon."

"He doesn't deserve to go to trial. He deserves to die! He *hit* her!" Nick said indignantly.

Eulalie made a decision. She reached out and placed a hand on Nick's arm. His muscles were tense with his fury, and he felt as if he'd been hewn out of granite underneath the rough cotton shirt he wore. Yes, indeed. Nick Taggart was the one, all right. "Please, Mr. Taggart. I appreciate your efforts on my behalf, but I don't want you to get into trouble."

Nick glowered at her. "He *hit* you!"

This recurring theme made Eulalie grimace and press her fingers to her tender cheek. She said, "Yes, he did. And his partner hurt Charles."

The other unconscious man groaned at that moment, and Junius put a boot on his chest to keep him down. Eulalie mused about how very effective extemporaneous frontier peacekeeping could be.

"Nick, we'll take care of these fellows," Sheriff Wallace said.

To Eulalie, it sounded as if he were attempting to placate a wild beast with soft words. Eyeing Nick, she allowed as how the sheriff might have the right idea. Therefore, she attempted a smile, discovered her face hurt too much to create a successful one, and used her voice instead. "Thank you *so* much, Mr. Taggart and—Mr. Taggart." Hmm. She wished Nick and Junius didn't share the same last name. "I really appreciate your coming to my rescue." Thinking about the oldest Johnson boy, she turned to Charles. "And you, Charles, how brave and strong you are!"

The dozen or so kerosene lanterns lighting the scene didn't render the night as bright as day, but Eulalie saw Charles's cheeks turn a bright and glowing red. She turned to

Mrs. Johnson. "I'm terribly sorry to have brought this trouble on you, Louise. You and your family have been so good to me."

"Pish tosh," said Mrs. Johnson. " 'Twarn't nothin' any Christian woman wouldn't do."

Eulalie could have disabused her of that naïve notion, but didn't. "Well, you've been wonderful. However, I don't want your children to have to defend my honor. It's not fair to you or to them." And she aimed to do something about it, too, if she possibly could.

"I don't mind," Charles said stoutly, if a little indistinctly. The poor boy's jaw was the size of a watermelon already. Eulalie cringed, feeling guilty.

"But where will you go?" asked Mrs. Johnson.

With a sideways glance at Nick, Eulalie said, "Um . . . perhaps Mr. Taggart and I ought to discuss the matter." This time Eulalie threw caution to the wind and batted her eyelashes at Nick.

The coy gesture didn't garner quite the reaction she'd intended. While Nick lost the maddened-bear-on-the-attack demeanor that had prompted the sheriff and his uncle to keep him securely held between them, the expression on his face changed to one of wary alertness. His gaze thinned, and he squinted at her as if he didn't trust her. This evidence of suspicion vexed Eulalie, but she wasn't able to pursue the matter because Mr. Bernie Benson barged up to the group.

"What's this I hear about someone attacking our precious cactus flower?" Bernie bellowed.

Eulalie noticed that his concern for her welfare hadn't prevented him from grabbing a notebook and pencil before he sought out the scene of the crime. She wasn't altogether fond of being referred to as a cactus flower, either.

"I'm fine, Mr. Benson," she assured him. She'd stopped

trying to smile, since the endeavor was painful and didn't seem worth the effort.

"And she don't need you," added Nick, back to sounding like an irritated bear.

"Tut tut, this is *news!*" cried Bernie with a flourish of his pencil. "Mr. Chivers is hot on my heels. Jerry Ballinger is at the Opera House right this minute, rousting him out of bed. When I heard our own beloved cactus flower had been injured by a couple of ravening beasts, I had to report on the story!"

"Ravening beasts?" said the man Junius had his boot on, lifting his head and trying to see. "Who you callin' a beast?"

Eulalie snapped, "You!" and the man subsided onto the ground again.

"What's this I hear about you shooting one of the villains, Miss Gibb?"

"For God's sake, don't write that!" said Nick. He reached for Bernie's notebook, but Bernie, for all his bulk, could move quickly when he wanted to, and he danced backwards, eluding him.

"It's news!" he said in an injured tone.

"It's all right, Mr. Taggart. I suppose Mr. Benson is right. This might be considered news." Eulalie heaved a long sigh. "But I'm not feeling awfully well at the moment, Mr. Benson. May I make an appointment to speak to you tomorrow?"

Bernie looked hurt. "But it's news! I have to be on top of the news. Besides, you'll be pleased to know, Miss Gibb, that I've been sending copies of the *Piper* all over the United States. I've even sent copies to Chicago!"

Eulalie almost cried out in her dismay. This was terrible! Curse all newspapermen for all eternity. If anything was needed to make her life complete, it was knowing that news of her stay in Rio Peñasco might reach Gilbert Blankenship. She only prayed he was still in prison.

"So you see," went on Bernie, "I have a wider readership than the town itself. And it's imperative that I gather the news as it happens."

"Nuts, Bernie," said Nick. "The damned paper comes out once a week. Nobody's going to scoop you."

Good point. Eulalie wished she'd thought of it. At the moment, she wasn't thinking of anything except how to stop Bernie Bensen from sending any more newspapers to his horde of Eastern friends. The fleeting notion that, if she shot him dead he wouldn't be able to do so, entertained her for only a second. She rejected it as being too drastic, although it still held some appeal.

It was Bernie's turn to sigh. "Very well. I'll visit you at noon, if that's agreeable with you, Miss Gibb."

"Fine," said Eulalie, and hoped everybody would go away now. She had some heavy thinking to do.

Stuffing his pencil and notebook into a pocket, Bernie eyed the two men on the ground. "Which one's the one she shot, Sheriff?"

Wallace pointed. "That one."

"He dead?" Bernie didn't sound at all distressed that the man might have been shot dead by Eulalie Gibb.

"Naw. Nick socked him."

Bernie said, "Ow."

"Want me to help you get these two galoots to the jail, Sheriff?" Junius offered.

"Yeah. Thanks, Junius. Then maybe you can go fetch the doc." Mr. Wallace turned to Eulalie and belatedly removed his hat. None of the other men standing around had bothered. "You need help, Miss Gibb? You want me to send the doc to see to your cheek?"

"Thank you very much, Sheriff, but I don't think that will be necessary. But I do appreciate everyone's help." While she couldn't smile, she could still appear gracious, and Eulalie gave it all she had as she swept a glance at her audience. The sound of shuffling feet and several "Aw, shuckses" greeted this display of her womanly charms, and she was satisfied she'd performed as well as might have been expected, under the circumstances. She wanted to get Nick Taggart alone, curse it.

"What happened?" a new voice said breathlessly.

Eulalie sighed again. Dooley Chivers. Her boss. Wonderful. He was going to take one look at her face, which was probably swollen and bruised by this time, and she was going to lose her job. Since she didn't believe in postponing unpleasantness, and since she figured she could use her considerable powers of persuasion on the softhearted Dooley, she turned and gave him the full glory of what she expected was a hideous sight.

Dooley skidded to a stop, churning up a cloud of dust. He stared at her, horrified. "My God, who did that to you?"

"That man on the ground," said Eulalie, indicating the still unconscious, formerly ravening beast. "I shot him."

"You did what?" Dooley blinked at the man and then at Eulalie.

"I shot him. And I'll shoot anyone else who dares to attack me, too." There. Let Bernie Benson make a story out of *that*.

"Christ," muttered Nick under his breath.

Dooley had seen her cheek. He goggled. "Good God, you can't sing like that!"

Bridling slightly, Eulalie said, "Please give me a chance, Mr. Chivers. I'm sure it won't take more than a day or two for the swelling to go down."

"What about the bruising?"

"Makeup," said Eulalie stoutly. "I'm an expert with makeup, don't forget."

"Hmm." Chivers appeared unconvinced.

She clasped her hands to her bosom, a gesture she'd learned at her mother's knee, and pleaded with him. "Please, Mr. Chivers. Don't allow this unfortunate incident to affect my employment. I really need my job."

"You can't fire her," Nick declared. "It wasn't her fault these two idiots attacked her."

"Well . . . I reckon that's true."

"And she's good, Dooley," said Nick. "You know she's the biggest draw you've ever had in the Opera House."

"Yeah, I guess that's true." He eyed Eulalie again and winced visibly. "But, Nicky, look at her."

"It's not her fault," Nick repeated in a measured and rather menacing voice. "Give her a couple of days off, and she'll be good as new."

"Exactly," said Eulalie, gratified to have received such staunch support from a man whose friendship she'd rather doubted until now.

"Well . . ."

"Dammit, Dooley, you know she's the best thing that's ever happened to your Opera House. Stop pretending you don't need her."

Dooley heaved a heavy sigh. "Well, I reckon you're right, Nick." He grimaced when he glanced at Eulalie again. "How long do you think you'll need, Miss Gibb? Before you're . . . you know."

"Now how in hell can she tell you that?" Nick barked before Eulalie could give an estimate of how much time her cheek would take to regain its normal size. "She don't know, and neither do you. I'll take her to Doc Canning tomorrow, and maybe he'll be able to tell her."

Defeated, Dooley said, "Reckon you're right, Nick. All right, Miss Gibb. I'm real sorry this happened."

"She is, too," growled Nick. "And don't forget, it's your damned Opera House that gave those sons of bitches the idea she was . . . available. And you sold 'em the liquor, too. You ought to post a sign or something."

"I made an announcement," said Dooley with something of a whine.

"Yeah, well, you'd better make it louder. Miss Gibb's a lady, dammit."

Eulalie could have kissed him. In fact . . .

She placed her hand on Nick's arm. He was no longer enraged, but his muscles were still hard as iron. Her heart began beating faster as she prepared to meet her fate—or what she hoped would be her fate, and that of her sister. "Mr. Taggart, I really need to speak with you."

He eyed her with misgiving. "Yeah? Well, go ahead. Speak."

Aggravating man! She lowered her voice, and made sure it throbbed just a bit. "Privately."

Nick said, "Uh-oh."

Chapter Seven

"There's no need to take that tone with me, Mr. Nick Taggart," Eulalie said when they were alone at last. Their surroundings weren't exactly conducive to the conversation Eulalie planned to have with him, and she'd have preferred it if she looked her best, but one had to make do when necessity arose. In this case necessity dictated they speak to each other in Mrs. Johnson's kitchen garden, as far away from the house as they could get.

Nick said, "Huh."

The wind had died down, and the night, while not quite black as the pit from pole to pole, was doing a good job of realizing that condition. The moon lay on its back and grinned down upon her from among the stars, and Eulalie was startled to realize that she'd come to enjoy the smell of the desert. The air was so clean here. There was no slaughterhouse stench permeating everything as there was in Chicago, and no odor of too many people in too small a space mingled with garbage and horse dung as there was in New York City. Out here, only the crisp fragrance of creosote perfumed the air.

And stars? She'd never seen so many stars in her entire life. Sometimes after she got home from work, she'd stare out her window at the sky and almost make herself believe that she could reach out and grab a handful of stars in her hands. She'd like to do that, and send them home to Patsy, so she wouldn't be frightened anymore—although why Eulalie thought a handful of stars would help her sister overcome her misery, even she couldn't have said.

Pressing a cold cloth to her cheek, Eulalie frowned at Nick. "I need to discuss something very serious with you, Mr. Taggart."

"Yeah? What?"

"The welfare of the Johnsons."

"What's wrong with the Johnsons?"

"Nothing! But for heaven's sake, Mr. Taggart, you must realize that I can't stay here any longer. Charles might have been seriously hurt tonight! I can't have that poor boy rushing to my rescue! He's only a child."

"Better not let him hear you say that. He did a pretty good job of holding those fellows off tonight."

"But he shouldn't have to do that."

"I agree, but it's not his fault you dress in nothing, sing at the Opera House, and then parade yourself all over town at night."

"I don't!"

Nick rolled his eyes.

"Stop doing that!" Eulalie cried, incensed. She'd hoped to have a nice, private chat with Nick, and that he'd be receptive to the suggestion she aimed to make to him, but now she wondered if she'd been a little too sharp with him these past couple of weeks. She hadn't pegged him as a particularly sensitive man, but, the good Lord knew, men were strange creatures. Maybe she'd hurt his feelings or something. "I have a very serious problem, Mr. Taggart, and I'm hoping you'll be willing to help me with it."

"What's your problem? The Johnsons? Hell, Miss Gibb, they aren't the problem. You are."

"I am *not* a problem!"

Another eye roll. Eulalie decided it would be better to ignore it.

"This problem concerns my welfare and that of my sister."

"Yeah? What's your sister's name?"

"Patsy. Patsy Gibb. She will be joining me in Rio Peñasco as soon as we can make arrangements."

"Couldn't she get a job in Chicago, either?"

His tone was more eloquent than his words, and Eulalie knew he'd begun to doubt her story. She decided to tell him part of the truth. "My sister suffered a horrible accident some months ago, Mr. Taggart, and is unable to work at all." It hadn't been an accident; it had been a cold-blooded assault, but Nick didn't need to know that.

"An accident?" He didn't sound quite as skeptical as he had before.

"A terrible accident. She was grievously injured, and is only now recovered enough to make the trip West."

"Why does she want to move West? Aren't there more amenities in Chicago?"

"She wants to move to Rio Peñasco because I'm here! Curse it, Nick Taggart, why are you being so obstinate? My sister needs me! And, unfortunately, I need you!"

He lifted an eyebrow. "Yeah? How do you figure that? Junius and I already see to it that nobody gets at you in the Opera House and afterwards."

"Yes. And I appreciate it very much." This was it. She sucked in a deep breath. "But I need to find a place for Patsy and me to live, and it wouldn't be fair to anyone for us to stay at the Johnsons."

Nick frowned. "You'd have to share a room."

"I don't care about sharing a room with my sister! I care about our safety."

Nick shrugged. "Don't know what to say about that, Miss

Gibb. The line of work you're in . . ." He allowed his sentence to trail off, but Eulalie got the impression he thought she ought to expect trouble.

"Listen to me, Nick Taggart. I know I can take care of myself. I proved it tonight when I shot that idiot who attacked me."

"Huh."

"And I'd have shot the other man, too, if poor Charles hadn't stopped him."

"That damned belly gun of yours only carries two bullets, Miss Gibb. What if you'd missed?"

"I carry a Colt Lightning Revolver, too, Mr. Taggart. Surely you haven't forgotten that."

"Of course, I haven't forgotten it, but I notice you didn't draw it tonight."

He had her there. She muttered, "I couldn't get at it. That awful man had me in a grip like iron."

"Anyhow, you'll have a lot of explaining to do if you shoot every man who talks to you dirty."

"I don't plan to shoot every man who talks dirty!" This wasn't going at all well. Eulalie ought to have expected Nick to be difficult. He always was. She sucked in a deep breath. "What I'm hoping is that you will agree to protect Patsy and me."

He didn't have a ready response to that. In fact, he only stood there—it felt more like a loom to Eulalie—and stared at her.

She ran out of patience at about the thirty-second mark. "Well?" she demanded. "What do you think?"

"About what?"

Obstinate man! "About protecting me! And Patsy."

"Like how?"

She huffed impatiently. "*I* don't know how! But the men

in this ghastly place seem to respect you, and do what you say. If everyone in town knew I was under your protection, I'm sure no one would bother me."

"Under my protection? Like how?"

She wished he'd stop saying *like how.* "If everyone in town knew that you were my . . . my bodyguard, no one would dare molest me. Or Patsy."

"Bodyguard? How am I supposed to guard your body?"

Her heart was pounding like a trip hammer, and Eulalie felt like battering Nick with her fists. She knew good and well the man wasn't stupid, but he was certainly pretending to be thickheaded this minute. "For heaven's sake, Nick Taggart! If everyone thought we were . . . together, no man would dare approach me with improper suggestions!"

"Together, eh?"

She couldn't recall the last time she'd heard him sound so cynical. Curses. Perhaps she'd misread his interest in her. Well, in her body. But she had to go on, because she really needed him. If some lout tried to break into her lodging after Patsy moved in with her, anything might happen. Poor Patsy was very fragile, both physically and emotionally, at the moment. "Yes," she said. "Together."

"Hmm. What exactly is in it for me, Miss Gibb?"

Here it came. Eulalie reached out and ran a finger along Nick's broad chest. "I could pay you."

"Yeah? With what?"

"Well . . . with money, if you'd like." She prayed like mad he wouldn't take her up on that suggestion, since money was the commodity she had least of.

He licked his lips, and Eulalie's heart soared. She had him! She knew she had him!

"I don't need money. I make enough money at the smithy."

"Well, then, perhaps I could pay for your services in some other way."

"Yeah? What other way?"

"With services of my own."

He took a step back, and Eulalie's arm fell to her side. Drat it, he wasn't supposed to have done that! He was supposed to have fallen under her spell, curse the man!

"All right, let me get this straight. You want me to protect your body, and in exchange, I get what? That same body?"

"Well, yes. I guess you could put it that way."

"I'm not marrying you," Nick stated flatly.

For some reason unaccountable to Eulalie, those bald words stung. She'd never let on. "I'm not proposing marriage. I'm proposing a carnal union. Your protection—of my sister and me—in exchange for my favors."

"Your favors, huh?"

"You seemed interested in them once." She hoped none of the hurt she felt inside leaked into her voice.

"I'm as interested in 'em as any other man. But I want you to know from the beginning that I'm not a marrying man. I'm not going to repeat my father's mistake in that regard. No, ma'am. There's no way I'm going to be at the mercy of a woman again in this lifetime."

"Well, really, Mr. Taggart! To hear you, one would think women are all terrible creatures."

He eyed her with what Eulalie could only term sardonic amusement. She stiffened.

"As far as I'm concerned, Miss Gibb—and this is based on my own experience, and I'm sure not all women are like this—but the only women *I've* ever had any truck with are sly, manipulative bitches. I wouldn't trust a woman any farther than I can see into the desert tonight. They take and take and take, and when a man doesn't give exactly what they want, they cry and carry on and make a man feel like two bits. That's pretty damned low, in my opinion."

Hmm. Interesting. Eulalie really knew nothing about Nick, the man, except that he was big and strong and helped out a lot of people in town. She'd like to hear more about his background—but not now. "You don't have to marry me, Mr. Taggart. I need your help, and I'm willing to pay for it the only way I know how. Patsy and I will probably need all the money I can earn just to survive."

"Hmm. Well . . ."

"And I was hoping that perhaps you might be able to suggest a place for us to stay when Patsy gets here. I really hate to remain at the Johnsons, especially after the altercation tonight. It isn't fair that small children should be put in jeopardy because I have to sing for a living."

"I don't think it's the singing so much as the costumes, if you don't mind my saying so, ma'am."

Eulalie was fed up with this shilly-shallying. She snapped, "Are you going to help me or not? I guess I can always ask somebody else to protect me. Lieutenant Fuller looked as if he might be willing to protect a lady." She hoped he wouldn't pounce on the word *lady* and use it against her.

"He lives at the fort," Nick pointed out, relieving the *lady* anxiety, if no others.

"Well, other women live at the fort!"

"Yeah, but they're married to men who are stationed there."

She lifted her chin. "Perhaps Lieutenant Fuller isn't as averse to marriage as you are, Mr. Taggart."

Nick seemed to get larger. His chest definitely expanded. Eulalie was impressed. "Do you mean to tell me you'd marry that fool just because you want somebody to protect you? Or . . . wait a minute. Do you *want* to marry Fuller?"

122

Eulalie couldn't understand how this conversation had got so far out of her control. She'd thought she had everything so well planned, and here Nick was twisting everything she said.

She stamped her foot. "I don't want to marry anybody! I already married the man I loved!"

Nick had been sucking in air, preparing, no doubt, to further harass her. When she told him she'd been married, the breath left him in a whoosh. "You're *married?*" He sounded stunned, unless that was her imagination.

"I *was* married," she said, peeved. "My darling Edward died four years ago."

"You're a widow?"

"Yes. I'm a widow."

"I thought your last name was Gibb."

"It is Gibb."

"But isn't that your sister's last name?"

"Yes. Gibb is our stage name."

"What's that? A stage name."

Eulalie heaved an enormous sigh. She hadn't meant to get into this. But she didn't suppose it would hurt anything. "Gibb is the name of my family. My great-grandfather, Mortimer Gibb, founded the Gibb Theatrical Company in New York City in 1834. We've been performing ever since. My husband's last name was Thorogood, but I've always been called Gibb, because I belonged to the acting company by that name."

"Oh." Nick scratched his chin. "I reckon that makes sense."

"Yes," said Eulalie. "It does. Now can we get back to the matter at hand?"

"I'll be damned. I didn't know you were a widow. So you've had experience, eh?"

She stiffened. "I don't know what you mean by *experience*, but if you mean do I know what men and women do together, yes. I do." Her lovely lost Edward had been a tender and gentle lover. She had a feeling bedtimes with Nick might be a trifle more exciting. Not that she meant in any way to disparage darling Edward.

"Hmm. So you'll become my mistress if I agree to protect you and your sister."

Bluntly put, but Eulalie couldn't argue with his conclusion. "Well . . . yes. In so many words."

"And you need a place to stay."

"Yes. With Patsy."

"And me."

"You'd live with us?" She hadn't counted on that.

He shrugged. "Don't know why not. I've got a place behind the smithy. It's big enough for two girls and me, I reckon."

"What about your uncle? I thought he lived with you."

"Well . . . we could probably work around that."

Eulalie doubted that. She decided to try a different tack. "Um . . . wouldn't people look at me askance if I lived with you without benefit of wedlock?"

The expression on his face could only be considered sardonic. "You're worried about that now? After you propositioned me?"

"I didn't proposition you! Not exactly." Frustrated, Eulalie went on, "Listen to me, Nick Taggart. My sister and I have been through a lot recently, and we might not be out of danger yet. I mean *Patsy* might not be out of danger. Because of her injuries and all, and the terrible suffering she's been through. We need protection. But we're not loose women, curse it! If I thought there was an alternative, I wouldn't have suggested this bargain."

His face lost its sardonic cast and became curious. "What kind of danger? Mind telling me about it?" He sneered a little. "I mean, if I'm going to put myself in danger for you, you might just mention what you're worried about."

Blast. She hadn't meant to get into *this*, either. "I doubt that you'll be in danger, Mr. Taggart. After all, you're a big, strong man."

"Yeah, but even a big, strong man isn't immune to bullets, so if you think—"

"Good heavens!" Eulalie tittered and couldn't believe it of herself. "I'm sure there's no danger of any shooting going on." She hadn't actually considered the possibility that Nick himself might be in danger if he took over the job of protecting her and Patsy. For probably the millionth time, Eulalie wished she'd been able to do more than hit Gilbert Blankenship over the head with a skillet. If she'd only had her guns then . . .

But it was no use wishing things were different from what they were, as she well knew. "Don't be silly, Mr. Taggart."

"Yeah? Maybe I don't think looking out for myself is silly, *Miss* Gibb."

Feeling defeated and wondering how it had happened so fast, Eulalie sighed. "Of course you don't. I didn't mean to imply that."

"Don't you two have any other family? Why don't you go to your family?"

Oh, dear. How could she explain her family? She loved them dearly—the remains of them—but she couldn't picture either Uncle Harry or Aunt Florence being of much use to her in the protection department. And she'd be hanged if she'd subject her cousins to Gilbert Blankenship's wrath. "I . . . we only have an elderly aunt and uncle. What could they do?"

"Hmm. What exactly is it you're worried about? A couple more drunks like those tonight?"

Eulalie's temper snapped like a dry twig. "Yes! Curse you, Nick Taggart, don't you understand? My sister is very fragile right now. If those two drunken louts had decided to break into a house where Patsy and I live when I'm at work, what protection would she have? Don't you understand? Even if they didn't hurt her, they'd terrify her, and her condition is too shaky for that. But if everyone in town believes you're living *with* us, then they'll surely believe Patsy and I are both scarlet women, and that would only invite more problems! *Why can't you understand?*"

Nick held up both huge hands, as if to ward off her hot words. "All right, all right. I understand."

Eulalie took heart. "So you'll do it?"

"First I'd better understand exactly what *it* is. I think that's fair, don't you?"

She sighed. "Yes."

"You want me to find you a place to live with your sister."

"Yes."

"And you'll reward me for protecting the both of you with . . . your favors."

The way he said the word *favors* made Eulalie think he didn't consider them such. How discouraging. Nevertheless, she said, "Yes."

"But you don't want the folks in Rio Peñasco to know we're . . . exchanging favors."

Her teeth clenched. "Yes. I mean, no, I don't."

"And your sister's sick."

"Injured."

"Injured. And she's in rough shape."

"Yes."

"And you don't want her bothered by men like the ones that are always trying to get at you."

"Yes." She pushed the word through her teeth.

"Hmm."

Nick stood there and thought. At least Eulalie presumed he was thinking, although what he had to think about she couldn't understand. The proposition seemed quite straightforward to her. She'd sleep with him. He'd protect Patsy and her. What could be simpler, really? If Nick didn't know the full extent of the problems she and Patsy faced, it didn't matter. Eulalie was sure nobody would ever find them in this place.

She recalled Bernie Benson's glee when he told her he'd been sending copies of the *Rio Peñasco Piper* hither and yon, and frowned.

But that was nonsensical. How could such a tiny, small-town paper ever reach the evil hands of Gilbert Blankenship? It couldn't. She hoped.

Finally Nick spoke. "I don't know, Miss Gibb . . ."

To her horror, Eulalie felt tears sting her eyes. She didn't want to cry in front of this man! She wanted him to think she was strong and indomitable and that she was only asking his help for her sister's sake. She didn't want him to think she was a conniving harpy like the other women in his life evidently had been. She clutched his shirtsleeve. "Please, Mr. Taggart. I don't know what else to do."

He huffed. "Yeah. Right."

"It's true! I can shoot any man who bothers me, but my sister can't. She's delicate. She's been horribly injured. She's fragile."

"Yeah, you've said that before."

Well, it looked as if Nick wasn't going to oblige her. Eulalie was surprised by how disappointed she was. Worse, she feared her reaction had more to do with his rejection of her as a woman than his refusal to act as Patsy's bodyguard.

And she still needed a bodyguard for Patsy. Drat it! She'd never be able to find anyone as suited to the task as Nick Taggart; she knew it in her bones.

Drawing her brisk, no-nonsense demeanor about her like a protective shield, she said, "Well, if you won't oblige me, I shall just have to look elsewhere."

"Hold on a minute. I didn't say I wouldn't do it."

"Oh?" She decided to hold off becoming happy until he clarified his position. His frown worried her a little bit.

"Let me make sure what's expected of me."

"Of course."

"You want me to find a place for you and your sister to live in Rio Peñasco."

She nodded and sighed heavily. They'd already covered this ground. "Yes."

"You want me to protect you and your sister from evil-doers."

"Well, that's a little dramatic, but yes. That's exactly what I want you to do."

"And in exchange for doing those things, I get to sneak in your back door at night and, uh, partake of your favors."

"Yes." He had a way of saying things that put them in the worst possible light. Eulalie didn't like it.

"And you don't expect me to marry you or bring you flowers or presents or cut your wood or wash your horse or do your shopping or—"

"I don't even *have* a horse," Eulalie cried, irked. "You're being silly, Mr. Taggart! All I want you to do is guard my sister and me and make sure nothing horrid happens to either one of us. We're two ladies alone in the world, and one of us is very weak, and the other one has to work and leave the weak one home alone at night! Is it so hard to understand that I might feel safer if I knew you were protecting us?"

"I guess not. But I want *you* to understand that I'm not at your command. I'll protect you, but I won't court you."

"Fine. That's fine with me." Again, Eulalie couldn't account for the slight pang that assailed her. She was only tired and bruised. That must be it. She'd steeled herself for all contingencies before she'd moved to this hellhole. The fact that a rough bumpkin didn't want to court her meant absolutely, positively nothing to her. Nothing. Zero.

"All right then, you have yourself a bargain, Miss Gibb. Only I wish you'd call me Nick. Every time anybody calls me Mr. Taggart, I look around for my father, poor man."

"Fine. And you may call me Eulalie."

"Eulalie. Pretty name."

"You really think so? I've always disliked it, but I was named for my favorite aunt, so I don't mind it too much."

"Hmm. Well, I reckon you'd best get to bed now. I'll talk to my uncle Junius, and we'll figure out some place for you and your sister to stay. What's her name again?"

"Patricia Anne. We've always called her Patsy."

"Patsy. All right."

"Thank you, Mr. . . . I mean Nick. I really appreciate this."

He grinned. "You'll be paying me, ma'am."

She sighed. "Yes. I will."

Nick looked her up and down, as if assessing his part of their bargain. "I'd take a little on account, but I expect you don't feel up to it."

Pressing a no-longer-cool cloth to her cheek, Eulalie said, "No. I don't."

"Too bad."

Men. They were all alike.

Except for Edward, of course.

★ ★ ★ ★ ★

When she finally got to her room that night and un-dressed, she tried to recall Edward's image to her mind's eye. It wouldn't come. She kept picturing Nick Taggart.

Annoyed with herself, Eulalie opened the top drawer of her dresser and dug under her underwear until she found the locket she kept hidden there. Snapping it open, she gazed at the miniature painting of Edward she cherished so greatly.

He'd been so handsome—in a pale, Lord Byronish way. He certainly wasn't massive, like Nick Taggart. Edward had been fine-boned and delicate. And his dark hair had always been a little long; poetically long, Eulalie had always thought. Looking at the picture tonight, in her state of pain and ex-haustion, Eulalie thought dear Edward looked just the slightest bit . . . affected? Good heavens, no. Not her beloved Edward.

Why, he'd been a gem among men. A loving, gentle man. A dear, really.

Anyhow, he'd been an actor, for heaven's sake, so he *had* to adopt roles. And if he played up his poetic good looks, that didn't mean he was affected! It meant he'd been a fine actor.

Of course, if he'd had Nick's deep, powerful voice, her fa-ther might have given him better parts, but that wasn't Ed-ward's fault. Eulalie shed her demure blue dress—covered in dust and dirt now, thanks to those two louts who'd tried to waylay her—removed her undergarments, and pulled her nightgown over her head. She stared at Edward's image as she sank onto her bed. The mattress rustled, having been made of corn shucks, according to Mrs. Johnson, but it wasn't uncomfortable.

Edward would have scorned such a bed. Eulalie sighed deeply. Dear Edward. He never could have imagined living in such a place as Rio Peñasco. He would be horrified to know she was here now.

But however much she disliked herself for it, Eulalie was rather glad she didn't have to depend on Edward in this present crisis. As much as she had loved him and would continue to cherish his memory, she had to acknowledge that Nick Taggart was going to be ever so much more effective as a bodyguard than Edward.

As she sank onto her pillow—on her right side, since her left cheek was so sore—Eulalie acknowledged grimly that life just wasn't fair. And, no matter how much she disapproved, there wasn't a blamed thing she could do about it.

Chapter Eight

My darling Eulalie,

Dr. Longworth tells me that I will be fit to travel in another week or so. I can't wait to see you again. The Hollands are such wonderful friends, and, of course, the family is a comfort to me, but I miss you terribly. I will feel much safer when we are both a couple of thousand miles away from the threat posed by Mr. Blankenship.

The scarring is terrible, Eulalie, as I feared it would be. Therefore, I have adopted the practice of wearing hats with heavy veils. I've almost stopped crying about my disfigurement, darling, except when I have to put on one of those awful hats.

I'm glad to know that Rio Peñasco isn't as ghastly as we feared it would be. I look forward to the day I can join you. I can hardly wait to meet all the people you've written to me about.

Lovingly, your sister,
Patsy

Nick Taggart awoke the morning after his altercation with Eulalie's attackers feeling better than he had for several weeks. He couldn't account for his good mood until he recalled his conversation with Eulalie the night before.

He'd won! By damn, he'd won! He was going to get to enjoy that spectacular body, and he wasn't going to have to pay with his life, the way his father and so many other poor dumb clucks had. He hoped Eulalie would be responsive to him. He didn't like a cold woman. Hell, if he wanted coldness, he'd get married.

Leaping out of bed, he hollered, "Junius! We got us a house to build!"

Junius had been in the kitchen of the small house they shared behind the smithy, making coffee. Nick sniffed appreciatively and decided his uncle had been cooking bacon, too. Good. Nick was hungry as a bear.

"What's that you said, Nicky?" Junius appeared in Nick's doorway, holding a mug of coffee out to his nephew. "Here's some brew."

"Thanks, Junius. You're a good cook."

Junius grunted and said, "Hell, what this place needs is a good woman."

"There is no such thing," growled Nick.

"Nuts. You can't judge all females by the witch your daddy married, son, and those daughters of hers. I think Miss Gibb is the right sort."

"That's who we have to build the house for."

"Oh?" Junius cocked a furry eyebrow. "You settin' up housekeeping with the woman?"

Nick had been stepping into his trousers. He looked up, horrified. "No!" His shudder was involuntary. "Shit, Junius, I'll never do that in this lifetime. You ought to know me better than that by this time."

"Reckon I do, son. But I still maintain not all women are evil."

"Maybe not, but by the time you figure out which ones are and which ones aren't, it's usually too late."

"My Pauline was a great woman, Nick. Too bad you never met her. Might have softened your opinion of females."

"Maybe." Nick had no doubt in his mind that his late aunt Pauline was a better person than his stepmother, but that didn't make her anybody Nick himself would want to live with.

His uncle chuckled and let the matter drop. "You aimin' to fix up a little adobe place for Miss Gibb?"

"Yeah, and there have to be two bedrooms, because her sister's coming to stay with her."

"Yeah? Interesting. She aiming on bringing the whole family out here eventually? We might could use us some entertainment in Rio Peñasco."

Nick shrugged. "Didn't sound like it to me. Just her sister. Her name is Patsy."

"Hmm." Junius didn't seem awfully interested in Patsy Gibb. "Come on in to breakfast. I have some eggs scrambled, and there's bacon. Joe Cameron's bringing his wagon in to the smithy today. Got to fix the axle."

"Thanks. Don't mind if I do. What's Joe done now?" Joe Cameron seemed to have accidents in his wagon on a regular basis. Last week he'd driven it into a dry arroyo and damaged a wheel rim.

"Drove it off a cliff, is what he said."

"A cliff? Where'd he find a cliff to drive it off of?"

"Mescalero ridge, I think he said."

Nick shook his head. "That takes some kind of talent."

Junius only chuckled.

It occurred to Nick, as he ate the breakfast his uncle had prepared, that since Miss Gibb wouldn't be able to work for a day or two, he might take her out to see the sights around Rio Peñasco. True, there weren't many of them, but there was a swampy area not far off where you could see lots of different kinds of birds. And there were the lakes said to be bottomless sitting among some pretty rocky hills. This time of year they were fairly dry, but the scenery was still kind of pretty to Nick's mind. He wasn't sure how a lady from New York City and Chicago might take them.

Hell. It was probably a stupid idea.

Nevertheless, he decided to pay a call on Miss Gibb. Just to reassure her that he and Junius would be building her a little house. Not because he wanted to see her or anything.

"You're twitchin' your shoulders and frowning, son. Got something on your mind?"

Junius's mild question startled Nick. He glanced up from his coffee cup. "Nope. Just thinking where to get wood to build the frame."

"We might could go up near Capitan."

"That's a fair hike."

Junius shrugged. "We could make it in a day if we don't mind traveling some in the dark. We could aim for a full moon, and that's only a few days off." He eyed his nephew with what Nick could only call a sly smile. "You might want to take Miss Gibb with us. Show her that not everything in these parts is desert. She ain't going to be singing for a day or two, is she?"

Nick frowned, praying that he appeared only to be thinking over his uncle's suggestion. As for himself, Nick wouldn't mind being out under the full moon with Eulalie Gibb, as long as she kept her mouth shut. Or, if not shut, as long as she didn't talk with it. But Nick couldn't cut enough wood for the frame of a house by himself, which meant Junius would have to go with them, and that would rule out any amorous activities.

"I don't know, Junius. It might be a little tiring on a lady."

Junius shrugged. "You could ask her."

"I reckon."

But when Nick slapped his hat on his head and set out to

Mrs. Johnson's house, he'd decided against taking Eulalie to the mountains. If he and Junius trekked to Capitan, it would be to work and work hard, and they'd both get hot and sweaty and would stink by the time they headed back home. Somehow, Nick didn't fancy the notion of Eulalie crammed into a wagon next to two smelly men, one of whom was he. Maybe after her sister got here, Nick would take them both to the mountains for a day trip or something. That might be nice, and it might give Miss Gibb—Miss Eulalie Gibb, that is—a softer opinion of him.

Not that he cared, of course.

Charles answered Nick's knock at the Johnsons' door. "Holy cow, Charles! Your cheek looks like one of those eggplants your mama grows."

Tenderly touching his cheek, Charles tried to grin. "Yeah. It doth. Hurth, too."

"I bet it does. Sorry you got knocked around, Charles, but you did a danged good job of slowing those two galoots down."

Charles blushed, thereby providing a colorful background for his eggplant cheek. "Thankth, Uncle Nicky."

"Sure thing, Charles. You aren't in school today?"

Charles looked displeased. "Ma wouldn't let me go. I wanted to."

Nick grinned. He was sure of it. Charles would be a damned hero. He probably wanted to parade his injuries in front of his friends. "Mothers can sure be a pain in the neck, can't they?"

"Nicky Taggart, don't you be putting ideas in my boy's head!" came the words, loud, from the kitchen.

The two males exchanged a meaningful glance, as if to agree that Mrs. Johnson had just proved Nick's point.

"You wanna thee Mith Gibb?"

"If she's up and about. I need to tell her something."

"Thure thing, Uncle Nicky."

And, as Nick paced the Johnsons' small front parlor, Charles went to fetch Eulalie.

He grimaced when she walked into the room. "Shoot, Miss Eulalie, that cheek looks sore."

She sighed. "It is. I could probably cover the bruise with makeup, but until the swelling goes down, I suppose Mr. Chivers won't want me to appear in front of an audience."

Nick wasn't so sure about that. Dooley was a nice enough fellow, but he wasn't exactly overflowing with the milk of human kindness. As long as Eulalie looked good in her costumes—and she did, damn it—he wouldn't give a hang if her cheek was a little chubby. However, he didn't want Eulalie to know that. The longer she stayed away from all those slathering, lust-crazed men, the better Nick would like it. He particularly didn't like it when Lieutenant Fuller in his damned snappy uniform showed up, because Eulalie always fawned over him, a spectacle Nick would sooner live without.

Although, he thought with a sense of satisfaction washing through him, pretty soon he wouldn't have to worry about things like that. Any man who got too close to Eulalie, including that damned encroaching lieutenant, would have to deal with Nick Taggart. The notion made his juices run a little too freely, and he cursed inwardly and hoped like fire that Eulalie wouldn't glance below his belt. To disguise his condition, he held his hat in front of him.

"Please, Mr. Taggart, sit down," said Eulalie graciously. "I'm interested in hearing what you have to tell me."

So he sat and put his hat in his lap. It was getting painful, hanging around with Eulalie. He'd sure be glad when he could assuage his condition—which meant that he and Junius had to get her house built *pronto*. "Junius and I are going to take a trip up to the mountains to get some logs, and we can begin building your house on Saturday."

It gave Nick a warm feeling in his chest when Eulalie seemed to brighten. "That soon?"

He nodded. "Yeah. It won't take us long once we get the frame up."

"How handy you and your uncle are."

She sounded as if she was honestly grateful, but Nick had learned long ago not to trust a female. He squinted suspiciously and said, "That's us, all right. We're a couple of handy fellows."

"Thank you very much. Patsy wrote to say she would be able to travel in a week or so. Since she wrote the letter two weeks ago, I suspect she's ready now. I can hardly wait to see her again."

"You two close, are you?"

"Very. I was afraid I was going to lose her a few months ago."

"After the accident."

She hesitated for only a second or two. "Yes. After the accident."

He probably shouldn't ask—and anyhow, he didn't really care—but he did anyway. "What kind of accident was it?"

Again, Eulalie hesitated. Nick felt his eyebrows draw together and endeavored to stop them. But this wavering on Eulalie's part seemed curious to him. Accidents generally didn't take a whole lot of thought to describe. He couldn't shake the feeling that there was more to Eulalie Gibb and her story than she'd let on.

"She was badly cut."

The nature of the injuries startled Nick. "Cut? Shoot, I'm sorry. How'd that happen?"

She drew in an audible breath and said, "Really, Mr. Taggart, it pains me to talk about it."

Since she put her hand over her astonishing bosom and shuddered when she said it, he guessed she meant it, although he wasn't totally convinced. "Hmm. All right, then, we won't talk about it."

She bowed her head. "Thank you."

It was the bowed head that did Nick in. He just hated it when women tried to act pathetic around him. He knew better than most that females could adopt that posture for manipulative purposes at the drop of a damned hat. "Yeah. Sure."

She frowned at him. "There's no need to take that tone with me, Mr. Taggart."

Before an all-out battle of words ensued, Mrs. Johnson entered the room and Nick had to stand up again. That's what gentlemen did, or so his stepmother had taught him. He never did understand why; maybe so he could be available if one of the creatures fainted. Nevertheless, he liked Mrs. Johnson, so he stood.

"How do, Nicky?"

"I'm fine, thanks. You?"

"I'm just fine. Sit, sit," she said, doing likewise.

"You should have let Charles go to school today, ma'am. How's he going to get to be lauded as a hero if he can't be around his friends?"

"Nicky Taggart, you're really something, you know that?"

Nick only grinned.

"How about I pack up a picnic lunch, and you take Miss Gibb out to the lakes to see the scenery, Nicky. It's about the only place around here that's got any pretty at all to it."

"Oh, please, Mrs. Johnson, don't go to any trouble," Eulalie cried before Nick could respond. He frowned at her.

Dammit, the lady had addressed the question to him, not her. "Uncle Junius suggested the same thing, Mrs. Johnson. That's mighty nice of you to offer to pack a lunch." He glared at Eulalie, daring her to contradict him.

She glared back. Figured. "Don't be silly, Mr. Taggart. It's entirely too much trouble for Mrs. Johnson."

"Nonsense," said Mrs. Johnson, who, from the expression on her face, was enjoying their little contretemps. Nick thought about glaring at her, too, but knew it would do no good. She knew him too damned well. "I think it'd be good for you to get out and about, Eulalie. You work too hard, and you're never out in the daylight. A little sunshine will do you a world of good." Her eyes had a mischievous twinkle in them when she turned to Nick. "And you, Nick Taggart. You need a day off. You work too hard, too."

Nick said, "Huh."

Eulalie said, "Well . . ."

Mrs. Johnson popped up from her chair. "Fine, then. It's settled. I've already got sandwiches made." And she bustled out of the room.

Still glaring, Eulalie said, "Honestly, Mr. Taggart, that woman has enough to do without packing picnic lunches for us!"

"She don't mind." Nick felt better about life now that he knew he was going to spend the day with Eulalie. Not, of course, that he admired her or anything. But if they were going to be bed partners, he figured it wouldn't hurt to get better acquainted. He only wished she wasn't such a thorny female. While her body was soft and lush, her personality was all spikes. Maybe Bernie had it right when he called her a cactus flower. He himself still thought of her as a prickly pear. On the other hand, all those barbs kept her interesting.

"Don't you ever work?" Eulalie demanded.

The question surprised Nick. "Sure I do. Junius and I are the local blacksmiths. We work all the time."

She sniffed. "I never see you working."

"That's because you only come out at night. Like a bat. Or a vampire."

"Well, really!"

That line had been used on him so often, it only confirmed Nick in his opinion of females. Any time a fellow said something they couldn't rebut, they'd say, *well, really!* in that snotty way. His faith in the ordered administration of the universe thereby restored, Nick sat back, content, and waited for Eulalie to get her traps together so they could ride out to the lakes.

The truth was, although Eulalie was loath to admit it, she was looking forward to spending the day with Nick Taggart. He was uncouth, true, and he didn't treat her like a delicate flower, as did Lieutenant Fuller, but she liked him better than any of the other men she'd met in Rio Peñasco to date, perhaps because of that very prickliness to his nature. She sensed he wouldn't lie to her, and Eulalie had good reason to value honesty.

They paid a visit to the smithy before setting out to the lakes. Eulalie had never seen a blacksmith at work before, and the sight of Junius at the forge made her think of Roman gods. She had a strange wish to view Nick Taggart there in his leather apron, bashing away at a horseshoe or a . . .

"What's that thing your uncle is working on, Nick?"

"He's pounding out a crick in the axle of that wagon." He pointed at a disjointed wagon resting next to the building.

"He must be very strong," Eulalie said, thinking Nick must be very strong, too. She was alarmed when a tiny thrill ran through her at the notion that some time in the not too far distant future, she'd be given the opportunity to investigate Nick's strength on her own.

"Yeah, old Junius is as strong as an ox." Nick grinned at his uncle, who winked at him as he pounded on the axle. Lifting it with some huge tongs, he held the strip of metal over the forge with one hand, wiped his sweating brow with a handkerchief held in his other hand, and said, "You two going to have a picnic?" He nodded at the basket Nick held.

"Yup. Just came by for the gig."

"It's where it always is," said Junius. "And Claude's out back, like he always is."

Giving Junius a bright smile, Eulalie asked, "Who's Claude?"

Nick answered her. "Claude's our horse. He's a lazy son of a gun, but he'll work when he has to."

Since he walked off, Eulalie waved at Junius and scurried after him. She rounded the corner of the building, saw a horse, and stopped in her tracks. "Good Lord! I've never seen such a huge horse in my life!"

With a grin, Nick said, "Claude's big all right. He's got to be, because sometimes Junius or I have to ride him. Either one of us would bust down a regular horse."

"What kind of horse is it?" Eulalie's knowledge of horses was severely limited.

"Belgian draft horse. They're big."

"If they're all as big as that one, I'd say they're huge." In truth, Eulalie had never ridden a horse before and didn't particularly want to. She'd always considered regular horses big and frightening. Claude was a blasted monster.

He seemed to be an amiable one, however. As soon as he spotted Nick at the fence, he trotted over, shaking the earth with each thud of a huge hoof. Eulalie didn't want to get any nearer than she had to, but Nick gestured for her to come closer. She shook her head.

"Claude's a friendly fellow. You're not afraid of him, are you?"

Eulalie thought about lying and decided against it. What was the point? "Yes."

Nick made a rude sound indicative of mockery. "I didn't think you were afraid of anything, Miss Independence."

Giving him an exasperated frown, Eulalie snapped, "Well, I'm afraid of horses, so now you know. Especially huge horses, like that one."

She had to admit, if only to herself, however, that Claude, munching happily on the carrot Nick had given him, didn't look as if he aimed to leap over the fence and trample her to death. In point of fact, he had a rather placid expression on his face—not that Eulalie knew the first thing about horses' expressions.

"He's a big baby," said Nick. "Really. Come on over and get acquainted. Claude's never snapped at anybody, and he'd rather sit up and beg than kick anyone."

The mental image of that monstrous horse sitting up and begging, as her uncle Harry's dog Ginger used to do, was too amusing for Eulalie. In spite of herself, she smiled. "Promise?"

"Yes." Nick sounded exasperated. "I promise. For Pete's sake, Eulalie, you don't think I'd sic a horse on you, do you? We have a bargain, remember? And I'm looking forward to cashing in on it."

Eulalie felt her face flame. "Well, really!" she said for the second time that day. She couldn't account for the sardonic expression that crossed Nick's face.

She did, however, approach Claude. Cautiously. She kept her arms at her sides.

"Pet his nose. Just stroke it gently."

"I don't want to pet him."

"Don't hurt my horse's feelings, Eulalie Gibb. Claude is very sensitive."

She eyed him slantways, decided he was joking, and kept her arms down.

"Honest. He's a nice horse. Here, give him a carrot. Hold it in the palm of your hand, like this." He demonstrated. "That way, he won't nibble a finger by accident."

The notion of that giant animal chomping on her hand made Eulalie shudder. Nick noticed and heaved a sigh.

"Shoot, you're one stubborn female, Miss Eulalie Gibb. You know that?"

"Nonsense. I just value my . . . fingers."

"Huh."

The sound of hoofbeats behind them made Eulalie turn. She smiled when she saw the two lieutenants galloping into town.

Nick muttered, "Shit. Not fast enough."

The two men pulled their mounts to a stop a few feet away from Nick and Eulalie. They didn't do any fancy rearing stops today, a consideration for which Eulalie was grateful, since she didn't care to be covered in dust any sooner than was absolutely necessary—and, since she now lived in Rio Peñasco, it would be necessary before the end of the day. She'd lived there long enough to understand that much.

"How-do, Miss Gibb," said Lieutenant Fuller. "Nick."

Nick said, "Hmm."

"Ma'am," said Lieutenant Nash, his face bright red. Eulalie didn't know if it was because he was hot or because he was embarrassed. She also didn't care a whole lot.

"You going to hitch that beast up to something, Nick, or are you just showing Miss Gibb the sights?" Lieutenant

Fuller couldn't have been said to sneer at Claude, but his face registered the closest thing to a sneer without producing one.

"Yes, as a matter of fact," said Nick stonily. "I'm going to hitch him to the gig."

"Oh? You two planning an excursion?"

Before Eulalie could confirm Lieutenant Fuller's assumption, Nick said, "Yes, and you aren't invited."

Giving Nick a frown, Eulalie said to Lieutenant Fuller, "Mr. Taggart and I are going to see some lakes that I understand are nearby. Mrs. Johnson packed us a picnic."

"And there's only enough for two," Nick added.

Eulalie got the impression that the lieutenant would have liked to tease Nick some more, but he didn't. Instead, he turned to Eulalie. "I heard about what happened last night, ma'am, and I wanted to offer my condolences and to ask if there's anything I can do for you."

"She don't need you," grumbled Nick. "I'm taking care of her."

"It never hurts to have more than one champion," the lieutenant pointed out.

Eulalie thought he was nice to offer, even though he'd probably expect payment of one sort or another if she accepted. Again, almost against her will, she appreciated Nick Taggart's basic honesty. Nick didn't offer gallantry. He accepted a job. Since, however, she had Patsy to consider, she equivocated. "Thank you so much, Lieutenant Fuller. I don't believe I need any other help at the moment. My sister will be coming to live with me soon, though, and it would be nice if a couple of brave, strong men like you two would keep an eye out for trouble." She lowered her lashes and fluttered them once, knowing the lieutenants weren't as cynical as Nick Taggart about such things. "I would certainly appreciate it."

"We'd be happy to do that, ma'am," said Nash, still red.

"Absolutely," confirmed Fuller. "What's your sister's name, Miss Gibb?"

"Patsy. Patsy Gibb. She'll be joining me soon."

"But right now," Nick said loudly, "we have to be getting on."

"I thought you had to hitch up the horse first," Fuller said sweetly. "Why don't you do that, Nick? We'll keep Miss Gibb amused in the meantime."

Nick muttered, "Aw, hell." But he led Claude out of the pasture and over to the barn where, Eulalie presumed, the gig was kept.

It didn't take Nick long to hitch Claude to the two-wheeled gig, and Eulalie was glad when he drove it out to the little group still standing beside the fence. She liked the two lieutenants, but she'd rather be with Nick. She considered this a rather odd circumstance, but didn't dwell on it.

Fuller helped her into the gig, Nick glowering at him the whole time. She smiled sweetly at the lieutenant. "Thank you so much."

The lieutenant bowed grandly. "Any time, Miss Gibb."

She waved her hanky at the two men as Nick clicked to Claude, and the gig took off in an easterly direction.

Nick said, "Asses."

"They're nice men," Eulalie countered.

"Huh."

Deciding to shelve that particular issue, Eulalie said, "How far are these lakes?"

"About five miles."

"Ah. It shouldn't take too long to get there, then."

"Naw. About forty-five minutes."

The ride was bumpy, and Eulalie held on to her hat with one hand and gripped the seat with the other, for fear one or the other would become dislodged and land on a cactus. She eyed the countryside with interest. For almost a month now, she'd been looking at what most people in town called nothing. As Nick guided the gig along the barely discernible path, she revised her own opinion slightly. True, it was rugged country. And there was precious little green anywhere. But the geological aspect of the desert was interesting, as it was broken here and there by deep crevices, some of which ran along for several yards, and looked as if the ground had cracked.

"What causes those enormous cracks in the earth, Nick?"

"Water."

"Water?" Eulalie turned to see if he was joshing her. Didn't look like it.

"Yeah. Come summer, we'll have thunderstorms and flash floods. You don't want to be caught in an arroyo during a rainstorm. Folks drown that way."

"That's difficult to imagine," murmured Eulalie. "Not that I doubt you."

"You'll find out," Nick said. It sounded more like a threat than a promise.

As they increased their distance from town, Eulalie noticed other signs of geological activity. "My goodness, what's that long, flat thing?"

"Mescalero Ridge. It's a little . . . ridge. A rock ridge."

"It's not visible from town," Eulalie observed.

"That's because we're in a valley."

Again, she turned to look at him. Again, he didn't appear to be joking. "Seriously?"

His mouth kicked up into a one-sided grin. "You'd never know from looking, would you?"

"No," she agreed. "You wouldn't."

"Come summer, you'll wonder why they didn't start

building on higher ground. We'll probably have at least one flood. Maybe more."

"Good heavens. If Rio Peñasco is so prone to flooding, why *didn't* they build on higher ground?"

Nick shrugged. "Maybe they founded the town in the wintertime. Or maybe they just couldn't tell."

As nonsensical as it sounded, Eulalie thought he'd probably hit on the reason. If one merely inspected the countryside with one's eyes, it all looked as flat as a pancake. It wasn't until you got out in it that one began to notice slight rises and dips. "What a strange country. I've never seen anything so . . ." She tried to think of a word that couldn't be taken as disparaging. "So harsh." She didn't think Nick could take exception to that.

"Reckon not, if you're from New York or Chicago."

Curious, Eulalie asked, "Where are you from, Nick?"

"Galveston."

"That's in Texas, isn't it?"

He nodded. "On the gulf."

"Is it like this there?"

"Naw. It's green and humid there. It's on the Gulf of Mexico, so it gets some huge blows, too. Winds so hard, they knock down houses and ruin ships. After one storm, two boats ended up in our yard, and we didn't live right on the water."

"Good heavens. I've heard about terrible storms like that."

"They're no damned fun. That's one of the reasons Junius moved out here."

"Is that why you're here, too?"

His mouth twisted into a grimace. "One of 'em."

Hmm. Interesting reaction. "Do you still have family there?"

"No." He hesitated for a second, then amended his curt answer. "My pa's dead. My stepmother and four stepsisters still live in Galveston."

"I see. Do you miss them?"

He looked at her with such incredulity that Eulalie guessed the answer before he said, "No!" in a voice loud enough to make Claude twitch his ears and Eulalie jump slightly on the seat.

"There's no need to shout," she muttered.

"You don't know my stepmother and stepsisters," he said grimly. "If you did, you'd shout, too."

"Hmm. I get the feeling I understand where your distrust of women originated."

"I don't distrust all women. I just don't . . . trust 'em."

"There's a difference?"

"Yeah. I like women, as long as I'm not involved with them." He slanted her a glance. "On a permanent basis, I mean."

"Perhaps you haven't been involved with the right women." Eulalie didn't know why she felt an urge to defend her sex. She knew as well as anyone that most women, because of the nature of the injustice by which the world ran, had no option but to manipulate men in order to get what they needed or wanted out of life. Her own experience had been vastly different from that of the bulk of her sisters. Her family honored all its members as valuable participants in the acting game. They had to.

And still the women in her family couldn't vote. Unfairness, which Eulalie had been very much aware of in recent months, attacked her and made her bridle.

"I doubt that's the answer," he grumbled.

That was enough for Eulalie. "And exactly why do you think that is, Mr. Nicholas Taggart?" she demanded. "You claim that the women in your family—*all* women, according to you—are sly, manipulative creatures who, through evil means, make men do what they want them to do. Well, what do you *expect* from an entire population that's rendered helpless, both socially and politically? How else can women achieve justice in this ridiculous world except through *men*. We can't vote. We can't hold office. We can't be police officers. We can't own property in some states and territories. We can't even keep our children if the men in our families turn out to be brutal drunkards and we try to escape! If the women in your family discovered that the only way they could survive in the world was to get you to do things for them, can you blame them?"

Her vehemence must have startled Nick, because he looked at her as if he'd never seen her before. Naturally, this reaction on his part fueled Eulalie's ire.

"Don't look at me that way! It's the truth! Do you know that if a man stalks a woman, like prey, and then brutally attacks her, he'll get a slap on the wrist from the authorities? Did you know that if a woman complains to the authorities because a man is threatening her, she'll be treated as if *she* were the crazy party or, worse, as if she *encouraged* the monster? Do you realize that—" She broke off suddenly, worried that she'd said too much.

His brow creased as he frowned. "Is that what happened to you, Eulalie? Did your husband hit you?"

Honestly startled that anyone, even someone who, like Nick, had never met her late husband, Eulalie said, "Edward? Good heavens, no! Why, Edward was the gentlest creature alive." In fact, although she didn't say so, if he'd been alive when Patsy had her trouble, he probably wouldn't have been a whole lot of help. Even thinking such a thing seemed disloyal, so she ruthlessly shoved the notion aside.

"But you sound as if you're speaking from experience. This couldn't have anything to do with the accident you told me about, could it?"

"I . . . prefer not to discuss it." Silently, Eulalie cursed her too-ready tongue.

"Hmm."

Neither of them said any more until Nick had driven the gig into an area of the countryside Eulalie wouldn't have known existed if he'd not taken her there. Short, sheer cliffs rose here and there, sheltering green and serene pools of water. Wildflowers bloomed on their banks, and to Eulalie, who was accustomed to the lakes and rivers of her Eastern roots, the beauty of the scene seemed not so much tranquil, but rather a rest from the savagery that was so much a part of the rest of this out-of-the-way area of the continent.

"Say," said Nick, breaking the silence that would have seemed eerie to Eulalie if she'd been alone. "Look there." He pointed, and Eulalie saw several big birds circling lazily in the sky over a lake. "Sure sign of spring."

"Really? What kinds of birds are they?"

"Buzzards."

Eulalie turned to stare at him. "You're joking, aren't you?"

His grin was wicked. "Nope. You can always tell when the weather's changed when the buzzards come back."

"Good heavens." Eulalie's voice was weak.

"Rough country."

"I should say so." She'd have to write Patsy about this.

It would be the last letter she'd be able to write because Patsy would be here before another communication from Eulalie could reach her. The notion made her heart leap with happiness. She'd have her family back again! Or at least part of it. And Eulalie was sure, now that she'd made arrange-

151

ments with Nick Taggart, that Patsy would be safe. For that alone, Eulalie would like to kiss Nick.

A sensation low in her belly surprised her. Good heavens, she hadn't felt that . . . that sense of excitement since Edward died. Did that mean she was a hussy?

Nonsense, Eulalie Gibb. It means you're human.

That was another thing women missed out on: access to their own sexuality. Eulalie, who possessed a passionate nature, although she tried to hide it so as not to give her audience the idea that she was easy, decided this was one of the most unfair of life's many inequities.

She was, however, anticipating her union with Nick Taggart with a good deal of pleasure.

Chapter Nine

Dearest Patsy,

By the time you receive this letter, I should be residing in a brand-new home, with a bedroom especially designed for you. Actually, both bedrooms will be a trifle crude compared to what you are used to, dear, but I know we can be happy here.

The two Mister Taggarts have agreed to build the house for us, and Mr. Taggart (the younger) has agreed to watch over and protect the two of us after you arrive in Rio Peñasco. The price is one I am happy to pay.

Eulalie thought about that last sentence and decided to leave it in.

I can hardly wait to see you again, Patsy. Please take care of yourself, do exactly as the doctor orders, and prepare yourself. Rio Peñasco is like nothing you have ever experienced! I actually enjoy it here, and I pray you will, too. At the very least, you will have peace and security.

All my love,
Eulalie

Two weeks and a couple of days after Nick took Eulalie to the Bottomless Lakes for a picnic luncheon, Eulalie's cheek had healed and Nick and Junius finished building a small

153

adobe house—with two bedrooms—for the Gibb sisters. Not only did everyone in Rio Peñasco understand that this was a declaration of Eulalie's status as Nick Taggart's special lady friend, but Dooley Chivers opened a betting book at the Opera House on whether or not Eulalie would ever trap Nick into marrying her.

"Wouldn't surprise me none," said Lloyd Grady on a cool Saturday night in May with the wind howling like a banshee outside the saloon. "She's small, but she's mighty determined." He rubbed his hand on his coat in memory of the time Eulalie had walloped his knuckles with her Colt Ladysmith.

"I dunno," said Joshua Pratt, caressing his bandaged thigh. "I can't see Nicky marrying any female that'd shoot a man for admiring her."

"Hell," said Lloyd, "you should oughta learned from what she done to me not to mess with her. She's a scary female."

"She only wants respect, gentlemen," said Lieutenant Gabriel Fuller. "She doesn't like to be manhandled." He didn't exhibit any particular happiness about the arrangement between Nick and Eulalie, though.

"Respect," muttered Lloyd, as if he wasn't sure what the word meant.

"Huh," said Joshua.

Nick strolled through the batwing doors of the Opera House at that moment and conversation stopped abruptly. He paused at the doorway to let his eyes adjust to the darkness indoors, then walked to the bar where Cletus Bagwell, who'd been bartending for Dooley Chivers ever since the Opera House opened, reigned.

"Sarsaparilla, Cletus," said Nick.

"Beg pardon?" said Cletus, blinking at Nick as if he wanted to make sure to whom he was speaking.

"You heard me. Give me a sarsaparilla."

"Sure thing, Nick." Cletus filled Nick's order. When he shoved the glass at him, he asked, "You give up drinkin' or something?"

"Nope. Just want a sarsaparilla is all," said Nick, sipping his drink. He didn't think anyone needed to know that he aimed to collect his first payment from Miss Eulalie Gibb after she got off work that evening. He guessed she'd have to have some supper first. But then . . . He closed his eyes. He'd been dreaming about this for more than two weeks, and he was ready. More than ready. About to bust, in actual fact.

He leaned against the bar, watching the men who would soon be watching Eulalie, and he felt a touch—only a touch—of irritation. For some inexplicable reason, he didn't fancy all these men getting a look at so much of her. Odd. He never minded when Violet shared her favors—for a price—with other gents in town. Why should he have this feeling of annoyance when he thought about Eulalie displaying herself in front of them?

His reaction made no sense to him. He decided he didn't want to think about it.

"So, Nick, you won, didn't you?"

Lifting his head from his contemplation of the floor in front of him, Nick saw Lieutenant Gabriel Fuller standing before him, and his heart lightened. "How do, Lieutenant." He tried to look innocent. "Won what?"

Fuller heaved a deep sigh. "Don't be coy, my man. I understand the fair Eulalie is now under your protection." He knocked on the bar and said, "Rye," to Cletus, who promptly filled the order.

That sounded mighty fine to Nick. He said, "Yeah. I reckon you might say so."

"Too bad."

155

Fuller's sidekick, Lieutenant Nash, also knocked on the bar, to no avail.

"For you, maybe," said Nick.

Nash said, "Cletus?"

"Indeed," said Fuller with another sigh. He took a slug of his whiskey.

Nash said, "Hey, Cletus!"

"She's got a sister," Nick told Fuller. "She's going to be arriving here in a couple of days. Maybe she'll take to you more than Eulalie did." He snickered.

Nash said, "Dammit, Cletus!"

"Huh." Fuller downed the rest of his drink, knocked on the bar once more, and Cletus appeared, as if by magic. "Hit me again, Cletus."

Cletus obliged and would have vanished, but Nash grabbed his sleeve. "Hey, Cletus, gimme a rye, too, willya?"

Blinking at the smaller man, Cletus said, "Oh. Sure, Lieutenant. You want something?"

Nash, whose face was red and whose ears steamed, said, "Yes. A drink."

Cletus obliged.

With a sigh, Nash turned, leaned against the bar, and watched Nick and Fuller.

"So what's her sister's name?" asked Fuller, sounding bored.

"Patsy. She's coming from Chicago, and Eulalie says she's an actress, too."

"Oh?" Fuller appeared slightly more interested.

Nick nodded and sipped his sarsaparilla. "Yup. Whole family's in the business."

"Really." Sipping thoughtfully, Fuller eyed Nick through slitted eyes. "But you have no interest in this sister of hers, right?"

Nick eyed him back, wondering what the man was up to. "Right." But if this upstart army bastard thought he could waltz in and sweep her off her feet, he had another think coming. Nick had made a deal with Eulalie, and he intended to honor it. He decided not to say so at the moment. For all Nick knew, Fuller's intentions were absolutely honorable.

In a pig's eye. However, that was neither here nor there. Griswold Puckett, the piano player, played a loud chord on the tinkly piano upon which Violet sat, looking pretty as a picture—and arousing no more than a brotherly sense of affection in Nick's bosom. Strange how that had happened so fast.

The room quieted for approximately ten seconds, and then a cacophony of applause broke loose. Everyone who'd been in Rio Peñasco for more than a day knew what that piano chord meant: Miss Eulalie Gibb, Rio Peñasco's very own Cactus Flower, was about to take the stage. As was usual, Dooley Chivers strolled out from behind the red velvet curtain and held up his arms for silence, which was achieved, more or less.

"All right, gents. Time to shut your yappers, 'cause the biggest sensation to come our way in a month of Sundays is about to perform for our delectation and enjoyment!"

Amid the whoops that followed this speech, Nash muttered, "Talks big, don't he?"

Nick looked down upon the lieutenant's curly head and said, "It means you're going to like it."

"I figured that out on my own," grumbled Nash.

Dooley said, "And now, gentlemen, here she is. Miss Eulalie Gibb!"

The curtain opened to the sounds of clapping, cheers, and stomping, and the kerosene lamps set on the stage illuminated Eulalie in all her glory. Tonight she wore her bright red outfit with the dyed-to-match ostrich feathers sticking out the back of it and making her look like a red peacock. She'd stuck another couple of red ostrich feathers in her hair, and she looked kind of like a lobster to Nick, who wanted to eat her up. It annoyed the hell out of him that so many other men did, too, although he couldn't think of anything he could do about it. Eulalie had flatly refused his offer to support her when he'd made it in a moment of weakness.

"Good heavens, Mr. Taggart!" She always called him *Mr. Taggart* when she was mad at him. "I'm not going to give up my means of livelihood!"

"But I'd be supporting you," said Nick, already regretting his rash impulse.

"Fiddlesticks. You've made your opinion of permanent relationships quite clear, and I'll not give up my independence for less. Than a permanent relationship, I mean."

"In other words, marriage," Nick growled.

Eulalie had only shrugged.

At the time Nick had told himself he was glad she'd saved him from suffering the consequences of his folly. Tonight, eyeing her audience as they lusted and slavered over her, he wasn't so sure.

But it was all right, he reminded himself. These lusty fellows might pant after her, but Nick Taggart was the one who had her.

Dammit, he wished he'd had her already; he'd feel more secure about this protection-for-favors thing. He supposed that, until they consummated the bargain, she still might be tempted to allow somebody else to protect her and her sister. He slanted a glance at Gabriel Fuller.

But no. Eulalie was too smart to fall for a blue uniform and a cavalry mustache.

The piano played the opening notes of *Champagne Charley*, and Eulalie started to sing and dance, and Nick forgot to think. Instead he, like every other male in the room, riveted his attention upon Miss Eulalie Gibb, who had the most magnificent voice and the lushest figure west of the Hudson River. east of it, too, probably, although Nick had never been back East, so he couldn't say for sure.

Eulalie could scarcely wait to get out of her costume. She was perishing from being so tightly bound. "It's those huge steaks," she muttered, struggling with her corset hooks behind the screen in her dressing room. "It's a good thing Patsy's coming the day after tomorrow. She'll cook for us, and I'll lose some weight."

"Don't lose too much," requested Nick, who liked his ladies with a little meat on their bones.

"I doubt that will be a problem," said Eulalie, who'd always had a tendency to gain weight when she didn't watch herself like a hawk. Of course, in Rio Peñasco, until the advent of her sister, she didn't have much of a choice. Mrs. Johnson, who fixed her breakfast and dinner—Eulalie had learned to call her three daily meals breakfast, dinner and supper in deference to prevailing custom—fussed at her if she didn't finish every morsel on her plate. And, since dinner came at midday, Eulalie ended up eating two dinners: Mrs. Johnson's and Vernon's. Small wonder she was getting fat. She'd end up like her aunt Florence if she wasn't careful.

"I'll help you work some of it off," Nick offered.

Eulalie peeked out from behind the screen to see him grinning at her. Hmm.

She'd been as nervous as a cat in a room full of coyotes—another bow to her new home—all day long, in anticipation of the night to come. She'd been to the local mercantile with Mrs. Johnson, who approved of the choices Eulalie had made regarding fabrics for kitchen, bedroom and parlor curtains.

And she'd purchased everything she could think of—and that she could come by in this out-of-the-way place—that two ladies living alone might need for their home, including sheets and pillowcases, cooking pots and dinnerware. Nick and Junius had made them a couple of sturdy bed frames in the blacksmith shop, and Mrs. Johnson and her daughters had stuffed some mattresses and pillows for her.

Eulalie, who appreciated the help of her friends more than she could say, had also used the Sears and Roebuck catalogue at the Loveladys' mercantile emporium to order regular pillows and mattresses. Not that the corn-shuck mattresses were uncomfortable, but poor Patsy would probably be driven crazy by the crackling noises they made. Ever since the incident, she'd been very jumpy.

Mrs. Sullivan, another local matron whose children went to school with Mrs. Johnson's, had agreed to sew up the curtains for Eulalie at a price that was much lower than Eulalie had expected. She still couldn't account for the way everyone in town seemed to accept her as just another woman making her way in the world.

"For heaven's sake, Louise, I sing in a *saloon*," she said as she and Mrs. Johnson left Mrs. Sullivan's little house, which sat on the edge of town where it garnered more than its fair share of wind-whipped dust and looked, as a result, even more derelict than most of the houses in Rio Peñasco.

"Pooh," said Mrs. Johnson. "Everybody out here knows what it's like for a woman trying to earn her own living. Some of us take in boarders. Some of us sew up curtains for other folks."

"Doesn't Mrs. Sullivan have a husband?"

"Ptaw," said Mrs. Johnson in disgust. "Her Hubert is about as useless as tits on a boar hog, if you don't mind the indelicacy."

"Not at all," murmured Eulalie, blinking in astonishment.

"Y'get to know people when you need 'em, like we do out here," Mrs. Johnson continued. "And Hubert Sullivan is stupid. He makes enough money, I reckon, but he also spends a lot on his drinkin'. Just because a woman's married, doesn't mean the man she's married to is worth a hill of beans. It's all in a person's character. For instance, I know you're a fine woman, Eulalie. So's Miss Violet at the saloon, but don't go tellin' the preacher I said so."

"Oh," said Eulalie, flabbergasted, although she, too, believed Violet was a fine woman, in spite of her profession. "No. I won't."

"Not that the preacher isn't as much a man as any other man in town, no matter how much he pretends he's holier than anybody else."

Egad. Eulalie wasn't accustomed to such plain speaking from members of her gender. Most of the women she knew had completely succumbed to the myth that females were helpless. Then again, most women she knew back East could *afford* to pretend they were helpless. These rugged Westerners were another matter entirely.

"At lest my Zeke, God rest his soul, was a hard worker," said Mrs. Johnson, her tone taking on a musing quality. "Not that it mattered. He died anyway, leaving his wife and children to fend for themselves. Which pretty much tells you exactly how much good a man is in your life, if you ask me."

"I suppose so."

"Nicky Taggart, now, he's another hard worker. And I have a feeling he's smarter than my Zeke, God rest his soul."

"Oh?" Eulalie's attention fixed on her companion.

"Yup. He's been through a lot, and I 'spect that if he ever gets himself attached to a female permanently, he'll be sure she's taken care of if anything ever happens to him."

"Really?" Eulalie didn't want to seem too interested, but lately whenever anyone mentioned Nick's name, she was all ears.

"Yep. He's a good man, Nick. Had a rough time with his stepma, and she kinda colored his attitude toward women, but he's still a good man. Can't seem to help himself." She chuckled.

Fascinating. Eulalie would have liked to press Mrs. Johnson further, but didn't want to be perceived as too interested in Nick Taggart. Not that the whole town didn't know what was going on between them—even if it hadn't technically started yet—but even out here on the frontier, appearances seemed to matter. Eulalie didn't think she'd ever understand the human race.

But Patsy would be here the day after tomorrow, and she could hardly wait to see her. When Eulalie had left Chicago, Patsy had been in bad shape and Eulalie had not wanted to leave her. But Patsy had begged her to find a safe place for them to live. So she'd done it, worrying the entire time. Patsy's recent letters made the decision seem like a sound one and eased Eulalie's mind a good deal. It was a shame about the scarring, though. Gilbert Blankenship deserved to die a slow, painful death for what he'd done to Patsy, and Eulalie wished she could watch it being administered.

Nick and Junius had provided her new home with an old stove that Nick had salvaged from an abandoned cabin, as well as a kitchen table and some chairs he'd built using wood left over from framing the house. Eulalie couldn't recall ever knowing two such clever and handy men as Nick and Junius Taggart. And she couldn't chalk up their expertise merely to the fact that they lived in the wild and woolly West, either. She had a feeling that her uncle Harry, for example, could never have built a kitchen table and chairs, even if he were

Cactus Flower

forced to exist in the wild. Not that Harry wasn't smart as the proverbial whip, but his expertise lay in cerebration rather than manual labor. And talk. Harry could out-talk a parrot once he got started. It amused Eulalie to mentally picture Harry and Junius telling tales to each other. They'd keep each other amused for a century or more.

As she watched Nick and Junius carry in a table, Eulalie's eyes feasted on Nick's bulging muscles, and indelicate visions supplanted the images of Harry and Junius chatting. Even though she'd been busy all day long, furnishing her new home, Eulalie had been unable to thrust the vision of Nick Taggart in her bed out of her mind. In fact, the very word *thrust* made her cheeks heat up. Good heavens. She must really be a loose woman to be looking so forward to her carnal union with Nick.

Or perhaps she was only human. It was difficult to say, what with established attitudes about women and all. Eulalie had read a good deal, however, and it was her studied opinion that established attitudes were stupid. Women were human beings. They not only deserved the same rights men enjoyed, they deserved the same freedom to enjoy their sexuality, curse it.

She hoped she wasn't just making excuses for what she was about to do with Nick.

But if she was, she decided defiantly, so what? Necessity was the mother of invention, after all, and Eulalie definitely needed Nick Taggart. So did Patsy. When Eulalie ran a list of the men she'd met in Rio Peñasco through her mind, she knew she'd selected the very most qualified candidate as protector of her body. And Patsy's. And, curse it, since Eulalie was the one earning the money to support the both of them, she might as well enjoy what she had to pay for their protection!

163

She hadn't quite convinced herself she was right by the time she kicked her last kick and left the stage for the final time that night. That, however, didn't matter. Whether she was a fallen woman or not, tonight would be payment time, and she was looking forward to it.

"Need any help?" Nick asked, his tone provocative.

"No, thank you." Eulalie might be anticipating what the night would bring her with uneasy pleasure, but she was also hungry. She vowed she wouldn't eat too much at the chophouse.

"Sure?"

"Yes, thank you." She'd probably be so nervous, she wouldn't be able to eat anything at all.

She wasn't. In fact, she tucked away fully half of Vernon's evening steak, beans and biscuits. Nick finished up what she couldn't eat.

Nick pushed away from the table and held out an arm for Eulalie. The twinkle in his eye should have been outlawed, Eulalie decided when she glanced up at him. To make up for his clearly pleasurable anticipation, she pasted on a stern expression and whispered, "Stop looking at me like that."

"How come?"

"Because you're embarrassing me."

"Huh. You parade yourself danged near naked in front of every male in Rio Peñasco every damned night, and *I'm* embarrassing you? I don't buy it."

"I don't care what you believe," Eulalie snapped. "It's the truth."

"Huh."

They hadn't left the chophouse by the time the door swung open and Bernie Benson made one of his customary, swaggering entrances. Nick eyed him with disfavor. "Hell, Bernie, you should of took to the stage instead of the press."

Bernie only grinned, his piggy eyes gleaming. "Don't be a spoilsport, Nick. I have some exciting news for Rio Peñasco's own precious cactus flower." He swept her an elegant bow, almost mopping the floor with his hat.

Every time anybody compared her to a cactus flower, Eulalie thought of sharp, painful spines. Nevertheless, she knew better than to complain. It never did to upset a newspaperman. They wielded too much power. Therefore, she smiled one of her patented smiles at Bernie. "How do you do, Mr. Benson?"

"I'm fine, fine," he said, plopping his hat back on his head. "I want you to see what I got in the mail today, all the way from Chicago, Illinois. Your fame is spreading like wildfire, Miss Gibb."

Eulalie stifled an irritated retort. She didn't *want* her fame to spread, curse it, especially not to Chicago or New York City. However, unless she wanted to explain her entire situation to the world, she didn't dare let on. She said, "Is that so?" in a voice she hoped didn't reveal her inner turmoil.

"Yes indeedy," said Bernie happily. "Here's a copy of the newspaper my friend H. L. May sent me from Chicago. My article about Rio Peñasco's Cactus Flower has hit the big time, my dear."

"She's not your dear," mumbled Nick unpleasantly.

Bernie only grinned some more. "H.L. sent an extra copy for you, Miss Gibb. He knew you'd want to see it."

Eulalie took the paper between her gloved fingers. She wanted to rip it to shreds and jump up and down on the remains. "Thank you so much, Mr. Benson."

"Now if you'll excuse us, Bernie, I'm going to see Miss Gibb to her new home."

"Ah, yes," Bernie said. "That goes in the next article."

"What does?" Nick demanded, frowning.

Eulalie's heart leaped unpleasantly.

"Why, that the citizens of Rio Peñasco have built their favorite cactus flower a new home, of course." He spread his chubby hands in the air, as if showing Nick and Eulalie the newspaper article he envisioned. "I can see it now. 'Rough-and-ready community opens its heart to its beloved cactus flower. Using the materials available to them, uncle and nephew build a house for their songbird.' "

Eulalie felt her brow wrinkle. "I . . . um . . . think you're mixing your metaphors, Mr. Benson."

Bernie tapped his hat. "Well, that's just the beginnings of an idea. I'll also write about how the women in town have taken to you, Miss Gibb." His eyes all but danced in their sockets. "And aren't you singing in church now, too?"

"Well . . . yes, but no more than anyone else sings in church. We all sing. Hymns, you know."

"Ah, but nobody else has a voice like yours," said Bernie in a faraway voice, as if he were creating yet another article in his head.

Eulalie wished somebody else would move to town. Somebody already famous. Somebody to make Bernie's attention veer away from her.

"And I hear your sister is coming to town, too, Miss Gibb. Is she an actress, too?"

"She used to be," Eulalie said cautiously.

"Give it a rest, Bernie. Miss Gibb is tired. She deserves to get a good night's sleep after working so hard."

To Eulalie's great relief, Bernie acquiesced, stepping aside so Nick could guide Eulalie out of the chophouse. "That guy drives me nuts," he muttered.

"I wish he didn't take his duties so seriously," Eulalie said, thinking of Patsy.

166

"Oh?" Eulalie felt Nick's gaze on her. "Don't you like being worshiped by Bernie Benson?" His tone mocked her.

Eulalie didn't blame him a whole lot. If she'd met up with Bernie Benson when she lived in New York, she'd have adored all the free publicity. At the moment, publicity was the last thing she wanted. "No," she said. "I don't."

She felt Nick shrug. "It's good for the town, I reckon. Folks are coming to see you from all over the place."

Oh, dear. Eulalie's heart fell. "Are they really?"

"Yup. Every day, more fellows show up. Bernie's spread the word far and wide about what he calls our cactus flower. I still think prickly pear is a better name for you." She heard the grin in his voice.

"You would."

They walked the rest of the way to Eulalie's new house in silence. The moon was waning, but still fullish, and Eulalie was amazed by how clearly one could see under its benevolent light. The night she'd been attacked by those two drunken louts, she couldn't see her hand in front of her face. This evening, she could clearly see to pick her way across the rocky ground to her home. Nick had even built a fence around the place, enclosing a whole bunch of dirt. But Eulalie didn't despair. Mrs. Johnson said that grass could grow here if a body took care to plant it deep enough that the first heavy rainfall didn't wash away all the seeds. Eulalie had dutifully sent away for a packet of grass seeds from Sears and Roebuck.

"Junius and I painted the place today," Nick said, pushing the gate open for her. "We used whitewash, so it will dry fast. We'll get some real paint as soon as we can."

"I see. It looks very nice. I can't thank you enough, Nick."

"Yes you can," he said, and Eulalie had no doubt what he meant.

She noticed that he and Junius had set out flat rocks from

the gate to the front door. The notion of planting a few rosebushes along the walkway appealed to her. "That looks nice,
Nick. You really outdid yourself."

"You haven't seen anything yet," he promised her.

Eulalie was getting just a little tired of his innuendoes, although she guessed she couldn't blame him a whole lot.
She'd been itching to get him alone for days now. She didn't
recall feeling this sense of anticipation when she'd married
Edward. Then again, when she'd married Edward, she'd
been seventeen years old and didn't have the least notion
what marriage entailed. Now she was getting the benefits
without the ceremony.

Since she didn't feel like thinking about that anymore, she
didn't.

Nick pushed the front door of her new house open. "Your
new home, Miss Eulalie Gibb. Hope you like it. Junius and I
did the best we could."

"I'm sure I'll love it, Nick. Thank you so—"

She got no further. Suddenly a lamp flared to life in the
little front parlor, and Eulalie nearly jumped out of her skin
when just about everyone she knew in town shouted, "Surprise!"

Before she was engulfed in happy hugs, she heard Nick
mutter, "Shit."

Nevertheless, it was a nice little party. Since it was a Saturday night, even the Johnson children were allowed to attend. Joining them were the Loveladys, Mr. and Mrs.
Sullivan and their brood, Mr. Huffington the minister (who
blessed the house), Mr. Chalmers the schoolmaster, the
sheriff, Dooley Chivers and both lieutenants. Mrs. Johnson
had set out a veritable feast on the table in the kitchen, which
she'd first spread with a tablecloth she'd made herself, with
the help of Sarah and Penelope.

"I helped sew the hem," said Penelope.

"I pinned it up," declared little Sarah.

"Thank you so much. You're both so nice to me." Eulalie gave them each a hug. As she did so, she glanced up to see where Nick was in the overall scheme of things. He and Junius were being congratulated heartily by Dooley Chivers and the two lieutenants. Junius looked happy as a lark. Nick looked rather like a thundercloud ready to burst and rain all over the party.

Thinking she'd worry about her weight after Patsy arrived, Eulalie indulged in a piece of cake and took one each over to Nick and Junius. "This was so nice of everyone," she gushed at Junius.

Nick, holding a cup of something that didn't contain alcohol, although Eulalie wasn't sure what exactly it was, looked at her as if she'd planned this entire party out of spite to thwart him. She didn't appreciate it, and showed him so by lifting her chin and pasting on her most defiant expression. He rolled his eyes.

"We're happy you come to stay amongst us," said Junius, oblivious to the silent exchange between his nephew and Eulalie. "Can't remember when we got a nicer surprise here in Rio Peñasco."

"That's what I just told her," boomed Bernie Benson. "To our own cactus flower!" And he lifted a cup filled with the same liquid in toast.

"To Miss Gibb!" the attendees said in unison, lifting their cups, too.

Was it lemonade? Eyeing it dubiously, Eulalie didn't think so. Where would anyone come by a lemon out here?

Somebody said, "Speech!" and the refrain was taken up by the rest of the group. Eulalie, perceiving no way out, stepped in to do her duty, to a rousing round of applause.

"I can't tell you how much I appreciate the warm welcome I've received in Rio Peñasco. All of you have been so kind to a stranger. I don't know how to thank you."

She heard Nick mutter, "Christ," and raised her voice.

"My sister Patsy will arrive on the stagecoach the day after tomorrow, and I know she will love you all as I do. Thank you *so* much!" She lifted her own cup then, fearless, took a sip of its contents. Whatever it was, it wasn't half bad.

It was probably heading toward three a.m. on Sunday morning when the last of the celebrants left the little now-white adobe house Nick and Junius Taggart had built for Eulalie and Patsy Gibb. Eulalie was pretty sure she was going to die from exhaustion. She didn't have a clue how Nick was feeling, but if he thought she was going to begin fulfilling her part in their bargain tonight, he was mistaken.

She kissed Junius on the cheek and hugged Louise Johnson as the two herded Mrs. Johnson's sleepy children out the door. "Thank you so much, Junius and Louise. This is the happiest day I've had in a long time." She meant it, even though she was so sleepy, she could hardly see straight.

Mrs. Johnson patted her cheek. "You get a good sleep, now, you hear? Church don't start until eleven this morning, and if you miss it, nobody will think a thing of it."

Church. Oh, sweet heaven, that's right. Eulalie had been religious—so to speak—about attending church services since her arrival in Rio Peñasco. No sense riling the natives, and all that. Besides, Eulalie took comfort from the rituals and hymns of the church, even the church in Rio Peñasco. At the moment, however, she wanted to attend a church service about as much as she wanted to walk barefoot from Rio Peñasco to New York City. She said, "Thank you, Louise. I shall try to attend."

As soon as she shut the door behind Louise and Junius,

Eulalie turned, expecting to find Nick Taggart behind her, ready to ravish her. She had a few choice words to say to him.

He wasn't there. As Eulalie went through the small house—parlor, kitchen, service porch, hall, first bedroom— she didn't find him anywhere. Had he given up and gone back to his own home behind the smithy? It seemed unlikely, Nick being a full-blooded and lusty male and all that.

When she finally pushed the door of her own bedroom open, she found him, sprawled on the bed, fast asleep.

With a sigh of relief, Eulalie decided that took care of that quite nicely, and she grabbed her nightgown and hied herself to Patsy's bedroom, where she changed, fell into bed, and slept the sleep of the innocent. Which she was, at least for the time being.

Chapter Ten

Nick awoke because some damned fool had shined a light in his eyes. When he opened his eyes, he discovered the fool was God and that Nick himself was spread-eagled on Eulalie Gibb's bed. Alone.

"Damn it!"

He stormed out of the bedroom, furious that his plans for the night before hadn't been achieved. Although he wasn't sure, he had a sneaking suspicion that Eulalie had known all about the party her friends had planned for her. Oh, very well. They were his friends, too, although they sure hadn't proved it by thwarting his purpose.

She was gone.

Nick looked high and low, feeling kind of frantic, although he figured he was being irrational. Finally, when he slowed down long enough to really *look* for signs of Eulalie's presence or absence, and possible reasons for either, he discovered a note she had set on the table in the kitchen. She'd set a little bowl of wildflowers on its edge to hold it down. Good thing she'd thought to do that, Nick thought ruefully, since it was the note's fluttering in the breeze he made as he barreled through the house that had caught his eye. He reached out to snatch up the note, realized that if he did that, the bowl of flowers would fall over and he'd feel like an ass, so he carefully moved the flowers and picked up the note.

Dear Nick, it read. *I've gone to church with Louise Johnson and the children. Please make yourself at home. Eulalie.*

"Make myself at home?" he asked incredulously to the universe at large, since no one else was there. "How the devil am I supposed to do that? I'm not even supposed to be here during the day."

Hell. Another day of frustration and misery. Nick stomped out of the house—via the back door and making sure nobody saw him—and scurried to the house he shared with Junius.

Junius, naturally, was in a jolly mood. Junius was always in a jolly mood, and Nick didn't understand it. Nor did he appreciate his uncle's good humor. Especially today, when Nick was feeling rather like a bear who's been deprived of sustenance for too damned long.

"Howdy, Nicky!" boomed Junius. "Beautiful day, isn't it?"

Nick wondered if the man was *trying* to irritate him. "What's so damned beautiful about it?"

"Why, it's Sunday, Nicky! A day of rest. We don't have to do no smithing today, and the house is built, and Miss Eulalie's sister will be coming to town tomorrow, and we'll have another lovely young lady to spruce up the place."

"Cripes," muttered Nick. He stomped to the stove and poured himself a mug of coffee.

"Here," said Junius. "Miss Eulalie gave me some of these buns Mrs. Johnson made up when I left last night." He eyed his nephew speculatively. "Say, where were you last night, Nicky? I didn't see you come home till right now, and you come through the front door."

Nick downed some coffee, glaring at his uncle over the brim of his mug. He didn't want to answer that question, mainly because he felt kind of like one of those wicked seducers out of the old-time Gothic novels his stepmother used to read when he considered his relationship with Eulalie. Or, rather, what he wanted his relationship with Eulalie to be.

"Nick? You didn't do anything you're ashamed to tell me about, did you?" Junius's normally sunny expression soured slightly.

Nick exploded. "Hell, no! I fell asleep on the damned bed, and she left me there to sleep."

"Ah. Well, that was right nice of her. You've been workin' mighty hard lately."

Nice of her, my hind leg, Nick thought bitterly. She cheated. He might have figured she would, since she was a woman, and all women were sneaks and cheats.

"You want to go to church with me?"

"Church?" Nick looked at Junius as if he suspected the man of having lost his mind overnight.

"Sure! Miss Eulalie will be there, and if we sit near her, we'll be able to hear her sing. She's sure got a pretty voice."

She had that, all right. And a pretty everything else. Nick had planned to explore it in depth the previous evening, but had been foiled, damn it.

In spite of himself, he offered a prayer of forgiveness for having blasphemed on the Sabbath. Then he cursed himself as a damned fool, and prayed again. He began to think of himself as hopeless.

"Come on, Nicky, change into a clean shirt and put on your Sunday suit, and let's go hear Huffington huff." Junius considered Reverend Huffington a little pompous, although he liked a good hellfire-and-damnation sermon as well as the next man.

Nick sat at the kitchen table, reached for one of Mrs. Johnson's cinnamon buns, and scowled at his uncle. "Huffington's an ass." Once more, he winced inside, although he stopped himself from asking for forgiveness this time.

"Yeah, that he is," Junius agreed amiably. He, too, reached for a bun.

Nick suspected it wasn't his first.

"But it's Sunday, Nicky. Gotta thank the good Lord for lettin' us live another day, I reckon."

This particular Sunday morning, Nick saw no reason to thank anyone for anything, but he didn't say so. What he said was, "Good bun." Had lots of cinnamon on it, and Nick liked cinnamon.

Junius nudged Nick's elbow. "Quit chawin' and get dressed, Nicky."

Nick heaved a huge sigh and stood, stuffing the last of the bun into his mouth. "Aw, hell, I reckon it can't hurt." And, as an added benefit, he'd get to see Eulalie and maybe walk her home or something. He'd be damned—*forgive me, Father*—if he'd let her get away again.

"Mebbe Miss Eulalie would like to come for dinner today after church, Nicky," Junius said. "Got me a brisket smokin' in the barrel out back, and Mrs. Johnson give me a mess of Swiss chard. I got some taters from the Loveladys' store, and I can't think of a better dinner than that, with a mess of pinto beans to go with it all."

Hmm. Maybe his uncle had a good idea there. "Brisket'll be ready at noon?"

"Noon or thereabouts. I 'spect the preacher'll get a late start this morning, seeing as how he got to bed late last night." Junius winked at his nephew. "And I don't think he was just sippin' cider out of that glass he was suckin' on all evening."

"Huffington was drinking booze?" Nick asked incredulously as he headed to his bedroom to change.

"Wouldn't surprise me none. The fellow likes a nip now and then."

"I'll be damned."

"You surely will be if you keep talkin' like that on a Sunday, Nicky Taggart."

Shit.

Eulalie was trying not to drown out the rest of the congregation as they sang *Washed in the Blood of the Lamb*, not one of her favorite hymns since the notion of being washed in anyone's blood disgusted her, when she saw Nick and Junius walk through the side entrance of the church. Junius looked like one of God's more hardworking angels, what with his cheerful demeanor and his muscles. Nick looked like he wanted to kill something. Eulalie suspected herself.

She kept singing. Even when Nick and Junius spotted her, standing with the Johnsons, hymnal in hand, and made a beeline to their little group, her soprano didn't wobble or squeak. She knew she should have taken a seat closer to the center of the church. She was too vulnerable here on the aisle.

Ah, well. She'd known ever since she and Nick struck their bargain that she'd have to face the music, so to speak, eventually. And, really, the notion excited her in a way that seemed out of place in church—not that God hadn't created the process to begin with when He created people, so to consider lust a sin was disingenuous at the very least.

That being the case, and because she knew her time had come, she smiled at both men and moved over to give them room. Naturally, Nick shoved himself into the pew—if a few rough-hewn logs could be termed a pew—ahead of his uncle. Because there weren't sufficient hymnals to go around, even though the congregation was extremely small, Eulalie offered to share hers with Nick. He grunted and took it from her, holding it so she could read the words and music. His hands looked odd holding the book, probably because they were so large and callused, more suited to handling a bellows and sledgehammer than a book of holy songs.

Junius sang as he did everything else: with great gusto. He had a nice, if untrained, bass voice. Nick didn't sing at all. He just stood there beside her, rather like a lowering mountain, holding the book. Eulalie wondered if he didn't like to sing, or if he was embarrassed to sing—some men were silly like that—or if he had a lousy voice. She'd like to find out. An image of Nick and herself singing in the evening while Patsy played the piano flitted through her head, but it was so absurd she thrust it away almost instantly.

The song ended, and everyone sat. Nick snapped the book shut and held it as he might have held a tool, on his knee next to his hat. Out of the corner of her eye, Eulalie saw that he'd tidied himself up for church and wore clean trousers, a white shirt, and a tie, vest and jacket. He'd also bathed and washed his hair, which was slicked back from his forehead. All in all, Nick looked quite respectable and very handsome. She almost wished she hadn't noticed the last characteristic.

Junius was also clean and tidy, but there was something about Junius that made him seem rather like a restrained madman even under the most favorable of conditions. Not that he was one—a madman, that is. But he had a certain quality of unearthly innocence and humor about him that set him apart from the rest of the world, and he always looked as if he might explode into song or dance or laughter at the drop of a hat.

Or maybe Eulalie was spinning fantasies. Wouldn't be the first time. She'd made a hero out of Edward, hadn't she?

Good Lord, where had that thought sprung from? Edward *had* been a hero. Just because he wasn't big and strong and . . . Eulalie gave herself a mental shake and told herself to stop thinking.

Since she couldn't trust her thoughts this Sunday morning, she tried her best to concentrate on what the people in front of the congregation were saying. There were a small herd of them, from the Sunday-school superintendent, Mr. Vallens; to the lay speaker, Mr. Whittaker; to the lady in charge of tidying the sanctuary, Mrs. Martin.

It wasn't the first time Eulalie had been struck by the resiliency of the human spirit. Fancy people coming all the way out to this frontier in the middle of nowhere and creating something resembling civilization out of absolutely nothing. Amazing. For instance, Mrs. Martin was every bit as fussy about her duties to the church as old Mrs. Perkins in the Episcopal Church had been back home in New York.

And Mr. Huffington delivered a most rousing sermon. It was a little too full of hellfire and damnation to suit Eulalie's taste, but there wasn't much to choose from out here, and she understood that Baptists were always prone to condemn their fellows. When she bowed her head in prayer, she cast a peep out of the corner of her eye at Nick, who was doing the same at her. Instantly she closed her eyes completely and felt herself flush. Blast!

What this church needed was a choir, Eulalie decided when the prayer concluded on a dolorous "Amen." Glancing around the congregation, she had a brilliant idea. After Patsy arrived—tomorrow, thank God—she and Patsy ought to organize a choir. That would take Patsy's mind off her problems and help to solidify their standing as righteous citizens in the community. It might also provide a little decent music in church on Sundays. Slanting a glance at Nick, she wondered if he'd be willing to sing with them. She was pretty sure she could count on Junius.

The notion of starting a church choir kept her entertained through the remainder of the church service, and when the congregation sang the closing hymn, *Come Thou Fount of Many Blessings*, she'd almost got over being nervous about what was to come. As soon as she turned to exit the pew and bumped into Nick's broad back, her fate came back to her with a crunch.

"I beg your pardon, Nick," she stammered, slapping a hand to her hat so it wouldn't fall off.

He eyed her over his shoulder. "Think nothing of it."

She thought he was being sarcastic, but couldn't tell for sure. Not that it mattered. She donned her brightest smile and proceeded to greet her neighbors and friends as they all filed out of the church. Mrs. Johnson was hot on her heels, followed by her five children.

Junius caught her eye as they milled toward the front door. "Hope you can come to dinner with us today, Miss Eulalie. I've got a brisket smokin' outside and everything's ready."

"Why, thank you, Mr. Taggart. How kind."

"Figgered you'd need a day or two to get settled before you're able to do much cookin'."

"Thank you. I'd be delighted to join you two gentlemen for dinner."

Junius gave her a beaming smile. Nick frowned. He would.

At the front door, Mr. Huffington smiled his flock out onto the street, shaking hands and slapping backs and acting generally like a politician, although Eulalie hadn't been told if he had any political aspirations.

"Good to see you, Nick. Junius," the minister said, smiling at the two men who, Eulalie gathered, were not regular church attendees.

"Gotta thank the Lord sometimes, Huff," Junius said genially.

"All the time's better," said Mr. Huffington with the barest hint of reproof in his voice.

Nick said, "Huh," and turned on Eulalie.

She wasn't quite ready for him yet. Holding out her hand to Mr. Huffington and doing her best to ignore Nick, she smiled sweetly and said, "Thank you for a most interesting sermon, Mr. Huffington. It was . . . um . . . quite rousing." Lord, she wished she'd thought her speech through before delivering it.

"Thank you so much, Miss Gibb," the reverend said, gushing slightly. He didn't release her hand. "I try to deliver a moving message."

"It was moving, all right," grumbled Nick, eyeing their clasped hands. "And now *we're* going to be moving."

Eulalie retrieved her hand, using slightly more force than was usually required. "Actually, Mr. Huffington, before I go, I wanted to ask you a question."

Nick heaved an aggrieved sigh. Eulalie shot him a repressive look. For heaven's sake, anyone would think he was her husband, the way he was trying to direct her life. Eulalie didn't appreciate him for it. The man was supposed to *protect* her, not order her around.

"I will be thrilled to answer any question you might propound, Miss Gibb," Mr. Huffington assured her.

Was he making sheep's eyes at her? Egad. Maybe Nick had a point. However, that was neither here nor there. "Have you ever considered forming a choir, Mr. Huffington? I should be very happy to help organize an effort in that regard if you believe your congregation would support it."

"A choir?"

Eulalie was surprised to find herself suddenly flanked by two matrons of the church. She blinked at them, hoping she hadn't done something wrong. "Er . . . yes."

"A choir?"

Good Lord, here were two more women, one of whom, Mrs. Fanning, elbowed her way past Nick to get at Eulalie. Mrs. Fanning was probably the only female in Rio Peñasco with the bulk to do so.

"What's this about a choir?" Mrs. Johnson appeared, leading her string of children. "We've been needing a choir for a coon's age."

Eulalie began to breathe more easily. Evidently she hadn't broached a forbidden subject. Modestly she said, "Well, I just thought it might be nice. And my sister would be happy to play the piano or an organ—if we could find one somewhere."

"My Samuel brought his family's organ from New Hampshire," said Mrs. Fanning. "I 'spect we might could donate it to the church."

"And Mrs. Sullivan can make choir robes."

"I'll be happy to direct," said Eulalie, wondering how her position as saloon singer would allow her to conduct choir practice once a week, but willing to do anything to be accepted in the community. Maybe the Rio Peñasco Baptist Church's choir could break with tradition and hold rehearsals at noon or something.

"Well, my goodness gracious sakes alive," said Mr. Huffington, looking slightly alarmed by the herd of women that was growing ever larger around him. "What an interesting suggestion, Miss Gibb."

"It's the same one we've been making for a couple years now, Huff," Mrs. Fanning reminded him darkly.

The minister flinched. It was a sensible reaction to the overpowering woman's aggressive posture. "Er . . . but no one ever offered to do the work before," he pointed out in a small voice.

Mrs. Fanning sniffed. It was Mrs. Johnson who said,

"Well, there's no sense hashing over what used to be. Now we have Eulalie." And suddenly Eulalie found herself being beamed upon by an entire townful of rugged Western matrons. Would wonders never cease?

When she was finally able to break free from the throng, Nick and Junius fell into step beside her as if they'd choreographed the move. She glanced from one man to the other. Junius's smile was as broad and bright as the sun. Nick still looked as if he wanted to murder someone. This time Eulalie had *no doubt* it was her.

"That was right nice of you, Miss Eulalie," said Junius with his customary vigor. "I wouldn't mind singin' in a choir myself."

"You?" Nick guffawed.

"I think that's wonderful, Mr. Taggart." Eulalie gave Nick a quelling glance. He remained unquelled, curse him.

Junius slapped Nick on the back. "And you can join, too, Nicky! You've got a great voice."

"Huh," said Nick.

But Eulalie's interest was piqued. "Really? What range do you sing, Nick?"

He squinted at her. "What's that mean?"

"I mean, are you a bass, like your uncle, or do you sing in the tenor range?"

Nick shrugged his massive shoulders. "Beats me."

"I reckon Nicky sings same as me," said Junius. "Belt out a few bars of somethin', Nicky."

Nick eyed his uncle with what looked to Eulalie like horror. "Not right here on the street, for cripes' sake."

Smiling inside, Eulalie guessed Nick Taggart, while a big, strong, masculine fellow, had one or two foibles. "We'll discuss it later," she said.

"Don't threaten me," grumbled Nick.

Eulalie laughed. "Thank you for inviting me to dinner, Mr. Taggart."

"Call me Junius, Miss Eulalie. Everybody does. I feel like an old man when you call me *Mr. Taggart* that way."

"Very well. Junius. And please, call me Eulalie."

Dinner was delicious. Eulalie had never tasted smoked meat until she'd moved West, but she liked it. And the pinto beans people served with everything were quite tasty, too, especially the way Junius fixed them with chilies and onions and garlic. At least she and Nick would smell alike when they consummated their deal.

The idea of consummation sent hot shivers up Eulalie's spine, and she endeavored not to think about it. It was difficult not to, however, with Nick eyeing her as if she were a piece of cake he aimed to devour as soon as the meal was finished.

A knock came at the door just as Eulalie took a last bite of brisket. It occurred to her to ask Mrs. Sullivan if her costumes could be altered slightly so as to make more room for her expanding tummy. Sternly she told herself not to be silly. The problem wasn't with the costumes. It was with her tendency to eat everything that was put in front of her. When Patsy got here, that would change. She hoped.

"I'll get it," said Junius, hopping up from the table and heading to the door.

Nick glowered, as if he expected whoever had knocked was going to try to impede him in his purpose for the day.

His eagerness amused Eulalie, although it also stirred the butterflies in her stomach to life.

"Come in, come in!" cried Junius when he saw who was at the door.

Mrs. Johnson took him at his word and stepped into the house. "Brought you fellows over a pie," said she, smiling at

Eulalie, who returned the favor, although she wasn't necessarily happy to see the pie. She had enough trouble resisting
meat and potatoes. She was a sucker for pie.

"Looky here, Nicky! It's a pie!" Junius sounded as if he'd
never seen a pie before.

Nick and Eulalie rose from the table and joined Mrs.
Johnson and Junius in the parlor. "Thanks, Mrs. Johnson.
What kind of pie is it?" Nick wanted to know.

"Cherry. I canned a whole mess of cherries last spring, and
this is the last of them."

"Oh, my," said Eulalie. "Cherry pie." One of her favorite
foods, and one she'd assumed she'd left behind in Chicago.
"Where did you get the cherries, Louise?"

"Why in the groves up near La Luz," said Mrs. Johnson.
"My Zeke, God rest his soul, and a few of the other men in
town planted those cherry trees. Closer to town here, we have
pecan and apricot trees, too. They were planted some fifteen,
twenty years ago. They're producing real well now."

"You've lived here that long?" Eulalie blurted out the
question before she thought about it. "I mean . . . good
heavens, Louise, Rio Peñasco must have been *nothing* fifteen
or twenty years ago." It was nothing now. Eulalie couldn't
even imagine what it must have been like then.

"You got that right, sweetie." Mrs. Johnson laughed, a circumstance for which Eulalie was grateful. She hadn't meant
to criticize Louise's adopted hometown.

So they all ate pie. Eulalie despaired of her figure.

Dusk was falling when Nick escorted Eulalie back to her
little adobe home. Eulalie's heart was racing like a road-
runner alongside a stagecoach. She opened the door and
looked up at him. "Um . . . are you coming inside, Nick?"

Nick glanced up the street. Then he glanced down the
street. Rio Peñasco was an exceptionally small town, but it

looked to Eulalie as if every single one of its inhabitants had decided to sit outside that evening and take the air. Nick said, "Hell, I'd better wait until dark."

Thank God. Thank God. Eulalie wasn't sure why she was thanking her Maker, since her reprieve was only temporary, but she did anyway. "Very well. I'll . . . see you later then."

"Yeah." He scowled at her. "And this time, you're going to have to start paying."

She sighed heavily. "Yes, Nick. I know."

He stomped off, and Eulalie retreated to her nice new, if small and fairly crude, home. Sinking into the sofa she'd bought from Fanning's Furniture, an infinitesimally small furniture store located along the row of business establishments running each side of the main street of Rio Peñasco, she looked around and decided life wasn't half bad at the moment. True, there was still Patsy and her problem to be dealt with, but all in all, Eulalie felt a sense of satisfaction she hadn't experienced since before Gilbert Blankenship darkened her life. She missed her family like crazy, but at least Patsy would be joining her tomorrow. And Uncle Harry had written that he intended to pay a visit to her before much longer. She smiled when she thought about what Uncle Harry, the quintessential city feller, would make of Rio Peñasco. Knowing Harry, he'd probably profess to love it.

She wished she had something to read besides the few books she'd brought with her from Chicago, all of which she'd read at least once already. Along with a choir, this town could use a public library. Eulalie wondered if Rio Peñasco was large enough to support such an institution, and decided that was one more thing she might as well look into. As long as she and Patsy were going to be living here permanently— her heart twanged painfully at the notion—the place might as well be as up to date as she could make it. As soon as Patsy was settled, Eulalie decided, she would just write to Mr. Dale Carnegie and see what he had to say about the establishment of a public library in Rio Peñasco, New Mexico Territory. It seemed to Eulalie remotely possible that, with care and a good deal of help, one day Rio Peñasco might actually grow up to be a real town.

Perhaps not. She supposed it would forever have its own personality. That wasn't necessarily a bad thing, but Rio Peñasco's personality was different from the personality of any other city or town she'd been in—and because her family traveled a lot, she'd been in tons of cities and towns. But that had been in the East.

A knock at her front door startled her. Who could it be? Not Nick, surely. Nick would use the back door, since he aimed to stay once he got here. With some trepidation, lest her visitor prove to be one of the more stubborn men who frequented the Opera House, Eulalie went to answer the door. She opened it a crack and discovered Bernie Benson surveying the front of her new house.

Opening the door wider, she said, "Mr. Benson, how kind of you to pay a call." She didn't really feel like entertaining the ubiquitous newspaperman, but she knew that she was obliged to placate the press. Her family had been dealing with reporters for decades.

"I can't stay," said Bernie, although he entered her house anyway. "I only wanted to bring you a copy of an article that appeared in a New Hampshire newspaper. I tell you, Miss Gibb, word of you and, by extension, Rio Peñasco, is spreading like wildfire."

Wonderful. Just what she wanted to hear. She said, "How nice," and wished she could think of some way to muzzle the man. Or, if not the man himself, at least his reportage of her own personal career. She'd come here to get away from publicity, not court it.

With a flourish, Bernie presented her with a folded newspaper. "I asked Clyde to send me two copies, so I'd be sure to have one for you."

"Thank you." Eulalie suspected her smile was sickly. "Er . . . I'm afraid I don't have much by way of refreshment to serve you, Mr. Benson. As you know, I only moved in yesterday."

"No refreshment required, Miss Gibb," he assured her. "I've accomplished my mission, and I shall now depart. I'd meant to bring it yesterday and forgot."

Well, there's a mercy. "Thank you very much for the newspaper, Mr. Benson." She offered him one of her charming smiles.

He swallowed and bowed. "Think nothing of it, Miss Gibb. I'm happy to be able to report your beauty and talent to the world."

Oh, good Lord. "I wish you wouldn't."

Bernie looked at her as if she were crazy. "Why not? Don't you want to be famous? After all, the more people hear about you, the more successful you'll be."

Eulalie would have liked to set him straight, but she didn't quite dare. Knowing Bernie, he'd advertise Patsy's tragedy to the entire world, and that might send Patsy into an even deeper melancholy than she was in already. She fought the urge to pummel Bernie and tried to convince herself that there was little chance that anybody who mattered would ever encounter one of Mr. Benson's articles. Eulalie prayed that she and Patsy would be safe. Thank God for Nick Taggart. She kept her smile in place as she waved Bernie off.

And then Eulalie began to think about the advent of Nick into her home and her bed. How should she greet him?

Should she remain clad in her Sunday best? Including corset, stays, corset cover, stockings, garters, chemise, and drawers? Or should she take the bulk of her armor off and put on a simple tea gown? That would be easier, but it might give Nick the wrong idea about her.

"Stop being an ass, Eulalie Gibb," she advised herself aloud. Nick knew exactly what she was: a woman in need of a man's support and protection, and one who was, moreover, willing to pay for those commodities using her best asset, said asset being her body. There was nothing wrong with that. Eulalie was only being more honest about her needs than most women, who required marriage before paying for the assistance rendered by the males of the species.

That being the case, and because Eulalie was honest and straightforward except when she couldn't be, she removed her Sunday dress, stepped out of her corset and stays, and breathed in a deep breath of relief. She simply *had* to stop eating so much.

The wavy mirror Nick had found for her and that she'd hung in her bedroom revealed she still looked good, in spite of a couple of extra pounds. Actually, she decided, her face looked better with her cheeks filled out a trifle. The dreadful tension of her final weeks in Chicago had killed her appetite. She pulled the pins from her hair and brushed it out. She'd been lucky when the gods were doling out hair, she guessed. Hers was red-gold and wavy and as thick as anything. Because she recalled that Edward had loved it when she wore her hair down, she opted to wear it down this evening, since men, being predictable creatures, probably had similar tastes in hair.

And besides all that, Eulalie was sick and tired of pretending to be someone she wasn't. She also suspected that Nick wouldn't care much how she was dressed when he came to call. In fact, he'd probably appreciate fewer clothes and impedimenta in the way of his ultimate fulfillment. Therefore, she grabbed her favorite wrapper, flung it on over her head, stabbed her feet into her wooly slippers, left her hair down, and donned her spectacles. If Nick was going to be a more or less permanent fixture in her life, he could jolly well take her as she was.

Then she grabbed *The Moonstone*, plopped herself down in the overstuffed chair that nominally went with the sofa, lit the kerosene lamp on the table Nick had fashioned out of an old apple crate, and settled in to read. She'd been at it for about a half hour when she heard a tentative tap on the kitchen door.

Eulalie rose from her chair, took a deep breath, prayed for strength, and walked through the kitchen to meet her fate.

She opened the door, and Nick stood there, hat in one hand and a little bouquet of wild flowers in the other. She looked at the bouquet, feeling stupid. "You brought flowers."

He shuffled his feet. "Figured it was the least I could do."

Gazing up at him, Eulalie thought that here was the man who'd built her a house and furniture and agreed to protect her and Patsy, and now he'd brought her flowers. Which he'd picked himself. She said, "Thank you," and stepped back so he could enter. She took the flowers and found a glass to put them in. "I'll put them in the parlor."

"Yeah. Fine." Nick set his hat on the kitchen table and watched her fill the glass and take it into the parlor, where she set it on one of the apple-crate tables.

She stood back and observed the flowers, smiling. "They look pretty."

"So do you."

And he took her in his arms and kissed her. Eulalie, who hadn't been held very much in recent years, melted.

Chapter Eleven

Nick left Eulalie's bed and home before dawn on Monday morning feeling better than he had in . . . hell, better than he'd ever felt in his life.

Eulalie had surprised him. Not only had she met him at her kitchen door wearing a big, shapeless blue thing and slippers, but she'd had her glorious hair unbound, and she'd been wearing eyeglasses. Eyeglasses! Miss Eulalie Gibb, the most glamorous human female ever to set foot in Rio Peñasco, New Mexico Territory, wore *eyeglasses!* What's more, she looked cute as a bug in them.

He hadn't wasted much time, but Eulalie didn't seem to mind. She hadn't demonstrated the least little hesitation in fulfilling her part of their bargain. Nick, who had been prepared for evasive tricks, was thrilled.

She's proved to be just as wonderful as he'd hoped she'd be, too. It occurred to him that Miss Eulalie Gibb might be the one female on the face of the earth that he might be able to stand being around for more than a couple of hours at a time. She didn't bear the remotest hint of a resemblance to the females with whom he'd grown up—the sly, malicious, manipulative cats that had masqueraded as family—his stepmother and stepsisters.

The blunt truth was that Nick hadn't wanted to leave her this morning. He said as much, shocking himself more than Eulalie, or he missed his guess.

"Don't be silly, Nick Taggart," she'd said as she shoved his trousers at him. She wore her big shapeless blue thing again, covering up her spectacular body that Nick had enjoyed every inch of during the night. "You're the one who said people will talk if they see that you and I have spent the night together. I'm having a hard enough time being accepted by the good ladies of Rio Peñasco without them all thinking I'm a scarlet woman."

"You're kind of scarlet this morning," Nick pointed out. He rubbed his chin. "Sorry. I shaved before I came over here."

"I know it. Thank you."

"Anyhow, they all like you. You're already accepted."

"Do you think so?"

"Hell, who do you think came to your party the other night?" He guessed, after last night, he could forgive her for letting him go to sleep at the party.

"Hmm. Maybe you're right."

"I'm right."

"Well, I'm pleased to hear it. Now go."

She'd knotted her hair on top of her head, too. In that blue thing and with her hair up and her spectacles on, she probably should have looked like a schoolmarm, but Nick's masculine tool reacted to her with the joy of experience and blissful memory, and he had a hard time getting his buttons fastened.

"I'll come over again tonight. That all right with you?" He tried to sound casual, but he didn't feel casual. He felt as if his entire life had just become . . . enchanted or something.

She frowned, as if she were mulling over his request.

Nick's delight faded slightly. "You and I have a bargain, don't forget," he said, his voice almost as hard as his cock.

"I know we have a bargain," she snapped. "But my sister

will be arriving today on the stagecoach, and I don't know if tonight would be the best time for you to pay another visit."

Damn. He'd forgotten all about the reason Eulalie had struck this bargain with him. For a minute there, he'd begun to think she might actually care about him a little bit. "Oh," he said. "Yeah, I guess you're right." Hell.

"Mrs. Johnson has asked us to supper with her, and we'll be home after that. Mr. Chivers let me have the evening off, and this is about the only time I'll have to spend with Patsy until next Sunday."

"Yeah. I know. All right. Not tonight."

She reached for his arm. "I'm not trying to be difficult, Nick. Truly, I'm not."

He eyed her closely for a moment before he decided she actually meant what she said. "I know it. I just . . . aw, hell, Eulalie, you were great. I . . . I'll be looking forward to our next . . . ah . . . meeting."

Did her cheeks just flush? By God, they did!

"Actually," she said, "so will I."

He swept her up into his arms. "Good. I want us both to be happy with this deal."

"Me, too."

He kissed her then, long, deep and hard, and by the time he put her down, he was as ready for consummation as he'd ever been in his life. And he wouldn't be able to fulfill his desire until another damned day had come and gone. Putting her down and plopping his hat on his head, he said, "I'll be at the stage with Junius to meet your sister."

She gave him probably the sweetest smile he'd ever received in his life. It shocked him a little, Eulalie generally being so prickly and all. "Thank you, Nick. That's very nice of you."

He stared down at her, wondering if this was an act or if

she meant it. "Hell, Eulalie, the stage only comes once a week, and it's about the most excitement we get here in Rio Peñasco. You know that."

"Yes, I do know that, but I still think it's nice of you and Junius to greet Patsy. She's had a very difficult time lately, and I know she'll be eager to meet you. I've written to her about you, you know."

"Oh, yeah?" He wasn't sure he wanted to know what she'd written. Probably something about him being a small-town hick or something like that.

"Yes. I told her how very kind you and your uncle have been to me. In spite of our shaky start."

"Aw, hell, it was nothing."

"No, it wasn't nothing. It was definitely something."

To Nick's horror, tears flooded her eyes. "Hey. There's no need for that." He never knew what the hell to do when women cried in front of him. He stood there, feeling solid and stupid and wishing she'd stop it.

"I'm sorry." She fumbled in her pocket for a handkerchief. "It's just that I miss my family *so* much, and Patsy has been through such a terrible ordeal. I'm happy, that's all. And . . . and . . ."

"Aw, hell, Eulalie. I know your life has been rough lately." He'd deduced that, actually, since she hadn't really told him much. But he'd come to appreciate her character, and he knew good and well that she was too strong and independent and smart to cry over nothing. Because he couldn't seem to help himself, he wrapped his arms around her again. "It'll be all right, Eulalie."

"Oh, Nick, I appreciate you so much."

His eyes, which had been closed as he held her close—he loved the feel of her in his arms—popped wide open. "You do?" Well, hell, how had that happened?

"Of course, I do. I don't think I could have survived here if you and your uncle hadn't been so kind to me. And Mrs. Johnson and her children. And Mrs. Sullivan. And the Loveladys. And . . . oh, everybody." She sniffled onto his shirtfront.

"Territorials stick together," he muttered, trying to think of something more brilliant to say. He failed.

"I guess they do." Sniffling again, she withdrew from Nick's arms, leaving him feeling cold and alone. "I'm sorry for being so silly."

"It's all right." He shuffled slightly, tried to come up with something to say that, if not brilliant, would at least make her feel better, failed at that, too, and left, damned near running to get away from those tears. Damn! He hadn't expected Eulalie Gibb, of all people, to cry at him. Maybe females really *were* all manipulative cats.

Somehow, he couldn't stand the notion of Eulalie being on the same level as his stepmother and stepsisters, so he decided that he'd make allowances in her case. Unless, of course, she ultimately proved herself false. He only hoped that, if it ever happened, it wouldn't be until he was tired of her.

He had the melancholy notion that tiring of Eulalie Gibb might entail the association of an entire lifetime.

Eulalie didn't have a notion in the world why she'd broken down in front of Nick Taggart, but her tears continued for a good ten minutes—or, more precisely, a bad ten minutes—after he'd left her that morning. She hadn't wanted him to go. She'd wanted him to stay and never leave her.

She was clearly losing her mind.

Or maybe she was just sick and tired of being strong all the time. It had felt wonderful during the night to give herself to Nick. He was so big and strong and protective. Eulalie felt safe with him. She'd also felt a variety of other sensations that surprised her a good deal. Edward, probably the tenderest man in the entire universe, couldn't hold a candle to Nick Taggart when it came to making Eulalie's body sing.

"I'm sorry, Edward," she moaned, mopping at her tears and curling up into a little ball on the sofa.

She realized at once that she wasn't sorry at all, and that made her cry harder. She'd loved Edward with all her youthful enthusiasm and innocent ardor. Well, she *did* have her family still. Until her mother and father died in that dreadful train wreck. Then she'd had Patsy and Uncle Harry and Aunt Florence and a couple of cousins.

Eulalie wished she could crawl back into her bed, pull the covers up over her head, and hide for the rest of her life. Everything was getting all muddled up. She'd believed it would all be so simple, because she and Patsy had planned and schemed and made detailed arrangements about how they were going to escape from the threat posed by Gilbert Blankenship, in Rio Peñasco, a village so far away from civilization that surely no one would ever find them.

And then she'd found Nick, who, for a price, had agreed to keep them safe. The problem was that, God save her, she'd realized last night in the heat of passion that it wasn't only lust she felt for him. God save her, she'd fallen in love with the man! A blacksmith! In Rio Peñasco, New Mexico Territory.

She ought to have known she wasn't the type of woman who could merely bargain her body for protection. She *had* known it. But she and Patsy had been *so* desperate, and she'd *so* hoped that she'd be able to keep her end of the bargain and not entangle her heart.

"Fool," she muttered, uncurling herself, knowing she had to get cleaned up and start her day.

By the time Nick and Junius knocked on her front door a little past noon in order to walk her over to the stage stop, she'd managed, by constant applications of cool, damp compresses, to get the puffiness around her eyes to subside. And her eyes no longer looked bloodshot. Eulalie figured that if she acted cheerful and happy—which she was, really—no one would notice the remnants of her crying jag.

She smiled at her escorts. "It's very nice of you to walk me to the stage stop."

"We're both looking forward to meeting your sister, Miss Eulalie," Junius said, grinning from ear to ear. "Is she as purty as you?"

She used to be. "Patsy is a lovely person," Eulalie said. "She had . . . um . . . an accident a few months ago that has left scars."

"I'm right sorry to hear that," said Junius. "That's a right shame."

"Yes. It is a shame. I believe she's rather sensitive about the scarring."

"Too bad," said Nick, who until that time hadn't said a word.

Eulalie glanced up at him and was slightly alarmed to see him scowling, as if he were in a vicious mood. After what they'd done together last night, Eulalie would have thought he'd still be feeling euphoric.

Then again, so should she, and she'd been crying all morning. She sighed at the fickleness of fate and human moods.

As they approached the stage stop, which was right outside the Loveladys' mercantile establishment, Eulalie noticed that quite a crowd had gathered. "Goodness, are all

those people here to meet friends and family arriving on the
stagecoach?"

"I think they're all here to greet your sister," muttered
Nick.

"Good heavens. Why?" Patsy would be terrified.

Nick eyed her as if he suspected her of being disingenuous.

She looked back at him and said, "What? Why are you
looking at me like that?"

"You mean to tell me that with all the friends you've made
here in town, you expected to meet your sister all by yourself?"

"I . . . I didn't think of it that way." She wished she had.
She could have warned Patsy.

Nick snorted derisively. "What kind of people do you
think we are? We stick by our friends here in the territory,
Eulalie."

If she'd felt stronger, she might have bridled. As it was, she
felt like bursting into tears again. Her reaction seemed stupid
to her. She said, "Yes. I guess you're right."

Nick said, "Hmm."

Junius looked at them and laughed merrily. It figured.

The stage was forty-five minutes late, which wasn't unusual. What seemed unusual to Eulalie was that practically
every person she'd met since she'd come to live in Rio
Peñasco remained with her, waiting for her sister to arrive.
What's more, they all seemed as excited as she that Patsy was
coming.

"I'm looking forward to meeting a sister of yours, Miss
Gibb," said the gallant Lieutenant Gabriel Fuller.

"As am I," echoed Lieutenant Nash, whom Eulalie had
begun to think of as something akin to a cocklebur. Wherever
Fuller went, Nash went also. Not that he wasn't a very nice

man—but Eulalie wondered what he'd do if suddenly deprived of Fuller's leadership. She envisioned him losing his anchor to this earth and floating skyward, to be blown away by the unceasing territorial wind.

"Thank you both very much," she said in her sweetest voice.

Nick said, "Huh."

"Is your sister a singer, too, Miss Gibb?" Fuller asked.

Eulalie's heart twanged. "We come from a theatrical family, Lieutenant Fuller, but Patsy won't be performing in Rio Peñasco. She expects to be keeping house for the two of us."

"How interesting." Fuller attempted to move a little closer to Eulalie, and was intercepted by Nick, who glowered at him as if daring him to take one more step. He didn't. After returning Nick's glower, he said, "Do you suppose your theatrical family will ever decide to visit the two of you here? It would be a real treat to have a troupe of entertainers perform for us."

Eulalie, thinking of her family, sighed. "There aren't many of us left, although I believe my uncle Harry intends to visit us once we're settled."

"That would be nice. You know the railroad is making travel to the territory much easier than it used to be."

She wondered if he thought she didn't know that, but she only smiled.

Nick said, "Huh," again. Fuller only smiled a superior smile at him.

Bernie Benson was there, of course, with his pencil poised. Spying him, Eulalie sighed again and hoped he wouldn't spread the word of Patsy's arrival too far and wide. She didn't dare ask him to keep Patsy's presence a secret for fear he'd learn the whole story and spread it all over the place. They'd both hoped to be anonymous, more or less, out on the frontier. From everything Eulalie and Patsy had read before their move here, people disappeared into the Western territories all the time and nobody ever found them. They undoubtedly didn't have a Bernie Benson dogging their footsteps.

"I hope you and your sister still plan to join us for supper, Eulalie," said Mrs. Johnson.

"Yes. Thank you very much, Louise. That would be nice. I'm sure neither Patsy nor I will feel much like cooking after she gets here."

"She's going to be right tuckered, is my guess," said Mrs. Johnson, nodding sagely.

"I'm afraid she will be." Eulalie chewed her lip for a second before reminding herself that no one here knew exactly why she'd come to Rio Peñasco.

"We're having a ham for supper, Miss Gibb," Sarah Johnson told her, gazing up at her with adoration. Eulalie couldn't quite account for the little girl's evident worship of a saloon singer, but she appreciated it. "And Ma picked a whole mess of summer squash to go with it. And taters, too. And she cooked a pie."

"That sounds delicious, Sarah." And there went her vow to stop eating so cursed much, too. Well, Patsy would soon take her in hand and make sure she didn't overeat. And if she couldn't stop her from overeating, she was a wonderful seamstress and could let her costumes out.

"I think I hear the stage," Junius said.

Eulalie's heart sped up. "Really?" She'd donned her eyeglasses, in spite of appearing in public in the daytime in them, and squinted toward the west, where the stage would come from. Roswell had gained access to the railroad in 1893, and served as a hub to all the villages and towns in an area almost two hundred miles in diameter. Eulalie couldn't imagine how

people got to Rio Peñasco before the advent of the railroad—
or why they'd want to. Covered wagon, she supposed, although that didn't answer the other part of the question. "I
don't see—Oh, wait! I see the dust!"

Excitement bubbled within her. In fact, so much excitement bubbled so enthusiastically that she grabbed Nick's arm
and held on tight. He glanced down at her, as if he didn't understand. Eulalie did. She'd begun treating Nick as if he belonged to her, and her reaction to excitement was automatic:
she wanted to share it with the person closest to her emotionally. And that person, unfortunately, was Nick Taggart. Idi-
otic Eulalie. However, she didn't see any reason to let him go.
After all, the more they were seen together as a couple, the
more people would be likely to understand that Nick was her
protector. That was her excuse, at any rate. The simple truth
was that she needed the human contact. With him, God save
her.

He didn't protest. Eulalie suspected it was because she
was pressing her bosom against his arm.

It wasn't long before Eulalie could decipher shapes in the
cloud of dust to the west. First she discerned two horses, then
another two, then numbers five and six, and then the bulk of
the stagecoach. She hugged Nick's arm tightly, forgetting to
be regretful that their relationship was a sham.

He said softly, "You all right, Eulalie?"

"Yes," she said, and only then realized tears were dripping
down her cheeks. "Oh, how silly!" she said, and she let go of
his arm and grabbed her handkerchief. To her amazement
and gratification, Nick put his arm around her waist and
hugged her to his side. How sweet.

After another few minutes, during which Eulalie tried and
failed to calm her nerves and Nick continued to hold her, the
stagecoach drew up in a dramatic flourish of horseflesh,

screeching wheels, and a huge flurry of dust. Eulalie noticed that everything connected with the coach, including the horses, driver, and the stagecoach itself, was the same reddish-beige that she'd begun to think of as the prevailing color of her new life—the color of dust.

Phineas Lovelady, the Loveladys' middle son, hurried to the heads of the lead pair of horses and grabbed their harnesses. Everyone knew the horses were too exhausted by this time to bolt or do anything else of an outlandish nature, but it was tradition, and Phineas took his job seriously.

Eulalie was vaguely aware of people cheering and clapping, and then the door opened—and there was Patsy! She peeked out timidly, a black mourning veil covering her face from forehead to chin. Eulalie tore herself away from Nick and rushed to the stage, where the driver had jumped down and was flipping the stairs to allow his passengers to exit.

Patsy said, "Eulalie?"

Eulalie exclaimed, "Patsy!" and reached out to help her down the steps. As soon as Patsy hit the dirt, the sisters were in each other's arms, and both were crying as if the world would end. Everyone in the crowd who had gathered to witness the touching reunion cheered, the ladies dabbing at their eyes with hankies, and the men sniffling surreptitiously. Eulalie couldn't recall being this happy in a long, long time.

And then Nick was at her side, saying something. Drawing away from her sister, she sniffled, grabbed her already-damp hankie, mopped her cheeks, and said shakily, "I beg your pardon?"

"Sorry to interrupt your reunion, ladies, but you're blocking the exit."

Blinking and glancing around, Eulalie realized Nick was absolutely correct. "Oh! I'm so sorry. Come, Patsy, let's move aside."

Patsy, dabbing at her own damp cheeks under her veil, complied. The rest of the passengers, their way now clear, climbed down the steps. They all smiled at the sisters, so Eulalie presumed they hadn't minded their delayed exit.

And then Patsy saw the crowd. She took Eulalie's arm and held on tight. "Who-who are all these people?" she whispered. The question held an edge of panic.

She rushed to reassure her sister. "They're all friends, dear."

"Oh."

Her reassurance hadn't succeeded; Eulalie could tell. Therefore, she increased the jollity in her voice, put an arm around Patsy's waist, and said, "But here, Patsy. Please let me introduce you to everyone."

"Oh, dear." No one else heard the two words, which had been uttered in a tiny, frightened whisper.

"Be strong for just a little bit longer, Patsy," Eulalie whispered back. "This won't take long."

"Thank you."

Eulalie squeezed her sister's waist, her heart aching when she realized how thin Patsy had become. Making her voice loud and cheery, she said, "First you need to meet the two Mister Taggarts, Patsy." She led Patsy down an aisle the townsfolk had created and that ended at Nick and Junius. Eulalie felt as though she were leading a wraith, Patsy was so frail. She smiled at her friends—and the very word *friends* almost made her cry again—and stopped before the Taggarts.

"Patsy, please allow me to introduce you to Junius Taggart and his nephew, Nick Taggart. The Taggarts were . . . uh . . . among the first people I met when I arrived in Rio Peñasco." She hadn't revealed the exact nature of their meeting because she hadn't wanted to alarm Patsy.

Junius yanked his disreputable hat from his head and swept a bow that would have done Uncle Harry proud. "How do, Miss Gibb? We're mighty happy to have you here. Miss Eulalie has been a bright spot ever since she come to Rio Peñasco."

"Thank you, Junius," said Eulalie, watching her sister with concern.

"How do you do, Mr. Taggart?" Patsy said in a very small voice.

"And this is Mr. Nick Taggart, Patsy. Nick has become a particular friend of mine, and he is always watching out for my welfare." She wasn't sure she should have said the *particular friend* part, because she didn't want people to get the wrong idea—or the right idea, perhaps—but she wanted Patsy to know how things stood.

"How do, ma'am?" said Nick, removing his hat with much less of a flourish than his uncle.

"Thank you so much for helping my sister, Mr. Taggart," Patsy said in her tiny, breathy voice. "She's told me of your many kindnesses."

"Think nothing of it," muttered Nick. Eulalie could plainly tell that he was uncomfortable being praised.

And then came the Johnsons and the two lieutenants, and just as Eulalie was preparing to go through the entire rest of the town, wishing all the while that fewer people had come to greet Patsy so as to spare her this ordeal, Patsy uttered a tiny, breathy squeak. And then she fainted.

Lieutenant Fuller caught her just before she hit the dust. "Good God," he said.

Eulalie figured he didn't know what else to say. "Patsy has been quite unwell lately, Lieutenant Fuller. Perhaps you can carry her to the house?"

She looked around for Nick, and realized he'd already

gathered Patsy's baggage together, and he and Junius stood just a couple of feet away, ready to escort the two ladies home. She appreciated them *so* much, and once again she realized that she'd never before met two such helpful people. She smiled gratefully. "Thank you."

And then, because she loved these people, her new friends, she turned and said to the crowd, "Thank you all for coming. I'm so sorry, but Patsy has been very ill lately. I expect the excitement was too much for her."

Mrs. Johnson hurried up to her. "Will you two be fit to come to supper tonight? I can send Clarence and William over with—"

Eulalie clasped her work-worn hand. "No. We'll be fine. Patsy will be fine. She'll want to come to supper at your house, Louise. She just needs to rest up a bit."

"Well, if you're sure . . ."

"I'm sure." And she kissed the older woman's cheek.

It annoyed Nick that Fuller got to carry the sister while he was stuck with the baggage, but he guessed it wouldn't do to fight the fellow for her. Worse, it annoyed him to realize that he wanted to carry Patsy because she was Eulalie's sister, and Eulalie loved her, and he wanted to be the one to protect everything Eulalie loved.

He had it bad, and it peeved the hell out of him. He'd sworn since he was a boy never to get entangled with a woman. His experience told him that, except for a few older widows like Mrs. Johnson, females were trouble. And here he was, wanting to play Sir Galahad for Eulalie Gibb. He'd believed he'd struck the perfect bargain with her, setting everything up on a businesslike basis. But no. Nick Taggart, the world's worst sucker, had gone and fallen for the woman. He made himself sick.

"Your sister doesn't weigh more than a feather, Miss Gibb."

Fuller sounded worried. He would, Nick thought uncharitably. Always trying to get in good with the ladies, Fuller was. And the bastard knew that the best way to win Eulalie was to care about her sister.

"She's been terribly ill, Lieutenant Fuller."

"Please call me Gabriel, ma'am. I'm off duty at the moment." He gave Eulalie one of his more charming smiles, and Nick would have leveled him except that Fuller was carrying Eulalie's sister.

Patsy stirred as they approached the small, whitewashed adobe home. "Wh-what happened?" She realized she was in the arms of a man, clapped a hand to her hat, and whispered, "Oh! Who are you?"

"Lieutenant Gabriel Fuller, ma'am, at your service." Fuller turned his charming smile on Patsy.

"You fainted, dear," said Eulalie, taking Patsy's hand. "Lieutenant Fuller was kind enough to catch you before you got all dirty, and he's carrying you to the house."

"How embarrassing," muttered Patsy. "But I do thank you, Lieutenant Fuller. Um . . . I'm sure I can walk now."

"Don't be silly, ma'am. We're almost there."

Nick snorted. Junius chuckled.

Eulalie ran on ahead to open the door. Standing aside, she ushered Fuller and Patsy into the house, and smiled at Nick and Junius. "Thank you all so much. I don't know what I'd have done without you."

"You'd probably have managed," Nick said churlishly. "You want me to put this in Miss Gibb's room?"

"Yes, please."

Eulalie didn't appreciate his comment. He could tell by her frown. He snarled, "In here, Junius," and led the way to

the bedroom Eulalie had designated as being for Patsy.
Junius followed with a grin.

Fuller put Patsy gently down on the sofa, but he spoke to
Nick. "Know your way around this house pretty well, eh,
Nick?"

Patsy murmured, "Oh, my."

Eulalie said, "Well, really!"

Eyeing him over his shoulder and irked that he should take
his rancor out on Eulalie, who was the only one who might be
hurt by his comment, Nick snarled, "Junius and I built the
place. Remember? I know where the bedrooms are."

"Right." Then Fuller returned his attention to the
women. "Sorry, ladies. I don't know what I was thinking. Of
course, the Taggarts know where everything is."

"Yes." Nick was pleased to hear the chill in Eulalie's
voice. "Thank you very much for taking care of my sister,
Lieutenant. But you'd probably best be getting along now.
Patsy and I have a lot of catching up to do."

Nick would have applauded, but his hands were full.

"Yes, ma'am." Chastened, Fuller bowed to Eulalie,
picked up Patsy's hand, and kissed it. "Please forgive me,
ma'am."

"Oh, no, Lieutenant Fuller. I must thank you. You were
so kind."

Nick decided he liked Eulalie a whole lot better than
Patsy. At least Eulalie, while spiky as a barrel cactus, could
see through some people's surface charm. He plopped the
trunk on the floor of Patsy's room and returned to the parlor
in time to see Fuller bow one last time and depart. He was
glad to see his back.

Turning to Eulalie, he said, "Is there anything else we can
do before we leave you two to catch up?"

Behind him, Junius said, "It's sure a pleasure to know

Miss Eulalie has some of her family with her now, Miss Patsy. She's been missing you something fierce."

"And I've missed her, too, Mr. Taggart. You can't imagine how much. Thank you so much for being such a help to her."

"Junius is just full of help," Nick muttered. He cocked an eyebrow at Eulalie.

"Thanks, Nick, I think we'll be fine now."

"All right. We're right close by if you think of anything else you need." He could have kicked himself as soon as the words left his mouth. Hell's bells, he'd spent the past fifteen years trying to get away from helpless females. He didn't need to make a capable, independent woman *think* she was helpless. In an effort to retrench, he said, "Although I doubt that you'll need us at all."

He heard Junius snicker.

"Thank you, Nick," Eulalie repeated. She narrowed her eyes at him. "We'll be fine."

So Nick grabbed Junius, and they left.

Chapter Twelve

Eulalie got a glass of water for her sister and sat beside her on the sofa. "Are you all right now, Patsy? You scared me to death when you fainted."

Patsy shook her head. "I'm sorry. I must have been more fatigued by the journey than I realized. That stagecoach is a rough ride."

"It certainly is. It nearly battered me to death, and I hadn't been through the ordeal you've been through."

Patsy set her glass on one of the apple-crate tables, and turned to embrace her sister. "Oh, my Lord, Eulalie, I'm so glad we can be together again! The Hollands took wonderful care of me, but I'm so happy to see you again!"

They cried in each other's arms for a few minutes, before Eulalie, feeling stupid, pulled away and wiped her eyes. "Good heavens, we never used to be such sillies."

Lifting her veil, Patsy mopped her eyes. "No, but I think we deserve to be silly for a few minutes."

Eulalie gazed mournfully at her sister's face. "The scarring really isn't so awful, Patsy."

Patsy heaved a sigh that was almost as big as she was and fingered the worst of her scars, a two-inch white pucker on her right cheek. "I feel so self-conscious. I know others have to endure much worse troubles than I, but . . . well, I'm not used to being . . . ."

She hesitated for so long, Eulalie said, "If you say you're

not used to being ugly, I may have to take a strap to you, Patsy Gibb. You could be scarred three times as badly as you are now and still be beautiful."

Patsy gave her a gentle smile. "That's because you love me, dear. I'm afraid the rest of the world might not be so kind."

"Bosh." Eulalie knew her sister was right, however. The world could be a cruel place. "I hope you don't mind, but I accepted an invitation to dine with the Johnsons this evening."

"The Johnsons? Was that the nice woman to whom you introduced me? The one with all the children? I remember you writing to me about her."

"That's the one, all right. She's one of the nicest people you'll ever meet, and she's generous to a fault. In fact," she said, realizing with surprise that she was going to tell her sister a truth, "I've found most of the people in Rio Peñasco generous and giving. And forgiving, too, since they don't seem to mind that I earn my living by singing in a saloon."

"At least that's all you had to do." Patsy looked searchingly at her sister. "It *is* all you've had to do, isn't it, Eulalie? You wouldn't pretend with me, would you?"

It was Eulalie's turn to sigh. "No, Patsy, I won't pretend. And I'll tell you the truth. Mr. Taggart—the younger Mr. Taggart, I mean—has agreed to act as our protector in exchange for . . . for my favors."

Patsy sagged on her end of the sofa. "Oh, Eulalie," she whispered, and she began to cry again. "I can't believe what we've come to. I'm so sorry I've put you through this. I feel as if everything is all my fault."

"Stop that!" Eulalie cried, aghast. "None of this is your fault! It's all Gilbert Blankenship's fault, and you know that. He's the villain of this particular drama." She took a deep breath and decided to admit another truth. "And besides all that, I . . . don't mind. You know, doing . . . that with Nick. He's . . . well, I like him. A lot. And . . . and, curse it, I enjoy it, too!" She felt her face flame and pressed her hands to her cheeks.

Lowering the handkerchief into which she'd been weeping, Patsy looked at her sister in wonder. "Eulalie . . . I can't believe . . . do you mean you've fallen in *love* with Mr. Taggart?"

Curse it. Eulalie took an agitated turn around the parlor. Pausing at the window, where she pushed aside the sheet she'd been using as a curtain until Mrs. Sullivan had the new ones finished, she gazed out into the amazing desert on which she now lived. She used to think there was nothing here. She knew better now. She took a deep breath and examined herself keenly, not wanting to fib to Patsy. "I . . . I'm not sure. I . . . oh, bother."

"It's all right, Eulalie. I know you must be confused. Mr. Taggart is . . . well, he's so unlike . . ." her voice trailed off.

"He's so unlike Edward," said Eulalie flatly. "Yes, he is. He's big and strong and tough, and poor Edward was frail and weak—not morally, of course." She felt compelled to defend her late husband and to remind herself and Patsy that she'd loved Edward madly.

"Of course," murmured Patsy.

Eulalie watched as her sister surveyed the small parlor in which she sat. Patsy said, "Mr. Taggart certainly seems to be a helpful man who is knowledgeable about life on the frontier."

"Exactly!"

"He's a blacksmith, you say?"

"Yes. He and his uncle both. Junius reminds me of Uncle Harry."

"Yes," Patsy murmured. "You said so in one of your letters."

Silence permeated the small room for a moment before Patsy broke it. "Mr. Nick Taggart is a very large man."

"Yes, he is."

"And he's awfully good-looking, too."

Eulalie lifted her eyebrows. "Yes, he is."

After what seemed like a million years of taut silence, Patsy grinned at her sister. "I don't blame you one little bit, Eulalie Gibb. Good for you! I hope you and Mr. Taggart keep enjoying each other for the rest of your natural lives!"

"Oh, Patsy!" And Eulalie ran to the sofa and threw her arms around her sister, and the two of them cried *again*.

When five o'clock rolled around, Patsy again donned her hat and veil, and Eulalie led her to the Johnsons' house, where Mrs. Johnson served the ham and squash and taters that little Sarah had promised. Eulalie knew Patsy would be embarrassed to remove her hat, but she also knew that the people in Rio Peñasco would find it more odd if she continued to veil herself indoors than if she revealed her scars to the world. The good Lord knew, Patsy wouldn't be the only person in town to show evidence of a cruel and quixotic world.

She'd warned Mrs. Johnson what to expect, and that good woman behaved as Eulalie might have expected. She didn't bat an eye, but greeted the sisters with a hug and a quick kiss each. Then she took their outer wraps and hats, handed them off to William with the order to hang them on the hall hooks, and led the way to the parlor. "You two just sit yourselves down in here, and I'll have William bring you both a nice cup of tea while my girls and I get supper on the table."

"Thank you so much," murmured Patsy.

Eulalie knew she felt self-conscious, so she smiled and

tried to act natural. "Is there anything we can do, Louise? We're not used to sitting around while other people work."

"Lord bless you! I know that, Eulalie Gibb. But you deserve to be waited on at least once in your life." She winked at Patsy and went to the kitchen, and Patsy and Eulalie sat on the flowered sofa that held pride of place in the small parlor.

"She's very nice," whispered Patsy.

"Indeed, she is. And her children are delightful."

At that moment, William Johnson made his way into the parlor very slowly, carrying a tray with cups, saucers, sugar, cream, and a teapot. He walked slowly, unaccustomed to this particular brand of social behavior. Because she felt a little sorry for him, Eulalie rose to help him.

"Thank you, William. You're quite the gentleman." She relieved the tray of the teapot, which was heavier than anything else.

He blushed a vivid shade of scarlet, but managed to set the tray on the table before the sofa without mishap. "Thank you, ma'am." He bobbed his head at Eulalie.

"Thank *you*, William."

"You're welcome," he said, and fled the room.

Patsy laughed softly. "Poor boy."

"They're all very nice children."

Mrs. Johnson entered the parlor and sat with a huff in the chair opposite the sofa. "My girls are going to set out supper, but I thought I'd come in here and take a cup of tea with you." She poured out tea and handed a cup to Patsy. "I hope you don't mind, but I invited someone to supper with us."

"Of course, we don't mind," Patsy said, taking the cup and saucer.

Eulalie knew she was lying, but she also knew there was nothing to be done. Besides, Eulalie suspected Mrs. Johnson had invited Nick and/or Junius—and the two of them were so much like family, it hardly mattered. She accepted a cup of tea with her thanks. "Who'd you invite, Louise?"

"Lieutenant Fuller."

Patsy's eyes widened. "Oh!"

Eulalie's eyes narrowed. "Oh?"

"Yep. I felt sorry for the poor man. He carried you all the way to Eulalie's house, and then got sent home. He's a nice fellow, and he looked so forlorn, I couldn't help myself."

Eulalie and Louise gazed at each other for a pregnant moment, each woman knowing that Louise was playing a deep game. Eulalie wasn't sure she approved.

On the other hand, this would give Patsy an opportunity to practice overcoming her shyness about being scarred. Lieutenant Fuller would most definitely act the gentleman. She said, "I see. That's . . . nice."

"It will be," said Louise with more assurance than Eulalie felt. "I'm sure we'll all have a good time. Or as good a time as possible, with five children at the table."

The sisters laughed a little out of politeness. Eulalie figured Patsy must be wishing everybody would leave her alone right about then.

She had no time to reflect on the matter, however, because a knock came at the door, and Penelope rushed to answer it. Eulalie had noticed before now that Penelope seemed smitten with the handsome lieutenant. He entered the parlor, carrying his cavalry hat in one gloved hand, and proffering a little bouquet of flowers in the other.

"I brought flowers for the ladies of the house." Somehow, he managed to include all the women in the parlor in his elegant bow.

He hadn't seen Patsy's face yet, Eulalie surmised. It

wasn't surprising, since Patsy had bowed said face and turned slightly so that he couldn't see her right cheek.

"Aren't you the one!" exclaimed Mrs. Johnson, laughing. "Such a gentleman."

"Thank you, Gabriel," said Eulalie, wishing he hadn't come.

"How very kind," murmured Patsy into her lap.

Eulalie prayed hard for her sister in that moment.

"Well," said Fuller, straightening and lapsing into a more relaxed attitude. "Flowers are kind of hard to come by out here, but Mrs. Magruder let me pick a couple of her roses and some of these white things."

"Daisies," said Eulalie. "They're very pretty."

She heard Patsy take a deep, sustaining breath, and glanced over. She wanted to take her hand and offer her a measure of courage, but she didn't want to appear obvious. Besides, she knew her sister would get through this. She only wished she could save her the awkwardness accompanying these initial meetings with strangers. Patsy was strong. She would survive. But she'd already suffered too much, both physically and emotionally. She didn't need to endure any more of life's vicious buffets.

Patsy turned and smiled up at Gabriel Fuller. Turning her attention to him, Eulalie recognized the moment of shock in his eyes when he saw Patsy's poor scarred face. It lasted only a second, and then his brown eyes warmed, and his grin turned into a pleasant smile. She honored him in that instant and breathed more easily.

"We're awfully happy to have you join us here in Rio Peñasco, Miss Gibb," he said after the briefest of pauses.

"Take a seat, Gabriel Fuller," said Mrs. Johnson, rising from her chair. Eulalie understood that she, too, had been figuratively holding her breath, waiting for Fuller's reaction to Patsy's tragedy. "I'll go fetch a bowl for these pretty posies.

You just take this chair here. I won't be sitting down much before we get supper on the table."

"Thank you kindly, Mrs. Johnson." Fuller handed over his fistful of flowers and stripped off his gloves as he sat. He put his hat and gloves on the table next to him.

"It's nice of you to join us for supper, Lieutenant," said Eulalie, searching her mind for suitable pre-supper chitchat. She was usually pretty good at this sort of thing, but her anxiety had taken up most of the room in her otherwise agile brain. "And the flowers are really pretty. I'm surprised roses do so well here on the desert."

"According to Mrs. Magruder, you have to be careful with them," he said. Eulalie got the impression he pounced upon roses gratefully, as if he, too, were unsure how to carry on a conversation with a scarred former beauty.

Suddenly all this shilly-shallying seemed stupid to Eulalie, and she decided to confront the monster head on. "Poor Patsy suffered a terrible accident, Lieutenant, as you can see, but she's ever so much better now." She reached over and took Patsy's hand. "And she'll only continue to improve now that we can be together again."

She felt Patsy's start of surprise, but then she sensed her relax, as if she were glad the monster had been dispelled. "Yes," she said. "I'm afraid I was badly scarred." With a rueful smile, she added, "The . . . er . . . accident put an end to my acting career."

"I'm very sorry to hear that, ma'am." Fuller added gallantly, "But I can't see that you have anything to worry about. You're still a lovely woman."

And then he blushed, charming Eulalie. When she glanced at her sister, she saw that her sister, too, found the ingenuous comment felicitous.

"Thank you, Lieutenant Fuller. You're very kind."

Patsy's smile still held its old beauty, Eulalie decided. Nothing could mar the genuine goodness of her sister, really. Not even Gilbert Blankenship.

Fuller walked the sisters home after supper ended and they had all thanked Mrs. Johnson profusely for her excellent meal and delightful hospitality.

"What a very nice woman Mrs. Johnson is," said Patsy.

Eulalie was pleased to note that she seemed calm and unembarrassed to be walking with Fuller. The two had been friendly over supper, and Fuller had made Patsy laugh twice, something of a miracle in itself, when he told her tales of his life on a frontier fort.

"Mrs. Johnson is a saint," Fuller agreed. "She's always got a kind word and a piece of pie for any of us poor bedraggled soldiers who find our way to town."

"You don't look very bedraggled to me," Eulalie commented dryly.

Fuller grinned. "I spruced myself up for the evening. Wanted to be presentable for two such lovely ladies."

Again Patsy laughed softly. "You're quite the gallant gentleman, Lieutenant Fuller."

"I do my best, ma'am."

He left them at their door with another graceful bow, and returned to Mrs. Johnson's house, where he'd left his horse.

Eulalie ushered her sister into their little house, and both ladies sank onto chairs in the parlor. Eulalie decided to see what Patsy had to say about the evening's entertainment before she commented. After sighing deeply, Patsy did.

"That was a wonderful meal. I'm surprised accommodations are so good here."

"Oh, my, yes," agreed Eulalie with a grin. "Why, we even have a restaurant, of sorts."

"Goodness."

"Its goodness is fair, actually, but the quantities are grand."

The comment brought a smile to Patsy's lips. The two lapsed into silence. Eulalie noticed a dreamy expression on her sister's face, and she wondered if Patsy was thinking about Gabriel Fuller or her old, carefree life in New York and Chicago. Civilization was trying its best to take over Rio Peñasco, but it had a ways to go yet, and Patsy was the product of a thriving metropolis. Eulalie hoped she wouldn't find life too harsh in the West.

Thinking that a little of nature's beauty might be appreciated under the circumstances, she said, "Would you like to take a couple of kitchen chairs outside, Patsy? The sunsets out here are really quite remarkable, and there may be a little of it left."

"I'd like that. Where's the wind you wrote so much about, by the way?"

Rising and heading for the kitchen, Eulalie laughed. "I thought I'd blow away the first few days I was here. Believe me, the wind was something hateful. But it seems to have died down some now that it's summertime. People tell me that the springtime is the worst time for winds, although they say the winter winds can be vicious, too." She picked up a chair and headed for the back door.

"I suppose there's nothing one can do about the weather," Patsy murmured, grabbing another chair.

"Not much, although people are planting trees everywhere they can think of to serve as windbreaks. Nick planted a little row of Lombardy poplars out back. I'll show you. He said they'd grow quickly."

"That was very nice of him."

"Yes," Eulalie agreed. "It was."

"I'm so glad you've found a protector, Eulalie. You've had

to be strong all by yourself for too long. God knows, I haven't been of any use to you."

Placing her chair against the back wall of her home and sitting, Eulalie said, "That's enough of *that* kind of talk, Patsy Gibb. You couldn't help what happened to you." She turned her chair slightly so that she was facing full west.

"Sometimes I wonder about that," said Patsy softly. "If I'd only been more firm with Mr. Blankenship when he first started coming around, perhaps none of this would have happened."

"The man's a lunatic, Patsy. It wouldn't have mattered what you did," Eulalie said firmly. She didn't want her sister to sink into a melancholic state. This was going to be hard enough on the both of them without having to battle bleak and wintry moods.

"Do you really think so?"

"Yes. I really think so."

Patsy sat with a sigh, her chair, too, facing west. "Perhaps you're right." She gazed into the firmament for a moment or two. The sun was low on the western horizon, and the clouds piling up in the deep-blue sky were edged with silver. The clouds themselves ranged from light pink to brilliant orange in streaks and slashes. "Oh, my, the sky is wonderful, isn't it?"

"It's the most beautiful sky I've ever seen. It's always beautiful." Eulalie hesitated, then added, "It sort of makes up for the landscape."

Patsy's low chuckle made her glad she'd said it. "Yes. I see what you mean, although I must say it's not as bad as I'd expected."

"Really?" Turning to assess the truthfulness of her sister's statement, Eulalie was surprised to find that Patsy appeared content.

"Really."

The sisters sat in silence, watching the western sky's landscape change as they observed it. Eulalie felt a strange sense of peace pervade her being. For so many months, she'd been tense and worried and anxious. The move to Rio Peñasco, for all her outer bravado, had been terrifying. The wide-open spaces she'd heard so much about had made her feel insignificant, as if she might be swallowed whole and no one the wiser if she weren't careful. She'd been frightened of the huge men she'd encountered here—starting with Junius Taggart and Nicholas Taggart—and she'd been terribly concerned that the ladies in the town would shun her because of her occupation.

But she'd discovered soon enough that the ladies in town were starved for companionship and new stories, and that the Taggarts and most of the other fellows in town might be rough around the edges, but they were good, decent people. In fact, although her heart ached when she admitted it, she loved one of them very much. And she was becoming accustomed to the vastness of the landscape. She didn't feel nearly as lost as she had when she first arrived. In fact, she had a funny feeling that she might find the tall buildings and constant trees of her home state of New York a little confining now.

She was lost in contemplation of the sky, which was rapidly losing its color, when Nick showed up. His approach was virtually silent, something of a miracle for so large a fellow. Eulalie presumed he'd seen Patsy and her in the backyard, because he didn't knock at the front door, but just appeared before them. His arrival was unexpected, and gave Patsy something of a start. Eulalie reached out and took her hand.

"It's only Nick, Patsy," she said softly.

"Sorry, ma'am. Didn't mean to startle you."

"Oh, no, Mr. Taggart, please don't apologize. I'd only been so lost in the sunset I didn't hear you approach."

"You ladies mind some company?"

Eulalie was a little surprised that Nick seemed ill at ease. She'd never seen evidence of anything other than pure masculine dominance from this quarter.

"I'm sure we would be happy for some company," Patsy said softly.

She'd averted her face, not that Nick could see her very well in the dark. But Eulalie knew that the moon and stars would soon be out, and then the night would be bright enough for Nick to discern Patsy's scars. Her heart gave another twang.

"Why don't you bring out another chair, Nick? You can set it here, next to me." That would put him a whole person away from Patsy and make her sister feel slightly less uncomfortable. Besides, she wanted to feel him near her. She was absolutely lost, she thought glumly. She was in love with a man who not only disparaged marriage as an institution, but who didn't have a very high opinion of women, either.

"Be right back," he said, and vanished into the kitchen.

"He's very nice, isn't he?" said Patsy after Nick left.

"Yes," said Eulalie, surprising herself. "He is." How she'd misjudged him at first, she couldn't imagine. She supposed she'd been so full of fear and trepidation, it had taken a while to allow herself the luxury of evaluating him by his actions. She'd been so determined not to be taken advantage of that she'd mistrusted everyone she met. She knew Nick had resented it, too.

With a sigh, she wished they could start over again, and this time get off on the right foot together. But, as she knew too well, life didn't work that way.

Nick placed his chair beside hers, and before she realized what she was doing she reached out for his hand. "Thanks for visiting, Nick. Would you like something to drink?" Since this wasn't New York or Chicago, the "something to drink" would have to be water, but Nick already knew that.

"No, thanks. Just thought I'd come over to see how you ladies are settling in." He gave her hand a soft squeeze, and Eulalie felt better about things.

"Everyone has been very kind to me," said Patsy. "And I can't thank you enough for the lovely house you built for Eulalie and me, Mr. Taggart."

"Aw, it was nothing," said Nick.

Eulalie believed he actually meant that. How odd that two men in Rio Peñasco, New Mexico Territory, could build an entire house in a couple of weeks and think nothing of it. When she considered how many people it took to build houses back home, and how long it took them to do so, her mind almost boggled.

As the sky darkened and the moon and stars began to shine, Patsy's reaction to the glories of these territorial heavens was everything Eulalie had anticipated. Nick continued to hold her hand, which she hadn't anticipated, but which she appreciated.

"My goodness," Patsy whispered. "I've never seen so many stars in my life."

"It's astonishing, isn't it?" Eulalie laughed gently.

"It certainly is."

"Guess I'm used to it," said Nick. "But it's real pretty."

In the distance a coyote yipped.

"What's that?" Patsy sounded wary.

"Coyote," said Nick. "There's lot of 'em out there on the desert."

"Oh, my, I've heard of coyotes," said Patsy.

"Kind of a lonely sound, if you ask me," said Nick. "But maybe that's my own fancy."

"I don't think so," said Eulalie. "They always make me shiver a little bit." She thought of something Patsy might enjoy. "Wait until you see the owls out here, Patsy. They're little spotted brown things, and they dig their nests in the ground."

"In the ground?" Patsy sounded as though she suspected Eulalie of teasing her.

"Yup," said Nick, taking over for Eulalie. "They're screech owls."

"That's right," agreed Eulalie. "None of your civilized hooting for these fellows. I made the mistake of walking up to an owl's burrow, and got screeched at for my efforts. What's more, the owl then dived at me and bumped my head. They have rather sharp talons."

"Good heavens."

"I suspect he was protecting his young. It's that time of year, when the owlets hatch," said Nick.

"True," said Eulalie.

"Reckon this is kind of rough country," Nick said, sounding slightly defensive to Eulalie's sensitive ears. "But I think those owls have the right idea. Too bad more human pas don't care enough to protect their kids."

Both sisters turned to look at Nick. Eulalie couldn't see him well, but she noticed the set of his jaw and wondered if his own childhood experience had given him a certain respect for the bloodthirsty nature of a father owl's protective instincts toward his young. Her heart ached a little, and she felt a compulsion to reassure him. "It is rough, but it's . . . oh, I don't know. I think it's marvelous, too. It's certainly not an easy country. Every plant has thorns, and every creature is poisonous or has claws or something. But you get used to it after a while. In fact, I've come to like it a lot."

"I'm glad," said Patsy.

"And I agree with you about some human fathers." Her brain had begun recalling and sorting through instances of human fathers' insensitivity to the welfare of their children. She'd seen it often enough in New York, and even out here, although to a lesser extent. She spared a moment to be grateful for her own male relatives, all of whom, except perhaps her cousin Josiah Gibb, who drank to excess, were responsible and caring individuals. "As for the land, I think it's funny that most of the native plants and creatures are either poisonous or full of spikes. I love it, but you have to be careful. We have scorpions, tarantulas, rattlesnakes, perfectly hideous insects called vinegarones, coyotes, and even the occasional cougar."

"Goodness, what a dismal topic of conversation," muttered Patsy.

Eulalie sensed her uneasiness, and decided she probably shouldn't have pointed out the relative harshness of Patsy's new home and the callous natures of some men. To make up for it, she said, "But the people here are wonderful. They make up for the . . . er, hardness of the country."

Nick wished she hadn't mentioned hardness. The only reason he'd come over here tonight was because he'd been in a state of semi-arousal all day long, and it was mighty uncomfortable. He'd been hoping maybe Patsy would be sleeping by this time. Glancing over to see if he might catch a glimpse of a yawn or another indication of impending exhaustion, he was startled when the moonlight revealed a terrible scar on her cheek. He turned away again instantly, but his heart had suffered a severe spasm. He hated when it did that. This was especially true since he'd been doing his very best since his sixteenth year to harden that organ against the manipulations of the female of the species.

He wasn't sure how Eulalie's sister's terrible scar could constitute manipulation, but he'd learned a long time ago to view all indications of feminine weakness with deep suspicion. Still, he wondered how she'd got that scar. Eulalie had told him Patsy had been involved in an accident. Could she have fibbed to him? It seemed mighty unlikely that a scar like that had been inflicted accidentally—unless hers was a circus family. That possibility hadn't occurred to him until now. Hmm . . .

"Say," he said casually, "you said your family acts, didn't you?"

"Yes," said Eulalie.

"Indeed." Nick heard the smile in Patsy's voice.

"Do any of them do any circus work?"

"Circus work?" Eulalie sounded puzzled. "You mean like trapeze acts and things like that?"

He was actually thinking of knife-throwers, but he said, "Yeah. Bareback riding. Sword swallowing. That sort of thing." He supposed a sword might account for that scar, but the notion gave him the shivers.

"No."

He glanced over once more and saw that both sisters were shaking their heads. Which meant they were either telling the truth or lying. Which also meant that, as usual, he didn't know what to believe.

Damn it! He wished like thunder that females weren't so damned difficult to interpret.

"Ah," said he. "Just wondered. When I was a boy, I wanted to run away and join the circus." He'd wanted to run away, at any rate.

"I understand that's a common ambition among little boys," said Eulalie.

"I suppose so."

He heard a rustling sound and turned to see Patsy rising from her chair. She kept her face averted from his vision, and again his heart crunched painfully. However she'd received that awful scar, it embarrassed her. Poor thing.

Unless she'd deserved it, he reminded himself. Even as he did so, he knew he was being irrational. Nobody deserved to be hurt like that. The Gibb girls might be female, but so far they hadn't exhibited the demonic attributes his stepmother and stepsisters had possessed in such abundance. He was still withholding judgment, but he sensed Patsy was more to be pitied than blamed for whatever accident had befallen her.

"I think I'm going to go to bed now," said Patsy, patting a yawn. Nick suspected she'd actually lifted her hand to hide that scar.

Eulalie rose, too. "Do you need any help, Patsy? I know you've had a difficult day."

"No, thank you. I'm fine." She hesitated for a moment, then Nick saw her straighten her shoulders, as if she were bracing herself for an ordeal to come. He realized he was the ordeal when she turned, faced him directly, and held out her hand to him. "I can't thank you enough, Mr. Taggart, for helping Eulalie and me. You've been wonderful. And so has your uncle."

He rose and took her hand. "It was nothing, Miss Gibb. Truly. Junius and I were glad to help."

After another couple of pleasantries, and after Patsy refused to allow Eulalie to follow her into the house ("For heaven's sake, Eulalie, you can't leave your guest.") Nick and Eulalie were alone at last under the starshine and moondust. Nick gazed up into the night sky and a sense of infinity enveloped him. For all the suffering people caused each other, the cold, sparkling universe didn't give a rap. Men were such fools—and women were, too—to think they mattered much when compared to all that up there.

Neither of them spoke for a few minutes. Then Nick's curiosity got the better of him. Softly, he said, "Is that scar on your sister's cheek the result of her accident?"

He heard Eulalie sigh before she spoke. "Yes. She's very sensitive about it. It is awfully noticeable, isn't it?"

"Well . . ." he thought about lying, and decided against it. Eulalie Gibb was the only woman he'd ever met who didn't need to be pacified with soothing fibs. "Yeah, it's noticeable, but it doesn't detract from her looks any." He thought that sounded crude, so he muttered, "If you know what I mean."

He was surprised when Eulalie reached for his hand. "I do know what you mean, Nick. Thank you."

Feeling a little unequal to her gratitude, he shrugged. "It's the truth. I'm . . . sorry it happened, but she's still a beautiful woman." *Just like you,* he silently added to himself.

"Yes. She is, isn't she?" Eulalie was clearly pleased by his assessment, and that made him feel better. After a moment, she added more softly, "But the scar on her face is only one of them. She has other scars on her body. Not to mention her soul."

"She does?" Nick was horrified to hear it. The story behind Patsy's so-called accident was beginning to sound less accidental with every piece of information Eulalie leaked to him. "What kind of accident was it, anyhow?"

Eulalie hesitated, and for a second or three Nick thought she might actually tell him. He was disappointed when she only said, "We don't like to talk about it."

"Guess I can't blame you for that," he growled, although it was the truth.

"It was horrid," said Eulalie somewhat defensively. "We didn't think Patsy would survive for a long time."

He only shook his head, imagining how horrid it must have been, and wondering when it would be suitable to ask Eulalie if he could spend the night. He didn't expect she'd appreciate the question right now, since she was still plainly recalling the tragedies of the past. He sighed deeply, wishing he knew more about good women. Until he met Eulalie, he hadn't been sure such an animal existed, but he'd almost changed his mind.

"Um, Nick?"

"Yeah."

"Would you like to come inside with me?"

The question so startled him, he nearly fell out of his chair. Because he didn't want to demonstrate too plainly how thrilled he was that she'd asked, he paused for a heartbeat to catch his breath before he slipped up and hollered *yes* at the top of his lungs. Damn. He had it bad. He was acting like a schoolboy, for God's sake. Feeling like one, too, if it came to that.

"Sure," he said, hoping he didn't sound as eager as he felt. "Don't mind if I do."

So he carried the chairs back into the kitchen, and the two of them retired to Eulalie's bedroom, which he'd been careful to build an entire hallway away from Patsy's.

She came to him sweetly and passionately and with total abandon, and before the night was over, Nick had come to the melancholy realization that he loved Eulalie Gibb. What's more, he was pretty sure he wouldn't survive if she ever decided to move back to Chicago again.

He was also sure she'd laugh at him if he told her about his condition.

Pitiful. He was totally pitiful.

Chapter Thirteen

Eulalie was delighted that Patsy fit into what passed for society in Rio Peñasco without any trouble at all. Her sister was a beautiful person inside and out, and as warm and generous and openhearted as a woman could be, so it wasn't surprising that the citizens of the town loved her. It was more of a surprise to Eulalie that Patsy seemed to overcome her embarrassment about her facial scars with relative ease, although Eulalie knew how much it cost Patsy to appear in public without her veil.

"I can't hide forever," said Patsy when Eulalie squeezed her hand one day as she left the house to do the marketing.

"You're being very brave," Eulalie told her.

Patsy shook her head. "I'm being practical. It's too hot here for veils."

And she smiled. Eulalie could only imagine the pain behind her façade, but she honored her for her grit and determination.

Gabriel Fuller helped. Although she'd never admit it aloud, Eulalie hadn't honestly expected the handsome lieutenant to be so gallant. She'd pegged him for a man who wouldn't appreciate a woman with defects of beauty, and had rather expected him to disappear once he saw Patsy's scarring. Perhaps she'd become too cynical during her life on the stage, but she'd noticed more than once that men didn't much care about a woman's character as long as she looked good.

But Fuller surprised her, and she was mightily gratified. As often as he could, he rode into town, and he always visited Patsy, even taking her for rides to explore the desert and the surrounding countryside. In fact, it seemed to Eulalie as if the two might be forming some kind of attachment. She prayed that Patsy wouldn't be hurt again.

"Lieutenant Fuller seems to have taken a shine to Patsy," she observed one day as she and Nick ate lunch in her kitchen. He had just finished whitewashing the fence and laying rocks out back so that she and Eulalie would have something akin to a veranda on which to place chairs and watch the sun set in the evenings. Patsy had proved herself to be an admirable cook, and this day Eulalie and Nick were feasting on sandwiches made with chicken left over from supper the night before. What's more, the sandwiches were made with bread Patsy had kneaded and baked her very own self. Eulalie, who had always assumed bread came from bakeries until she moved West, was impressed with how well Patsy had taken to their new life.

As soon as she'd asked her question, it occurred to her that she and Nick were becoming as comfortable together as a pair of old shoes, and she acknowledged that he had become necessary to her emotional well-being. Was it wise to have allowed herself the luxury of loving him? She chided herself for her astounding stupidity. Of *course* it wasn't wise.

But what had wisdom ever to do with love? Not a blessed thing, and she knew it. How discouraging.

"Yeah? Well, I guess he's not a bad fellow," said Nick.

She eyed him closely as she chewed and swallowed a bite of sandwich. "I thought you thought he was an ass."

"He is an ass. But he's not a bad sort of an ass."

"You're silly, Nick Taggart."

"Maybe. I don't like it when he goes to the Opera House and drools over you."

The statement startled Eulalie. "He doesn't drool over me!"

"He does, too. They all do."

"Nonsense. Anyway, I suppose that's part of the act. I'm supposed to look good on stage. Otherwise, what's the point?"

Nick squinted at her. "Huh."

Eulalie rolled her eyes. "Would you like a piece of peach pie?"

"Yeah, thanks."

So Eulalie brought him a piece of peach pie. She decided not to have one herself, since she'd eaten one last evening after supper, and she was attempting to regain her self-control regarding food. It was a difficult thing to do, Patsy being such a good cook and all, but she didn't want to get fat and have to get new costumes.

Oh, whom was she trying to fool? She didn't want to get fat, because it would break her heart if Nick decided he didn't want her any longer because she was a tub of lard and eschewed her company for that of Violet or one of the other girls at the Opera House.

She was absolutely pathetic.

The ubiquitous Bernie Benson helped Patsy to fit in, too, although both sisters wished he'd desist. He not only wrote about her arrival in town, but started writing about both sisters as if they were a team or something. He sent articles entitled *Sisters in Beauty Grace the West* and *Cactus Flower and Prairie Rose Bloom in the Territory* and *Delightful Duet Dare Desert*, and after Eulalie and Patsy sang a duet in church, *Songbirds Soar on Sunday*. Eulalie couldn't think of a way to still his pen, short of murder, so she only prayed that Bernie's

prolixity wouldn't ever get anywhere near Gilbert Blankenship.

One day Patsy, looking up from the article she'd been
reading, said, "I wish he'd stop writing these articles."

Eulalie heaved a big sigh. "I've thought about telling him
why we'd rather he didn't, but . . ."

She got no further. Patsy paled visibly and whispered,
"No!"

Reaching out and patting her sister's hand, Eulalie said, "I
won't." And she despaired.

Three weeks after Patsy's arrival, the sisters received a
communication from back East that delighted them both.
They'd gone to the Loveladys' mercantile and dry goods
store, which also served as Rio Peñasco's post office, to re-
trieve their mail and pick up supplies Patsy needed in the
kitchen. Eulalie took one look at the envelope in her hand and
felt her spirits soar.

"It's from Uncle Harry!" she cried to Patsy, who was
eyeing some bolts of fabric.

Patsy instantly turned her attention away from tablecloth
material and hurried over to her sister. "Oh, good! He writes
the most entertaining letters."

"Glad you're happy about it," said Mrs. Lovelady.

Eulalie, who knew how people were in this out-of-the-way
corner of the territory, smiled at her. "Oh, our uncle Harry
makes everyone happy. He's such a charmer." Because she
knew Western etiquette by this time, she opened the envelope
then and there, so that Mrs. Lovelady wouldn't be left to
speculate about the contents of Harry's letter.

She was glad she'd done it when she read the first para-
graph. "Oh, my! He and Aunt Florence and the cousins are
going to visit us!"

"They are?" Patsy's eyes went as round as saucers, then

filled with tears. She hastily yanked a handkerchief out of her pocket, mopped at her eyes, and whispered, "How wonderful."

Eulalie felt a little bit like crying herself, although she didn't. She'd missed her family *so* much. "I wish we had a hotel in Rio Peñasco." Then she smiled at Mrs. Lovelady so that good woman wouldn't think she was belittling her town.

"Funny you should say that," said Mrs. Lovelady. " 'Cause the mayor and the sheriff are talkin' about building us a hotel in town, right across the street."

"Really?" The news came as a huge surprise to Eulalie, who couldn't imagine why anyone would do such a thing in so small a community.

"Yep. Seems as to how the railroad's coming to town, and pretty soon we're going to be having us a lot more business."

"The railroad?" This news came as rather a shock. Eulalie had expected Rio Peñasco to have remained isolated from the rest of the United States for a good deal longer than this. "That's . . . er . . . wonderful. When is it expected to be built?"

"Hear tell they're going to start next month. They're hopin' to get the tracks laid before next summer. It's not a long stretch they have to lay down. Only about forty or so miles between here and Roswell."

"A year," Eulalie mused. And what would she and Patsy do then? Move on? The notion made her heart ache. How strange. When she'd first arrived in Rio Peñasco, she'd believed herself to have landed in the closest thing to hell she could imagine. And now she didn't want to leave. Of course, a good deal of that reluctance sprang from her relationship with Nick Taggart, unfortunately.

Life just kept playing tricks on her. Cursed life.

However, in a way, that would make moving on easier. Since wherever she went, she'd go with a broken heart, she didn't suppose it made much difference where it was.

Unless, of course, Patsy and Lieutenant Fuller got married. That notion came to her out of the ether and stunned her for a moment before Patsy nudged her and said, "What else does he say? When are they coming?"

Startled out of her gloomy contemplations, Eulalie cleared her throat and scanned the missive in her hands. "They're coming the first week in October. That gives us a couple of months to prepare for them."

"I'm so glad they're coming." Patsy clasped her hands to her bosom. "I miss everyone so much."

"Yes," said Eulalie. "So do I." She turned and gave Mrs. Lovelady one of her most spectacular smiles. This smile wasn't the kind she aimed at men, but the kind she leveled at women to let them know that she valued their friendship. "Thank you so much, Mrs. Lovelady. I guess Patsy and I will have to figure out where to stash everybody."

"Oh, la, a couple of 'em can stay here," she said, flushing a little under the influence of Eulalie's smile. "We've got room since the girls got married and moved to Roswell."

"Really?" Patsy impulsively reached across the counter and took Mrs. Lovelady's hand. "Thank you *so* much, Mrs. Lovelady!" Her eyes began to drip once more. Releasing the other woman's hand, she again applied her hanky to her eyes. "Everyone here is so kind. So very kind."

"Yes," said Eulalie, still smiling at Mrs. Lovelady. "They certainly are."

And Eulalie went back to reading the mail while Patsy again perused the bolts of fabric. There was a letter from Mr. and Mrs. Holland, the couple who had let Patsy stay with them in Chicago until she was well enough to travel to Rio

233

Peñasco, as well. This letter contained news of a different nature, and which made Eulalie feel a little sick.

According to John Dearborn, Mr. Blankenship was released from prison on July 10, my dear. I'm sure he no longer poses a threat to you or your sister, but I felt it would be wise to let you know. I don't know what the police are thinking to allow such a monster out on the streets.

Eulalie didn't, either, but she was very grateful to John Dearborn, an actor friend in New York City, and Mrs. Holland, for the information about Blankenship. She prayed harder that none of Bernie Benson's articles about the Gibb sisters would find their way into Blankenship's evil hands.

But perhaps his obsession with Patsy had faded during the six months he'd spent in prison. If he were sane, it undoubtedly would have; she understood prison had that effect on most people. Unfortunately, Eulalie placed little confidence in Gilbert Blankenship's sanity. A sane man wouldn't have done what he'd done to Patsy. A shiver ran up her spine.

That night after her performance, Nick saw her home. Eulalie was especially thankful she'd made her arrangement with Nick as she curled up after making sweet love with him. He stroked her body with his big, work-roughened hand, and she thought she'd never felt so safe and protected.

Feeling the need to tell him how much she honored him, but not wanting to admit her love for fear of frightening him away, she murmured, "Thanks for helping so much, Nick."

"Hell, it's nothing," he whispered into her hair. And he squeezed her more tightly. "I get paid well."

She heard the smile in his voice and knew he didn't mean his words to sting, but they did. She was such a fool. She chose not to say anything more, but shut her eyes and drifted off to sleep.

And she saw Gilbert Blankenship. And that knife. And Patsy on the floor. And she saw herself pick up the cast-iron skillet from the stove, and she saw herself bash Gilbert Blankenship over the head with it. As he fell, the knife skidded across the floor, and Eulalie ran for it and picked it up. It dripped with blood. Patsy's blood. And she screamed. And screamed. And screamed.

"Eulalie, what the hell?"

Nick's croaky voice finally penetrated the bloodred horror in Eulalie's sleep-fogged brain. She awoke with a start and with another scream poised on the tip of her tongue. Petrified with terror, she threw her arms around Nick and sobbed onto his broad, warm shoulder.

A timid tap came at the door of Eulalie's bedroom. "Eulalie? Eulalie, are you all right? Mr. Taggart, is my sister all right?"

"Reckon she had a nightmare, Miss Patsy."

Eulalie felt, rather than heard, the rumble of Nick's voice, as her ear was pressed to his massive chest by this time.

"Um . . . should I fix some hot cocoa?" asked Patsy tentatively.

His arms still wrapped securely around Eulalie, Nick said, "Reckon it couldn't hurt." As Patsy's footsteps faded, he leaned over and whispered in Eulalie's ear, "Eulalie?"

Her panic subsiding, Eulalie swallowed hard and nodded. Embarrassment had started overtaking her fright. Damn Gilbert Blankenship! Bad enough he'd scarred her sister for life; now he was invading Eulalie's own dreams. "Sorry I was so stupid."

"Didn't sound stupid to me," muttered Nick. "Sounded like you were scared to death."

"N-nightmare," said Eulalie shakily. "I don't usually have them."

"Reckon that one was a whopper."

She pulled back a little, but Nick didn't release her. She looked up into his face. The room was dark, and she could only see his eyes shining down at her. She loved him so much in that moment, she hurt with it. Worse, she wanted to tell him the whole story—but it wasn't hers to tell.

"I feel like an idiot," she said after another moment or two.

"Nuts," said Nick.

And she loved him a little more for that.

At last, feeling strong enough to let him go, Eulalie said, "I'd better find a handkerchief and wipe my face. Can you get the lamp?"

"Sure." Nick lit the bedside lamp, and Eulalie allowed herself one last view of his magnificent torso before she reached for her wrapper and pulled it on. Then she went to the dresser and withdrew a clean hanky, which she used to good purpose.

A minute later, Patsy again knocked softly on Eulalie's door. "Hot cocoa is ready."

"Thank you, Patsy."

By that time, Nick had arisen and donned his clothes. Eulalie knew he'd go home after drinking his cocoa, and she wished he wouldn't. She wished he could stay with her forever.

That, however, wasn't part of their bargain.

They trooped out to the kitchen to find Patsy stirring the pot of hot cocoa. As soon as she saw Eulalie, she laid her spoon aside and came over to hug her. "What happened, Eulalie? I've never heard you scream like that."

"Nightmare," said Eulalie. "I can't remember ever having such a horrid dream."

"I'm so sorry. What was it about?"

Eulalie hadn't told Patsy about the letter from Mrs. Howell, and she didn't feel like confessing now, in front of Nick. "I . . . can't really remember. All I remember is being frightened nearly to death." A quick glance at Nick told her he didn't believe her.

Patsy, thank God, was more gullible. "I'm so sorry." And she gave her another squeeze and rushed over to the stove to save the cocoa from boiling over. "You two sit at the table, and I'll serve you some of this. Would you like a slice of pound cake to go with it, Nick?"

"Yeah. Thanks. That sounds good."

"Eulalie?"

"No, thank you. I'd better not."

"Why not?" Nick lifted an eyebrow at her.

Eulalie sighed and patted her tummy. "If I keep eating so much of Patsy's good cooking, I won't be able to fit into my costumes."

Nick opened his mouth, presumably to say something, then shut it without doing so. He said merely, "Huh."

Frowning, Eulalie wondered if he'd been going to say something about her weight. All things considered, Eulalie was in considerably better shape than the other women who worked at the Opera House, and she resented Nick's assessment of her overall chubbiness. "I'm not fat, Nick Taggart, and you'd better not tell me I am," she said firmly. She might love a man who didn't love her, but she wouldn't allow him to insult her, even silently.

"Huh?" Nick looked at her with a puzzled expression.

"Don't 'huh' me," Eulalie said, feeling a little ridiculous.

"I don't think you're fat," said Nick.

"Hmm."

"In fact, I think you're kind of skinny."

"Here we go," said Patsy cheerfully, placing two mugs of steaming cocoa on the kitchen table. After setting a thick slab of pound cake and a fork before Nick, she got another mug of cocoa and took her own place at the table, smiling brightly at Nick and Eulalie.

As much as she loved her sister, Eulalie could have wished Patsy had stayed at the stove a minute longer. Eyeing Nick closely, she tried to determine if he was fibbing or being honest about her state of skinniness. She couldn't. With a sigh, she said, "Thank you, Patsy."

"Yeah," said Nick. "This looks good." He forked up a morsel of cake and chewed blissfully.

Eulalie took a sip of cocoa and wished she'd taken a piece of cake, too. "Delicious cocoa, Patsy."

"Thank you."

"Why don't you two have some cake?" Nick asked after he'd swallowed his second bite of cake. "It's really good, and you both need a few more pounds on you." He squinted at Eulalie. "And if you can't fit into those costumes, I say that's a good thing."

Eulalie stared at him, astonished. "A *good* thing? How could that be a good thing? I'd lose my job!"

Nick ate another bite of cake before he responded. "Yeah. I guess."

He didn't sound as if he considered the loss of her job anything to be worried about, and his attitude irritated Eulalie. "For your information, Nicholas Taggart, I *need* my job."

Patsy patted her hand, which was gripping the table hard. Glancing at her, Eulalie realized she shouldn't continue the argument, for Patsy's sake. Drat!

Nick said, "Huh." How typical.

As Nick polished off his second slice of pound cake, he realized with dismay that he didn't want to leave Eulalie alone with her sister. He wanted to go back to bed with her and hold her in case she had another nightmare. Damn it, it was his job to protect her, and that included saving her from hideous terrors in the nighttime.

The trouble was, he didn't know how to ask her if he could stay. If there was one thing he didn't want, it was to know that she didn't care to have him hanging around. And if he asked to stay and she told him to leave, he'd feel like a kicked dog.

This agreement they had was all well and good as far as it went but, Nick thought bitterly, it didn't go far enough. True, most of the people in town had figured out that the two of them were together and, therefore, the likelihood that any of the men in town would dare accost her was slight; still, their arrangement felt too damned . . . temporary. It was an extremely odd fact, but for the first time in his life when contemplating a female, he didn't like the notion of a brief interlude of passion. Strange as it seemed, and as much as it worried him, he craved more than a temporary alliance with Eulalie Gibb.

He figured he'd get over it, given enough time—which was the whole point, damn it.

Well, he guessed it wouldn't hurt to put the matter to Eulalie. He could turn it over to her. Make it seem as if he were doing her a big favor. That was better than having her think he was a lovesick puppy.

How had he, a strong and independent man who knew better than to allow a woman to determine his happiness, sunk so low? He didn't have a clue, but he didn't like it.

As Patsy rinsed out the mugs and his plate at the sink, Nick leaned across the table and took Eulalie's hand. He re-

sented her expression of alarm. Nevertheless, he forged on-
ward, "You sure you want me to leave? Are you going to be all
right?"

She gave him one of her more brilliant smiles. "I'll be fine.
Thank you, Nick."

"You sure?"

"I'm sure."

"You won't have another bad dream?"

Retrieving her hand, she hugged herself. "I'm . . . pretty
sure I won't."

He made a decision. If she kicked him out on his ear, so be
it. He gave her a scowl that he hoped curled her liver. "Nuts.
You're worried. I'll stay."

To his surprise, she didn't instantly bristle and lash out at
him. Rather, she appeared grateful—unless that was his
imagination. She said, "Thank you, Nick," and he guessed he
wasn't imagining things. His heart felt lighter.

The two of them retired to bed, where Eulalie subsided
into his arms as if she were a soft and cuddly kitten instead of
a prickly pear. Nick decided he'd worry about the state of his
heart and sanity later. Everything felt too right just then for
such dismal contemplations.

Eulalie was getting mighty tired of singing at the Rio
Peñasco Opera House. She didn't mind singing, but she
hated having to parade herself in front of a roomful of sali-
vating men night after night. Her only consolation was that
Nick was there. Every night. Sometimes Junius came with
him, but Nick himself never, ever allowed her to be alone
anymore before that mob.

Her love for Nick grew every night when she looked out
over her whistling, stomping audience and saw him, eyeing
her audience as if daring any one of them to step out of line.

No one ever did. She considered this a most unfortunate circumstance—not that the men were behaving themselves, but that she loved Nick Taggart more every day.

It became a habit for the Gibb sisters to have dinner with Nick and Lieutenant Gabriel Fuller—sometimes Junius joined them—and then Nick would walk Eulalie over to the Opera House while Fuller—and sometimes Junius—sat on what passed as the back porch of the little adobe house and chatted, until the men went home.

"I'm sure you'd rather be alone with Gabriel, Patsy," Eulalie said one day as she set the table while Patsy stirred the savory stew she was preparing for their evening meal. She had cornbread baking in the oven.

Patsy laughed softly. "I don't mind, and neither does Gabriel. In fact, Gabriel has told me more than once that he honors Nick and Junius for being such good guardians for us. He says he feels guilty that he has to be away so much, attending to his duties at the fort."

Eulalie noticed that her sister's cheeks had turned a pretty rosy pink, and she wasn't sure if the lieutenant or the kitchen's heat was responsible. She suspected the former. In truth, Gabriel and Patsy seemed to have formed quite a bond. Eulalie prayed that Gabriel wouldn't turn out to be a false hope. So far, he appeared to be solid as a rock, but Eulalie knew better than to assume anything when it came to men.

Or women, either, she supposed. The notion surprised her. But Nick had let slip enough tidbits from his childhood to make her realize that men weren't the only rats in the world.

Damn his stepmother and those rotten stepsisters of his anyhow! If it weren't for them, Nick might have asked Eulalie to marry him ere this.

The thought almost made her drop the plate she held.

Good Lord, she didn't mean that! Did she?

"No," she murmured aloud. "I didn't."

"Beg pardon?"

Realizing she'd spoken out loud, Eulalie hastened to say, "Nothing. Nothing at all."

But it wasn't nothing. It was something, and that something was completely deplorable. Eulalie Gibb did *not* need to be married in order for her life to be complete. Such thinking was not merely old-fashioned, but faulty into the bargain. All Eulalie had to do was look around her if she found herself doubting it. Why, when she lived in New York City, she might have searched for three weeks before she found a husband who was worth his salt. Even here in Rio Peñasco, an outpost of the frontier, where one would expect men to feel a greater responsibility toward their wives and families than men did back East, she could see evidence that such wasn't always the case.

Anyhow, she and Nick Taggart had nothing in common. True, they seemed to share a similar sense of humor. And she'd also discovered that they enjoyed the same books, which had amused her at first. She hadn't believed anyone living out here in the middle of nowhere could read at all, much less read for pleasure. But Nick did. What's more, he shared with her. When he and Junius received a shipment of books from San Francisco, he'd immediately brought over a copy of *The Picture of Dorian Gray* for her and Patsy to enjoy. When they were through with it, Nick had swapped *Dorian* for Arthur Conan Doyle's latest compilation of Sherlock Holmes stories.

She was still mulling over the insanity of falling in love with a man who abominated the very thought of marriage when Nick knocked at the kitchen door, and her heart soared. Stupid heart. To make up for it, she was short with him when she greeted him. In point of fact, she didn't speak at all, but merely glared at him and stepped aside to let him enter.

He eyed her warily as he removed his hat and came inside.

"Good evening, Nick," Patsy called from the stove, where she was scooping stew into a serving dish.

"How do, Miss Patsy?" Taking a wide path around Eulalie, he marched to the front door and hung his hat on the stand he'd built for the purpose.

Eulalie huffed and followed him. Drat the man! Here she was spoiling for a fight, and he was trying to avoid her. He turned away from the hat rack, saw her standing there with her hands on her hips, and he rolled his eyes. Eulalie resented that.

"What did I do now?" he asked in a resigned, world-weary tone of voice.

"What do you mean by that?" she demanded, knowing as she said it that she was being unreasonable.

"You're in a fuss."

"I am *not* in a fuss!"

"Whatever you say." And he walked around her to go into the kitchen.

The evening didn't get any better after Gabriel Fuller arrived. He and Patsy were as cozy as two lovebirds together. Now he, Eulalie thought bitterly, didn't seem to mind showing his affection for a woman. *He* didn't seem to think that all women were sly and untrustworthy. *He* didn't even care that Patsy, the object of his attentions, was badly scarred.

Neither did Nick, but that wasn't the point. The point was that Eulalie Gibb, a woman who until recently, had believed herself solid, sensible, and infinitely sane, had allowed herself to care deeply for a man who didn't care deeply for her. It was a lowering realization, and she didn't like it one little bit.

Unfortunately, she couldn't seem to do anything about it. Her heart refused to be dictated to by her brain. She wished the two would coordinate better. They always had in the past. Neither her heart nor her brain had suffered a single qualm when she'd married sweet Edward Thorogood. She should have thought they'd function better as she grew older and gained experience, but they clearly didn't, drat them.

She endeavored to maintain a cheerful demeanor with Patsy and Gabriel during supper. She couldn't seem to help being cold to Nick, probably because she felt somehow cheated by him—which was ridiculous, and she knew it. Understanding her own culpability only aggravated her further and made her snappish. It occurred to her that Nick couldn't win with her that night, and that made her angrier yet.

The most annoying circumstance of all was that Nick seemed merely amused by her foul mood. He was impeccably polite to her all during the meal, and spoke kindly to Patsy, and was even gracious to Gabriel, which was a departure. Nick generally treated the handsome lieutenant with some degree of condescension.

But the uncomfortable—for Eulalie, although everyone else seemed to enjoy it—meal ended at last, and Nick waited patiently while Eulalie donned her hat and grabbed a shawl. They set out for the Opera House in silence, Eulalie stamping along the dirt road next to Nick, who was perfectly relaxed and comfortable, curse him.

He left her in her dressing room. She got the impression he was eager to escape her bad temper, and she had an irrational impulse to throw something at him.

"What in the world is wrong with you tonight, Eulalie Gibb?" she demanded of her reflection in the mirror.

But she knew the answer to her question. She was feeling persecuted and abused because she'd fallen in love with Nick

Taggart. *How the mighty have fallen,* she mused as she wriggled into her tight sapphire-blue costume with the dyed-to-match ostrich feathers. The blue went well with her eyes, and she harbored the no-doubt futile hope that Nick would be impressed with her looks. Not that he hadn't seen enough of her often enough to know what she looked like. And if he hadn't fallen madly in love with her by this time, she didn't suppose seeing her all gussied up tonight would tip the scale.

Frustrated almost beyond bearing, she hurled one of her high-topped shoes across the room. It banged against the far wall with a satisfying thwack, and she decided that she felt calm enough to perform. She'd allow herself another tantrum later.

Chapter Fourteen

Nick didn't have any idea in the world why Eulalie was mad at him. Not that she needed a reason. Nick had learned long, long ago that women were totally irrational and prone to behave in odd ways for no discernible motive.

This fit of temper on Eulalie's part kind of surprised him, though. In spite of their rocky beginnings—which, he'd finally admitted to himself, weren't entirely her fault—he'd begun to think of her as a woman unlike the others he'd known in his life. And, although he hated to own up to it, it would break his heart to discover she was just like the other members of her sex.

"Hell," he muttered as he trotted down the stairs to the saloon. Violet greeted him warmly.

"Never see you anymore, Nicky," she purred, rubbing her bosom against his arm.

"Yeah, I guess not," Nick said noncommittally. He didn't want to tell Violet that she wouldn't see him again, either, in the way she meant. After having begun his affair with Eulalie, the notion of bedding another woman didn't appeal to him. Which was one more indication that he's lost his mind, he supposed. Shit.

"I miss you, Nick," Violet said wistfully.

"Aw, hell, Violet, you see me all the time." He knocked on the polished mahogany bar and Cletus Bagwell appeared before him. "Sarsaparilla, Cletus."

"I swear Nick, have you stopped drinking, too?" Violet's big brown eyes widened.

Yes, he had, actually, because he wanted to be fully aware of his surroundings while Eulalie was performing. And even while she wasn't. If anything happened to Eulalie—God forbid—Nick was determined that it wouldn't be his fault. "Yeah, I reckon I have kind of given up the booze," he muttered, grabbing the foaming glass Cletus set before him.

Dooley Chivers, his ever-present cigar dangling from the corner of his mouth, moseyed over. Nick suspected Dooley wanted to get Violet mingling again since she wasn't going to make any money off Nick that evening. Or any other girl, he thought with a sigh. Damn, it was pathetic what had happened to him since he met Eulalie. No booze. No other women. Hell, he might as well marry the female and put himself out of circulation forever.

"Evening, Nick."

Horrified by his last thought, Nick didn't respond to Dooley's salutation immediately.

Marry? Him? Nick Taggart? The notion was so appalling, he had to swallow a couple of times before he got his voice to work. "Evening, Dooley," he said at last in somebody else's voice.

"You sick tonight, Nick?"

Nick swallowed again. "What? Sick? Hell, no." He'd gone insane, was what the matter was. Holy Moses. If he were a Roman Catholic, Nick knew he'd be crossing himself.

Dooley subsided against the bar with a satisfied sigh. "Miss Eulalie's got us another packed house for her show tonight," he observed happily. "She's the best thing that's ever happened to the Opera House."

"Yeah," said Nick, taking another long pull at his sarsaparilla and wishing it was whiskey. She was the best thing that had ever happened to him, too, and he didn't know what to do about it.

Marry her?

Nick waited for the involuntary shudder of revulsion that inevitably attacked him whenever he thought about the married state. He waited some more.

Then he downed more sarsaparilla and decided he was in even worse shape than he'd supposed. The shudder never came.

Eulalie gave herself one last look in the mirror, adjusted a shimmering blue feather, dabbed a tiny bit more rouge on her left cheek, picked up the parasol that went with this particular costume, and removed her spectacles. She looked absolutely shameful and, therefore, perfect for her job. "This is it, Eulalie Gibb. Give 'em hell."

She always tried to encourage herself before venturing forth onto the stage of the Opera House. While she'd been performing for her entire life, beginning as a five-year-old child when she danced to wild applause in Vaudeville with her mother and father and aunts and uncles, and progressing through both dramatic and comedic plays in various venues, the Opera House was an entirely different kettle of fish. It didn't frighten her so much any longer, now that she had Nick Taggart guarding her, but she still felt a degree of nervousness before her nightly performances.

She tripped down the back steps that led to the stage and stood aside, waiting for Griswold Puckett to play the opening chord of "The Man Who Broke the Bank at Monte Carlo." She and Griswold always lined up a week's worth of opening numbers on Saturday mornings so that Eulalie didn't have to spend any more time at the Opera House than she had to. Not that she didn't appreciate both her job and Dooley Chivers.

Still, the atmosphere in the Opera House induced a degree of melancholy in Eulalie that she tried to avoid. Her life, while it had eased a good deal since Patsy's arrival, was still a trifle precarious. She didn't want to add dampened spirits into the already volatile mix of influences with which she was struggling.

There wasn't any time to think about it now, however. Dooley announced her name, the audience cheered, and Eulalie could scarcely hear Griswold's chord through the din. Nevertheless, as she was a consummate professional, no matter what the venue, she took her place onstage, the curtain opened, and she burst into song.

The first person she always looked for in an evening was Nick. As Eulalie had expected, he'd stationed himself by the bar, in back of most of her audience, so that he could keep an eye on everyone. Eulalie's heart throbbed for an instant when he winked at her. Damned stupid heart.

Knowing she was an idiot didn't slow her down. With a high kick and a twirl of her lacy blue parasol, Eulalie paraded before the crowd, listening for any abatement of their enthusiasm. She didn't perceive any. Good. Her job was secure for another while, anyway.

After her first number, Griswold played the introductory chords of *Lorena*, a solid old tearjerker that never failed to elicit strong emotions from the drunken patrons of the Opera House. Eulalie doubted whether any were veterans of the Civil War, during which the tune had been introduced, but they all loved it anyway. Eulalie always made sure to put an extra dollop of pathos into the song. It amused her to see how many of her audience had to dab their eyes with the big red bandannas most of these men used as handkerchiefs. She'd never yet been able to make Nick cry with her dramatic renderings of certain songs, but she kept trying.

Lorena passed by without Nick batting an eyelash, and she launched into *The Man on the Flying Trapeze*, a number to which she did several energetic kicks and dance steps. Her audience loved it, although Eulalie noticed that Nick apparently did not. She judged this reaction by the scowl on his face and the hand he kept on his firearm. Well, she thought bitterly, she couldn't help it if he didn't like what she had to do for a living. If he wanted her to quit singing and dancing in front of a bunch of half-drunken cowboys and worse, clad in scandalous costumes, he could jolly well marry her.

Good God! Eulalie almost fainted when that thought crossed her mind. She instantly shoved it out again and concentrated on her performance.

To thunderous applause, *The Man on the Flying Trapeze* ended, and Griswold immediately played the opening chords of a number that always made everyone laugh, *The Cat Came Back*. Eulalie was halfway through the song, and was creeping across the stage in her best imitation of a cat and tipping a wink at her audience—something she did every time she sang this particular number—when she stopped dead in her tracks, stood up straight, and very nearly died on the spot.

Eulalie screeched, *"You!"* Absolute terror engulfed her.

Confusion ensued.

Gilbert Blankenship smiled at her from the second table from the back of the saloon.

Nick's heart almost stopped when Eulalie screamed and ran off the stage. Pandemonium broke out among her audience, with people hollering and whispering, leaping to their feet, looking around, drawing weapons and obviously worried. Since Nick had seen the man to whom Eulalie had reacted so violently, he kept his gaze fixed on him as he drew his

Colt out of its holster and fired off one round into the floor-boards of the poor, abused Peñasco Opera House.

Instantly, every man in the audience save one hit the floor.

"Christ, Taggart," muttered Dooley Chivers.

Nick ignored him. "Quiet, everybody!" He pinned the one man who hadn't had sense enough to flatten himself on the floor—the one who'd frightened Eulalie—with the most vicious stare in his repertoire. He moved toward him, stepping over and around the bodies that were the inevitable result of gunshots in the saloon, keeping his Colt aimed at the bastard's chest. "Who the hell are you?"

The man's eyes opened wide, and he appeared a trifle worried. It was a sensible response, since Nick had every intention of killing him. Nobody frightened Eulalie Gibb and got away with it. Holding his hands up in a gesture of surrender, the fellow said, "Name's Gilbert Blankenship, and I didn't do anything!"

That would probably have been the end of everything right then, given Nick's intentions, except that Sheriff Wallace shoved through the bodies at that moment and put his hand on Nick's arm. "That's enough, Nick. I'll take it from here."

"Now listen here, Sheriff—"

"I'll *handle* it, Nick." Then, in an instant of unexpected brilliance, Sheriff Wallace added, "You ought to go see to Miss Gibb."

Nick was torn. He really, really wanted to kill this Gilbert Blankenship fellow. But he also knew that Eulalie needed him. He said, "Aw, shit," jammed his gun back into its holster, and turned to find Eulalie.

His feeling of alarm and dread intensified as he took the stairs three at a time, and he was running by the time he thundered to a halt before Eulalie's door. It was locked. "Eulalie!" he hollered. "Eulalie, damn it, let me in!"

"Are you alone?"

Sweet Jesus, was that her? The Eulalie Gibb that Nick had known to be as prickly as a cactus ever since she arrived in Rio Peñasco? That squeaky little voice sounded like that of a frightened mouse. "It's me, and I'm alone," he said, attempting to soften his tone, a difficult task, since he still labored under murderous impulses.

"Are you sure?"

What the hell was going on here? "Of course, I'm sure, dammit! Now open the damned door!"

He heard what sounded like someone tiptoeing to the door, and the bolt being drawn back. Then, very slowly, the door opened a scant half inch, and he saw one of Eulalie's gorgeous blue eyes, huge and wary, peek out at him. "It *is* you," she whispered, sounding relieved. "Thank God." And she swung the door wide and threw herself at him.

Nick never minded having Eulalie in his arms, but at the moment he wanted answers even more than he wanted her. He carried her into her room and set her gently on her feet. Still clinging to him, she glanced at the door. "Lock it. Please lock it, Nick."

So he locked it, Eulalie never letting go of his arm, even though he knew a well-placed kick would shatter the frame. But that didn't matter, since he had his Colt with him. And so, he noticed, glancing at the array of weapons Eulalie had set out on her dressing table, did she.

Picking her up and sitting on a chair in the corner and settling her on his lap, Nick said sternly, "All right now, Eulalie Gibb, what the hell's going on?"

"Oh, Nick, I'm so frightened!"

"Yeah, I can tell you are. Why?"

Suddenly Eulalie jumped from his lap. "Oh, Lord! I can't wait around here! I have to get home and warn Patsy! My God, I should have done that first! I was just so scared."

Without even bothering to step behind her screen, Eulalie ripped her costume off and threw it on the floor. "What's the matter with me? I shouldn't have panicked like that!" She halted, holding her street dress in front of her.

Nick, who would have enjoyed the show under any other circumstances, frowned. "Calm down, Eulalie, and tell me what's going on."

"Help me, Nick," she pleaded. "Go warn Patsy. Please! She has to be warned!"

"Damnation!"

His roar stopped Eulalie in mid-panic. She jumped six inches and dropped her dress.

Heaving himself out of his chair, Nick picked it up for her and plopped it over her head. "If it's that Blankenship fellow you're worried about, he's not going anywhere. The sheriff has him."

Eulalie heaved the most gigantic sigh Nick had ever heard and seemed to wilt as he buttoned her dress up the back. "Thank God," she whispered.

And then she turned in his arms and burst into tears. Nick, who had come to expect damned near anything from Eulalie except normal female vapors, was appalled. "Hell, Eulalie, don't do that."

She shoved herself away from him, swiping madly at her wet cheeks. "Sorry. You're right. I can't cave in now. I have to get to Patsy. Help me, please, Nick. Get my stockings and shoes while I take down my hair."

He did as she asked, and noticed that her fingers trembled as they fumbled with the gewgaws in her hair. She seemed unable to control them and ended up yanking feathers, pins, and hair with abandon. He hated to see her beautiful hair treated so disrespectfully, so he caught her hands in his. "Hey, slow down. Why don't you put on your shoes and stockings, and I'll take your hair down."

"Thank you."

Her eyes still dripped, he noticed. This wasn't good. In point of fact, it was very, very bad. Eulalie was having a fit about that man downstairs, and for the first time since he'd met her, was acting like one of his step-relations.

A knock sounded at the door, and Eulalie let out a small shriek.

"It's only me, Miss Gibb." Nick recognized Dooley Chivers' voice. "Are you all right? You durned near give us all a heart spasm when you screamed like that."

Eulalie sucked in a shaky breath. Before she could use it, Nick said, "She's all right, Dooley, but I'm going to take her home now. Is the sheriff still with that Blankenship fellow?"

"Is that the man's name? Yeah, Wallace took him over to his office."

"Thank God," whispered Eulalie, pressing a hand to her heart.

Eyeing her, Nick made a decision. He still didn't know what the hell was going on or who Gilbert Blankenship was in relation to Eulalie Gibb, but he wasn't going to allow the man to bother either Gibb sister if he could help it. And he could. "Say, Dooley, will you send somebody to fetch Junius? Ask him to meet Eulalie and me at her house."

"Junius?" Eulalie said dazedly.

"Sure thing, Nick. Take care of yourself, Miss Gibb."

Nick felt Eulalie swallow before she said, "Thank you, Mr. Chivers." Her voice sounded better. Stronger, although still somewhat strained.

"I'll take care of her," Nick growled. He didn't know if Dooley heard him, but Eulalie did. She reached up and squeezed his hand.

"Thank you, Nick."

"You're welcome."

He'd got all the pins and things out of her hair and she'd put her shoes on by that time. While Eulalie wrapped her hair into a knot and pinned it in place, Nick got her shawl and put it around her shoulders. "Now," said he, "what the hell's going on, Eulalie, and don't leave anything out. You can tell me all about it while I walk you home."

She clung to him like a limpet, a circumstance that worried Nick. This didn't seem like the Eulalie he knew and—God save him—loved. "Please wait until we get home, Nick. This is more Patsy's story than it is mine. And I really don't think I could stand to tell it more than once."

Nick didn't like it, but he agreed. He supposed it was for the best, since he wanted to be alert in case anybody tried to jump them. He'd have scoffed at such a possibility until tonight. Tonight, he wasn't sure of anything any longer, and the moon was new, and it was black as India ink outdoors. "Do you expect this Blankenship bastard to have friends hanging around?"

"Friends?" Eulalie sounded startled. "Why, I . . . don't know. Why?"

Why? Because he was debating whether or not to carry a lantern, given the relative blackness of the night. "Just wondering, is all."

"Oh. Well . . . I doubt it. I don't think he has any friends."

"All right." Still, he opted to forego the lantern. He didn't want to give any lurking villains a better target than he could help, just in case Blankenship had acquired friends since Eulalie had last seen him.

They heard a soft murmur of voices before they saw Patsy and Gabriel Fuller. Nick heard Eulalie suck in a quick breath.

"They're outside," she whispered, as if their being outside was one of the worst things that they could be.

"Probably spooning on the back porch," observed Nick with some satisfaction. He tolerated Fuller ever so much better now that he knew the lieutenant's interest lay with Patsy and not Eulalie.

"But she can't be outside," Eulalie cried softly, speeding up until she was practically dragging Nick behind her—quite a feat, given the differences in their sizes.

"Whatever you say." And Nick scooped her up and covered the last few paces to the Gibb sisters' house more quickly than Eulalie could have done.

Fuller jumped to his feet when Nick suddenly erupted into the backyard and set Eulalie on her feet. "Shoot, Taggart! I thought you were an outlaw or something," growled Fuller. He nodded at Eulalie. "Ma'am."

Patsy, too, was on her feet. She stared at her sister in trepidation, "Eulalie! What's the matter? Why are you home so soon? Why is Nick carrying you?" Nick put her down, and Patsy rushed over and threw her arms around Eulalie, who embraced her back.

Nick eyed the two sisters and felt slightly disgruntled. He really wanted to know what the devil was going on here.

Eulalie released Patsy and held her at arm's length. Watching her fiercely, as if she feared for the state of Patsy's nerves, she said slowly and deliberately, "Gilbert Blankenship has come to Rio Peñasco, Patsy. He was at the—"

She didn't get to finish telling her where Gilbert Blankenship was, because Patsy uttered a sharp gasp and crumpled to the ground.

"Patsy!" Eulalie tried to catch her sister's body, but only succeeded in being borne to the earth along with her.

"Shit," muttered Nick.

He and Fuller both reached for the sisters at the same time. Nick managed to get Eulalie on her feet, and Fuller picked Patsy up and headed to the kitchen door. "Good God," he said under his breath.

Nick couldn't have agreed more.

Eulalie rushed to the kitchen to get some water, as Lieutenant Fuller laid Patsy on the sofa in the parlor. Nick, who felt kind of useless, followed Eulalie. "Anything I can do?"

"I don't think so." She glanced at him and smiled tentatively. "Thank you, Nick. I'm so glad you're here."

And he didn't feel useless any longer.

By the time Patsy recovered from her faint, Junius had arrived. When she did open her eyes, she started crying and wringing her hands and generally behaving in a way that shocked Eulalie, who had always known her sister to be strong and resilient—and thank God for it, or she wouldn't have survived this long. Eulalie's relief was great when Gabriel Fuller wrapped his arms around Patsy and held her during the storm. She was also extremely grateful to Nick, who held her hand as they both watched helplessly.

After what seemed like hours, but was really only minutes, Patsy regained her self-control. Using the huge handkerchief Fuller had offered her, she mopped her cheeks and eyes and blew her nose. "I'm sorry," she said in a sniffly voice. "I was just so . . . shocked. And afraid." She gazed beseechingly at Eulalie. "Oh, Eulalie! Whatever will we do?"

Run? To Eulalie, that seemed like the only option, but she dreaded it. She didn't want to leave Rio Peñasco. She didn't want to leave Nick Taggart.

Anyhow, if Gilbert Blankenship had found them once, he could surely find them again. Unless, of course, the sisters found a town with no newspaper.

She didn't answer Patsy's question immediately, since her thoughts were in such a turmoil.

It was Nick who spoke next, in a voice that snapped with disapproval and suspicion. "Who the hell is that man, Eulalie? And what kind of hold does he have over you?"

Eulalie looked at him with surprise. "Hold? He has no hold over me. Or Patsy, either."

She heard Patsy take a deep, ragged breath. "That's not true, Eulalie. These men deserve to know the truth. I . . . I don't care anymore. They need to know everything if they want to help us." She looked suddenly at Gabriel Fuller, who still held her in his arms. "But maybe they don't. I mean . . . oh, dear, I didn't mean to presume."

Eulalie decided it was time to take charge. It was a demonstration of how much Gilbert Blankenship's presence at the Opera House had rattled her that it had taken her this long to do so. Over the past few years, she'd become adept at directing others. She cleared her throat. "Actually, this is exactly why I made arrangements with Nick. Mr. Taggart." Oh, dear. She really had to get a hold on her nerves. "This possibility, I mean. And to protect us from others, of course."

Nick said, "Of course." He sounded quite sarcastic about it.

"You don't have to make any arrangements with me," declared Fuller, shooting a glower at Nick, who rolled his eyes. "I'll kill the man if you want me to."

"The sheriff might have something to say about that," growled Nick.

"Well . . ." Fuller appeared slightly chagrined. "Maybe so."

"No maybes about it," Nick said. "I already tried to get rid of the bastard, and Wallace stopped me."

The two men glared at each other. Drat it, her control was slipping again. Eulalie said loudly enough to squelch any further comments from the male contingent in the room, "Would you like to tell the tale, or do you want me to do so, Patsy?"

Patsy bowed her head and whispered, "You tell it. I . . . can't."

So once again Eulalie cleared her throat. Then she began the story.

"Very well. As you gentlemen all know—at least Nick and Junius know, because I told them, and I assume Patsy told you, too, Lieutenant—Patsy and I come from a long line of theatrical people."

The men nodded.

"The Gibb Theatrical Company was established by our great-grandfather in 1834, over sixty years ago, in New York City. We practically grew up on stage."

"Yeah, you told me that before," said Nick, scattering her thoughts. Junius reached over and patted his arm, as if to tell him to calm down.

She scowled at him. "That may or may not be the case, Nick, but please stop interrupting me."

He rolled his eyes again, and she went on. "We traveled a lot on the east coast and, of course, performed before all sorts of people, most of whom appreciated our work and enjoyed our performances and left us alone. It was an enjoyable life, and we both got a marvelous classical education."

And that had nothing to do with the matter at hand, she realized when she saw Nick shift restlessly in his chair. She was clearly putting off the hideous revelation, and she told herself to stop it. She took a deep breath. "About three years ago, a man named Gilbert Blankenship saw our company when we put on a play in Pittsburgh, Pennsylvania. He . . . he . . ." She hesitated, trying to think of a way to put such a strange situation into words. Then she decided *to the devil with it* and just went ahead and said it. "He formed an unnatural attachment—really, I suppose one could call it an obsession—for Patsy."

"I didn't even know him," said Patsy in a pitifully wavery voice. "I just began receiving notes and flowers from someone who seemed to believe we had some sort of . . . relationship. A relationship of a romantic nature."

"And you didn't?" Nick lifted his eyebrows, and Eulalie experienced a strong urge to slug him in the solar plexus with her fist. She didn't, primarily because she knew from intimate experience that Nick's solar plexus, if hit by her, would probably break her hand.

"No," she said firmly. "She did not. At first we couldn't figure out who 'G. Blankenship' was. That's how he signed all his notes and letters. Then, gradually, we became aware that the man seemed to be following our company. Everywhere we went, there he was, too. He followed us from Pittsburgh to Philadelphia to Chicago and back to New York. He became more bold, too."

Patsy shuddered and tears leaked from her eyes again. "I swear to you that I did nothing to encourage him. I didn't even realize who he was until he accosted me one day as Eulalie and I were shopping at Macy's Department Store."

"Yes," Eulalie said, the memory making her skin crawl and her mouth tighten. "He stepped right in front of us in the hosiery department and demanded to know why Patsy hadn't answered his last several letters."

"It was awful. He created an embarrassing spectacle. I was . . . alarmed."

"Horrified," Eulalie corrected. "We both were. And we couldn't understand the man's reasoning. He honestly seemed to believe that he had some kind of romantic bond with Patsy. It was uncanny. At first, we thought someone must be playing a bizarre joke on us, although we didn't know why anyone would do so."

"Wait a minute," Nick said, his gaze flipping between the two women. "Do you mean to tell me that this fellow you'd never met believed you *had* met? And, not only that, but that he and Miss Patsy were involved with each other somehow?"

"Yes," said Eulalie firmly. "That's exactly what I mean. It's exactly what happened. He thought that he and Patsy were in love with each other."

Nick said, "Huh," and his frown was a picture of puzzled incredulity.

"It sounds crazy," admitted Patsy.

"It *is* crazy," said Eulalie. "And it's the absolute truth. Gilbert Blankenship is crazy."

"It was . . . horrid," said Patsy.

"It certainly was. I . . . wasn't as alert as I ought to have been," Eulalie said, guilt gnawing at her insides. "I'd recently lost my husband, and I fear I wasn't recovering from my grief as well as I'd expected to."

"How could you have?" asked Patsy gently. "You and Edward were perfect for each other. You had such a warm and special marriage. You were crushed when he died. You're not at fault for anything regarding Gilbert Blankenship. He's the one who's insane. He must be."

"But I should have seen how mad Mr. Blankenship was and tried to do something." She noticed that Nick's frown had intensified for some reason.

"What could you have done?" Patsy said reasonably. "None of us expected him to do what he did."

"What did he do?" asked Fuller.

"Well, a lot of things, really." Eulalie heaved a big sigh. "For one thing, he continued to write and send flowers, but his communications changed. From what had sounded like devoted, if unreciprocated and unasked-for love, he started threatening Patsy with harm if she didn't respond to his communications. He demanded that she go away with him."

"Go away with him?" said Nick.

"Yes. He said he was going to marry her and take her away from the life she lived. He evidently believed that acting was somehow sinful, and that Patsy was being forced to work with the company against her will."

"If all that's true, he really does sound loco," Nick observed.

"It's true, and he is. We went to the police, but they said there wasn't anything they could do." She glanced at each man in turn, and frustration pushed her to raise her voice. "I know it sounds unbelievable. It *is* unbelievable! But it happened exactly as I'm telling it to you. Gilbert Blankenship somehow convinced himself that he and Patsy were in love and that he was supposed to rescue her from the clutches of her family. Her evil family."

Patsy shook her head and uttered a low moan. Fuller squeezed her shoulders and asked softly, "What happened?"

Eulalie suspected Nick anticipated her answer to Fuller's question, because his expression softened and his gaze fixed on Patsy's scarred face. "He broke into our flat one night."

"He broke into your flat?" Fuller asked, evidently dumbfounded.

Eulalie nodded. "Yes. He broke in. I'd been feeling poorly and was in bed. Patsy answered his knock at the door, and he rushed in. He . . . had a knife."

"It was a huge knife," said Patsy. "The police told us later that it was one of those big hunting knives that men use to skin deer. A Bowie knife, one of them called it."

"Jesus," whispered Nick.

"And he said he was going to kill us both because we'd treated him so badly. He said he hated me in particular, because I was the one keeping Patsy from him."

"He would have killed both of us, starting with me," Patsy said, her voice shaking like an aspen leaf in a high wind. "But Eulalie stopped him."

"How'd you do that?" asked Nick, transferring his gaze to Eulalie.

Did she detect a note of approval in his voice? Probably not. "I heard him from my bedroom and tiptoed out to see what was wrong. I saw Patsy turn to run from him, but he caught her and . . ." She swallowed the huge lump that always formed in her throat when she remembered that hellish night. "And he stabbed her. She tried to fight him off, but he kept slashing at her arms and her face, and he . . . he stabbed her in the side and in the stomach." She had to stop speaking and gather her nerves before she could continue.

"I picked up a heavy cast-iron skillet from the kitchen stove. By that time, Patsy was on the floor and he kept stabbing her. Again and again. I hit him over the head with the skillet. But he'd already cut Patsy badly. I didn't get to him in time to save her from that damned knife." She was too caught up in the horror of the past to realize she'd used a bad word before three gentlemen until it was too late. They didn't seem to care. "There was . . . there was so much blood, you see. There was blood everywhere. I've never seen anything like it. It was . . . it was awful."

Gabriel Fuller's arms tightened around Patsy. "My God, the brute!"

"That's putting it mildly," said Eulalie, feeling shivery and cold and wishing Nick would put his arms around her as Fuller was doing with Patsy.

"But didn't you press charges against him?" Nick asked.

"Of course, we did!" Eulalie frowned at him. "The judge gave him six months for breaking and entering our apartment and for aggravated battery against Patsy."

A trio of masculine voices said in an incredulous chorus, "Six months?"

"Six months. For almost murdering Patsy. And that's all."

"But that doesn't make any sense," said Nick.

"No," Eulalie agreed. "It doesn't."

"But why so light a sentence?" asked Fuller.

Patsy, her head hanging and her hands squeezed together in her lap, said, "Who knows?"

Eulalie felt her lips tighten. "*I* know."

Patsy sighed deeply.

"You do?" Nick lifted an eyebrow in inquiry.

"Yes. The judge saw that Patsy was an actress, and he came to the conclusion that she'd led that monster on. That she'd encouraged him somehow."

"And I *didn't!*" Patsy cried, her voice trembling.

"No. She didn't. Neither of us had ever seen the man in our lives until he began . . . stalking Patsy. Like prey in the forest." She sucked in a huge breath and, not for the first or even the hundredth time, felt as if the injustice of it all would make her explode. Because she knew that screaming would only annoy the men, she said merely, "The laws don't favor women. It's terribly unfair."

"I should say not," muttered Fuller.

"And now he's here," whispered Patsy.

"And now he's here," Eulalie confirmed. She shut her eyes and wished Gilbert Blankenship to the devil.

"How'd he find you here in Rio Peñasco?" Nick asked.

Eulalie's eyes popped open again. She couldn't escape from her problems that easily. "I don't know, but I suspect Mr. Benson."

"Bernie?" Nick's brow furrowed. "Why Bernie?"

"He's been sending copies of his newspaper all over the country and its territories. I was afraid one of them might get to Gilbert Blankenship. I can't imagine how else he could have found us. Everyone in the family knows better than to have anything to do with him."

"Hmm." Nick appeared to mull that over for a moment. "I suppose it's not that hard to track somebody if you know where the rest of the family is. Your family doesn't keep itself under wraps. If a fellow tried, he could probably steal mail or whatever."

Patsy's face drained of the little color it had heretofore possessed. Eulalie gazed at Nick, feeling vulnerable and helpless. "I . . . never thought of that." She buried her face in her hands. "Oh, my God, what are we going to do?"

And then she felt Nick's arm go around her, and she didn't feel quite so alone and defenseless.

"I'll protect you, Eulalie. You know that."

"But how?" She lifted her head in time to see a meaningful glance pass between Nick and Gabriel.

"For one thing, you won't be alone. Ever. I'll be by your side every day."

"And I'll be by Patsy's side every night, while you're singing at the Opera House," declared Fuller. "I'll see to it."

"Can you do that?" Patsy asked in a little voice. "What about your duties at the fort?"

Fuller gave a derisive snort. "What duties? Don't worry. I'll be here every night while Miss Eulalie performs. If I can't get away, I'll be sure to send Nash."

"Do you think he'd mind?" Patsy asked.

"Mind?" Gabriel looked at her as if she'd gone mad. "He'd love it."

Patsy blushed a little and said, "How kind."

"And you'll watch them during the day?" Gabriel directed the question at Nick.

"Yes. And so will Junius. They won't be alone for a second."

Chapter Fifteen

Nick and Junius Taggart and Gabriel Fuller were as good as their word. Every day, either Nick or Junius, whichever man could be spared from their smithy, escorted Patsy and Eulalie wherever they needed to go.

And everywhere they went, they met Gilbert Blankenship. When they went to the Loveladys' mercantile store, Gilbert Blankenship was there. When they went to visit Mrs. Johnson and her children, Gilbert Blankenship lingered across the street, watching, watching, watching. Eulalie discovered that constant worrying was an asset to what she had perceived to be a threatening weight problem. Now that Blankenship had found them, she was so nervous, it was all she could do to swallow a bite or two of whatever meal she was supposed to be eating.

Nick spoke to Sheriff Wallace, who spoke to Gilbert Blankenship, but nothing came of it.

"Damn it, Sheriff, the man's stalking those two women as if they were a couple of antelopes and he was a cougar. He shouldn't be allowed to do that."

"I can't make the law, Nick. You know that."

"Shit. There are people in the U.S. of A. who say there are no laws in the damned territory."

"I know that's what folks say, but that's not how I run this town."

"Hell."

So Nick went to the mayor. Mayor Graveside's expression matched his name in the gravity department, but he couldn't offer much assistance to the beleaguered Gibb sisters, either. "I'm sorry, Nick. I reckon I can get a town council meeting together and see if we might could run the feller out of town. Mebbe even tar and feather him, if it comes to that."

"Good idea," said Nick, sensing a bright spot in the dilemma.

"But you know damned well the feller can just wait until dark and come back again. Rio Peñasco's small, but it ain't that small. There's strangers all over the place, especially with the cattle runs starting up."

Nick knew it. Nick hated it.

"Why don't I just gun the bastard down?" he asked Eulalie, Patsy, Junius and Gabriel Fuller one night as they all sat at the Gibbs' kitchen table eating the fine roasted chicken and potatoes Patsy had prepared for supper. "That would solve our problems."

"I'd love it if you would," said Eulalie. "But you'd get into trouble, Nick. Everyone from the sheriff to the mayor to Mr. Chivers would know it was you who killed him."

"Hell, I don't think I care much," mumbled Nick around a bite of potatoes.

"But I do," said Eulalie.

He shot her a speculative look, but didn't continue along that theme.

"I 'spect the gals will be all right 'slong as we keep watching them," observed Junius. "Blankenship can't get at 'em while we're around."

"True," said Fuller. "But . . ." He glanced at Patsy, obviously troubled. "But how long can we keep this up? My captain is . . . well, he's getting a little impatient."

"Oh, dear," murmured Patsy unhappily.

Eulalie shut her eyes and sent a silent prayer to God, begging Him to solve this problem for them. "I'm so sorry to have involved all of you in this mess."

"We don't mind," said Fuller stoutly.

"Hell, no," said Nick.

"Watch your language before the ladies, Nicky," warned Junius.

Nick grinned at his uncle. It was the first time Eulalie had noticed even a hint of humor in his expression since Gilbert Blankenship showed up in town.

"I have an idea," said Patsy, startling Eulalie, who was generally the one with the ideas in the family.

"Oh?" came a chorus of voices around the table.

"If you have to return to your duties at the fort at night, Gabriel, perhaps I can go with Junius and Nick to the Opera House. That way I'll be protected while Eulalie performs."

"But you need your sleep," Eulalie protested.

"I don't mind losing a little sleep if it means staying alive," Patsy said dryly.

Good heavens, Eulalie had never heard her sister sound so caustic. Patsy was the sweetest, dearest of women. Her hatred of Gilbert Blankenship edged up a notch for causing her sister to lose her prior innocence.

Nick and Junius exchanged a glance, then turned to Fuller. "What do you think, Lieutenant?" Nick asked in a neutral voice.

Frowning, Fuller said, "I don't know. I don't like the thought of her in there. In the saloon." Apparently he feared he'd been undiplomatic, because he hastened to add, "Not that there's anything wrong with you performing in the Opera House, Miss Eulalie, especially with the Taggarts watching over you, but . . ."

"I understand," Eulalie assured him. "But if you can't stay

with her, perhaps it would be better for Patsy to remain with me. She can stay in my dressing room."

"Better that she stay with us," said Nick. "Under the eye of everyone. Nobody will let Blankenship do anything to her as long as we can see both of you."

"I have an even better idea." Without so much as a warning, Fuller left his chair, took Patsy's hand, and knelt before her. Her eyes opened so wide, Eulalie feared they might pop out of her head. "If you will do me the honor of becoming my wife, Patsy, you can come with me to the fort and be protected by the entire First Cavalry of the United States Army."

Patsy gasped.

So did Eulalie.

The Taggart men goggled. Nick said, "I'll be damned," in an awed sort of voice.

Her face flushing a becoming pink, Patsy said, "Lieutenant! I . . . I don't know what to say."

Fuller fumbled in the breast pocket of his uniform. Eulalie had noticed something lumpy residing there, but she'd had no idea it was a little jewelry box until Fuller withdrew it, opened it, and showed Patsy a plain gold band with one tiny diamond set in it. "It's not expensive, Patsy. It's nowhere near good enough for you, but . . . well . . . I've thought about this for weeks now, and . . . well, curse it, I love you, and I want to marry you."

Fuller's face was as red as Patsy's by the end of his speech.

Eulalie pressed a hand to her cheek, and felt tears sting her eyes.

Patsy swallowed, hesitated for a moment, and said, "Well, then . . . yes. I will marry you." And she threw herself into Fuller's arms.

Eulalie had to grab her handkerchief from her pocket and

wipe her eyes with it. She was so pleased, she didn't know what to say.

However, Patsy and Gabriel's engagement didn't solve the problem of Gilbert Blankenship, and well Eulalie knew it. After swallowing her tears and taking a deep breath, she said, "I think that's wonderful, and I'm sure you'll be very happy together. But that still leaves the time between now and when you get married and go to live at the fort. So, until that happy event occurs, I suggest we do as Nick suggested and all walk to the Opera House together. Then, when we get there, Nick can escort me to my dressing room, and Patsy can stay with Junius—and Lieutenant Fuller when he's there." She glanced around at her companions. "Is that all right with one and all?"

They agreed that it was. So Eulalie and Patsy cleared the table and washed the dishes—because men didn't do things like that, Eulalie thought darkly—and they all set out for the Opera House.

As they'd expected, Gilbert Blankenship was there, smiling blandly at anyone who came near his table, which was closer to the stage than usual, a circumstance Eulalie didn't like, but couldn't do much about. She did notice that the sheriff was nearby, though, and that made her feel better. She knew Nick had talked to Wallace about Blankenship and, although there was nothing of a preemptive nature that Wallace could do about him, at least he was aware of the potential danger.

"They ought to pass a law," she grumbled as she and Nick climbed the stairs to her dressing room. "Men ought not to be allowed to harass women as that man has harassed Patsy."

"Sounds like you have a point, but I don't know what to do about it."

"I don't suppose there's anything *to* do. As long as women

are treated as second-class citizens with no rights, we're simply stuck with the way things are. It's terribly unfair."

Nick said, "Hmm."

Eulalie suspected he didn't dare say more for fear she'd snap at him. And she might. Ever since Gilbert Blankenship showed up in Rio Peñasco, her temper had been short. But, curse it, she had every right to a short temper. And, curse it, she was also correct about women being treated unfairly by the laws of the land. Which were enacted by men. Curse them, as well.

The show that night went without a hitch. Eulalie was ever so glad to see that Junius and Fuller kept Patsy between them during the entire performance. She was less glad to see Gilbert Blankenship smiling at her throughout her act. She wished she could just shoot the devil herself and be done with it, but she knew she'd only get herself arrested if she did anything so dramatic.

She hated most men because of Blankenship. Except for Nick Taggart, whom she couldn't help but love. And she hated that, too.

And so their waiting game commenced. August had rolled over and died, and September had come to the territory, as it had to everywhere else in the world. However, in the territory, there didn't seem to be much difference between summer and autumn, Eulalie noticed. Patsy and Gabriel Fuller had to wait until the circuit judge rolled around before they could be married, a circumstance neither appreciated. The judge was expected any week now, but the wait was hard on everyone.

"Back East, the nights would be getting a little nippy by this time, wouldn't they?" she asked Patsy one evening as they were getting ready to trek to the Opera House.

"You never know. I guess these are what they call the dog days of summer back East," Patsy murmured. "It might still be warm there. I suppose someone will write when the leaves start to turn."

Eulalie heaved a sigh. "The fall leaves are so beautiful."

"Yes, they are."

"I wonder if the leaves will turn here."

"I don't suppose anyone will know until more trees are planted," Patsy observed.

"True." There were some advantages to living out here in the middle of nowhere, but now that Gilbert Blankenship had come to town, Eulalie was hard-pressed to recall any of them. "Nick tells me there are aspen trees in the nearby mountains that turn yellow in the autumn."

"Hmm."

Patsy didn't seem to mind the inconveniences of the territory. She'd told Eulalie all about her grand passion for Gabriel Fuller, and Eulalie was happy for her, even as her own heart hurt because she didn't have a grand passion of her own.

Well, she *did* have one, but it wasn't reciprocated, which made it not at all worthwhile. In point of fact, the realization that Nick didn't love her as she loved him made her very sad, although she tried her best to disguise the unhappy truth. It wasn't Patsy's fault that she'd found true and abiding love and Eulalie hadn't. Eulalie had once had Edward, hadn't she?

Still and all, she couldn't help but wish Nick loved her as she loved him. However, as her uncle Harry used to say, although he invariably credited the bard for the sentiment, "If wishes were horses, all men would ride."

Every time she thought of that old saw, she detested it more.

★ ★ ★ ★ ★

For the tenth night in a row, with time out for Sunday when Eulalie didn't work, Nick and Junius clustered around Patsy Gibb. Gabriel Fuller had joined them this evening, too. Now Patsy was seated demurely on a chair in the very back of the Rio Peñasco Opera House. Nick was getting sick of this nonsense. If there were any justice in the world, he could just shoot Gilbert Blankenship dead and get it over with. The world would be a better place for it, and so would Eulalie and Patsy Gibb.

He couldn't do that, however, because if he did, *he* was the one who'd get arrested and locked up—and for a worse charge than breaking and entering and aggravated battery, too. For doing the good deed of ridding the world of a cowardly bastard who stalked women and tried to kill them, *he*, Nick Taggart, would be charged and probably convicted of murder. Nick had got it straight from Sheriff Wallace himself, and he knew that Wallace wasn't a man to joke around about stuff like that. In actual fact, Nick had yet to see a single vestige of humor in Rio Peñasco's sheriff, who was remarkably dull for so young a man.

Nevertheless, every night as he stood guard over Patsy in the Opera House and watched Gilbert Blankenship like a hawk, his fingers itched either to shoot the man or wrap themselves around Blankenship's throat and squeeze until the bastard choked to death. It didn't help his overall state of mental health that the woman he loved—God save him— pranced around half naked on the stage in front of Blankenship and every other slavering, lust-crazed man in town. She was so damned good at what she did, Nick was surprised nobody in the audience had grabbed her and made her his wife long ere this. He suspected this was because Eulalie had heretofore been bent upon protecting Patsy. He feared that as soon as Patsy and Fuller married, Eulalie, too, would be taken away from him. The thought made his belly clench and his heart hurt.

Damned bodily organs. They never misbehaved like this before he met Eulalie.

He entertained the idea that perhaps Eulalie might be persuaded to marry him, Nick Taggart. That notion lasted approximately thirty blissful seconds before it popped in his face like a soap bubble.

Hell, she'd never marry him. She was a lady from New York City and Chicago. What would she want with a rough frontier blacksmith like him?

She could do a lot worse, he told himself. And he was right. The unhappy truth was that she could do a hell of a lot better, as well, and Nick knew it.

Things had come to a pretty pass when he, Nick Taggart, a man who knew better, had allowed himself to fall head over heals in love with a woman so far above him, he might as well be reaching for the moon and stars. "Aw, hell," he grumbled, and lifted his mug of sarsaparilla to his lips and took another swig.

"What's the matter, Nick?" asked Junius, who remained his jolly self in spite of the peril threatening the Gibb sisters. Junius never let himself worry about anything. If crises arose, he dealt with them, but he didn't allow them to ruin his mood until necessity claimed his attention. Nick wished he could cultivate Junius's attitude.

"Nothin'. Just getting sick of this waiting game, I reckon."

Patsy, who kept her right hand firmly ensconced in that of Gabriel Fuller during these nightly vigils, patted Nick's arm with her left—the one with the ring on it. "I'm so sorry we're putting you through this, Nick. It's unfair to all of you."

"Not your fault," grunted Nick, feeling guilty. "It's that

fellow's." He tilted his head toward Blankenship, whose table this evening was even closer to the stage than it had been the night before. Nick wasn't sure if Blankenship's position in the room meant anything to anyone except himself, Eulalie, and the rest of their little group. He knew for a fact that Blankenship made Eulalie as skittish as a newborn colt—and he also knew that she took her foul mood out on Nick, who didn't deserve it. Still, none of this was her fault, either. Every ill that had recently visited the Gibbs and the Taggarts and Fuller could be laid directly at the feet of Gilbert Blankenship.

Which brought him back to the problem of not being able to rid the world of Blankenship, who was a louse and a menace and wasn't an asset to anybody or anything. Didn't seem fair somehow.

So he kept watching. He'd watch Eulalie for a while, then he'd turn his attention to Blankenship. Then he'd watch Eulalie some more. It was a stupid way to spend his nights, but there didn't seem to be any help for it. He absolutely hated feeling helpless.

On a Thursday night in mid-September, the house lights went down, Griswold Puckett played the opening chords of a bouncy melody called *The Sidewalks of New York*, Eulalie started singing in her beautiful soprano voice, Nick took a gulp of sarsaparilla, and Gilbert Blankenship rose to his feet and calmly shot Eulalie Gibb.

Patsy screamed. Junius bellowed. Gabriel Fuller leapt to his feet and whipped his gun from its holster. Bedlam broke out in the Opera House.

Nick's heart stopped beating for a second, and then soared into his throat. Without thinking, he raced to the stage, fairly throwing men out of his way to get there. He didn't even think about Patsy or Gilbert Blankenship or anyone else. He only needed to get to Eulalie. Her scream had ripped a hole in his heart, and he prayed as he'd never prayed before, that the scream meant she still lived.

"Eulalie!" he bellowed, thrusting Dooley Chivers aside. *"Eulalie!"*

She lay as still as a stone where she had fallen. Since there was hardly anything to her costume, Nick saw that the bullet had hit her leg. She was bleeding like a stuck pig, but a leg wound probably wasn't fatal. Even as he grabbed his bandanna and wadded it up in order to press it against the wound to stanch the bleeding, he thanked God for small favors.

"Doc!" he called out, his thundering voice cutting through the hubbub like a hot knife through butter. *"Doc!* Get the hell over here!"

"I'm comin', Nick. No need to swear."

Nick glanced up from Eulalie's leg to see Dr. Canning, and he thanked God again.

"What happened?" Eulalie's strained voice cut through the red haze in Nick's brain, although not enough to affect the tone of his voice or soften his choice of words.

"That filthy bastard shot you."

"Oh." Her face was stark white under the lights, which Dooley Chivers had caused to be turned up. "It hurts."

"Yeah. Well, that's what happens when you get shot. It hurts."

His heart hurt, too, it hammered so hard in his chest, but he supposed he might have been a little rough on her when she frowned at him. "There's no need to take that tone with me, Nicholas Taggart."

"Sorry."

The doctor, a burly man who was puffing by the time he climbed the stairs onto the stage, tapped Nick on the shoulder. "Move aside, Nick. Let me see what's to be done here."

"Patsy?" Eulalie asked in a weak voice. "Is Patsy all right?"

"Patsy?" Nick said as if he'd never heard the name before. "Patsy." Then he remembered. "Aw, hell."

Although every sinew in his body cried out to hold Eulalie, he surged to his feet and looked out over the crowd. He didn't see Patsy. He didn't see Junius. He didn't see Gabriel Fuller. The relief he felt when he realized this phenomenon was probably due to the men having hustled Patsy out of the Opera House and to her home suffered a quick death.

Gabriel Fuller, his face as white as Eulalie's, shoved the batwing doors open and stared at Nick, who still stood on the stage. Nick could scarcely hear Fuller when he said the words, but he understood them just fine. "He's got her."

Nick hovered over the table on which Eulalie lay. Doc Canning had given her a hefty dose of laudanum and sterilized his instruments, and was now digging the bullet out of her leg, while Nick watched, tense as a spooked jackrabbit, and wishing it had been he who'd taken the bullet instead of Eulalie.

"She's going to be all right, Nick," Dr. Canning said for approximately the five hundredth time. "Stand back a little, will you? You're in my light."

"Shit," said Nick.

Gabriel Fuller sat in a chair against the far wall, his head in his hands, looking as if he'd just lost the woman he loved—which he had. Every time Nick glanced at him, he harbored the no-doubt treacherous wish that Blankenship had shot Patsy instead of Eulalie. That he'd shot *anyone* instead of Eulalie, actually.

A light knock came at the operating-room door and Junius

opened the door and slipped in. Fuller lifted his head from his hands for the first time since they'd gathered in the doctor's office, and he sent Junius a hopeful look.

Junius nodded. "I found out which way they went. Toby Beech says he saw him throw her on a horse and climb up behind her. They headed out towards the draw."

Fuller leapt to his feet. "What are we waiting for? Let's go after them!"

Junius put a steadying hand on his shoulder. "Hold your horses, young feller. The sheriff's getting some men together. We'll have us a posse and ride out to get your lady back and arrest Blankenship, don't worry."

"Don't worry?" Fuller's voice was chock-full of scorn.

"We'll get her back, son," Junius assured him. "And at least Blankenship can be arrested now." He glanced at Nick. "Nicky? You comin'?"

Nick cast an anguished glance at the table where Eulalie's still form lay, covered from neck to hips by a white sheet. The doctor had cut her fishnet stocking away from her leg and looked up from his work with a sour expression on his chubby face. "Yeah, Nick. Go do something useful, will you? You're just getting in my way here."

"Aw, hell," muttered Nick. With one last glance at Eulalie—he wished he dared kiss her, but didn't want to do so in front of the other men—he reached for his hat, which he'd flung on a nearby table, and slammed it onto his head. Marching with purpose toward his uncle and the door, he growled, "Let's go."

So they went.

Chapter Sixteen

The night wasn't as black as Gilbert Blankenship's filthy soul, but it was doing a fair imitation of that condition when the posse from Rio Peñasco left town and headed out toward Black Water Draw, where it was assumed Blankenship had taken Patsy, at least to begin with. For all anyone knew, he might have gone several yards and cut off in another direction, although that was doubtful. Gilbert Blankenship hadn't been in Rio Peñasco long enough to understand the terrain. The moon helped minimally in guiding the posse's path, as it was relatively full. Clouds scudded across the sky, however, often obliterating both moon and stars.

Since Junius and Nick owned one horse between them, Nick, who was bigger than Junius by a hair or two, rode Claude. A Belgian draft horse, Claude was by far the largest horse in Rio Peñasco. Junius borrowed a horse from Sheriff Wallace, and Nick prayed he wouldn't break the poor animal's back. Both Nick and Junius were too large to be especially elegant horsemen, but they could ride as well as they needed to. Nick was grateful for Claude, who was not merely large, but a placid, steady creature.

They didn't dare force their horses to a gallop. The landscape was far too treacherous to consider doing anything so foolish. If there was one thing they didn't need it was for a horse to snap its leg in a gopher hole. Nick's nerves leaped and skipped like the ballerina dancers his stepmother had forced him to watch in Galveston a million years ago, only not nearly so gracefully.

Fat lot of good he'd done tonight in the protection department. Nick castigated himself for a good quarter mile before becoming aware of Junius beside him, whistling softly. He cast his uncle a reproving glare. "Hush, Junius. We don't want to warn the bastard we're on his trail."

"Hell, Nicky, don't you think he's going to hear the horses? My whistle ain't gonna do no harm."

"It's harming my nerves, dammit," growled Nick.

Junius stopped whistling.

As they drew closer to Black Water Draw, Nick rode his giant horse up to the sheriff. "If he's in the draw, we probably better dismount, Wallace. If we ride in all at once, we're going to spook him, and God alone knows what he'll do to Miss Gibb then."

The sheriff looked as if he didn't care to have Nick preempt him in the suggestion department, but he couldn't very well fault Nick's logic. "All right. I'll send Sandy on ahead to see if they're in there." Sandy Peete was the smallest, slyest fellow in Rio Peñasco. What's more, he'd had lots of practice in the spying arena, having spied for the Union during the Civil War when he was no more than a lad. "If he's smart, he won't camp there."

"He's not smart," said Nick. "At least not about the territory."

The sheriff said, "Huh," and beckoned to Sandy.

Nick grabbed Sandy's arm before he set off on his little pony. "Be quiet, Sandy. Don't spook the bastard."

Sandy, who looked like an elf next to Nick, turned a scornful glance Nickward. "I know what I'm doing, Nick Taggart."

Nick heaved a sigh. "I know, I know. Sorry."

But he didn't like it that it was Sandy who was checking out the draw and not Nick himself. He didn't trust anyone to have the same sense of urgency about this matter that he possessed. He knew it wasn't Eulalie with Blankenship, but he also knew that if anything happened to Patsy, Eulalie would never forgive any of them—including himself. He didn't think he could stand having Eulalie hate him. She might never love him, but if she ever found reason to detest him, Nick had a feeling he'd never recover fully from the blow.

As the posse milled about on the desert, waiting for a report from Sandy Peete, Nick figuratively chewed his nails. His heart hammered away in his chest like a woodpecker after a bark beetle, and his nerves tingled and twanged like banjo strings breaking. He was just about to tell the sheriff he was going after Peete, when Sandy emerged out of the blackness. Nick expelled a huge gust of air and went to intercept Sandy before the sheriff got to him. "Well?" he demanded, trying to keep his voice down.

"Where's the guy from?" Peete asked. "The idiot's built himself a big fire in the middle of the wash. Didn't he think anybody would be after him?"

"Hell, how should I know?" growled Nick, although relief nearly knocked him over backwards. "He's crazy, I think. And he's from back East."

"Ah." Sandy nodded. "I reckon that explains it."

"All right," said Sheriff Wallace, attempting to take control of his posse. "We'll have to dismount and a few of us go in and get the girl back."

"I'm going," said Nick, his voice announcing his purpose and daring Wallace to deny him the privilege.

"So am I," announced Gabriel Fuller, likewise adamant.

"Reckon I'll go, too," said Junius.

The sheriff glared at the three men, removed his hat from

his head and slapped his leg with it, and said, "Aw, hell." But he knew better than to argue. "All right. Sandy, lead the way."

So Sandy led the way. It was slow going, since the men had to maneuver over rocks, cacti and boulders to get into the draw, and neither Nick nor Junius were as slim and snaky as Sandy Peete, nor were Gabriel Fuller and the sheriff.

Nick was first to top the rise encircling the draw. Using Sandy's pointed finger as a guide, he tentatively lifted his head to peer into the draw. By damn, Peete was right. There, big as day, were Patsy Gibb, pressed back against a boulder and hugging her knees to her chest, while Gilbert Blankenship added fuel to the fire.

Turning, Nick pressed a finger to his lips. "I'm going to try to creep down in there."

"Be careful, Nicky," Junius advised. "Don't forget he's got a gun and ain't afraid of usin' it."

"I won't forget." How could he? Eulalie still lay wounded in Doc Canning's office, and he, Nick, wasn't there to supervise. The sooner Blankenship died, the sooner Nick could get back to the woman he loved.

"I'm the sheriff, Taggart," Wallace reminded him. "I should be the one going in there."

He didn't press his point when Nick looked at him. Even Sheriff Wallace, who could be stubborn and humorless upon occasion, knew better than to buck Nick Taggart when he looked like that. The sheriff held up his hands in surrender and said, "Shit. All right, Nick. Just don't blame me if the son of a bitch shoots you."

"I won't." And Nick started slithering down the side of the hill toward the campsite. He heard someone behind him and turned, determined to kick whoever it was in the head. When he saw Gabriel Fuller on his belly, slithering along in the same direction, he changed his mind. After all, Fuller had a stake in Blankenship, too. A big one.

It was slow going. For one thing, even though it was dark, they tried to keep themselves hidden behind rocks and bushes—and the bushes in the area were low-growing shrubs like creosote and prairie grass and cacti. For another, the ground was rough and rocky, and it took a good deal of effort to keep from dislodging pebbles and starting landslides. Fortunately for both men, Blankenship was unfamiliar with the hazards of territorial life, and Nick figured he couldn't be expected to differentiate between the progress of a man and, say, that of a startled jackrabbit or lizard.

Nick was approximately fifty or so feet away from the fire and felt as if he'd been crawling over rocks and spiky plants for a century at least, before he could make out the words being spoken by Patsy and Blankenship. He heard Patsy's voice first.

"This is insane, Mr. Blankenship. Don't you realize I want nothing to do with you?" Her voice sounded ragged, as though she'd worn it out screaming or crying. "And why did you shoot Eulalie?" Nick heard her sob. "Oh, why did you do that?"

"She tried to keep you from me," Blankenship said calmly. "Naturally, I had to get rid of her."

"But I don't want to be with you!"

"Don't be silly. I'll take care of you better than anyone else ever could."

"Take *care* of me!" Patsy cried. "You nearly killed me!"

Nick watched as Blankenship turned from the pile of wood he'd been stacking and looked at Patsy. Nick supposed he'd been adding to his supply for several days, because wood wasn't easy to come by out in this part of the world. So. Evi-

---

dently, the bastard had planned this abduction in advance. He clearly didn't know what he was doing, or he'd have developed his scheme more fully. He hadn't taken into account the territory itself or the territorials who inhabited it.

"That was punishment. You were misbehaving and had to be taught a lesson."

"You're crazy," Patsy whispered.

"That's not nice." Blankenship frowned at her. "I don't want to have to punish you again, Miss Patsy. I want us to have a nice, happy life together."

"A happy life? You're . . . you're insane."

Blankenship set the log he'd been holding aside and reached into his scabbard to withdraw a knife. "It's not nice to call people names." He felt the knife with his thumb. "I don't want to have to punish you again."

Patsy pressed her head to her knees, evidently deeming it prudent to stop calling Blankenship names. Nick agreed, although he hoped to be able to tell the bastard exactly what he thought of him soon.

"Do you know what they do out here to things they want to mark as their own?" Blankenship asked pleasantly.

Patsy shook her head.

"They brand them. I've decided the best way to keep you in line and to make everyone understand that you belong to me is to brand you."

Nick heard Fuller's hiss of breath and poked him with his elbow. They couldn't afford to show themselves yet; they were still too far away. And Blankenship had not merely his knife, but a gun as well.

Patsy lifted her head and gaped at Blankenship. "Brand me? You're going to *brand* me?"

"Yes. I thought I'd do it with this." He held out a piece of metal. "It's a pretty shape. A cloverleaf. I think it's supposed to be a seal. You know, in wax. But I had it soldered to this piece of metal to use as a brand. I think it's a good idea."

"He's a lunatic," whispered Fuller.

"Shh," said Nick.

They'd worked their way to the bottom of the hill. Nick slowly and carefully stood up. He reached out to help Fuller do likewise. Blankenship, wearing thick leather gloves, was holding his "brand" to the fire.

Worried and looking as if she were about to faint or break down or both, Patsy slowly got to her feet, too. "What are you doing?" she asked.

It looked fairly obvious to Nick, but he supposed there was no harm in keeping Blankenship talking. If he were involved in conversation with Patsy, he'd be less likely to hear Nick and Fuller sneaking up on him. Nick hoped like fire Fuller wouldn't decide to shoot Blankenship. Patsy was too damned close to take a chance on that.

"Why, I'm heating my branding iron, of course," said Blankenship.

"You don't need to do that," said Patsy. "I'll go with you without that."

"Oh, but this is necessary. You see, this way everyone will know that you're mine, and they won't try to steal you away again."

"That bastard," muttered Fuller in Nick's ear.

Nick couldn't fault him for the sentiment, but he wished the man would keep quiet. No wonder the army had undergone so much trouble with the Indians, if they were all this noisy on secret assignments. It looked to Nick as if Blankenship was about satisfied with his branding iron, which was glowing red in the fire.

They weren't going to have much time. Nick and Fuller were still at least twenty feet away from Blankenship and

Patsy. Nick wished Patsy would do something instead of merely standing there, awaiting her fate. Eulalie would have killed Blankenship by this time—or at least tried to. But Eulalie was one of a kind, Nick supposed, and Patsy couldn't be faulted too much for playing the role generally assigned to women in society. Which meant she aimed to continue standing there like a helpless lamb while Blankenship, the wolf, stalked her.

"Ah, that looks about right." Blankenship stood, admiring the glowing end of his makeshift branding iron. "I think the thigh would be a good place to brand you. And perhaps your arm, as well."

Finally, Patsy decided to take her fate into her own hands. She shrieked, "You're a maniac!" and she rushed away from the boulder against which she'd been huddled. About damned time, Nick thought.

Startled, Blankenship said, "What are you doing?"

By that time, Patsy had skirted the fire and retrieved a big pot. In the meantime, he and Fuller had picked themselves up and were running like stampeding cattle towards Blankenship.

"Drop it!" Nick hollered. He retrieved his Colt and tried to aim and run at the same time.

Blankenship whirled around. His eyes widened, and he dropped his branding iron and fumbled at his waist for the gun he'd stuck into his belt.

"Halt!" roared Fuller, who had already drawn his own gun.

"*Gabriel!*" shrieked Patsy. Nick didn't mind that she ignored him. He understood.

"Stay where you are!" cried Blankenship, having found his gun, which he now aimed at Nick and Fuller.

Because neither man was a fool, they both stopped. Nick,

panting slightly said, "Drop it, Blankenship, and let the lady go. She doesn't want to go anywhere with you."

"Nonsense," said Blankenship, and Nick could scarcely credit the fact that he sounded honestly offended. "We're going to get married. We've been planning this for months."

Oh, brother, now what? "Then put the gun down, and let's talk about it, all right?" The absurdity of the situation didn't escape Nick. Here he and Fuller were holding guns on Blankenship, and Blankenship was holding a gun on them. In the meantime, Patsy cowered in the background. Stupid, stupid, stupid.

But wait. Patsy wasn't cowering any longer. In point of fact, she had moved. Nick didn't want to stare, but he was pleased to note that she seemed to be sidling around behind Blankenship while he was occupied in holding Nick and Fuller at bay. While her action might well prove useful, at the moment, it wasn't at all, since if either Nick or Fuller pulled the trigger, Patsy might well be on the receiving end of a bullet. He decided to try to keep Blankenship's mind on other matters.

"I understand you know the Gibb sisters from Chicago, Blankenship." He tried to keep his tone conversational.

"Yes, that's where we met."

"Is that where you cut her up?" snarled Fuller.

Nick hissed at him to shut up. He didn't want the man to get riled.

Fuller, clearly too irate to take hints, didn't. "What kind of man cuts a woman with a knife? A coward, is what kind. Put the damned gun down!"

"Oh, I see," said Blankenship, focusing his attention on Fuller. "So you're the one who's been trying to steal my Patsy. You're an idiot if you think you can break our bonds of love."

Patsy, as pale as a frosty window, had made her way behind Blankenship. Now, obviously straining weak muscles, she lifted the pot, a cast-iron number that must weigh a ton. Nick prayed for her, even as he wished the noble lieutenant would stop being so damned noble and shut up.

"Cut it out, Fuller," he muttered out of the corner of his mouth.

The lieutenant shot a malignant glance at Nick, as if he didn't know why he should do any such thing.

"You're both wrong about Patsy and me. We love each other. We're going to get married. And I'm going to mark her, so that no one will ever doubt that she belongs to me."

At that moment, Patsy made her move. With a stumbling rush, she lifted the pot and bashed Blankenship on the shoulder with it. Nick figured she'd been aiming at his head, but didn't quite make it. It didn't matter. Blankenship staggered sideways, and his gun discharged into the dirt. Patsy, exhausted by her recent efforts, sank to the ground along with her pot, which made a dull thump as it hit the dirt.

Both Nick and Lieutenant Fuller fired at the same time. Nick didn't know whose bullet connected, or if both did, but Blankenship howled out in pain and fell into the fire, where he continued to scream.

"Shit," Nick murmured. He wanted the fellow dead, but he was a humane man and didn't care to see even vile creatures like Blankenship suffer unnecessarily. Before he was able to ascertain whether or not Blankenship might be rescued, another shot rang out, and the man fell back into the fire, limp as a rag. Dead, Nick presumed. When he turned his head to look, he saw Fuller stuff his gun back into his holster and head for the crumpled form of the woman he loved. Then, as the lieutenant and Patsy embraced, Patsy weeping pathetically against Fuller's formerly blue uniform, Nick pondered the spectacle of Gilbert Blankenship, roasting in the fire he'd built in order to brand Patsy Gibb. *Brand* her, for God's sake.

A small avalanche announced the arrival of the posse. "Jesus, Nick, we were watching the whole thing. We didn't dare shoot for fear of hitting the girl."

"Yeah, me, too," said Nick as the smell of roasting meat filled the air.

"God, we'd better get him out of the fire," said Wallace, wrinkling his nose and looking uncertainly at Blankenship's legs, which were the only parts of him not being cooked.

"I expect you're right," said Nick. "You want to get one leg and I'll get the other?"

"Yeah, I reckon."

So they hauled the remains of Gilbert Blankenship out of the fire, and Nick decided he'd never look at the annual Rio Peñasco barbecue supper the same way again.

The posse didn't bother taking Blankenship back to town. For one thing, they didn't want to wait until he quit smoldering, and for another, none of them had any interest in exerting so much effort on so puny a specimen of humanity as he. Therefore, using tools Blankenship himself had brought, they dug a shallow grave, rolled him into it, and covered him up with dirt. So that there would be no possibility of any sparks escaping the hole and igniting prairie grasses, however unlikely such a contingency might be, they rolled a few boulders over him.

"I expect those rocks won't keep out the coyotes," muttered Nick.

"Well, that's all right," said Junius in his usual jolly mood. "By the time they dig him up, he'll have gone out."

When the posse rolled the last boulder over the grave, Nick's nerves had begun screeching like seven untuned fiddles, he was in such a state about Eulalie, who, as far as he knew, was still under the knife in Rio Peñasco. Before the posse reorganized itself to ride back to town, he grabbed his uncle.

"Let's go, Junius. I've gotta make sure Canning isn't slicing off her leg."

Junius patted him on the back. "She'll be all right, Nicky. Canning might be slow, but he's a good-enough doc."

"For Rio Peñasco," Nick observed sourly. He knew good and well that Canning had never gone to medical school. Canning, like most of the doctors who set up practice in the western territories, had got his training by serving in the United States Army. He supposed that might give Canning experience in digging out bullets, but he didn't like to think of his Eulalie suffering under Canning's knife.

"Well, sure," agreed Junius, as if that went without saying.

Nick mounted Claude, and Junius mounted the poor horse he'd borrowed from the sheriff, and the two took off towards Rio Peñasco before the rest of the men knew what they were about. The sheriff didn't try to stop them, which Nick considered sensible of him.

Eulalie knew she was home when she awoke, because she recognized the pretty curtains Mrs. Sullivan had sewn for her and the chenille bedspread she'd bought from the Loveladys' store. But Nick wasn't there. And neither was Patsy. Rather, she recognized the stocky form of Dr. Canning, who was placing a bottle of something on her night table. Her leg hurt like thunder, too.

Where was Nick? Eulalie wanted Nick. She wanted him so badly, and she felt generally so horrid, that she very nearly succumbed to tears.

"Oh! She's awake."

Who the devil . . . ? Eulalie turned her head and frowned at where the words had come from. Was that Mrs. Johnson? She couldn't tell for sure because she wasn't wearing her spectacles. "Louise?" she croaked, alarmed when she heard her voice. Was she sick? Is that why she was lying in her bed with the doctor in residence?

And then it all came back to her.

"Gilbert Blankenship," she muttered, her heart sinking and beginning to ache along with her thigh, where he'd shot her. He'd *shot* her!

"I'm afraid so, dear." Mrs. Johnson placed a cool, damp cloth on Eulalie's forehead.

Eulalie appreciated the woman's ministrations, but she wanted information more than she wanted damp rags. "Patsy?" she whispered, hoping she wouldn't have to add any more words to her question, since she felt remarkably weak. She supposed that happened when a body got shot. Damn Gilbert Blankenship to perdition.

Mrs. Johnson didn't answer. Eulalie, who had allowed her eyelids to drift downward, opened them again instantly. "Louise?"

With a sigh, Mrs. Johnson said, "The men went after them. I'm sure she'll be fine, and they'll bring her back here safe and sound."

"He got her?"

"I'm afraid so, dear, but you know Nicky. He and that lieutenant feller and the sheriff and a whole posse rode out of here a couple of hours ago. Junius Taggart found out which way the man rode with your sister. I'm sure the posse will prevail. They know their way around out on that desert, you know, and I can't feature that feller who snatched Miss Patsy is any match for them."

Perhaps. But it only took one bullet. Or a well-placed knife thrust, and both Louise and she knew it. Eulalie couldn't help it; she started crying. She'd tried *so* hard to keep her sister safe, and this is what it had come to. Gilbert Blankenship, who had been the plague of both their lives ever since he'd seen Patsy on stage three years earlier, had come back to haunt them. And he now had Patsy.

Louise Johnson tutted and patted her hand. "There now, Eulalie, don't cry. Nicky won't let any harm come to your sister. He wouldn't dare."

Dr. Canning came to Eulalie's bedside and loomed over her. "Listen to Louise, Miss Eulalie. Nick Taggart will bring her back. And you have to stop worrying, or you'll make yourself sick. We have to watch out for infection when it comes to bullet wounds. Won't do to allow yourself to get weak. Here. I'm going to give you another little dose of laudanum."

Eulalie thought about protesting, then realized that to do so would not merely keep her in pain, but would be for naught. She couldn't do a blessed thing to help her sister now. She'd done what she could already, and it hadn't been enough. She whispered, "Very well," and resigned herself to sleep. Sleep was better than wakefulness right now. Oblivion was what she needed. Sweet unconsciousness.

She prayed she wouldn't dream.

Nick burst through Eulalie's front door, and was instantly brought up short. The whole damned parlor was filled to bursting with citizens of Rio Peñasco. What's more, they were all on their knees, and the preacher, Reverend Huffington, was in the process of exhorting God to help Eulalie heal and help the posse find Gilbert Blankenship and bring Patsy back safely.

"Lord, in your infinite mercy, save our sister Eulalie Gibb!" he cried in his most portentous tones. "Father in heaven, allow our sister Eulalie to heal completely and rejoin your flock! And bring Miss Patsy back to us, Lord!"

Nick couldn't argue with the sentiments, but he didn't have the patience to hang around in the parlor praying while who knew what agonies Eulalie was suffering. He skirted the kneeling mob and made his way to her bedroom, where he tried for silence as he opened the door and stuck his head around the jamb.

Louise Johnson saw him first, and her face broke into a stunning smile for a moment, before the smile faded and she looked a question at him. "Patsy?" she mouthed.

"She's safe," said Nick in a rumbling whisper. He'd never been much good at whispering, his voice being as big as the rest of him.

"Thank God," whispered Mrs. Johnson.

Carefully closing the door behind him, Nick tiptoed into the room, at which activity he was about as successful as he was when attempting to whisper. Doc Canning glanced over his shoulder at him, saw his face, which probably looked as scared as he felt, and gave him a small smile. Nick felt moderately encouraged.

"She's doing pretty well, Nick," said Canning. "The wound was clean, and the bullet came out easily enough. I disinfected the wound, and I don't think the bullet was in there long enough to poison her. If we're careful and infection doesn't set in, she'll be right as rain in a few weeks."

Nick had made it to Eulalie's bedside by this time, and was looking down upon her with a heart full to bursting. At the doctor's words, he shut his eyes and thought, *thank God, thank God, thank God.* Naturally, because he was a man and a blacksmith and all, he didn't say the words aloud.

Nevertheless, he was ever so grateful, both to God and to Doc Canning, whose hand he grabbed now, startling the man into dropping a tongue depressor he'd been about to stick into his black bag. "Thanks, Doc. You did a good job."

"For Pete's sake, Nick, be careful." But Dr. Canning looked pleased as he stooped to pick up his errant tongue depressor.

Nick grabbed a chair from Eulalie's dressing table and sat on it. "I'll just sit with her for a while." His eyes dared either the doctor or Mrs. Johnson to challenge his right to do so.

"Well . . ." Mrs. Johnson appeared doubtful.

"I'm staying here," growled Nick.

"Nick?"

The tiny voice startled all of them. Nick jumped a yard and instantly fell to his knees beside the bed. He grabbed Eulalie's hand. "You're awake," he said.

Eulalie said weakly, "Patsy?"

"She's all right. Fuller's got her, and he's bringing her back right now."

"Thank God," whispered Eulalie.

"And Patsy herself. She conked Blankenship over the head with a big pot. Well, technically, I reckon she got his shoulder, but . . ." He shut up, figuring nobody needed to know all the details.

"And Blankenship?"

"Dead."

Eulalie's eyelids fluttered. "Thank God."

Nick supposed it wasn't very nice to thank God for someone's death, but he didn't blame Eulalie one iota. He said, "Yeah. He's buried in Black Water Draw."

"How appropriate."

He grinned and squeezed her hand. Glancing around, he decided it was time for the doctor and Mrs. Johnson to skedaddle. What he had to say to Eulalie next was embarrassing and he didn't want witnesses.

But he'd made up his mind, as he and Junius rode back to town as fast as they could, given the blackness of the night and the perils of the desert, that he was sick of the way things were. As much as the notion of marriage made his stomach hurt, still more did the notion of losing Eulalie make his heart hurt. He aimed to make certain there were no more doubts in anybody's mind about his union with Eulalie. He was tired of other men ogling her as she pranced about half naked on that damned Opera House stage. She was going to stop doing *that* from now on.

Besides, her sister was going to marry that idiot Fuller, and Nick feared that Eulalie might decide to move back to New York or Chicago or somewhere equally far away from him, if he didn't do something radical to secure her presence in Rio Peñasco and, therefore, his life. He knew it sounded dramatic, and drama made him sick and reminded him of his stepmother, but the truth was that he didn't think he'd survive if he lost Eulalie. If he could help it, he wasn't ever going to find out.

Therefore, he intended to propose marriage to her. Right here. Right now—or soon as he got rid of the other people in the damned room. He scowled at Mrs. Johnson and Dr. Canning as he resumed his chair. "I'll take over now," he said.

Doc Canning rolled his eyes. "You aren't a doctor, Nick."

Nick heated up his glower some. "Neither are you."

"Tsk," said Mrs. Johnson. She said it with a smile, though, and took the doctor's arm. "Let's leave Nicky and Eulalie alone for a minute or two, Doc. I have a feeling Nick has something important to say to her."

The doctor appeared puzzled for a second, but Mrs. Johnson yanked him toward the door. Nick blessed the woman as a saint.

As soon as the door closed behind the doctor and Mrs. Johnson, Nick opened his mouth to demand that Eulalie marry him. A gentle snore smote his ears, and he shut his mouth again with a click of teeth. He stared at his beloved.

The damned woman was asleep!

He muttered, "Aw, hell," crossed his arms over his chest, sat back in the stupid little dressing-table chair, and decided he'd just wait. But he'd be damned if he'd leave this room until she agreed to marry him.

Chapter Seventeen

Three weeks after Gilbert Blankenship shot Eulalie and died as a result, Eulalie and Nick, Patsy and Gabriel Fuller, along with Junius Taggart, Sheriff Wallace and Mrs. Johnson and several other leading citizens of Rio Peñasco, stood on the boardwalk outside the Loveladys' mercantile establishment. Eulalie still had to lean on Nick for support, although her leg was healing nicely. Anyhow, Nick was big enough to handle her weight. Thank God he favored women with meat on their bones! She didn't fancy spending the next however many years of her life married to a man who carped at her about her weight.

"This is so exciting," said Mrs. Johnson, who was wearing her best hat, the one with pink flowers on it.

"Shore is," agreed Junius, who was in an even better mood than usual this fine autumn morning. "We don't gen'ly get real, live actors visitin' Rio Peñasco."

"I'm so happy they could come." Patsy dabbed her eyes with her handkerchief.

"I am, too," agreed Eulalie. "I'd hate to get married without the family present."

"I'm glad mine won't be," muttered Nick, who kept his arm around Eulalie as if he feared she might break if he let go. That was fine with her.

"You will, too, have family present," Eulalie chided him. "I'd like to know who Junius is, if he isn't family."

Nick swapped a big grin with his uncle. "Aw, hell, Junius isn't family. He's a friend."

"Nicky was kind of unlucky in his family," Junius said in a confiding tone and winking at Eulalie. "But I don't hold that against him none."

As ever when the stagecoach was expected, the first herald of its arrival was a cloud of red-brown dust in the west that gradually resolved itself into six horses and then the stage itself, barreling towards Rio Peñasco amid the thunder of horses' hooves and rattling wheels and the cheers and applause of the town's citizens. Even before the stage came to a stop, members of the Gibb Theatrical Company braved the dust to lean out of the windows and wave to the assembled crowd.

"There's Uncle Harry!" Patsy cried, pressing her hands to her cheeks in an ecstasy of delight.

"And I see Aunt Florence!" announced Eulalie, similarly enraptured.

"And there are Marcus and Horatia and Irving!"

"It looks as if your whole family decided to pay a visit," observed Nick.

"Yes," Eulalie said joyfully. "I'm so happy!" And she burst into tears, proving yet again that she was still a little weak from her recent ordeal. Nick didn't seem to mind, which proved to her once more, if further proof were needed, that he was the most wonderful man in the world.

Eulalie Gibb and Nicholas Taggart, and Patsy Gibb and Lieutenant Gabriel Fuller were united in holy matrimony on November 3, 1897, in the little Baptist church in Rio Peñasco, New Mexico Territory, in a ceremony conducted by the Reverend Thomas P. Huffington. The church was full to the rafters with attendees. Eulalie, who was accustomed to performing in front of an audience, told Patsy she didn't need to be nervous.

"But there are so many people out there," Patsy said in something of a whimper.

"They're all our friends, Patsy. They love you."

"And there's Gabriel," said Patsy, perking up a trifle.

"Yes," Eulalie agreed. "There's Gabriel." And there was Nick, too. Eulalie's heart trilled like a meadowlark in the springtime.

Uncle Harry escorted the sisters down the aisle. When they entered the little church on either side of him, Eulalie couldn't help but think that Nick was the most handsome man present, although Gabriel appeared quite spiffy in his uniform. Eulalie, who knew how much Nick disliked public displays like this one, was thrilled to see him smiling at her, as if he didn't mind being the spectacle of the day. She loved him more than ever.

Other members of the Gibb Theatrical Company provided music for the ceremony, with Gibb cousins Marcus and Horatia singing, accompanied on the piano by Aunt Florence. The two little Johnson girls acted as the brides' attendants. Junius was Nick's best man, and Lieutenant Willoughby Nash served the same role for Gabriel Fuller. The Johnson boys were groomsmen. Outside the church after the ceremony, representatives from the First Cavalry, swords crossed, created a canopy of sorts, under which both happy couples, arms entwined, walked toward the Rio Peñasco Opera House, which was closed today in honor of the event.

"Figgered it was the least I could do," said Dooley Chivers, his cigar drooping. "After all, she was shot right there on the stage." Since Dooley was, this day, losing the greatest draw the Opera House had ever seen, Eulalie, along with everyone in town, considered this a magnanimous gesture on his part.

Bernie Benson wrote several articles, both about the wedding itself and about the participants therein. He expected an influx of citizens to the village of Rio Peñasco once they read his vivid prose. Nick told him not to hold his breath, but Bernie was nothing if not optimistic.

The party lasted far into the night. Uncles Harry and Junius discovered in each other kindred spirits. Aunt Florence's interest in Junius couldn't have been more obvious, and it was reciprocated with gusto.

"I swear, Nick, I'm glad people usually only get married once in their lives," whispered Eulalie as the two lay together, sated and very much in love, after sneaking away from the party about three in the morning. "I didn't think I could go through this more than once."

"Hell, I hadn't planned on getting married *that* often," muttered Nick. He did it out of a sense of obligation, however, and didn't really mean it. He loved his Eulalie.

She didn't see it that way. "Curse you, Nick Taggart." She smacked his naked arm lightly.

With a deep chuckle, Nick turned and captured her luscious body in his huge arms. "But now that we're married, I'll be damned if I'll ever let you go."

She hugged him back, hard. "You'd better not." After a moment of delicious intimacy, she whispered, "But I'm still wondering, Nick. Since you hate marriage so much, why did you insist that we get married?"

"Me? Did I insist?"

She smacked him again. "Yes, you did, and you know it!"

He thought for a while. Then he contemplated the nature of the disclosure he could make. Then he remembered his stepmother and stepsisters. And then he realized that Eulalie

Gibb bore no resemblance whatsoever to that flock of pernicious females, so he decided to just go ahead and admit it.

"Aw, hell, Eulalie, I love you."

There. The truth was out. Nick waited for her scorn.

She tightened her arms around him. "Oh, Nick, I love you, too. I love you so much, I can hardly stand it."

He drew away slightly and stared at her, confounded. "You mean it? You love me? Me? Nick Taggart? Blacksmith?"

"Yes!"

"Well, I'll be damned."

But he wasn't. He was blessed, and so was his wife.

And so, when they arrived, were their children, who grew and thrived in Rio Peñasco, New Mexico Territory.

About the Author

In an effort to avoid what she knew she should be doing with her life (writing—it sounded so hard), for several years Alice Duncan expressed her creative side by dancing and singing. She belonged to two professional international folk-dance groups and also sang in a Balkan women's choir. She got to sing the tenor drone for the most part, but at least it was interesting work. In her next life, she'd like to come back as a soprano.

In September of 1996, Alice and her herd of wild dachshunds moved from Pasadena, CA, to Roswell, NM, where her mother's family settled fifty years before the aliens crashed. She loves writing because in her books she can portray the world the way it should be instead of the way it is, which often stinks. She started writing books in October of 1992, and sold her first one in January of 1994. That book, *One Bright Morning*, was published by Harper in January of 1995 (and won the HOLT Medallion for best first book published in 1995). Alice hopes she can continue to write forever!